# The Story
# of Light

# The Story of Light

## Hannah Spencer

MOON
BOOKS

Winchester, UK
Washington, USA

First published by Moon Books, 2014
Moon Books is an imprint of John Hunt Publishing Ltd., Laurel House, Station Approach,
Alresford, Hants, SO24 9JH, UK
office1@jhpbooks.net
www.johnhuntpublishing.com
www.moon-books.net

For distributor details and how to order please visit the 'Ordering' section on our website.

Text copyright: Hannah Spencer 2013

ISBN: 978 1 78279 207 9

A CIP catalogue record for this book is available from the British Library.

Design: Stuart Davies
www.stuartdaviesart.com


Printed in the USA by Edwards Brothers Malloy

We operate a distinctive and ethical publishing philosophy in all
areas of our business, from our global network of authors to
production and worldwide distribution.

# CONTENTS

# Prologue

Do you ever feel as if something is missing? A yearning, a sense of loss? A longing for a place once called home, which is now nothing but a shade of memory?

There are other signs as well – a fleeting recognition of a place, a face, familiar but yet unknown. Feelings, thoughts, that seem older than time. A strange affinity with a place, an age, a language. A love of history, a disconnection with the modern world.

After death, the soul drinks from the River of Lethe, Forgetfulness, so all memories are erased before life begins anew. But sometimes, a soul drinks from the Pool of Mnemosyne, Memory. The result; a remembrance of the past – fleeting, like a half remembered dream, lost in the sands of time, the only clues as to a life once lived.

I used to think that life was simple. You are born, live then die, gone forever leaving nothing but memories in the people you leave behind. I now know that this is not true. Aristotle once said that what is eternal moves in cycles – stars, days, years, cultures, Ages. The soul is eternal, and lives and dies in a constant flux.

The universe is constantly changing, but the changes are governed by eternal and unchangeable natural laws which cause it to revolve eternally, without beginning and without end. Its parts manifest, disappear and are created anew in the undulating pulse of time. And so our soul manifests in many different bodies over the course of eternity. Behind the scenes, infinite sources influence and guide each one, playing a complex game so all fulfil the purpose of many lifetimes.

Everything – men, gods, animals – is part of a grand and infinite plan, and each and all are guided by a greater power than can ever be imagined, for a purpose that can never be comprehended.

I was about to set out on a journey. With hindsight, I had been preparing for this journey all my life. Everything I'd done, everyone I'd met, had all given me something – some insight, some knowledge, which I would come to need on the way. I was drawn to authors such as Jean Auel, Mark Chadbourn, James Redfield and Paulo Coelho. In this modern age there are no sages, wise men or mystery schools to teach initiates of our sacred wisdom. Instead, these writers became my early teachers, sowing the seeds for what was to come. Books, poems, sacred texts, the internet, they have all helped to replace the teachers – the Truth has become democratised. The sacred wisdom of all cultures and all ages is available to all those who wish to hear.

The world has become smaller, many barriers have been broken. The input of wisdom from many cultures, combined with twenty-first century quantum mechanics, psychology, biology and astrophysics forms a Truth transcending that previously known.

But conversely, many barriers have sprung up between countries, faiths, cultures and ideologies. In another eternal cycle, as the world comes closer together, so it slowly falls apart. This fact was to be central to the journey I was about to undertake.

Here is the story of who I am, and who I used to be.

# PART I

1

# Chapter 1

*All men dream, but not all dream equally.*
T.E. Lawrence

It started with a dream. Such an incongruous thing, little did I realise how much it would change the course of my life. Everyone has had dreams like this, they seem so meaningful, important, evocative, and when you wake up you can't stop thinking about them. This was one of those. I now know it was the first move in a new game, the pieces on the board being arranged lifetimes ago.

It had been an ordinary day and an ordinary Friday evening. When I got up from the sofa to go to bed, I had no inkling of the dramatic change of events that was about to unfold. I was asleep within seconds, it seemed, and I was immediately transported through time and place to reach a whole new world, a new existence, a new life that was somehow a part of me.

What I saw was a snapshot of a life. I saw people and places, I felt joy and sadness, love and loss, all the things that come as a life is played out. I felt a profound sense of purpose and destiny, and a surety that comes only from the utmost confidence in the gods. The unshakeable beliefs that this person held seemed, even in my dream, intensely profound. Modern life I found frustrating, stressful and exhausting, and the contrast with what I was experiencing could not be more stark.

I'd had vivid dreams before, of places, journeys and people, they'd been magical, mythical almost, but nothing like this, not in the slightest. This was different. Real. More like a long forgotten memory, if that could be possible. And even in my dreaming state, I doubted it.

I felt a name, whispered across aeons of time. *Brigid.*

When I was a child I was called Brig – a childish pronunciation of Bridget, the nickname had stuck throughout my life. Was this person me? Unsettling confusion filled my mind.

My vision clarified, like mist burns away in the morning sun. I saw beautiful mountains swathed in snow. Rocks, harsh against the background landscape. I smelt the sharpness of the clean air as I breathed deeply in pleasure. I saw moors, trees and heather, then I saw with delight a patch of gorse bushes, blazing yellow in the summer sun. They were alive with bees and tiny black beetles, the sound of their busy foraging filled my ears. I'd always loved to see the gorse flowers, I remembered.

*Remembered?*

I heard water rushing down a nearby hillside, then the distant screech of a hawk far up in the sky. I had a feeling that I'd never really felt before, a sense of belonging and peace, a sense of *home.* The word hammered in my mind.

But before I could fully absorb this intense memory, I became aware of something else, a problem. A piece of the puzzle was missing, something that meant this life had been unfulfilled. Towards the end of the scene, something subtly changed in my dream. Hope gave way to despair and a flickering light, striving against the darkness, was finally extinguished. I felt a disquieting chill as if a cloud had suddenly covered the sun. Something had been lost. I had failed in something, something important, desperately important. The sense of overwhelming failure surrounded me like an impenetrable black shroud.

And I saw what it was, that missing piece – vague, blurred, hovering just beyond the edges of my vision, I was aware of a blazing light, multi-coloured and transcendent, incredible in its majesty. When I tried to see what it was, it vanished and was replaced by a stream of other images. I saw a smith hammering frantically at an anvil, the blade of a sword glowing red. A man bent low over a horse's neck, galloping fiercely across a moor. The flame of a candle in utter darkness. Stars wheeling overhead in an eternal cycle. A bright green horned snake with a leafy twig in its mouth. A cavern entirely filled with swarming bees, the sound almost deafening.

Then I was walking through a glade of trees, verdant and glowing, the scent of apples filled the air. A particularly juicy red apple hung just above my head and I reached up and picked it, its flavour filling my mouth as I bit into it. Then I saw that it had split exactly in two, and the five seeds in the centre formed a pentagram.

Next I saw a strange being, I couldn't tell if it was man, beast, vegetation, or a combination of the three, and then a woman bathed in light. She placed her hand on my brow, I was overwhelmed by dazzling light and felt myself spinning, out of control, back through aeons of time to my normal life.

On that point between dreaming and waking, when the two worlds seem to combine, I heard a voice, deep and profound. Words of intense power filled my bedroom and my mind, piercing my thoughts, my feelings, my soul, the most defining words I had heard in my life. But as is often the case, although the voice was clear I just couldn't understand what it had said.

I woke then and lay in bed, my head reeling with the feelings, emotions, sights and sounds of the place I'd visited.

*My home.*

The powerful surge of emotion I felt was too much to describe. An immense yearning filled my mind and I felt tears of loss and desperation prick against my eyelids. I had to find this place.

With hindsight, I think I'd been looking for it all my life. I'd always loved travelling, I anticipated childhood holidays with great excitement, always loving to see new places, and later I travelled all around Britain. But I could never quite connect with any of the places I visited; after a few days the excitement would pall and the disconnection would return. I would want to move on. I hadn't yet reached the place I called home.

But now, if only in a dream, I'd finally found it.

The sense of revelation I felt was intense. Then, in that time, that place, *that life,* I'd been the embodiment of hope, of destiny.

But something was lost. Something vital. I felt again that crushing sense of loss, of failure, of despair.

I thought for a long time about those words I'd heard. Their meaning was driven deep into my heart and I tried and tried to recall them, but it was in vain. They were vital, I knew, but they just would not come.

After three hours, replaying the dream constantly in a vain attempt to remove it from my thoughts, I finally got out of bed. In that movement, I was forcing myself back to the real world, away from the world of dreams and destiny. Back to my real life where I had bills to pay and a career to get on with. It was the invention of a dreaming imagination unhindered by rationality, I told myself firmly, the only explanation I could logically think of, or rather, believe.

It was already mid-morning, I realised. I hadn't stayed in bed this late for years. At least it was Saturday.

I went out onto the landing and jumped. That damned angel, huge, ceramic, ugly and tasteless, glared at me balefully. It had never failed to startle me since Anna, my flatmate, had brought it home a fortnight before. She insisted it would give psychic protection or something, but I hated the damn thing. I walked past it with irritation. Her weird and wonderful acquisitions were taking over the flat, it seemed.

I made some coffee, a Kenyan ground blend. I'd even bought Fairtrade which pleased Anna, but I actually just liked the taste of it. I put the jar carefully back in its rightful place, between a pot of rosemary and some other flowering plant – Anna was quite obsessive about feng shui or whatever it was.

The strong black drink restored my senses somewhat to the present time, but the effect was only temporary. My mind was still constantly returning to the scent of gorse, to the sharpness of clean, unpolluted air, to that *feeling* – hope, happiness, surety, an easy confident peace. I'd never in my life felt such an intense feeling of *being*.

I flicked aimlessly through the TV channels, trying to settle my mind, and then picked up the book I'd been reading, Yann Martel's *Life of Pi*. I loved reading modern fiction, it was a way of escaping from the harsh realities of life. For some reason, I always seemed to choose books that imparted a profound spiritual message, exploring life and its meaning. They were nice stories, I always told myself. That was all. Nothing more. Real life wasn't like that at all.

Of course, it was more than that, much more. They were planting seeds in my heart and soul, seeds that were germinating, deep down in the dark earth, slowly pushing upwards until the time came when they would burst forth into the light.

But this time was yet to come. The part of myself that I so vehemently denied was still struggling in vain to make itself heard.

*It was only a dream,* I kept saying to myself. I did not believe in the power of dreams, I was a scientist, university educated, not a credulous, superstitious nutter. I thought dream interpretation was ridiculous. I knew that dreams were the brain's way of repairing damaged cells and consolidating memories, nothing more.

I didn't learn any different for a long time.

I finished my coffee and immediately poured myself another. I was supposed to be meeting Tom later that morning, I really had to get myself going. We'd been introduced by a friend last year – *'You're perfect for each other'* – a statement I'd heard so many times before. I'd always been too involved in work to seriously think about settling down, and Tom was the same, but our fairly low-maintenance relationship seemed to be holding together quite well.

I had a quick shower and forced myself out of the door, and half an hour later I walked into the cinema entrance. Tom did not look happy. He was standing with his arms folded, fidgeting impatiently, then marched over when he saw me.

'Can't you ever be on time?' he growled. 'I've been waiting for you for fifteen minutes.'

I sighed. As if it mattered – the film hadn't started yet anyway. 'Sorry, darling. You know how it is, time flies.' I failed utterly to sound contrite.

'Well, I've got our tickets, we'd better go in else it'll be over.' He looked away, still angry, but I could see he was already forgetting his annoyance. I put my arm round his waist and smiled, unusually subservient. I just wanted to have a nice time today.

Tom hesitated, then smiled back. His unruly hair flopped over his face, making him look quite boyish. 'I am glad to see you though, Brig.'

He hugged me to him, a silent apology, his outbursts rarely lasted more than a few minutes. Then we went into the darkened room. Films weren't really my thing, I preferred to be outside doing things but Tom was a film buff, he'd set up his own film company after quitting his City job, and I felt obliged to humour him.

It was a French-language film with subtitles, based on the wartime resistance, a deep arty thing that Tom had insisted would be awe-inspiring, but I couldn't make myself focus on it. A landscape, a sound, a subtle gesture, all kept pulling my thoughts back to my dream, insistent reminders of it were everywhere. Eventually, I settled back in my seat and let the memory wash over me again, revelling in that feeling of perfectness and life.

Tom nudged me roughly some time later. 'Have you been asleep?'

I opened my eyes and saw the credits rolling. Nearly an hour had passed since I'd entered my reverie.

'We didn't have to see it, if you didn't want to. Joey was dying to see it, but I said I preferred to go with you.' Tom was looking genuinely hurt.

'No, no, I just had my eyes shut for a minute,' I hastily reassured him. 'It was very good, really, very moving.' He looked more pacified and I breathed a sigh of relief, then stood up before he questioned me on the details.

We whiled away the rest of the afternoon walking round the local park, making the most of the sunshine. I forced my mind to forget my dream and concentrate on now. The park was full of kids playing football and keep-fit joggers, typical of a Saturday afternoon. I focussed on the feel of the sun on my face, on the wind, of the smell of the lake which was full of beautiful white swans. A child with a bag of bread brought all the birds flocking. Ducks dashed here and there, seagulls swooped down to snatch crusts, and the majestic swans swam in between the fray, dodging discarded drinks cans and carrier bags and effortlessly taking pieces of bread from the smaller birds.

Then as soon as the bread was gone, the birds vanished. The last seagull snatched an overlooked crumb from beneath a floating beer can before too winging away, leaving behind a strange sense of emptiness.

'I used to love feeding the birds,' said Tom, looking enviously after the happy child. So did I, I thought. When had the dreams and joys of childhood been replaced by the grim realities of adult life? Tom's expression told me he was feeling exactly the same way.

'Let's get ice cream!' I suddenly said. We went to a small kiosk and bought two cones, then just wandered, childlike, with not a care in the world.

'It's lovely out here, really,' I said, licking the remains of the ice cream from my fingers and kicking a Coke can to the edge of the path. I wasn't sure if I was talking to Tom or myself.

This was my home, I told myself firmly, and I was happy here.

I looked at a few tree stumps, still flecked with sawdust, and Tom followed my gaze. 'They're cutting down the ash trees, trying to contain that new disease that's wiping them out.'

I nodded as a cloud drifted in front of the sun, chilling the air. There were a lot of strange viruses emerging nowadays, no one really knew why. As a biochemist, that's what kept me in work.

There was a piercing shriek behind us and we turned. A small girl wobbled past on a shiny tricycle, squealing with delight. One of the hundreds of CCTV cameras swivelled to watch her go.

Tom looked at her as well for a long moment. 'I love the idea of having kids,' he said, a strange wistfulness in his voice.

I was surprised – we'd never spoken about children before. 'It's easy to let work take over, and then you look back at your life and you've got nothing.'

He took my hand and looked at me with a strange, intense look. The background noise faded away, it was just me and him, alone in the world, and a flicker of excitement rose in me. He wasn't about to propose, was he?

Then the feeling died, a feeling of panic replaced it. Like most people, I'd dreamed of my wedding day, a beautiful house, rosy-faced children. But somehow, not with Tom.

After a long, heart-stopping moment he turned away. Had something of my thoughts shown in my face? The background noise returned, the world re-emerged. We walked on in silence, my thoughts in confusion. Had he really been about to propose? Or was it my imagination?

He loved me, I knew, but did I feel the same? I didn't know. I thought our relationship was easy going, convenient but not serious, I'd never had an inkling that Tom wanted more.

The feeling of turmoil and disconnection returned with a vengeance and I suddenly longed to escape, to get far away from here – from London, from Tom, from everything.

This is my home, I told myself again.

*No, it isn't.*

# Chapter 2

*I have been a tear-drop in the sky, a glittering star,*
*A word in a letter, a gleaming ray of light.*
Taliesin

The night passed without incident. Sunday I had set aside for work, and I spent all day in front of my laptop analysing three weeks worth of data and formulating equations.

My results were looking good, the potential new vaccine for the influenza virus was showing signs of promise, and I was really pleased. I'd been lucky enough to get a job at the highly renowned PharmLab after leaving university, but the pressure to succeed could be overwhelming. I'd put a huge amount of work into my pet project and was hoping for a significant leap forward. Simon, my boss, would be pleased when I told him tomorrow. Maybe, anyway. I could always be hopeful.

I looked over the data one last time, mindful of Simon's opinion, and finally closed down my laptop. I'd done well, the results looked good. Life was going well.

For the next two days I managed to focus wholly on work, the real world, the things that mattered. I was not going to let my life be dictated by a dream. I paid the rent, cleaned the flat, even to Anna's standards of perfection, and then changed the light bulb on the stairs that had gone months ago. As I'd expected, Simon found loads of faults with the results, but even he'd seen the potential and I was stupidly grateful for that.

I felt proud of myself. I'd taken control of my life, forced shut this disquieting door that had inexplicably opened in my mind and soul. The dream was forced to the sidelines, where it waited, patiently. It was on the third day that it made itself known again.

I could hear water flowing from an ornamental fountain as I walked through the park to the bus stop, and as I passed it I heard a loud screech. It was probably only a seagull, but it sounded just like the hawk of my dream. In an instant I was torn back to it, the images blazed vividly in my mind and the intense, desperate yearning made tears come to my eyes. I shook my head, trying to dispel that terrible longing, but to no avail. A woman looked at me strangely, opened her mouth as if to speak but changed her mind and hurried past. I struggled on, my eyes blurred with tears and my breath catching in my throat from suppressed sobs.

When I got home, exhausted by the rush of emotion, I flung myself in the shower, turning the radio up loud to try to force the terrible feeling from my mind. After half an hour, I felt sufficiently better to venture into the living room.

'Bad day?' asked Anna sympathetically.

'The usual,' I said. I couldn't elaborate. I forced my emotions deep inside with a superhuman effort and sank down on the sofa with a groan, staring rigidly at whatever trash Anna had on the TV. Anything to take away this maelstrom of feeling.

Anna got up and returned ten minutes later with a plate of toast, dripping with butter and honey. She put it carefully on my knee. 'You ought to eat something, at least.'

I smiled my thanks and began to nibble at it. No matter her rather ridiculous ideas on the world, she was certainly a good friend. My favourite comfort food served its purpose and soon I began to feel relatively normal again. Normal enough to put the incident down to stress and the long hours of the past few days.

*It was only a dream.*

So why did I feel as if it was trying to tell me something?

The rain poured under the collar of my coat as I waited with futile hope at the bus stop. Any minute, it would appear round the corner. *Please,* I added. The icy water trickled down my back and I tried to pull my coat tighter, but it just seemed to make things worse. The weather lately was really getting nightmarish, the impact of global warming apparently. I looked at my watch for the twentieth time. Why did they bother to print timetables? I looked down the road again.

Finally, it was here. I could already see it was standing room only, and I shared a look of mixed resignation and relief with the other soaked passenger.

'After you,' he said.

I squeezed into the aisle, water dripping onto the floor, and one of the monitoring police officers – it doubled as a school bus – shuffled backwards to stop himself getting wet. I smiled a resigned apology, plugged my iPod into my ears and turned up the sound.

Twenty minutes later I finally arrived at work, ran up to the building and swiped my pass at the door. It flashed red – denied – and I cursed and swiped it again as water splashed down my neck from the leaking gutter. On the fifth attempt it relented and flashed green, and I propelled myself in towards the next door. Each one needed a pass to open it – safety and security and all that – but the Big Brother mentality did nothing to improve my mood today.

I hung my sodden coat behind the door in the open-plan office and sat down at my computer. The bad start had killed all my enthusiasm. I opened my Inbox and scanned the list of messages but baulked at opening any. They could wait until later, I decided, and I got up and went into the lab. My experiments from the day before were now ready to analyse. The new influenza virus, an unusual and highly contagious strain which had suddenly appeared in the East, was rapidly spreading around the world and the results would be highly important. I rather liked the idea that I was doing my bit for mankind.

I picked up my test tubes and began to separate the test samples from the controls, but after a few minutes I gave up and went out again, finding it impossible to concentrate. I just couldn't afford to make any mistakes, I could already feel Simon's disapproving appraisal of the results.

I went to the drinks machine for a cup of coffee, grim but just about drinkable, then went back to my desk. I opened the files containing the data I'd already collected, then closed it again in frustration.

I stared at the screen for a while, then opened a search engine for scientific research. After a moment's hesitation, I typed in 'reincarnation'.

I didn't know why, obviously there would be nothing. But I was shocked when several hundred hits immediately appeared. It seemed that reincarnation had attracted attention from scientists worldwide. I opened a few of the files that came up – research papers published by serious and objective scientists, not just the theories of nutters and crackpots.

Still not entirely convinced by my peers' surprising endorsement, I read about many scientifically credible cases of reincarnation, backed up with substantial proof. In one case, a young girl had claimed to remember her previous life and her death in a car crash. When taken to the neighbourhood where she'd lived, she recognised her once husband and correctly remembered his pet name for her, his favourite food, and places they'd been on holiday.

I read many other examples of similar stories, all presenting overwhelming proof of their validity, and then I stared at the screen, lost in thought. I wasn't ready to change the beliefs of a lifetime – if there was one thing I prided myself on, it was my strength of mind. I wasn't going to be swayed by a few stories. But still, some niggling voice made me search further.

I searched on Google for more information and over the next hour I learnt that all ancient cultures believed in reincarnation. The idea that life is continually cycling is actually the norm, in both ancient religions and modern esoteric mysticism. The concept of travelling like an arrow from nothing, to life, to death, and either nothingness again for scientists, or alternatively heaven or hell for the religious types, is actually relatively recent.

*If* this was true, then what was the purpose of this constant cycling? It seemed the answer was that all souls are travelling on a journey, an ever-journey home, to immortality. When after many lifetimes a soul reaches a state of perfection, it escapes this constant cycle and reunites with the divine light from whence it came – Nirvana or heaven.

The door slammed behind me and I jumped, checking guiltily over my shoulder that no one was watching. I wondered how long my soul had been cycling. If it ever had. Which of course it hadn't.

I found that Pythagoras, the Greek philosopher, mathematician, astronomer and scientist, was a key figure in the reincarnation story. He developed a theory of the immortal soul and its transmigration into human, animal, vegetable and non-living objects, and he believed he himself had lived as a Trojan warrior and a rock in previous lifetimes. His ideas went on to influence great sages such as Plato, Socrates and Aristotle, and through them, the whole of the Western world. And I thought he'd just invented a triangle.

I took a mouthful of coffee. I winced – it was stone cold. I realised guiltily that I'd been engrossed in my reading for over an hour. What was wrong with me today?

I stood up and went back to the drinks machine, thinking about what I'd learnt as the machine whirred and spat a steaming cup into my hand.

I stared at the swirling steam and wondered what it must be like to exist as a rock. It had never occurred to me that they may have thoughts, feelings, awareness of their own. I imagined how it would feel – constant, solid and changeless over aeons of time, watching the rise and fall of the dinosaurs, the evolution of mammals, the first humans descending from the trees and gradually developing into what we were today. A hundred million years flashed before my eyes on fast forward, like I'd called up some ancient universal memory, and I shivered. Then the steam dissipated and I saw I was being watched.

'Solving the mysteries of the universe?' Bob always sounded so sarcastic, I thought with irritation. Why couldn't he just get on with his own work? I gripped the polystyrene cup harder and felt it crack slightly under my fingers.

'What, Bob?' 'You seem to be finding that coffee particularly fascinating.' He smirked derisively.

'I was thinking. I have a lot of results to think about.' I hoped he noticed the emphasis on 'results'. I went back to my desk before he could reply, checked round guiltily for observers and then typed 'Pythagoras' into Google. From the many hits I learned that Pythagoras developed his reincarnation theory from contact with the Celts of Western Europe. Far from being backward barbarians, the Celts were at the forefront of spiritual and mystical thought.

A strange and intense feeling of familiarity washed over me, as if somehow I already knew this. An image burst into my head for a split second. My computer screen faded and I saw a bearded, robed man exuding an air of wisdom and intelligence, deeply in discussion with someone I couldn't see. He looked away for a second, absently rubbing a deep, half-healed wound to his face before beginning to speak again, an expression of dawning realisation spreading across his face. I was aware of a rough wooden building and smelt rich wood smoke.

Then as soon as it came, it was gone, like a bubble rising to the surface of the pool of memory, bursting outwards to be no more. I shivered again. It must be the residual damp in my clothes, I reasoned, I really ought to do some work. In a minute.

Pythagoras set up esoteric schools in Greece to teach his new theories and his ideas were studied by mystics and scientists throughout the Dark Ages, influenced the Renaissance scholars, and now were the fundamental principle behind New Age thinking, Aquarianism, and many other mystical beliefs. In short, Pythagoras was the most influential figure on the spiritual history of Europe.

'Morning, Bridget.'

I jumped, recognising the voice behind me with a flash of panic. I hastily clicked the vaccine results onto the screen and turned round.

'Morning, Simon.''How do the results look?' he asked pointedly.

'I'm just interpreting them now,' I said, moving a few numbers around at random. 'They're looking good, very interesting.''OK, will you let me have the report by tomorrow at the latest? I can take it to the meeting.' He looked down his nose at me. 'There's not been much going lately, it seems some people are just not pulling their weight.'

A wave of anger surged through me. How dare he speak to me like that? I slaved on this project, I really did. Simon just didn't like me. Come to that, he didn't seem to like anyone.

'Most people would be very happy with my work. Most people would think I'm *slave-driven*.' My voice rose. The office became very still.

Simon's eyes grew hard. 'Well, maybe you could spend a little less time *slaving* on what you're doing,' he said quietly. With a last sharp look he walked away and I took a deep breath. There had been rumours circulating lately about the company's struggling finances and job cuts, the last thing I wanted was to get into the boss's bad books, even more than I already was.

I desperately needed to concentrate now. I went back to the lab and quickly finished analysing my samples, and then settled down to number-crunching. But because of my carelessness and lack of focus, I realised late in the day that I'd made a slight but devastating error in my analysis. I had to start again.

I let out a sigh of frustration. I couldn't afford to leave before I'd finished, not after this morning, and I stayed at my desk as the office gradually emptied around me. Soon I was alone, the only sounds were the hum of the air conditioning and the tapping of my keyboard.

Eventually, after a mammoth effort, I had the report finished. It was rushed, I knew, but I hoped it was not too obvious. I quickly emailed it to Simon, hoping he would notice the time – nearly nine o'clock – and gratefully turned off my computer.

The rest of the building was deserted, not even a security guard in sight, and my footsteps rattled on the tiled floor. I was glad to get outside – there was something quite spooky about this normally busy building at night.

I walked quickly to the bus stop, desperate to get home. The rain was still pouring down and I was soon drenched again. At least the bus was empty and, a minor miracle, on time. I watched the rain lash against the windows, glowing orange in the street lights, while the only other passenger, a hooded teenager, flicked through various rap songs on his iPod. How could he stand it that loud, I thought, thinking how old that comment made me seem.

I hoped Anna would be at home. My cooking was functional rather than artistic, and I was desperate for something delicious to make up for the terrible day. As I opened the door with a sigh of relief, I knew I was in luck. I could smell lasagne – my favourite. That was the first good thing to happen all day. It smelt mouthwatering and I was suddenly famished – I'd had only coffee all day.

'Hi Anna,' I called.

'You're late, Brig,' she said coming out of the living room, her phone to her ear. 'And you're soaked,' she cried, taking in my rats tails and dripping coat. 'Take that thing off, dry your hair and sit down,' she ordered.

I threw my coat down, resisting the urge to chuck it over the gloating angel, and went into the living room. I could hear Anna talking in the kitchen. The room smelt of lavender and something else, the result of the dozens of candles adorning the room, and I took an appreciative deep breath. Anna owned a small shop selling hocus-pocus stuff – candles, crystals, meditation aids and all other strange things – and she brought home a lot of samples. Although it was just fairy-tale science, I had to admit I found the aromatherapy very soothing.

She came back a moment later. 'I was just talking to Jenny, we're going to that protest at the weekend. Another nuclear power station – can you believe it!'

She walked to the window and shook her head in agitation. 'As if we're not destroying the world fast enough.' The one thing that got Anna's knickers in a twist was the desecration of her beloved earth.

'Nuclear power's the future, Anna. It's cleaner, more efficient, we can't rely on solar panels. The world has to move forward.''No, no! Look at Chernobyl, Fukushima! It's a disaster waiting to happen! We've got to stop it!' She looked at me like I'd suggested napalming the rainforests, and I sighed and collapsed on the sofa. 'But you need someone to moan to,' she stated, her familiar calmness restored.

'Today's been a total nightmare. Everything went wrong, I had to get a report to Simon and completely messed it up. I just couldn't focus at all today. And you know what Simon's like, he'll just rip it to pieces tomorrow.''He likes things done well, that's all.' Back in her comfort zone, Anna was like a rock in the midst of a turbulent sea.

'But he just criticises everything, everything seems to be a problem to him. I do it one way, he wants it done another. How do you cope with people like that?' My stomach rumbled.

'Do you actually mean, how do you convince someone that you're right and they're wrong?' Anna took a steaming dish from the oven and my mouth started to water. 'Because that's what most arguments bottle down to, isn't it?''No...'

'Yes,' countered Anna. 'Everyone wants people to see the world their own way. The answer's easy. Just accept that you're wrong, whatever you argue about. You're wrong, they're right.''I'm not wrong!' This wasn't the sympathy and consolation I wanted.

'Just accept you are, even when you're not. Do things their way without complaining.' Anna smiled gently. 'See what happens, it really does work. Amazingly so.'

Anna put a plate of hot lasagne in front of me. 'When it got to eight o'clock, I thought you'd need it.' I smiled at her gratefully. The smell of my favourite meal was mouthwatering, and I took a forkful with barely restrained relish. She fixed me with an appraising look then rearranged the candles, moving them nearer to my chair. 'They're all beeswax, so totally natural.' Now I noticed the delicate honey scent amid the lavender, and the weight of the day began to slip away.

'You're working too hard, you need to get out and relax a bit.''Tell me about it,' I said between mouthfuls, feeling better by the minute.

'And I know the perfect thing. Tomorrow, we're having a night at the shop, someone's coming who specialises in past-life regression. You ought to come along.' She said it casually. I hated that sort of thing and she knew it.

I felt a sudden jolt as if the floor had shifted under my feet. I couldn't believe the coincidence, that she should happen to mention the very thing that had been taking over my thoughts.

'Oh yeah? What's that about, then?' I tried to keep my voice casual.

'It's a woman I've had dealings with before, she's called Lucy Luck.'

'Lucy Luck?!' I spluttered, almost choking on my mouthful of food. 'Wasn't that a trained gorilla in a film?'

Anna giggled. 'No, not her. She's very well-known, she can read people's minds and lives like a book, you really ought to meet her.'

I made the decision there and then. Maybe something

ridiculous like this would convince my mind of its fallacy, get me back onto the realities of life. And with a name like Lucy Luck, it would definitely be good. 'OK, I'll come along. What time is it?'

Anna did a double-take, it was the last thing she was expecting. At least I shocked her, I thought smugly. 'Um, around six thirty, it should last a couple of hours or so.''OK. I'll leave work early and get there.'

If nothing else, I would have some new ammunition to goad her with. I'd never held any credence to Anna's stranger beliefs, and she in turn derided my firm belief that science held the answers to everything. We were as unlike as two people could be, but we'd shared a flat together since university despite our lives taking dramatically different turns.

On my second night at university, I'd been walking back from the Students' Union around three in the morning, alone, very drunk, and hopelessly lost until I saw an elaborately dressed fairy coming towards me. With utter relief I recognised her as living on my floor. Anna had willingly shown me the way back to the halls, retrieved my remaining shoe from the road and reminded me which room I lived in. Our friendship had survived through thick and thin ever since.

Anna piled the empty plates in the sink. 'So how's Tom? I haven't seen him for a while.'

'Stressing over his film, it's not going that well.' My mind was drawn back to my confused and conflicting thoughts about our relationship. 'I think he's questioning things, really, wondering if there's something missing in his life.'

Anna picked up on the hesitancy in my voice and looked at me sharply. 'He hasn't asked you to marry him, has he?' She smiled to lighten her serious question, and I sat back in my chair.

'I don't know what he's thinking. The other day, I thought... I don't know, like he might.''Well don't marry him.'

Anna's adamant response shocked me and I looked round at her. 'Why not?' I asked defensively. I knew he wasn't perfect, but still.

'The course of life should come from your heart. Your heart is telling you not to do it, that's obvious. If it was the right thing to do, you'd be full of happiness that he might propose, and you're not. He's not where your future lies.'

I knew that, really, but where else would my life lead? I wanted to be happy, like everyone, and sometimes second best was better than having nothing at all. I began to peel an orange, and when it was obvious the subject was closed Anna settled down on the sofa, picking up a book.

'What are you reading?' I asked, more to break the silence than from interest. Anna always seemed to read sham science books – astrology, ghosts, ley lines – nothing I could bring myself to be interested in.

'It's called *The Word*, it's about gemantria,' she replied.

'You what?'

'Gemantria. It's the concept that all letters have a corresponding number, and adding up the numbers in a name or a word gives its sum value. Other words with this same value give an insight into the hidden aspects of the personality and soul. It gives a new dimension to the meaning of a name.'

'OK, sounds good.' I picked up my own book. I could never understand how she could fall for this stuff.

'It's an ancient practice, and people like to find the hidden spiritual qualities of themselves,' she answered in defence. 'It's one of our most popular books. It's an ancient belief that a name is sacred, chosen by the Gods, the most defining aspect of a person. Once given, a name is eternal, can never be taken away.'

Again I shivered. That whispered name resonated once again across aeons of time. *Brigid.*

'So what would my name mean, then?' I asked, hoping I sounded casual.

'I'll work it out for you, pass me that pen.' I handed her a pen off the table and she began to write.

'B equals two, R, eighty, I, nine... D, G, E, T, that adds up to... 207!'

I was none the wiser. 'Meaning what?''There's a table of meanings at the back, I'll just look it up.' She flipped through the pages. 'Hang on, 207, it means 'body of light', it's a very auspicious number.'

Anna looked at me, a look I couldn't interpret. 'That's one of the most powerful meanings a name can have. It suggests that you have a great and important future ahead of you.'

That was the last thing I wanted to hear. 'It means nothing, Anna, it's not real. They're just numbers, and my name was chosen at random out of a baby book.'

'Nothing ever happens at random, nothing. Maybe you should think about that, about where your future lies.'

*Something is missing. Something important. Something I have to fulfil.*

Anna was still watching me and I felt an urge to tell her everything, about the dream, about Brigid, about Pythagoras, about the strange feelings and visions I was having. She would know what to do.

'What is it?' she asked quietly.

I opened my mouth to pour my heart out.

'I'm not sleeping well, that's all. I just need an early night.' I stood up decisively. I was a scientist, rational and logical. I didn't believe in dreams, past lives, gem-whatever, or any other rubbish that Anna seemed so taken in by. I was proud of my sudden burst of strength.

# Chapter 3

*Whatever is, has been already, and whatever is to come, has been before.*
Ecclesiastes 3.15

One email from Simon, flagged as urgent. Great. *Come and see me,* I read. No please, no well done, those results were fantastic. My irritation flared.

'Bridget, that report. Sit down.' I perched on the edge of a chair.

'It seemed to lack your usual care and attention. In fact it was terrible.'

*So it was obvious then.* 'I'm sorry, I'm a little tired, that's all.' I tried to sound contrite.

'It can't go to the Board as it is, it'll have to be delayed until next week's meeting now. I just can't understand why you've presented the results that way. The stats are all wrong, the interpretations, it's a disaster.' He thumped his fist on the table to emphasise his point.

That's so unfair, I thought indignantly, it wasn't that bad. Why was Simon always like this?

'That was the best way,' I said as calmly as possible, considering my rising temper. 'There were a couple of minor errors, I admit, but the results are correct.' 'No.' He barely even looked at me. 'That way will not do. You will have to put it right.'

I remembered what Anna had said, just accept you're always in the wrong. I took a deep breath. 'OK, how do you think I should do it?' No antagonism, no sarcasm, I felt like an over-eager puppy.

Simon looked up at me and leant forward. The most positive reaction so far, I thought with some surprise.

'Look at Bob's work,' he said. I couldn't help my lip curling in revulsion, but still nodded facetiously.

Twenty minutes later I knew exactly how Simon wanted the data presented. I would do it his way, it was easier, after all. I made a positive start with good intentions, but then ended up just sitting staring into space, seeing rolling hills covered in blazing yellow gorse in my mind, wishing I was anywhere but here.

After who knew how long, I felt a prickling on the back of my neck, and turned to see Simon standing at the far end of the room, staring at me. I felt a sharp flicker of panic. How long had I spent daydreaming? And how long had he been watching me?

I turned back to my computer and forced my mind onto my report, but the ominous prickling feeling stayed with me.

At five thirty I went to the toilets to freshen up and change. I'd never been one to dress up, I was more comfortable in walking boots than heels, so I'd just brought a different top and smart jeans.

I opened the door and was greeted by laughter and the overpowering smell of perfume. The department technicians, collectively known as The Ladies, were preparing for a night out.

'Careful with that hairspray, Sheila! Last time you set the fire alarm off!'

More raucous laughter followed and I smiled politely at their mirrored reflections.

'What do you think of that new guy, Dave? He's a bit of alright, he is! If only I was ten years younger!' Sheila was liberally applying lipstick and pursed her lips experimentally.

Only ten years? Dave had only just finished college – even I thought he was young.

'So, where are you going, Bridget?' Four pairs of eyes fixed me inquisitively. Any fuel for a gossip, I thought.

'I, um....' I couldn't think of an answer. I just couldn't admit the truth. 'Just out for a drink with a friend,' I finished lamely. There was an almost audible sigh of disappointment and The

Ladies turned back to their mascaras and eye shadows. I could practically hear the gossip spreading.

'...Bridget's been to a past-life regression...''...Bridget's a reincarnated superhero...''...Bridget's spending too long staring at her test tubes...'

I quickly made my escape and headed to Anna's shop, almost running to release the build-up of frustration inside me. I'd always used exercise as a way of releasing energy, I found it much more therapeutic than indulging in alcohol or chocolate like most of my friends.

I was surprised to see so many people gathering outside the shop. Past-life regression was obviously a very popular subject. An A-board on the pavement advertised the event luridly. I took in the collection of strange objects in the window – angels, fairies, gemstones, books, feathers – everything in the genre of weird stuff, it looked like a display for a child's bedroom. Then I plucked up my courage and went in.

I was met by the aroma of lavender and incense – evident, but not too overwhelming. Gathered inside were the usual mystical characters, all with flowing dresses, dangling jewellery, perfumes, and who all seemed to know each other. I shuffled my feet awkwardly and half felt like leaving again. I glanced round then fixed my eyes somewhere near the ceiling with contemptuous disdain. *Bunch of crackpots.* A few people glanced at me then returned to their conversations.

'Brig!' Anna came quickly towards me, beaming. She was wearing a long, rich green dress that swished round her legs as she moved. 'I thought you'd changed your mind!'

I smiled tightly, masking my discomfort. *Anna, you look like a leprechaun.* 'So where's Mystic Meg then?'

Anna gave me a look of irritation. 'She's on stage already. Come and sit down.' She led me into a back room where rows of rapidly filling chairs were facing a raised platform.

Lucy Luck actually looked surprisingly normal. She was

wearing black trousers and a smart top, with blonde hair in a tidy bun and black square-framed glasses. She wouldn't have looked out of place in a bank or an office.

'Not quite Mystic Meg, is she?' Anna smirked at my obvious surprise. 'I saved you a seat near the front.' We sat down, and when everyone had taken their seats Anna made the standard introductions and left the stage to the star performer.

'Everyone in this room has walked the world before,' she said in a melodious, almost haunting voice. 'Who would like to know how they once lived?'

Almost every hand in the room went up. Every one except mine. I settled back in my seat with a careful look of disinterest on my face. The last thing I wanted was people thinking I actually believed in this stuff. Lucy Luck's eyes roamed across the rows, settling on my face for a little longer than necessary before selecting a woman in the row behind us. She walked up onto the stage, and sat in the provided chair.

'What's your name?' Lucy asked.

'Alice,' replied the woman, smiling nervously and rubbing her hands together. She appeared to be mid-thirties and was smartly dressed.

'Do you believe you have lived before?' she asked seriously, removing her glasses, her eyes locking mesmerisingly on Alice's face.

'I think... yes. Maybe.' She seemed confused, her prepared answer forgotten under the hypnotising gaze. 'I feel like I was someone... lost.'

Their eyes remained silently locked together for a moment and the room grew palpably more silent. The shuffling of feet, chairs and bags stopped. Everyone in the room could sense that events were unfolding in a way they hadn't anticipated.

Lucy took hold of Alice's hands tightly, as if absorbing some deep spiritual essence from her. Despite my deliberate scepticism, I watched fascinated.

After a few minutes, Lucy began to speak. 'You lived on the south coast, you had just married your childhood sweetheart and your lives were fresh and full of hope and promise.' The melodious voice entranced everyone in the room and I could almost see a vision of her perfect life.

'But then the Spanish came, the Armada threatened England's future. Your husband went aboard one of Drake's ships, despite your pleas for him to stay. He said that your future, and your children's future, was worth fighting for. You wept uncontrollably as he left your home and sailed far across the sea, determined that he would do his bit for his country.'

A solitary tear rolled down Alice's cheek.

'He never returned. You stood on those lonely cliff tops, gazing out to the sea for weeks on end, hoping against hope that your love would return.'

I stole a look around the room. Everyone was mesmerised.

'How do you feel now? Are you happy with your life?'

'My boyfriends, my relationships, they always feel... dull, meaningless,' Alice answered hesitantly, her eyes glistening.

'You're still waiting for your lost love to come home to you, as you waited on that lonely cliff top, so long ago.'

The tears were coursing openly down her cheeks. 'I feel as if I'll be alone forever,' she burst out, now sobbing uncontrollably.

'True love can never be lost, not through time nor place. Your love tried to return to you. He has never forgotten you, and now he is close, he has almost found you. Soon you will be together again. His place in your heart will not be left empty.' Lucy squeezed her hands firmly and then handed her a tissue. Then Anna led Alice away into a side room.

I was surprisingly moved. I, and probably everyone else in the room, had been expecting something light-hearted and entertaining, but it could not have been further from the truth.

When Lucy asked for another volunteer, the show of hands was substantially less. I wondered if people didn't really want their souls opening up like a book.

Two more people went up on the stage, but they received readings far less emotional than Alice's – one lived as a farm labourer during the Great War, and one was a Saxon nun. Not surprising, I thought. The dramatic ones had kept their hands down.

Then Anna gave a final speech and people started to drift away. As I got up from my seat, Anna waved me over to her.

'Come and meet Lucy, she's asked to see you.' 'An unrelenting sceptic, can't she resist the challenge?' I hung back, it was a meeting I didn't want to make, but Anna refused to be swayed and I was dragged into a back room.

'This is my flatmate, Bridget.'

Lucy Luck fixed her eyes on mine. I'd never seen eyes like them, a dazzling electric blue which seemed to pull me into them. I felt suddenly dizzy and forced myself to break eye contact – it felt like my soul had been laid bare to her gaze. I realised then why Alice had been so off-balance.

'Do you believe you have lived before?' she asked, her honeyed voice lulling me into a state of relaxation.

'No,' I answered stubbornly, studiously avoiding her gaze. She caught at my hand, pulling me nearer. Her eyes caught mine, unblinking, and this time I couldn't look away, try as I might.

'Your soul is strong, powerful,' she said. 'Your will is the strongest I have ever encountered. You remember, don't you? Your soul remembers.'

'I don't remember anything,' I insisted. 'It was a dream, that's all.'

'Was it?'

The question hung in the air palpably.

'Dreams are how the Gods speak to you.' Her grip on my hand grew stronger, more urgent.

'There are unseen forces guiding you. Don't try to fight against them. Listen, believe, trust. I can see the battle within you, and this battle will destroy you, destroy everything. *Listen.*'

I tried to pull away but I was locked in the depths of her eyes and couldn't move.

'The power within you, locked in your heart, is immense, but it must be freed. Follow The Path that is laid out in your heart. Follow your intuition. Reason is only the voice of man, but intuition is the voice of the Gods.'

Her words resonated deeply within me, within the very fibres of my being. My mind began to reel. *Once I used to think like that.*

'You lost your way, a long time ago. You shut your mind to the world, because of what happened then.'

*That feeling of failure, of something unfulfilled.*

'You're denying who you are, what you are. And you feel that loss, deep within you.' I felt as if I was drowning in the intensity of her gaze.

'Are you happy?' she asked. In response, I felt tears begin to prick at my eyes.

'You must learn to feel again, to *be* again. You must find your way home.'

*Home.*

I tore myself away and almost ran from the room. Anna had been watching the exchange in silent puzzlement and followed me out. With a huge effort I managed to compose myself and turned to face her.

'Are you OK?' she asked.

'Fine,' I said through gritted teeth. 'I just want to go home now.'

I remained alone in the dark and deserted shop until Anna was ready to leave, trying to focus on anything but that heart-wrenching encounter. At last Anna set the alarm and we went out into the street. The stars were shining above our heads, visible even through the glare of the street lights.

'So what did you think of her?' asked Anna hesitantly. She was aware that something momentous had taken place.

'It's just psychological manipulation, that's all. She probably just picked up on that woman's insecurities, through her body language or something, and now she's convinced her to fall in love with the next guy she meets.' I tried to sound dismissive, but my voice lacked conviction.

'What about what she said to you back there? What was that about?'

'The same, trying to pretend she has some deep and profound insight into the world. It was like she was trying to hypnotise me, is that her trick?' I snapped my answer with more venom than I intended.

'You think you're so perfect, don't you, believing in nothing but your precious scientific theories? Just when I thought you might be starting to understand.' Anna was blazing, she looked at me with utter contempt.

I looked at her in shock, I'd never seen her as angry as this before. 'Anna...''Look at what's in front of you, see the truth for what it is. I know it's stupid to expect you to see anything further than your own nose, but you could at least try. *Think*.' She kicked a Coke can savagely, sending it flying into the street.

'Anna...' I tried again.

'You're *blind*, completely *blind*. Scientists are supposed to be open to new ideas, that's how progress is made. It's no wonder Simon's fed up with you. Sometimes I think you're the most irritating person I've ever met.' She wrapped her arms around herself, a defensive barrier, and walked faster.

Something inside me snapped. 'I live in the real world, Anna! The Real World! Not some ridiculous fairy tale! If people are so deluded with their boring, pathetic lives that they want to believe they're some born-again hero, that's up to them. I'm too intelligent for that!'

Anna walked on in angry silence. It was a real effort not to continue my rant, but inwardly I was fuming. I knew what was real, and I knew a lot better than her. There was no way I was falling for her laughable ideas.

But at the same time, a quiet thought niggled annoyingly in the back of my mind.

*She was right.*

# Chapter 4

*If the music of life seems discordant to us, we should not blame the*
*master musician but ourselves. We are the discordant instrument*
*which spoils its beauty.*
The Hermetica

The rain lashed against my face as I ran, faster and faster. Water
squelched in my trainers as I jumped puddles and dodged pedes-
trians. Whatever I was running from, I was leaving it far behind.
Everything that had happened in the past few days had built up
like a tidal wave in my mind, and the pressure was unbearable.
I'd always found I could think better when I was moving, and
running was the cure for all my problems. The detritus began to
clear from my mind, blown away by the wind and left far behind
me.

An hour later, tired, happy, free and relaxed, my muscles
aching delightfully, I got back to the flat feeling much more able
to face life. I idly browsed a few travel websites. I'd spent a
fortnight in Norfolk with Tom not so long ago, it had satisfied my
wanderlust for a while but now it was back with a vengeance.

I couldn't go away, though. I had too much work to do, too
many commitments, and after looking wistfully for a while I
closed them down with a sigh.

I'd cook tonight, I decided, and hastily rustled up some
salmon fillets with new potatoes and broccoli from the market. I
knew Anna extolled the virtues of Omega-3 fatty acids. I steeled
myself and even bought organic.

'Mmm, you've been cooking,' she said happily as she came
through the door. 'I'm starving!'

We talked for a while, mending our friendship, not that it took
much.

'I forgot to say,' said Anna, pulling something out of her
pocket. 'Lucy gave me this last night, she said it was for you.'

The last thing I wanted was more reminders of the previous night, but she handed me a piece of card which was ornately decorated with a never-ending and symmetrical design of Celtic knotwork. I took it reluctantly, at least it was something fairly benign. On it was a short message, the first letter of each line ornately illustrated.

*May the road rise to meet you,*
*And the wind be ever at your back.*
*May the sun shine warm upon your face,*
*And the rain fall softly on your fields.*

I read the ancient Irish blessing slowly. The words evoked a strong feeling inside me, exactly what I didn't know, as if on some deep level they were speaking to my heart.

'Lucy said it was important that you understand it, that it would guide you forward.' Anna was looking at me hard, waiting for my response.

I put the card on the table without comment and carried on eating. I ignored the pricking of tears behind my eyelids.

'I'm going to an event in Glastonbury in a fortnight,' Anna said after we'd sat in silence for a while. 'A festival, to welcome the new Age.'

'What's that about, then?' I suppressed a yawn.

'The new Age of Aquarius, which dawned at the start of the third millennium. It's said it'll lead to a new spiritual dawning for mankind.'

'Isn't that just some nutty, New-Age thing?' Out of habit, I couldn't help but deride her weirdo ideas. My eyes strayed towards the TV remote.

'Actually, it's scientifically proven fact, the cycle of the Ages is as real as the cycle of day and night. It's this thing called Precession of the Equinoxes, an astronomical cycle of 26,000 years.' Anna paused, making sure I was paying attention, and I made an effort to look interested. She wasn't convinced, she'd seen it too many times before, but continued anyway.

'One of the Zodiac constellations houses, or contains, the sun at all times, and the sun shifts into another constellation every month. This constellation is what your star sign is.'

'What, star signs are actually a real thing?' I couldn't help but be interested at this snippet.

'Yes, they are. If the sun is in Leo on your birthday, that will be your star sign.' She was enjoying the rare experience of my full attention.

'But the thing is,' she continued, 'in this cycle of the Great Year, the sun very slowly shifts from one constellation to another, and all the star signs will be shifted round by one month. So in the next Age, someone born on your birthday will be a Cancer rather than a Leo.

In the present Age, the sun on the key date of 21 March, the Spring Equinox, is in the constellation of Pisces, the fish. But it's now shifting into Aquarius, the water-pourer, which will house the sun on the Equinox for the next 2,000 years.''So now, we are in the Age of Pisces, which will soon be the Age of Aquarius? And this shift is what denotes the start of this new Age? It's actually real, not just imagined by weirdos?' I couldn't help adding this last bit.

'Yes, ask any astronomer, it's as real as anything.'

'So what does it mean then? Why does it matter?'

'Precession of the Equinoxes, the upheaval of the heavens, relates to times of great change on earth. That has been believed since time immemorial – people in Egypt, Mexico, Peru and loads of other places, they all believed in the periodic devastation of the world, directly caused by the shifting of the stars. The ancient belief was that the earth is a mirror image of the heavens; 'as above, so below,' as they said. And there are many books published recently...'

Anna was getting engrossed in one of her notorious lectures

and I held my hands up to stop the tirade. I knew from experience it could go on for a long time. I didn't mind a conversation about *normal* things, but this?

'You're losing me now, the scientist in you has died again.'

'It is true though. Just turn on the TV.'

'Gladly,' I said, picking up the remote.

'No, really, just look at the news. Wars, floods, famines, tsunamis, pollution, global warming, the bulldozing of the rainforests, over-fishing, mass extinctions, the world's falling apart. You can see it happening, all around you. We can all feel it.' Anna was referring to her group of nutty psychic friends.

'The Maya prophesied that the world would end in 2012, and it looks like they won't be far wrong. The world is dying, slowly but surely.''Sometimes you seem a bit too obsessed with our destruction of the world.' Her constant lecturing did grate on me somewhat.

'When I was seven, we'd gone on holiday to Cornwall, there'd been an oil leak from a ship. All the beaches, the rocks, everything was covered in it. We found loads of birds washed up, all matted with filth so they couldn't move, just left to die because of man's carelessness. I remember the hopeless despair in their eyes, begging someone to do something. It was the most awful thing I'd ever seen.' A tear trickled down Anna's face, the memory still raw. 'I promised then that I would.''Oh Anna, that's awful! I had no idea.' I finally understood what drove her. 'But the world has to progress, we can't live in the Stone Age forever.'

When she didn't answer I stood up and took the plates to the kitchen. 'So what are you going to do about it?' I asked.

We can help change things, we can increase the earth's spiritual resonance, make things better, put things right. I'm determined to do something, to make a difference.'

I sighed. 'Don't be ridiculous, Anna. How can one person change the future of the world?'

# Chapter 5

*Faustus: Have you any pain that tortures others?*
*Mephistopheles: As great as have the human souls of men.*
Christopher Marlowe

I walked quickly through the deserted streets into town. I wished I was at home on the sofa, but Tom was desperate for a drink to unwind after work. Anna was having a DVD-and-Duvet evening and I was jealous of her curled up in the warm flat with her cookies and ice cream.

There was no one about except the last few harassed-looking commuters, heads bowed against the weather, hands deep in pockets. I glanced up at the clock on the bank – 7.20, five minutes late already, and now I had to pull my hands from my warm pockets so I could text him.

Outside a shuttered and grilled bookshop was a man standing on an upturned crate, shouting at the passers-by. A small gathering of followers surrounded him and two yellow-jacketed police officers were eyeing him, one speaking into a radio. Most people were hurrying past them, eyes averted, as if they might be ensnared by a Siren's spell. These religious fanatics were every-where these days. I begrudgingly realised Anna was right – the End Times were firmly fixed in people's thoughts.

Arranged around them were home-made signs with pictures of emaciated, sad-eyed children, bomb-damaged buildings, war planes and burning forests. All were topped with the stark words, THE WORLD HAS LOST ITS WAY.

I glanced at them as I hurried past, but I must have hesitated long enough to suggest I was interested and one of the preacher's groupies walked in front of me. I made to dodge round him but my feet tangled together – I was unaccustomedly wearing heels – and I nearly ended up on the pavement. He took advantage of my indisposition to force a leaflet into my hand.

'Save the world, before it's too late.'

I took it without speaking, glaring at him, and glanced at it. The final line jumped out at me:

**AND SO THE WORLD SLOWLY FALLS APART.**

I screwed it up and put it in my coat pocket. There was litter everywhere but I still didn't want to add to it. When I reached the corner I heard shouting, and looked back to see one police officer grappling with the nutter, the other chasing after his scattering groupies. I carried on – this was an everyday occurrence round here. Obviously free speech was not considered appropriate tonight, it may cause the assorted drunks and clubbers to retaliate against the Establishment.

I reached the spot where I'd arranged to meet Tom and stood under a lamp post. There was no sign of him yet and I stood awkwardly for a moment, shuffling my feet. For want of something to do I fished the leaflet out of my pocket and smoothed it out. It was saying the same sort of thing as Anna had. The two of them were probably friends, I thought spitefully.

I looked up and down the street. Tom was still not in sight, just two giggling girls staggering up the road, arm in arm for support, and I read the leaflet again.

The coming of the **millennium** has been marked by **violence, fear, prejudice and intolerance. Global wars** have broken out – each country believes that they, uniquely, are on the side of the right and **denounce all others** opposing their thoughts, **fearing** an attack on their way of life.

Man's great **gifts of innovation and invention** have developed **new weapons**, spy planes, remote-operated drones capable of **wiping out entire towns** in one fell swoop. Insurgents race to arm themselves, learn **bomb making**, acquire **radioactive** material. Other countries are developing their own nuclear programmes, striving for a weapon which could **destroy an entire city**, or even a country, in an instant.

**Fear, distrust and paranoia** are rife – every stranger or foreigner is looked at with suspicion – is he a **terrorist**, is that a **bomb in his rucksack?** Individuals and authorities are **ostracising and persecuting** those who appear different, a potential threat, in the desperate struggle to **unify and harmonise** themselves and provide a secure front to **face the enemy.**

The **paranoia** runs deep – everyone is **afraid**, afraid of losing the things they hold dear, the things that define who they are.

**WHY?**

For without these things they are nothing, non-existent, because they have already lost the one thing that makes them **human**, the voice of **God** whispering in their ear.

To substitute for this disconnection, the loss of their place in the divine hierarchy, they try to establish **a new and bitter hierarchy** in the world of men. And in doing so, man wilfully **ravages the natural world**, fighting to impose his way of life on the rest of the world.

**The world as a whole is becoming sick.** Global temperatures are rising, rainforests are burning, species are becoming extinct at unprecedented levels.

**BUT IT IS NOT TOO LATE. WE CAN STILL PUT THINGS RIGHT.**

It ended with particulars for a festival or gathering from what I could make out, called *Love Yourself, Love Your World*.

It was in Glastonbury in a fortnight, and I almost laughed out loud when I realised it actually was the same thing Anna had been on about.

'You look pleased about something.' Tom had appeared behind me. He snaked his hands round my waist and nuzzled my neck.

'Oh, I was just reading one of the nutters' leaflets, I was

accosted back there,' I said dismissively, smiling back at him. He wasn't so bad, really. I tried to imagine what our children would look like.

'You look an easy target, you should try dressing a bit more fiercely,' he joked.

'What, black hair and head-to-foot leather? I'll attract more nutters than I frighten.''You'd look good though,' he said seriously, eyeing me up and down as he imagined it.

I punched his arm. 'Stop it!' I giggled. He was fun to be with, I thought. Perhaps I could see myself settling down with him.

'What did your nutter want, anyway?''Just to save the world, the usual.''Was it one of Anna's friends?' Tom looked at me with a smile to share the joke, but I felt annoyed. What gave him the right to criticise my friend like that? I forgot I'd been thinking exactly the same a moment before.

'Sorry, I didn't mean...' He took in my distinctly unamused look.

I waved my hand dismissively. 'Gerald's, is it?'

I walked into the nearby bar with Tom following, now I was wishing I'd made more of an effort to stay at home.

Tom handed me a vodka and Coke a moment later. 'I thought you'd like some chocolate to cheer you up,' he said, putting two packets of Maltesers on the table. His look of tender concern made me feel terrible and I squeezed his hand by way of thanks.

'So, the new film's not going too well?' I started munching the Maltesers.

'Well, it's coming on OK, but we're having problems with some of the scenes. They just don't seem quite right, somehow.' He took a swig from his pint glass. 'I'm desperate to make it work, I really am, we've put so much into it.' He chewed his thumbnail distractedly.

'You just have to keep going, one foot in front of the other. You never fail until you give up.' I'd heard this pep-talk so many times from one of the research managers.

'I shan't give up, it's my dream, my heart's desire. My dad always said to me, 'never give up on your dreams.''

That struck deep into my heart. But my dream was different, obviously. It was just a product of a sleeping imagination, not my heart's desire. I took a long drink from my glass and noisily crunched Maltesers, if only to drown out the persistent voice that screamed otherwise.

Tom rambled on about some inconsequential problems that I had no real interest in, and his words washed over me. Was that the most interesting thing he had to talk about? I looked at him closely. His hair had fallen over his eyes, he really needed a haircut. Somehow his hairstyle made his ears stick out like a cartoon character.

*What am I doing here?* The words spoke clearly in my mind. I'd always thought I was happy – life was easy, I had no real cause for complaint, no great hardships. I had friends, family, a flat, a successful job, a loving boyfriend. I was healthy and fit. I had everything I ever wanted, and more. Many would say I had the perfect life.

But I was lacking in something. A spark, a challenge, a real sense of meaning. It was only later that I realised this, although on a deep unconscious level I'd known it for a long, long time.

'You're very quiet, Brig.' Tom looked at me with concern.

'I'm just tired,' I lied. 'I'm not sleeping well.''Bad dreams?'

I hesitated. 'Yeah, something like that.'

'Do you want to go home?' he asked.

*Home.* The only place I wanted to be.

'What do you think about reincarnation?' I blurted before I could stop myself.

He raised his eyebrows in askance. 'Some of us were talking about it at lunch,' I added by way of excuse.

'Yes, I've always believed in it.'

It was my turn to be surprised.

'It was, um, one of the Greeks who brought the idea to

popular belief, I forget his name.''Pythagoras.'

'Wow, you've done your homework! Not one of your usual subjects of interest, is it?''Why do you believe in it?' I asked, avoiding the question.

'Why not? The soul is immortal, I was taught that at Sunday School. After death, it goes on to a new life. Either in heaven or on earth, to me it works both ways. Eventually I'll go to heaven, but probably not after this lifetime. I feel I've got a few lives to go yet!' He drained his glass and laughed. 'So why the philosophical discussion?'

I felt lost. I was envious of Tom and his assured, confident beliefs. Anna too. Everything I believed in, the solid and unshakeable pillars of science, reality and reason, my safe and orderly world that I knew and understood, was being slowly but surely dismantled. And I didn't like it one bit.

'I don't see how it's possible,' I said doggedly, pulling the shreds of my beliefs around me like a tattered security blanket. I knew and understood the world. I was a scientist, that's what we did. 'There's no scientific evidence that the soul exists. Life is a series of chemical reactions, that's all. When it's gone, it's gone.''Can you really believe that?' Tom's gaze was intense. 'Can you really believe that you're nothing but atoms and molecules? What about your feelings, hopes, dreams, memories? Do they count for nothing?'

He picked up the last Malteser. 'Remember when we went to Dorset in the spring? On one of your 'have to go away somewhere' trips? We walked through that wood in the evening and found that tree tied up with ribbons. And from there we could see across the whole valley, the sun was shining on the mist from the river, the birds were singing, the lambs were playing in the field below. It was simply perfect. And you said, 'If God exists, he's here, now.''

Tom leaned over and took hold of my hands, a surprisingly intense gesture as we both remembered our shared experience of perfection. 'You could feel it, the sacred power in that moment. And so could everyone else, hence the ribbons.' His voice was gentle, but firm. 'The soul, the spirit, it's real.' 'If it can't be measured, it can't be real.' The greatest dogma of the devout scientist.

Tom shook his head slowly. 'There's more to life than that, a lot more. Everyone knows that on some level. Even you.'

That night I had another dream. Every night I'd been hoping I would relive it, that incredible experience, and every morning I woke up disappointed. It wasn't that dream again, but it still stuck in my mind.

I dreamt that I was hanging from a beam by a thread, and I was trying to reach the next rafter. I desperately needed to spin a web, and must fix the thread at two points to start. I swung across to my intended target and fell back down again. Time and again I tried, always failing, growing ever more desperate.

Then I realised I was being watched. Far below on the floor lay a man, huddled against the wall for warmth. He was dirty, ragged and hungry, I would have thought him a common vagrant if not for the air of authority and confidence about him. He'd arrived late that afternoon, near collapsing through the door with exhaustion. The wind and rain blowing in had disturbed me on my fragile thread. He'd not moved from his spot since, and now he was watching my progress intently as if his world depended on it.

I kept on trying – I had no choice. And eventually I made it, I reached the far beam. The relief I felt was immense and I paused for a moment in thanks. From then on it was easy, I soon had my web built and I hung in the centre, satisfied and happy with my work.

The man never once took his eyes off me, and he also seemed happy once I'd finished. He rose the next morning, the air of despair and failure replaced with purposefulness and determination. He looked at me again and nodded, before leaving with a spring in his step.

I woke up with a start, with the face of Lucy Luck in my mind and the repeating words, *Listen! Listen! Listen!*

# Chapter 6

*Tear off this cloak of shadows, these shackles of decay, this living death, this conscious corpse. Empty yourself of darkness and you will be filled with light.*
The Hermetica

I was at work before eight and quickly analysed yesterday's results. My disconnection had vanished, my drive had returned. Life was going well again.

Remembering Anna's advice, I wrote the report exactly as Simon wanted and begrudgingly saw it was actually better for it. He would be pleased, I knew he would. I'd put in extra effort to make up for everything that had gone wrong lately, and the project was really going forward. The vaccine would soon be ready for trial, and it was something that would help the world a lot more than selling crystals and incense. I smiled happily as my fingers raced over my keyboard.

I looked up and saw Simon. 'Morning, Simon! I've got the latest results, they're looking really good!'

He didn't look as pleased as I'd hoped. He didn't look pleased at all. 'Come into my office, please.'

My heart sank. Something was wrong. I looked around the room as I stood up, aware of a sudden drop in the noise level. Everyone was busy working, pointedly oblivious to the exchange.

'Bridget, you've probably heard, the company's having problems.'

*Oh no.* I nodded mutely.

'We have no choice but to make redundancies. I'm sorry. Lately you haven't been yourself, your work standard has dropped. I'm sorry,' he repeated. He leant back in his chair, a big, shiny, leather contraption to showcase his authority.

'You've been an asset to the company these last few years, but,

I don't know if it's a blip, or if you've lost your motivation. I'm afraid there's no other option. I will of course supply you with a reference for your next post, and will arrange your redundancy pay immediately.' He concluded his carefully prepared speech.

I felt like I'd been kicked in the stomach. It hurt, it physically hurt, and I stared at him open-mouthed. He was waiting for me to say something, but my mind was blank.

'Thank you,' I said at last, my mouth on autopilot. 'I've enjoyed it while it lasted.'

He nodded, and seemed to be waiting for something else – pleading, begging, tears? My thoughts began to order themselves and I took a deep breath.

Instead of arguing, just accept you're wrong, that's what Anna had said. Accept Simon was right. Perversely, I felt like laughing. Arguing wasn't going to do any good anyway. 'Well, thanks for everything,' were my eventual last words.

Simon nodded again. 'Take the rest of the week as holiday time, your money will be transferred into your account next week.' He held out his hand and I shook it numbly then walked out of his office.

Everyone fixed their attention to their screens, carefully oblivious to my presence. I picked up my coffee mug, my pens, the strange angel-like thing that Anna had given me for my last birthday, the half-eaten packet of biscuits in my desk drawer.

The rest of the things – paper clips, notepads, scribbled notes, an apple, I left where they were. As I walked across the room for the final time, not one person met my eyes, her whose career was ruined.

In all these years, did no one care enough to even acknowledge me? I thought about it, and decided, no. I'd never made any true friends here. They were colleagues, we got on well enough, but friends, no. I wasn't going to miss anyone here.

So that was it. It was over, my future, my dreams, my aspirations. I shut the door on all that and walked out into the day, wondering what on earth I would do now.

I went to the nearby park where I sometimes ate my lunch. I'd never been here this early in the day before, it was full of mothers with prams and old couples walking slowly around the paths. A keep-fit class of overweight women in tracksuits jogged slowly past me, red-faced and sweaty, led by a fit young man jogging easily backwards.

'Keep going! Round to the left! Well done Michelle!' They disappeared from sight but I could still hear his shouted commands.

I flopped down on a bench and pulled out the packet of biscuits, eating four in a daze. The sun was shining warmly and I lifted my face to feel it beat down on me, grateful for its comfort. For the first time in ages, I had nothing to do. No purpose, no meaning. I was nothing. The future felt bleak and desolate.

I tried to think positively – I could easily get another job. What with the new and sinister viruses popping up all round the world, biochemists would never be in surplus, but I just couldn't get any enthusiasm for the idea so I stopped thinking all together.

I sat there for a long time without moving, concentrating on what was happening around me to block out my desolate thoughts. The gentle kiss of the breeze on my skin contrasted with the heat of the sun. I closed my eyes and listened to the chortle of a baby, the rustle of the leaves, the laboured footsteps of the joggers returning.

I noticed that for some reason there wasn't much litter scattering the park, and wondered why. Then I saw an elderly man with a bin bag methodically picking up pieces of rubbish. He nodded as he passed me. 'Doing my bit,' he answered my questioning look.

A bumblebee droned past my ear – a rare occurrence according to the media, which claimed all bees were dying out from some unprecedented disease. I noticed buds were forming on the trees already, that fallen leaves had been scattered on the paths by birds, that a tiny, gnome-like statue was hidden in a flower bed. Things I'd never noticed before.

How many people did notice? None? I realised how many little things I passed every day, but had never had time to notice.

I began to think.

I began to feel.

I began to *be*.

My life had been turned upside down, and now my feelings did the same. I now had time, freedom and peace, and I began to feel happy and free. Don't argue, accept Simon was right, Anna had said, and I began to see how right she was. The stress and pressure of my job had weighed heavily on me, I realised, grated on my spirit relentlessly. I looked back at the glass and concrete building I'd just left, ugly in contrast to the green and leafy park, and felt sorry for those still stuck inside.

I looked at the passers-by, harassed and hasty, no time to lose. Late for work, deadlines to meet, staff to hire, losses to explain. I empathised with them.

Then I noticed something else. All these people had another thing in common – all were walking with their eyes fixed firmly on the ground, and all had the headphones of iPods stuck in their ears. They were all subconsciously trying to block out the world. Beyond their own immediate problems and concerns, it was to them non-existent. Ironically, considering the smallness of the globe nowadays, we'd all shrunk ourselves to within four solid walls of concrete.

With so much to fit into so little time, I realised paradoxically, that life just flashed past us, so fast we couldn't grasp it.

Had I been like that, too? With my head down, blindly rushing through life, entirely oblivious to the world? Yes, I had.

This, I realised in that moment of stillness, was the problem the world faced. We'd all lost touch with the world, and lost touch with ourselves.

I thought of Lucy Luck, and my dream. And the words

written on her card. The revelation was so dazzling I laughed out loud. Events were moving out of my control, no matter how hard I was trying to prevent it. Maybe it was time to simply accept it. Accept I was wrong. Even when I thought I wasn't. And let the road rise to meet me.

A man was aimlessly walking past my seat, one of the city's many homeless. The loose sole of one laceless boot scraped on the tarmac with each step. He looked startled as I laughed, then he smiled back as I beamed at him.

'Have a biscuit,' I said, offering him the packet.

'Having a good day, miss?' he asked, revealing several missing teeth.

'The best of my life!' I answered.

He offered the packet back. 'Keep them,' I said.

'Thank you, miss. God bless you.'


'What will you do now?' asked Anna.

I wondered again whether to tell Anna of my dream. Of all my friends, she alone would understand. But I didn't want to seem like some irrational nutter, deciding my life on account of a dream. I was a scientist after all, I couldn't bring myself to think otherwise.

My mind said, *find another job, and quickly. Salvage your career.*

My heart said, *follow your dream, find that place. Follow The Path home, to your destiny.*

I decided to let the road rise to meet me.

'I'm going travelling,' I said.

# Chapter 7

*Thou livest, thy soul is strong, thy body is enduring and great. Thy face doth penetrate into the house of darkness, thou dost not see the whirlwind and the storm.*

The Egyptian Book of the Dead

The tannoy announced half a dozen arrivals and departures as I waited in the ticket queue. Early morning commuters vied with tourists and holiday-makers dragging oversized suitcases through the constant rush and bustle of the station. The buzz was infectious and I grinned at Anna.

'You're never happy unless you're going somewhere, are you?' She gave me a knowing smile. 'Maybe this time you'll find what you're looking for.'

The familiar rush that I got only from setting out to destinations unknown made me laugh. 'Maybe, this time.' Anna's veiled comments and her smug know-it-all attitude, once so tedious, could not spoil my happiness today.

When I had my ticket we walked over to platform two, heading north. We stood patiently in the queue for the bomb detectors – it was like an airport now since the last terrorist attack. The bombs had devastated two stations and getting onto a platform was like getting into Fort Knox now.

Two rows across, a young man with dreadlocks was arguing ineffectually with security, his rucksack emptied out onto the counter. Like everyone else, I ignored him. What did he expect? – they always went for the weirdos. We looked normal enough to make it through with only a cursory check and then we merged with the throng.

Carrying only a rucksack I nipped easily through the crowd, looking with sympathy at a couple trying to manoeuvre three suitcases, a holdall, two pink rucksacks, a doll's pram and three young children. A suited man barged into the woman as he

49

rushed across the platform, knocking a bag from her hand. He threw an apology over his shoulder without pausing.

The woman struggled to retrieve it without losing her grip on the bewildered children and Anna went to her aid. 'I'll get it for you, which platform do you want?' 'Platform two.' The woman smiled her thanks.

I went back and took a suitcase as well and a moment later we were all stationed on the platform.

'Brig!' I looked over my shoulder and saw Tom almost running down the platform, dodging tourists and commuters. Anna saw him as well and turned towards me.

'I'll head off then,' she said quietly. 'Good luck.'

I took a deep breath.

'Brig! Don't go!' Tom had now reached me, he had his hands on my shoulders in an imploring gesture. 'Let's go away together,' he said desperately. 'I can have time off, we'll go for a few weeks, anywhere you like, it'll be perfect!' He almost shook me in an effort to make me understand.

I thought he was going to cry and I looked round uncomfortably. A few people hastily looked away from us.

'It's only a couple of weeks or so, Tom. That's all.' I tried to sound as gentle and reassuring as I could, but we both knew it was more than that.

The train pulled into the platform with a hiss and the doors slid open. There was a flurry of movement as people disembarked and the couple nearby gathered their luggage and children.

'I don't know what's been happening with us lately,' he said defensively. 'I thought we had something special, really special. I've never loved anyone like I love you.'

I didn't know what to say. A surge of indecision hit me. Perhaps I was wrong, perhaps my life, my future, did lie in London. Tom looked at me, his eyes so desperately pleading that my decision was almost made.

The platform was empty. The guard was looking up and down then blew his whistle. I was still carrying my rucksack, it was only three steps to go.

'Don't go.' A tear slid down Tom's cheek, unnoticed.

The doors hissed, at the top of the train they were already shut. I was frozen with indecision. Tom stretched out his hand, touched my arm with an infinitely gentle gesture. The door began to move.

'I'm so sorry, Tom.' I wasn't sure if he'd even heard as I leapt for the door. It was shut before I could turn round and then our eyes locked through the thick glass. The pain in his face told me how wrong I'd been.

I watched the landscape flash past as the train sped north. My rucksack, the only thing I had with me apart from everything I carried inside my mind and my heart, was on the floor next to me. I couldn't decide how I was feeling, my mind was in turmoil. By the time it pulled into Newark, I'd almost decided to get off and go back.

I sat tight, waiting for the doors to hiss and signal it was too late, but the sound didn't come. Then came an announcement that the train would be delayed, there'd been a cable theft on the line. An angry murmur rippled through the carriage.

'It's disgraceful, absolutely disgraceful!' complained one woman in a high, affected voice. 'They should come down on these criminals, lock them up, every one!' 'Good luck to them, I say,' muttered another man. 'Not like there's any other work for them to do. Government's own damn fault.'

I shifted in my seat. Perhaps this wasn't meant to be, perhaps I was meant to go back? The pain had begun to recede with the miles, along with my feelings of regret. I'd really hurt Tom, I knew, but the feeling was being slowly replaced with hope, excitement and jubilation. *I was going home. At last, after so long.*

But Tom, my future, my life, I was throwing it all away, on a whim. The Voice of Reason railed against it. *Get off the train, while there's still time. Go back home!*

The Voice of my Heart said, *go home!*

I didn't know what to do. Either way I was irrevocably losing something, something I would never again get back. On the one hand I was throwing my life away, and on the other hand – *my life, again.*

The delay stretched on. I was both dreading and hoping for the hiss of the doors, the sound that would signify the choice was out of my hands. Twenty, thirty minutes, and still I couldn't decide. I picked up my rucksack, just in case.

It was only a few weeks, I lied to myself. Then I could get back to normal. I could have it both ways, really. I waited and waited, the delay not a moment too long. As the other passengers grew increasingly angry, my thoughts swirled and stewed.

The dreaded announcement came to a collective cheer – five minutes to departure. Five minutes to decide the course of my life. Four minutes. Three minutes. Follow your heart, I'd been told, follow your intuition. I looked forward, and I looked back. So much had changed lately, I felt that after a lifetime of searching, for what I didn't really know, the doorway had finally opened, the way forward had been lit up. Two minutes. The world seemed brighter now, more meaningful, I'd finally found my way out of the prison I didn't know I was in. One minute.

I sat back down, my decision made. The doors hissed and closed. There was no going back now. I settled back in my seat, there was now nowhere to go but forwards. Every aspect of my old life was now over, blown away like so many fallen leaves, as I recommenced the journey which had been lifetimes in the making.

It was a journey into the unknown, I'd set off with no idea of where I'd go. But then, I mused, all great discoveries were made when people stepped off the beaten path and walked into the unknown, where no one, least of all themselves, had ever walked before.

And as I left my old life behind, I subconsciously began to leave my old ways of thinking behind. Like a snake shedding its skin, I became a new person on that train. I had the strange feeling that I'd just awoken from a long deep sleep, one that had lasted for my whole life.

When the train entered Newcastle station, I picked up the rucksack which now contained my entire life and stepped onto the platform. The old Victorian station was quiet in between rush hours and there were no bomb scanners here, I noticed, just a dozen Transport Police patrolling the platforms. Obviously either the terrorists or the government considered the Northerners not worth bothering with.

I went to a small cafe and sat in the window, watching the people rushing past. All looking at their feet, all with headphones in their ears. It was still not yet midday, but already it felt like a lifetime had passed since I'd left London that morning.

I didn't really want to stay in Newcastle, my heart was craving open spaces and wilderness. I found the bus station and scanned the departure board, looking for interesting places. One seemed to leap out at me – Alnwick, the county town of Northumberland, a place I'd often heard of but never visited. My decision was made.

I people-watched for a moment then picked up a newspaper off a bench. There was more trouble in the Middle East; not only Iraq and Afghanistan, but now Pakistan, Syria, Iran and Libya were in-fighting, jockeying for supremacy in the bitter hierarchy. The threat to Western security was palpable, and questions were being asked as to what we should do about it.

I'd always assumed that the Western countries were the world's liberators, but now I began to wonder. Was it just paranoia and the desire for control that created an imaginary threat? I began to feel quite depressed – there wasn't one good thing reported in the paper. Not one positive event at all. Apart from the Middle East, it reported a hurricane threatening the east coast of America, droughts, global warming, the plight of the honey bee, diabetes, cancer, freak weather conditions which now seemed to be the norm, the list just went on. It seemed Anna was right, the world really was falling apart.

Then I saw something tucked into a corner, like the tiny voice of Hope left in Pandora's Box. An upcoming festival, *Love Yourself, Love Your World*. The organisers touted it as a universal message of peace and unity, advertised around the world. I felt awful that I'd derided Anna's heartfelt mission. She was right, someone had to do something. It seemed no one else was.

The bus arrived a few minutes later. 'Single to Alnwick please,' I said.

I watched the landscape whizzing by. Soon I saw the sea, a bright blue haze dazzling in the sunshine. Small fishing smacks bobbed in the distance, and further out was the North Sea ferry, thick smoke billowing from its engines. For an instant I had a glimpse of a sandy beach full of playing children. Then we passed a power station and the sun was blocked by the mushroom cloud of white smoke.

Fields turned to moorland, and soon the bus entered Alnwick. I felt the familiar buzz of arriving at a new place, this time stronger than ever. I took my meagre belongings and stepped off the bus. A guest house or a bed and breakfast was first, I wanted to stay here and explore this new area. There was no hurry. I had all the time in the world.

An hour later, my room secured and my rucksack offloaded, I was again walking the streets. I was handed a leaflet for the castle by a brightly dressed young man who looked like a court jester.

'See where Harry Potter was filmed! Did you like those films?''No,' I said. I wasn't twelve.

'Oh... well, there's loads of other things to see here. It's the only castle in the country owned by the same family for more than five hundred years.''Really? What about Windsor?' I asked seriously.

'Um, well...' he shuffled his feet nervously. 'It's worth a visit,' he finished lamely.

'OK, I'll do that,' I reassured him, and he bounced off to his next victim, a Chinese woman with a camera. 'See where Harry Potter was filmed!'

I carried on along a footpath which led to the open moor. I could see across the wilds of the county in the rapidly fading light. Grey silhouettes of hills, trees and rocks stood out in the twilight, and I could see a herd of cattle settling down for the night. The air resonated with peace and stillness, and from many miles away I could hear the barking of a dog.

I absorbed the peace for a moment longer until the almost obligatory fighter jets roared overhead, tearing the tranquillity asunder, then I turned and went back to the town. The street lights were on and the pubs were opening their doors, loud music periodically blared out into the streets in a stark contrast to the peace of a minute before.

I found a small restaurant that specialised in pasta and went inside. I was starving – I hadn't eaten since Newcastle. It was quiet inside, I was immediately given a table and ordered a spaghetti carbonara. The couple at the next table were arguing furiously in whispers and I strained to hear what they were saying.

The woman threw down her napkin and marched out of the door, leaving the man looking distinctly embarrassed. He carried on eating with deliberate concentration, for all the world as if nothing had happened. I shared an amused glance with the waiter and he shook his head slightly.

I reflected on the first day of my new life as I walked back to the guest house, and then scanned one of the provided newspapers. I skipped over the tinder box situation in the Middle East looking for something more positive, then saw an article on archaeology which caught my eye. I'd always been fascinated with history.

There had been an excavation in Iraq, recently freed from the Saddam regime. Iraq was once the ancient kingdom of Sumer, and an amazing temple complex had been discovered. It was over four thousand years old and, the archaeologists reported excitedly, it had been built on no less than seventeen earlier buildings – the site had been sacred since time immemorial. It was a similar custom, apparently, to ancient Egypt, where a building was not considered sacred unless built on the foundations of a previous sacred building.

My phone buzzed and I jumped. Anna.

'Are you there yet?'

'I'm in Alnwick,' I said.

'Never heard of it.''Up north of Newcastle.''Tom's been round, he's so upset. I told him he shouldn't ring you, but I thought I'd let you know.' There was no accusation in her voice, just matter-of-fact. I wondered if she agreed with what I'd done, but the feeling of doubt returned nevertheless.

'I just need some time,' I said. 'It's only a few weeks, then I'll be back to normal.'

We both knew that wasn't true.

'It's your journey, you have to walk your own way.'

I was about to respond to her cryptic comment when the phone went dead. I tried the usual things – smacking it, shaking it, shouting at it – before giving up. I'd heard about the problem, something to do with satellite interference, but hadn't bothered to read into it. The main fact, that it wasn't the work of terrorists, was enough to keep most people happy.

My thoughts kept turning to Tom over the next few days. Should I ring him? I couldn't bear to think of his face when I'd got on the train, but at the same time I knew our future wasn't together. Every time I picked up my phone, I decided against calling. It would only make things worse.

Although the landscape round Alnwick was very much like that in my dream, it didn't feel right. And soon, the familiar unsettled feeling returned. I wanted to move on. My heart said, *go further north, you're not there yet.*

I looked at the map in the bus station. The only major place to the north was the ancient market town of Wooler, The Gateway to the Cheviots – the wilds of the north which separate England and Scotland. The area was the spiritual centre of the Iron Age North, the number of ancient sacred sites had no equal anywhere in the country. Hundreds of hill forts, cairns, standing stones and stone circles were built there.

The bus was already waiting. My heart said, *take it.*

'Wooler please,' I said to the driver.

'Single or return?''Single.'

I reached Wooler late in the afternoon, and from here I had my first vision of the panoramic landscape. I saw the sharp hills, stark, brooding and menacing against the darkened sky, heralding one of the heavy rainstorms for which the area is well known and respected. Here, the hills tolerate trespassers who respect their space, their might, their strength. Those who do not, pay the price. I saw the swathes of heather across the wild landscape, smelt the sharp tang of the moorland air. Far up in the sky, the tiny speck of a bird soared on the air currents.

The first spots of rain began to fall heavily, rapidly gaining in intensity. Within a few minutes rivulets of water were running down my face and soaking into my clothes, but then just as suddenly the shower passed over. The sun broke out from behind the clouds and the area was transformed. Gone was the menacing, warning facade. The hills glowed green in beautiful contrast to the tumultuous black clouds behind them, the sun was lighting up every blade of grass. The gorse and heather blazed brightly and the moorland scent grew suddenly stronger, carried on the droplets of rain. A gossamer sheet of cobwebs stretched over the grass, each strand shimmering with an infinite number of tiny water droplets as if they were bejewelled with diamonds.

The beauty of the land resonated with my soul. I'd never been here before, yet every inch of the landscape was familiar to me, as the place where, so long ago, the story had started.

The land spoke to me, it welcomed me back. I felt the same feeling that I had in my dream, only this time it was stronger, more defined. I felt that I belonged here, that this was where I was meant to be. The feeling of peace, of belonging, swept over me so strongly I was overwhelmed by it. Tears filled my eyes, but they were tears of happiness. I had reached the destination my soul yearned for, by following my dream, and by understanding its message.

At last, I had finally found the place I had been looking for for so long. The place of my soul. The place that I called home.

# Part II

# Chapter 8

*Be not afraid of growing slowly, be afraid only of standing still.*
Chinese proverb

A final agonised scream tore through the air before fading into the night. A moment later, a second sound arose – the high-pitched wail of a newborn. At that instant a blaze of light – the death throes of a mighty star – shot across the heavens towards the distant sea.

High on the hillside, the Druid leant on his staff and watched, a vigil he had maintained for many long nights. He nodded to himself. His wait was over.

'She has come,' he said.

\* \* \*

Brigid gazed across her homeland from her special secret place, drinking in the rugged landscape, the hills reaching far into the distance, revelling in the raw power she could feel in the fierce, untamed landscape. She shifted slightly and wrapped her arms round her knees – the alcove, high up on the hillside, was small and cramped. She heard a voice nearby and tensed, fearful of discovery, but luckily it came no nearer. It was unlikely she'd be seen here anyway – she'd only found it herself by chance, it was completely enclosed except from the front.

Brigid pushed her legs out and relaxed, the pressure and strain of her lessons seeping from her body. She counted back carefully, it was six days since she'd had a moment of spare time and she was determined to enjoy her rare snatched moment of solitude. She'd known it would be hard, the training as a priestess of Ceridwen, the Great Goddess, but it was easy to resent the constant strain and she often wished it could be just a little easier.

In the far distance she could see the sea, the edge of the world, and she shuddered. She'd been told stories when she was young of great monsters, sucking whirlpools, a sheer drop where the water poured over into nothing, and the sea had always frightened her. She was glad she was seeing it from the safety of her hilltop.

The wind whipped at her hair and clothing and she could see clouds gathering on the distant horizon. A storm is coming, she predicted, and felt cold. She knew from bitter experience that it wouldn't be possible to see two paces in front of her when the cloud and fog came down. Her homeland was harsh and unforgiving to those who didn't respect it.

In the distance she saw people, nothing but specks climbing a distant hillside. She idly wondered who they were, where they were going and why. She drank in the crisp clean air and reached out with her mind to touch the furthest hilltops, expanding her soul to cover all she could see.

In her mind's eye she flew across the expanse of moor, saw the people getting bigger and bigger until she could see them clearly. They were peat-cutters, three men from an isolated farmstead. They struggled up the steep hill, driven forward by necessity and the need to survive, clawing their existence from the body of the hillside. Brigid could see their lined, worn faces, prematurely aged by the harsh, unforgiving elements.

'We'll cut peat until the sun disappears behind yon hill,' said one, the eldest. 'We've done well today.'

The other two men nodded in response, not wasting precious energy by speaking.

Brigid turned from the men and flew further, across the hillside where they were heading and saw the scars where more peat had been removed. Then, faster, she crossed hill and dale in a blur until she reached the far horizon. The wilderness seemed to stretch for ever, an endless chain of hills, moors, rocks and rivers. She hovered there for a moment then began to return, shrink and contract back over the way she'd come.

The three men had reached their destination and dropped their tools from their backs. The youngest was already at work.

'One full carry each,' instructed the eldest. 'Then back to yonder farm.'

Then Brigid was back in her rocky alcove, looking outwards again. Were these journeys, which she'd undertaken ever since she could remember, a part of her imagination or real? She was never quite sure.

How much time is passed? I'd better return to the rath, she thought reluctantly. The school and home of the Druids was on the very summit of the Sacred Hill of Cernunnos, she had a good distance to walk and was due at lessons at noon.

She squeezed out of her alcove, brushed the dust and grit from her woollen dress, then ran her fingers through her long, dark hair to tidy it somewhat. The wind immediately whipped it round her face again and she pushed it back irritably, wishing she could stay here longer. She started to walk quickly back across the hillside – someone may see her looking idle.

Glancing up at the sun, she saw with a start that the day had progressed further than she'd realised. Guiltily, she began to walk faster – Cathbad would not be amused if she were late. He was one of the most respected Druids in the north, advisor to the king at Maelmin, the town at the base of the Sacred Hill, and she was a little afraid of him.

As she rounded the hill she could see the buildings of Maelmin far below. Tiny wisps of smoke rose from roofs and dots indicated animals and people going about their daily lives. Out of habit she looked for her family's home, her home until her twelfth winter.

Her keen eyes picked out the round building on the edge of the main settlement. She could see two dots outside – people, she thought – and she felt a pang of yearning for her family. Her mother would be grinding grain now; she'd done so every morning since Brigid could remember. Was that her she could see? As much as she strained her eyes, she couldn't tell. She'd been permitted no contact with anyone outside the rath for half a year after she'd begun her training, and even afterwards her sparse contact with her family and her former life had become formal and chaperoned.

'You are chosen for a higher purpose in life, to serve the Goddess,' Cathbad had explained. 'Your family is now all the realm, and no person should have a higher place in your affections than another.'

But it had been a huge wrench to be separated from her family, her younger brothers and sisters, her friends, in short all that she knew, to go to the bleak and unforgiving rath where most people were strangers. During those first hard and lonely days and nights, she'd realised what her family meant to her.

She looked down the hillside again, thinking about them. What were they doing? Were they thinking of her? She longed to see them again. She could run down the hillside now, into the town, to where her mother would be working, fling herself into her arms, be a child again.

But she knew she couldn't.

She doggedly returned to her path and trudged onwards up the hill. She was chosen for the Path of the Goddess and she tried to shoulder the burden as best she could, no matter how hard it seemed at times.

A moment later she saw the stone wall of the rath crowning the summit, surrounding over a hundred ancient buildings – not even Cathbad knew when it had been built. She always felt a flutter of awe at the sight, it was designed specifically to display the power of the Druids and their Gods, and she was proud to be a part of this select group. She'd never understood how the ancient builders had pulled all those huge stones to the top of the mountain, and wondered secretly if magic was involved. On her first day at the rath she'd looked up at those walls with mixed incredulity and fear, knowing her life would never be the same again.

The caul had been over her face when she was born – a sure sign that she was destined to walk the Path of the Gods, and the Druids and also many others, albeit unseen, had been watching her for a long time.

'Training for the Druid Path begins at twelve winters,' Cathbad had said as she struggled up the rocky path beside him, the first of many times she would make this journey. 'Younger trainees cannot grasp fully the true, subtle insights of our philosophy. The Path is hard, very hard, you must develop intelligence, thought, insight and intuition to gain a true understanding of our world.'

Brigid had nodded, too out of breath to speak. Her blood pounded in her head and she leant her hands on her knees for support. She longed to rest but Cathbad barely seemed to notice the ascent. She didn't want to seem weak in front of him so she doggedly plodded on. Cathbad was watching her closely and was pleased with her determination. Although she didn't realise it, her training had already begun.

Brigid broke from her reverie and glanced up again. How did the sun move so fast? She began to run along the narrow path towards the stone walls – she couldn't afford to dally any longer. A small shape darted in front of her path, barely noticeable in the corner of her eye, before disappearing into the undergrowth.

'Probably a rabbit,' she said to herself as she ran, although it didn't seem quite the right answer. Immediately she put it from her mind. Since the earliest days she'd been taught the importance of concentration and ignoring all petty distractions.

The strange shape watched her run across the hillside from a patch of gorse, wondering, examining and scrutinising, as it had watched her go many times before, although she was entirely unaware of its presence. As she disappeared behind the stone walls, the shape nodded to itself, satisfied with what it saw.

# Chapter 9

*The Goddess Isis is with thee, she never leaves thee. Thou art not overthrown by thine enemies.*
The Egyptian Book of the Dead

'You are late,' stated Cathbad as Brigid ducked through the low door to his building. He looked at her without smiling and Brigid shuffled her feet. The Shadow-Stick outside, Cathbad's own invention which marked the movements of the sun, had told her it was well past noon.

'I'm sorry, the day has passed further than I realised,' she answered awkwardly. She had no further excuse, and it would never occur to her to invent one.

Cathbad accepted her answer without comment and turned back to his work, and Brigid breathed a sigh of relief. Although still a little frightened of him, she'd come to know the wise, intelligent and kindly person behind the austere facade, and regarded him with almost reverent awe. She didn't want him to be angry with her.

'You are to copy these messages for me,' instructed Cathbad without looking up. 'They are from the rath of the Brigantes.'

He pushed them towards her dismissively. He knew of Brigid's growing emotional dependence on him and did his best to discourage it. The girl must learn to stand on her own two feet.

Brigid took the sticks of wood and studied the marks and grooves of Ogham script notched into them. Between one and five lines of differing lengths and angles made up each vocal sound. She thought it fascinating that these lines could speak words to those who could understand. 'And indeed,' Cathbad had said, 'no one would suspect that these sticks conveyed messages, or be able to understand them if they did.'

'Here are fresh sticks,' he said, handing her a bundle. 'Make sure you can understand everything you carve, I will ask you to explain their meanings later.'

Brigid took her knife from her belt and began to carefully make notches on the wood, painstakingly recalling the meanings of each different symbol.

A second figure appeared in the doorway. It was Emer, a priestess and healer from the land of Albany, far to the north.

'Cathbad, you must come,' she said, glancing at Brigid. 'There is a problem.'

Cathbad rose immediately, as if expecting the summons. 'Carry on with your writing, Brigid. I will return shortly.'

As soon as he was gone, Brigid looked up from her work and stretched. The writing took a great deal of intense concentration. She wondered what was happening outside and how long she would have to write for. But after only a minute she forced her mind back to her work – Cathbad may return any minute.

But in the end she was finished long before he returned, and had deciphered both the obvious and esoteric meanings of the scripts – even the secret language itself contained secrets. It seemed there was trouble brewing between their kingdom and the Brigantes – war, even, had been alluded to, and Brigid felt a sick feeling of dread. She knew all too well what that would mean.

The heavy hide drapes were pushed aside and Cathbad ducked through the doorway. She jumped to her feet. She knew immediately that whatever the problem had been, it hadn't been resolved well. Although there was nothing outwardly obvious in his demeanour, she could sense an undercurrent of anger and frustration.

'You may go now,' he said. 'We will finish this lesson tomorrow. Go to your instruction with Emer.' Brigid nodded, made the correct obeisance to the great Druid and gladly went out into the sunshine.

Cathbad sat down and sighed. The negotiations were becoming increasingly difficult, it was taking all his considerable skill to prevent an all-out war. The emissary who'd just arrived had absolutely refused to see reason, it seemed the Druids of the different kingdoms were splitting into factions, and Cathbad understood well the disaster that would entail if a united ideal could not be maintained.

He'd hoped to speak with his pupil of these matters – this, after all, was just the beginning. The approaching calamity was written in the stars, he knew their whole world could be destroyed by what was brewing. And he'd also seen Brigid's future written in the stars.

She was chosen. The future of the realm would one day fall on her shoulders, and he'd been chosen to prepare her for her destiny. Cathbad sighed again and pulled absently at his beard, not for the first time wondering if he was up to the task the Gods had laid on his shoulders.

As Brigid crossed the rath she saw the familiar profile of Rhod, facing his workbench and busy hewing wood. Her heart jumped and her breath caught in her throat, and as if in response he turned towards her. His dazzling and rather shy smile crossed the distance between them and Brigid smiled back, overjoyed that he'd noticed her.

Brigid started towards him, hoping to perhaps speak to him, but at that moment Emer appeared around a corner and she abruptly changed direction. Rhod also turned quickly back to his task. Although their relationship was little more than shared glances and shy words, it was strictly forbidden. Druids could marry but relationships were not permitted for trainees – they were not considered mature enough to separate personal feelings from their duties.

Despite their imagined discretion, Emer and most of the Druids were aware of the developing situation. Emer looked at her pupil and shook her head slightly. That bright look of excitement and longing in Brigid's eyes was obvious to anyone.

67

She hoped the infatuation would soon run its natural course, else action would have to be taken. Hard as it was, personal sacrifice was a key feature of the Druid life.

'Greetings, Emer.' Brigid made the obeisance to her teacher and then smiled.

Emer returned the greeting warmly, putting aside her misgivings. 'The new stocks of healing plants we gathered are now dry and ready to store. We need to pack them away.'

As Brigid ducked through the entrance to Emer's hut her nostrils were greeted by the aromatic scents of dozens of different plants. She picked out betony, rosemary, thyme and juniper, combined with the harsh yet not unpleasant smell of wood smoke from the drying fire in the centre of the hut. She was looking forward to the afternoon – she had a great interest in healing, and also this task would be quite easy.

Emer unobtrusively studied her pupil as she deftly crumbled the stems and leaves to fine powder for storage in small leather packets. At least she's not so infatuated she can't focus on her work, she thought. 'What sicknesses can we heal with thyme?' she asked. Her pupil's mind had a tendency to wander, and Emer would give her something worthwhile to think about.

Brigid looked at the mass of shrubby stems she was picking the small leaves off. 'It's good for pains in the head and the stomach. And for sickness in the lungs,' she added.

'And what else?'

Brigid hesitated, looking at the fire for inspiration. 'For damaged muscles and joints, when mixed with fat and applied as a paste,' she eventually suggested.

'Well done. Now juniper, what's that used for?'

The lesson went on for most of the afternoon until all the herbs were stored away.

'You've done well today, you'll make a good healer one day,' said Emer, smiling with pride at her charge. Brigid grinned. The rare and welcome praise made her efforts seem worthwhile.

'Emer, what is the sea?' she asked suddenly. 'When I was younger, we were told it was the end of the world, to cross it was to disappear into nothing. Is that right?'

'No,' Emer replied, a slightly condescending smile on her lips. 'That's a story used by old women to amuse children. It's just water, past it are other lands. Across those lands, other seas and then more lands still.'

Brigid flushed as she realised her naivety. She worked hard to maintain an air of wisdom and now felt slightly foolish.

'Does anyone live in those lands?' she asked to cover her mistake.

'Yes, many people. They often come here, to Prydain, to trade and to follow the paths of wisdom. But they rarely travel this far north, they mainly settle in the south. Although there is an island in Albany, Ynys Druineach, the oldest and greatest of the Druid training schools, thousands of years old. People travel from across the world to study there. It's the location of the greatest wellspring of the life-force of the Goddess in the world.'

But Brigid's mind was filled with thoughts of fantastic and mythical places and she barely registered Emer's words. Years later, she would come to greatly rue her lapse.

'What are those other lands like?' she asked eagerly.

'Some are very hot, some are very cold. To the north is a land of ice, permanently frozen. Travellers say it's inhabited by giants made of ice, they cross the land and destroy everything in their path, but I don't believe that's true. The travellers get a bellyful of meat and mead in lieu of a good story. It doesn't mean it has to be true!'

Brigid laughed at the ridiculous story, and Emer met her eyes and laughed too. Their lessons were always lighter and more relaxed, Brigid couldn't imagine laughing with Cathbad.

And from then on, although she retained her sense of awe of the ever shifting sea, she was no longer afraid of it. She knew it for what it was, not what she imagined and feared it to be. She had learned an important lesson.

The moor was buzzing with energy and birds were twittering among the thick patch of gorse bushes. Brigid breathed in the strong scent of the bright yellow flowers with delight. The deep, resonant hum of bees told her she wasn't the only one to appreciate them. The sun beat down on her and she shut her eyes and raised her face, letting its heat penetrate deep into her skin. A sudden gust of wind swept across the moor, whipping her long hair into a frenzy, and she relished its cooling touch. Twice in two days she'd been able to escape the rath, the Goddess was truly favouring her.

She reluctantly opened her eyes and picked up her baskets. She was supposed to be searching for bilberries but the rare freedom was too tempting to pass up; now she was wandering freely without any thought for her task.

'Fill two baskets, that'll last for the next two days,' she'd been told that morning, and Brigid had nodded seriously, carefully masking her delight at her task.

With a sigh she made a half-hearted attempt to calm her hair and continued along the path. She could see a patch of berries over to the left, it wouldn't take long to fill the baskets.

Then her sharp eyes picked out an unusual shape amongst the loose scree. She knelt down and saw it was a perfectly formed seashell, the patterns picked out exquisitely, just like the shells the traders brought. The only difference was it was made entirely of stone.

Brigid had never seen anything like it before and she turned it over in amazement. She knew seashells were made by living animals, but stone was not living, so how could it be?

It must be a sign from the Goddess, she decided. She would take it back to the rath, the Druids would be able to interpret its meaning.

As she knelt she heard the sound of men's voices approaching and crouched down further behind the gorse, then crept into the thick bushes. Two men appeared, walking along the path which she'd been following. They were unkempt and scruffy, had obviously spent a long time living rough. With a gasp, she pushed herself deeper into her hiding place, ignoring the scratches of the sharp thorns, her heart beating faster. She recognised the men – they'd been outlawed by the Druid Council some time previously, forbidden from contacting or coming near the town on pain of death.

One of the men stopped abruptly, looking sharply around him. 'Did you hear something?'

His companion also stopped. 'No, nothing,' he replied quietly.

Brigid froze, hardly daring to breathe. These men were outside the Druid Law; if they saw her, alone and defenceless, there was no telling what they might do.

They both looked around, as alert and wary as the deer she often saw, then one man turned towards her hiding place. Her adrenaline surged. She must run, there was nothing else for it, and her muscles tensed in readiness.

But on the instant of discovery a small shape darted across the path and into another clump of bushes. Both men turned to look at it. 'A rabbit,' the first stated. 'That's what it was.'

The second nodded with relief, their illegal foray was undiscovered. They both relaxed and returned to the path.

Their voices grew quieter and Brigid also relaxed and crawled from her hiding place, putting the shell carefully into the pouch at her belt. She slowly raised her head and watched the men walk away. Another pair of eyes also followed their progress from its refuge in the bushes.

If I hadn't found that shell, I would have walked right into them, she thought to herself, feeling it again reverently. It must be a gift from the Goddess, sent to protect me.

But what were the men doing here? It must be the growing threat of war, the raiding and robbing that preoccupies the

Druids and leaders, it's making them reckless. No one has time for them any more, she thought.

It brought home to her how real the problem was. The moorland no longer seemed a place of freedom, it felt lonely and dangerous and she suddenly longed for the safety of the rath.

The men were out of sight and she leapt to her feet and raced down the hillside, careless of her steps. The erratic motion caused the stone seashell to jolt free and fall to the ground. Hearing it drop, she half turned and tried to stop, caught her feet in a rock and crashed hard to the ground. Winded and with bruised arms, she struggled to sit up. She found the stone and picked it up, breathing hard from shock and exertion. Then, as her body recovered, her breath stopped in her chest and her blood turned to ice.

Directly in front of her, no more than five paces away, was a yawning chasm. A sink hole, a hazard of iron mining, they sometimes opened up because of instability underground. She'd been warned of these many times, they were a death trap for unwary people and animals, and she'd been a heartbeat from suffering this fate. She looked at the stone in renewed respect – it truly was a gift from the Goddess. She would keep the stone with her, always.

# Chapter 10

*If it must be so, let's not weep or complain, if I have failed, or you,
or life turned sullen. The flag stills flies and the city has not yet
fallen.*

Humbert Wolfe


Brigid's long hair hung in sodden rats tails, and she made an
ineffectual attempt to push it from her eyes before it was blown
straight back. She was soaked through – the rain had been driven
through her meagre clothing which offered no protection against
the wind, and she was feeling fed up and churlish, and
immensely jealous of the people sitting snug by their fires in the
valley below.

It had been raining heavily for several days, the bare rocks
were slippery and treacherous. This, coupled with the strong,
bitterly cold wind lashing across the exposed hillside made the
climb particularly unpleasant – the strongest gusts made it
difficult to even stay on her feet.

'Why is the rath on the top of this hateful hill?' Brigid spat
bitterly to Emer, who was struggling upwards at her side. Why
couldn't things be easy for once? Since she'd encountered the
outlaws three moons before, Cathbad had decreed that none of
the younger Druids were to leave the rath alone. This was only
the second time since then that she'd gone out, and her eagerly
awaited excursion to the town had become insufferable. At that
moment, she hated her life. Her legs were aching, her boots were
blistering her feet, and she thought bitterly of the easy life she'd
given up.

What if she went away with Rhod, left the rath? Although
they spent little more than fleeting stolen moments together,
their love was true, Brigid knew it. They'd spoken of going away
and starting a life together, albeit only in carefully contrived jest.
They would have a home, warm and dry, a normal, happy,

simplistic life that at the moment seemed so very appealing.

Her bitter smile told Emer exactly what she was thinking, and she sighed in resignation. Her pupil still had a very long way to go.

Brigid raged against her Path – anything would be better than this hellish existence. A tear of frustration ran down her cheek, it was immediately lost in the rivulets of rain but it wasn't missed by the sharp eyes of Emer.

'This is the home of Cernunnos, Brigid. The King of Beasts, the God of the Green, the Woods and the Wilds, our God. This is where his spirit manifests.' Emer's patient voice was whipped away by the wind and Brigid struggled to hear. Emer knew that the iron mental discipline of the Druids, the ability to keep a positive light in one's heart and mind took years to develop; she had to be patient with Brigid.

'You think it's hard to climb the hill – think of the people who built the rath, generations ago. Their efforts enabled our way of life to exist. If they'd complained and given up when it got difficult we would have nothing.'

Brigid took the gentle chastisement to heart as she struggled on. She slipped and fell, bruising her hands on a rock, but she tried to force her pain and despair from her mind. She tried, she really did, but sometimes it was just so very hard. She bit her lip and forced herself back to her feet.

Emer put her hand on her shoulder, a gesture of both comfort and respect. 'The Road is not always easy, Brigid. There are hard and difficult times, but these trials are necessary for your soul, mind and body to learn the lessons you will certainly need to know on The Way.'

Brigid nodded, trying to swallow the lump in her throat. 'I know, Emer. I'm trying to learn.'

They struggled on in silence, the effort too much for talking. As they reached the rath entrance, as if in spiteful mockery the rain stopped and the sun broke through the clouds.

'Come with me, I want you to see something,' said Emer. She'd been wondering how best to demonstrate this lesson. 'See the blacksmith at work.'

Sweating under the blazing heat from the furnace, the blacksmith heated a shaft of iron until it was glowing white-hot, aided by his son who tirelessly worked the bellows. Brigid stood back near the door but the heat thrown out from the forge was still near unbearable.

When the iron reached the crucial point, the smith pulled it from the furnace and hammered it franticly, red-hot sparks flying. Despite his haste, each blow was still carefully and skilfully placed, years of experience and failure telling him exactly how to proceed. Brigid shrank back, a little afraid of the flying sparks, but the smith and his boy were oblivious to them.

The iron cooled and was heated again, the process repeated over and over until gradually the sword began to take shape. After many carefully placed final strikes from the hammer, the smith was satisfied. The sword was plunged into a vat of cold water and steam exploded upwards; then the smith held up the finished article, a tired grin of triumphant pride on his face.

'You see how this masterpiece of craftsmanship was made?' said Emer to her pupil, gesturing her forward. 'It is only through the trials and fires of the furnace, the heat and the punishment of the smith's hammer, that plain iron can be transformed into the beautiful object you see here.''It's incredible,' breathed Brigid, reaching with her fingers to touch it.

'This is how the soul develops, forged in the furnace of life. This is why your training is hard – you are on a divine journey towards the Goddess, and you must face hard trials along the way. But just as the iron can withstand the hammer and the heat, so you can survive the trials that the Gods place in front of you.'

Brigid turned the sword over in her hands. The experience was burned into her mind, she wouldn't forget it as long as she lived. She knew she'd just witnessed something amazing, incredible, divine. She now understood why iron-working was one of the most sacred professions.

'Did you see how the smith knew exactly where to strike the iron?' Emer continued. 'He would never damage or break his creation. And the Gods would never expect you to face anything you're not capable of or ready for. You can always overcome your trials, if you have the will.

'You always have the option of the easy way out, Brigid. You can return to the town and live an easy, simple life. But if you desert the Path, the Gods will desert you.'

Emer fell silent. She knew her pupil very well, she knew she was thinking of abandoning her Path, and that she may try to act on her wishful dreams. Her pupil needed to understand exactly what consequences her actions would have.

The terrible warning sunk deep into Brigid's soul. She felt a shiver at the thought of what that would mean, and resolved to remember this lesson for the rest of her days. She silently repeated the words, engraving them indelibly in her heart.

*If you desert the Path, the Gods will desert you.*

# Chapter 11

*Nothing in life is to be feared. It is only to be understood.*
Marie Curie

A mass of violets carpeted the Wyldwood with a swathe of shimmering blue. The rain had at long last stopped, and spring was beginning to stir from her long sleep. The sweet flowers would make a lovely fragrant addition to honeyed fruit – her favourite food, Brigid thought with pleasure, but then her mind clouded over with worry.

She glanced at Cathbad who was at her side, hoping that the rising surge of fear was not obvious to the great Druid. She was to spend the night here, alone, with no company but the nocturnal animals. The ancient and primeval forest was huge, many days' travel across, and the thought of being left here alone was starting to seem positively terrifying. There was little real danger, just the imaginary. Some animals were potentially dangerous – the bears and wolves for example, but mostly they didn't venture near people.

She'd been here many times, Cathbad had taught her the different trees and plants and their various uses, and the signs and tracks of the many animals that lived there. In truth she should know and understand the wood well, but now it seemed to take on a sinister atmosphere.

'This, here, is a spindle tree,' said Cathbad, stepping a short way from the path. 'It's very rare, but the wood makes the best spindles for spinning yarn.'

Brigid looked at it closely, making sure she would recognise it again. 'Its stems are square,' she noted.

'That's right,' said Cathbad, pleased with her observation. 'That's the key to recognise it, even when the leaves are gone.'

They returned to the path. Brigid automatically scanned the forest as she walked, recognising fourteen woodland plants in a short distance. Although she'd spent a lot of time in the woods when she was a child, gathering berries and food plants, she'd never realised the diversity of the life there. If she wasn't looking for it, she simply didn't see it.

She thought back to her early life and realised how much of the world she'd never noticed or thought about. She'd learnt from her own experience that many people were only aware of the small fragment of the world that particularly concerned them, and were entirely ignorant of the rest.

This, she reasoned, was why the Druids were trained in such a diverse range of skills; they must have their eyes open to everything to truly understand the world.

They reached a clearing where a rude shelter of poles and skins had been constructed, a hunter's lodge. Here she would stay until Cathbad returned the next day. She'd relaxed whilst in her reverie, but now the feeling of dread and fear reawakened deep in her stomach and she fingered her stone seashell nervously.

'Try to enjoy the peace and solitude,' Cathbad told her quietly, looking at a foraging blackbird rummaging through the leaf litter. 'Listen to the animals and birds, try to identify what's here with you. There's nothing here to be afraid of, nothing except your own imagination. Nothing here will harm you.'

He looked at her closely, assessing her emotions and her fear. 'Are you afraid?'

'A little,' she admitted, not wanting to appear weak but at the same time wishing she could be excused from her ordeal. She almost wished the outlaws were still at large – she'd never be made to do this then – but they'd been captured two moons ago.

Cathbad noted the flash of mute appeal in her eyes before she looked down at the ground. But that was only to be expected.

'Fear is the most detrimental emotion that man possesses,' he told her tersely. She was seeing him as a protector, emotionally depending on him far too much. 'It's essential for Druids to understand and conquer fear.'

Brigid nodded silently, her eyes fixed on a singing robin. Cathbad noted the slight tremble of her hands and continued his instruction. 'Fear only comes through unknowing and misunderstanding. Instead of fearing something, try to feel what it's feeling, think what it's thinking. Then your fear will evaporate like the spectre it is.' He must be severe, he thought. She had to learn.

He turned and left her, striding from the glen without looking back.

Brigid looked after him in panic, she hadn't thought he would leave so soon. She was now alone. Already it was growing dark in the dense forest, although it was still some time until sunset. The trees, once familiar and benign, took on a sinister air, their branches loomed towards her like taloned limbs. Her panic grew and she thought to run after Cathbad, beg him not to leave her. He wouldn't be far away yet.

Then she forced herself to focus. She couldn't do that, she must do something positive. Soon she wouldn't be able to see at all, so she quickly gathered wood for a fire, both for warmth and for protection and safety.

When it was burning well she ate the cold meat and bread she'd brought with her. Outside the circle of dancing flames, the wood was now completely dark. She could hear the nocturnal creatures coming to life around her. Large beetles buzzed through the air, attracted to the light of her fire, and twigs crackled as larger animals moved. A large snap coming from very close behind her made her jump, and instinctively afraid, she huddled closer to her protective fire.

'I must listen, learn, understand,' she told herself firmly, trying to calm her beating heart. 'It's nothing to be afraid of.'

She listened carefully, heard footsteps trotting through the undergrowth.

A controlled haste. It sensed me here and was afraid, she

deduced, and felt suddenly better. They're more afraid of me than I am of them.

Understanding this, she began to relax and feel more comfortable in the depths of the untamed forest. A moth bumped into her head, and then another. She pushed them away and watched them flying around the flames.

A chilling screech indicated the presence of an owl. These small owls hunt moths, she remembered. This was a creature that benefited from her presence.

Something large came towards the clearing, slow and lumbering. A bear, she worried, but knew in the rational part of her mind they'd never come this close to her or her fire. She forced down her natural fear – she'd go and see what it was. She took a burning branch from the fire and crept towards the sound. The creature stopped, listening, and she held the branch out in front of her. She saw the silhouette of a large badger, illuminated for an instant before it dashed off into the darkness. They live deep underground, digging holes with their big powerful feet, she recalled. She held the branch lower and saw its footprints in the soft ground, the large claws clearly visible.

She returned to her fire, now using it for warmth rather than comfort, and continued to listen to the sounds of the woodland creatures. Eventually she fell asleep and was awakened by the sound of birds singing.

She waited, enjoying the peace as the birds foraged and sang. A blackbird hopped around the clearing as she watched, searching under the leaf litter for insects. It came up close and cocked its head towards her, fixing her with its beady eye before picking up a morsel of bread she'd dropped. It looked at her once more and then flew away. It was a rare period of oneness with nature and she was sorry when, all too soon, Cathbad returned.

He looked at her closely, noted her aura of tranquillity and peace, and was pleased. 'Never again will you fear something which you do not understand,' he said.

# Chapter 12

*'Tis all a chequer board of nights and days,*
*Where destiny with men for pieces plays.*
*Hither and thither moves and mates and slays,*
*And one by one back in the closet lays.*
Omar Khayyam

The rain and wind buffeted against the two women as they hastened across the valley. A young boy had come to the rath pleading for help for his mother, who was very sick. He was close to exhaustion and had been given a bowl of hot food and a bed before they set out into the inclement weather.

'There's the house, Emer!' Brigid's keen eyes picked out a glimmer of firelight through ill-fitting door drapes and they quickened their steps. Neither felt the inclement weather as they hastened to their duty.

The sick woman, Rhian, was lying on a bed, pale and weak, cold despite the warmth of the house. She turned her head and smiled faintly at their presence. Brigid, despite her limited experience of death, could sense that her hold on life was very tenuous. A small baby, a few days old, lay in a basket crying pitifully, hungry and untended. Emer squeezed Rhian's hand and felt her forehead.

Puerperal fever. She offered a silent prayer to the Goddess, Ceridwen.

'You have a sickness from birthing,' she said. 'But it's not serious, we'll soon have you cured'.

Rhian tried to sit up but Emer pushed her back down. 'It's too late,' Rhian whispered. 'I know there's no hope. Will you see that my baby's cared for? My sister lives across the valley, she's recently birthed – she can care for her.'

'You will care for her yourself,' Emer told her firmly. 'You will recover yet.' She went to the door, signalling Brigid to follow.

'I need wild thyme, ramsons and betony, will you gather them for me?'

Brigid nodded, mentally retracing her journey and recalling where she'd noticed these common woodland plants.

'I'll go at once, I know where they are,' she said, already on the path. Rhian would recover now, she was sure of it, Emer could heal any sickness. In the two years since Emer had decided Brigid was ready to aid her in her healing, she'd never known her to fail.

'I'm afraid though, this case has progressed too far,' Emer said quietly, so Rhian wouldn't hear. 'If I was called yesterday I could have helped her. You see she's given up hope, she's expecting to die – the only real cause of death.'

Emer looked sadly into the distance, it always hurt when her treatment failed. 'You must gather the herbs anyway – there's still hope while life hangs on.'

Brigid soon returned and Emer made an infusion of the herbs. Even in her short absence Brigid could see Rhian had deteriorated. She fingered the stone seashell that she still carried everywhere and sent a heartfelt plea to Ceridwen. She couldn't die, she thought desperately. They had to save her, they *had* to, Emer must know what to do. Brigid had to force tears back as she threw more wood on the fire to drive the chill from the sick woman.

When she fell asleep, both women watched over her silently, each offering prayers to the Goddess. Brigid asked desperately that Rhian be cured. Emer serenely asked for the strength to overcome the ordeal – for the woman, her baby and her family – whatever the necessary outcome must be.

The sun set, night fell, the fire burned low. Neither stirred from her vigil. The baby had also fallen into a fitful sleep. Then, in the darkest hour of the night, Rhian at last stirred.

'Why, it is day already,' she said, her voice stronger. 'See how the sun shines!'

Brigid looked at Emer to share her gladness – their treatment and prayers had worked, she was better! But Emer pressed

Rhian's hands tightly, infusing her with spiritual strength for the great journey she was now certain she was to undertake. Brigid looked back to the bed with confusion – why was Emer not rejoicing?

Rhian's burst of strength was short-lived. She closed her eyes a moment later and her breathing quickly grew weaker. Brigid stared at Emer in panic, willing her to do something, but she held her silence as Emer's gaze remained on Rhian.

And then the moment came. They both felt a sudden flash of energy, a burst of spiritual light. Emer bowed her head, wishing her soul a safe journey, and Brigid did the same, the tears already coursing down her cheeks.

The light rapidly faded. The spark of life was gone.

Distraught tears flooded down Brigid's face and her body was racked with sobs. The salty tears soaked into her dress as she buried her face in her arms, but she didn't notice and didn't care. She raised her head and looked with blurred eyes across the hillside from her secret alcove, but the view she loved seemed now harsh and unwelcoming. She rested her head on her knees again, gaining no comfort from her homeland.

Why had she died? Why had the Goddess failed to help? It was so unfair, she couldn't understand it. It was the first time she'd ever witnessed a death, the first time she'd witnessed the inexorable progress of fate that all people, no matter how wise, must succumb to.

She thought of the baby, now orphaned, and then of her own mother, also lost to her. She yearned for her, the one person who, as all children unerringly know, could heal all hurts. It was hard, too hard, she wished she could leave it all behind. The Path of the Goddess was too much for her.

Or she could go away with Rhod. The idea was still toying in her mind and the thought lessened her tears a little. He had kin in a nearby town, he was a carpenter, not a Druid, there was nothing holding him here. Maybe a life with him was her true destiny; maybe that was why Ceridwen had allowed them to meet.

Rhod had only spoken of it two days before. After checking no one was watching, he'd grabbed her hand and dragged her behind his workshop, so hard she'd almost fallen. Giggling with excitement and surprise, she'd feasted her eyes on his tanned skin, his thick blonde hair and rippling muscles, breathed in the musky scent of his body. She loved him, she knew it. He'd kissed her once, bold and daring, the memory quickened her pulse. Rhod saw her pupils dilate and smiled knowingly.

'Let's go away together,' he said insistently. 'We can live in Dunholm, I can get work easily.' It wasn't the first time he'd tried to make her give up her calling.

'The Druid Path is my destiny,' she countered, shyly but firmly. She could hardly bear to refuse him. 'We can't be together, it's forbidden.'

She reached up and stroked his long hair to soften her refusal but Rhod looked away, his lips tightened into a thin line. At the sound of approaching voices, he turned and walked away without a word, and Brigid looked after him with mixed feelings. She'd done the right thing, the Goddess was her destiny.

But now, she was not so sure.

Brigid crept from her secret alcove and walked slowly back towards the rath. Tears still blinded her eyes and she walked with her head down. This time, she didn't even notice the small darting shape which followed her.

It was time for the daytime meal when she passed through the walls and everyone was heading towards the vast central hall.

'Brigid!' Mair, another trainee Druid, came towards her with a smile. 'Where have you been? Come and sit with us!'

Brigid could think of nothing to say and was propelled along by the crowd. The babble of noise in the hall struck her forcefully and she flinched. How could anyone bear to be happy today? She wished she hadn't come back to the rath.

She sat down at one of the long benches and dutifully took a bowlful of steaming broth and some bread. She couldn't face eating, she just couldn't, and just stirred it round in the bowl, the conversation washing over her.

'Don't you like it, Brigid?' asked Mair, trying to draw her into the conversation. 'Gwen's cooking this week, I thought she makes broth better than anyone, even me!' A ripple of laughter rose but Brigid couldn't smile.

'I'm not hungry,' Brigid managed, forcing her spoon to her lips. Mair shrugged and returned to her conversation.

From across the room, Emer watched her closely. She hadn't realised how sick Rhian would be, Brigid should have been introduced to the concept of death in a more gentle way, but there was nothing could be done now. She would have to talk to her, explain the spiritual facts of life and death which the Goddess had obviously decided it was time for her to learn.

# Chapter 13

*Raise a stone, there you will find me. Cleave a piece of wood and here I am.*
Gospel of Thomas

'Why did the Goddess allow her to die?' asked Brigid desperately. 'Why did she not save her?'

'She died because the Goddess saw fit to call her back to her bosom, that her time on earth was at an end.'

'But it's not fair!' she cried. 'Leaving her poor baby all alone, making her family suffer. How could she do that?'

Emer had thought carefully about how she was going to explain this. The Goddess, with her infinite wisdom, had a reason for everything, even what people considered bad or wrong. In life, the nights were as important as the days.

'We may never understand the true reason, but we must still accept in our hearts that it is right and necessary. The trials are a part of our soul journey, the flames of the furnace which forge the soul.'

The awe-inspiring memory of the forged sword came back to Brigid, and for the first time that day, she didn't feel like crying.

Emer could see that her words were having the desired effect. When her pupil had lifted herself from her despair, she could move on to the more important aspects of the lesson. She got up and threw some wood on the fire to give her time to think.

Brigid watched the sparks leaping high, flaring for a second before dwindling into nothing. The smoke swirled upwards and disappeared through the central roof hole.

'You're worried about the baby, but you shouldn't be,' she continued. 'The Goddess has a great future planned for her, that's obvious by this severe ordeal at only a few days old. Her future doesn't lie here, where her life would be to sew, spin, cook and grind grain. The harder the ordeal, the greater the reward. The child will overcome her ordeal, and achieve greatness because of it.'

Emer's eyes were filled with a fervent belief, a certainty that everything, no matter what, happened for the greater good of the world. They locked onto Brigid's face and she was filled with the same surety. It was a hope that would never leave her, ever.

'Each life has one purpose,' Emer continued. 'To learn. Our trials must be accepted and embraced, not shied from. You can try to run and hide from The Path, but The Path will never leave you behind. No one can escape their destiny, no matter how hard they try.'

*If you turn from the Path, the Gods will turn from you,* thought Brigid, and felt that same shiver race down her spine.

'But surely, not everything can happen for the best? Some things must just be bad?'

Emer stirred the fire and then sat back down. Her pupil's questions of late were forcing her to analyse her own beliefs, in truth she'd been learning as much as Brigid. Just as the analogy of the sword had suddenly come to her as they were climbing the hill, so she had a flash of inspiration to explain this latest question.

'I will tell you a story from Albany which I heard long ago.' She settled back in her seat and Brigid leant forward. She still loved to hear stories, as did all people, the reason why their gentle instruction was so favoured by teachers realm-wide.

*A man was riding hard across the moors, travelling to the High Court of Albany in the city of Edin. Although the road was rough and treacherous, Cian couldn't let up on his speed for a moment. He was on an important mission, to deliver a hard brokered message of alliance and peace between the two great kingdoms of the north. Trouble had been simmering for a long time, and all-out war was now just days away.*

*One of his mount's iron shoes was coming loose, and as he'd half expected, it was eventually cast. There was no blacksmith for miles around, and Cian's decision was made instantly. He had to push on regardless.*

*The horse soon began to suffer, its delicate hoof bruised and sore, and Cian eased up slightly to save its discomfort, although he could ill afford to do so. But even so, when it stumbled on an exposed rock, it couldn't correct its balance and fell hard, throwing Cian to the ground.*

*He leapt up at once but saw his mount was injured. Its leg was badly strained, he could see its flanks heaving with shock and pain. What was he going to do? The future of the realm depended on his completing this journey, but his horse was now crippled.*

*He had one option. He gave his mount a quick, reassuring pat on its nose and began to run, the quick jog-trot men use to cover long distances with minimal effort. It was not quite dusk, and he had until daybreak to reach Edin. He tried not to think about the huge distance left to go. As a professional messenger, he was expected to make long and difficult journeys in exceptional time, no matter what the obstacles. He knew all the trade routes, moorland paths and brigands' routes like the back of his hand, and despite everything he made good progress. He had to get there, he had to, and he trusted that the Gods would guide his feet.*

*Just before dawn, his prayers were answered. A farmstead. With a bursting of joy, he ran to the door with renewed energy.*

*'Help me, please!' he cried to the old man who met him, barely able to stop himself hopping from foot to foot. He rapidly explained the situation and the old man gladly lent him a horse. All men hoped war would not come.*

*He galloped hard, clinging grimly to the horse's back, pushing it to its utmost limits, and an hour after sunrise he reached the High Court.*

*But he was too late. The king had already left. Cian had failed. War broke out.*

*It was soon over, but it was not a happy time for Cian. He'd* failed in his task, threatened the future of the kingdom. He was outcast and soon became destitute, reduced to begging on the streets of Edin for scraps of bread.

But throughout this time, seven turns of the seasons in all, he never lost the light of hope, peace or justness in his heart.

One day, sitting huddled on the road as usual, he saw an old man. The face was familiar – it was the farmer who'd lent him the horse, what seemed a lifetime ago. He didn't recognise Cian, barely noticed the bundle of rags nearby. But as he approached, Cian saw a man following him. His instincts were sharpened by the cut-throat life of the outcast and he began to rise, but the robber had already grabbed the farmer's purse, thrown him to the ground and was running. Before he'd gone ten paces, Cian had lunged from his spot, knocked the robber down and retrieved the farmer's purse.

When he learnt of Cian's unfortunate circumstances, as well as their previous acquaintance, the farmer offered him a place in his own home. His deep understanding of the moorland, learnt through his days as a messenger, stood him in good stead and he soon became as respected a farmer as he had been a messenger.

The farmer's son had gone to Edin long before to seek his fortune, and had become prosperous as a trader. His eldest daughter was of marriageable age, and in time an alliance was made. Cian returned to Edin with his bride to a position of honour and respect.

In time, he became known to the king himself. His new, respected position, together with his great knowledge of the realm, legacy of his days as a travelling messenger, his farming knowledge, and his understanding of the town and its under-classes, legacy of his time as a beggar, made him a unique asset, and the king shrewdly resolved to have him on his council.

Eventually Cian became one of the most respected law-givers in Albany. He spent the rest of his days in Edin, in a position of unequalled renown, and even today his laws are still respected.

Brigid was leaning forward in her seat, enthralled by the story.

Emer was a gifted story-teller and her lilting, melodious voice was a delight to listen to. She saw in her mind the messenger galloping hard across the moor, urging his mount ceaselessly before being thrown to the ground.

'You see how he didn't give up on life?' asked Emer. 'He trusted that the Gods were still beside him, despite his misfortune.''He was undergoing a test!' exclaimed Brigid. 'It seemed to cost him everything, but in the end his failure became his greatest success.' She looked into the fire with wonder, her despair forgotten. 'Imagine his horse had not cast its shoe that day! He would have remained a messenger all his life, with no great hardship, but also no real success.''You see then, if you walk The Road with the light in your heart, no matter what, everything will always work out for the best.' Emer filled two wooden cups with hot water and added some herbs. The sweet scents of chamomile and rosemary perfumed the air. She handed one to Brigid who sipped the tea with appreciation and gazed into the swirling, steaming liquid.

'Why is it that everything that lives must die?' she asked. 'Why does the soul not live in just one body for all time, instead of in many bodies?'

Everyone knew that after death the soul would pass into another body, and so continue living forever, but only the Druids actually knew the reason why.

'As you well know,' said Emer, 'every living thing is made of two parts, the body and the soul. The body is the house of the soul for a short time, and when its life purpose is fulfilled the body dies and the soul is released. When the time is right the soul will enter another body to live again. The body returns to the ground after its death, to provide nourishment for new life.''But *why* is this?' asked Brigid impatiently. She'd known that all her life.

Emer gave her a sharp look and Brigid dropped her eyes contritely. 'All life mirrors that of the Goddess and her son

Cernunnos, the God of the Green, the two life-giving forces. The soul belongs to the Goddess – it is eternal and can never die, just like her. The body belongs to the God and is born, lives and dies, just as he is born in the spring and dies in the autumn.'

Brigid remembered the spring festival of Beltaine half a moon before, which re-enacted the Sacred Marriage of the Goddess and God. 'So Beltaine celebrates the unity of the God and Goddess, the body and soul, into one being, so life can flourish in the spring? Life can't exist unless a body and soul have come together?'

Emer started at the quick intuition of her pupil, then quickly masked her surprise. 'Yes, that's exactly right,' she said casually. 'Cernunnos is the spirit of all things green – the plants, trees and herbs – which flourish after his marriage in spring, the marriage which provides him with the life-force of the Goddess. Without that the world would be barren and dead.'

Emer stood up and went to the wood pile in the corner of the room, picking up a log. 'Do you see how the small fungi grow from the decaying wood?'

Brigid looked with interest at the mass of mushroom-like growths protruding from the broken end of the log. 'They are the life which comes from the death of the God!' she exclaimed. 'When Cernunnos' spirit died in this wood, its body became the food for the mushrooms!'

Emer had to work even harder this time to mask her astonishment and pride in her pupil. 'This is the circle of life. Life is nourished by death, which in turn is nourished by life. The key Truth of our philosophy.' Emer's voice held an unaccustomed warmth, and Brigid saw with pride that her teacher was pleased with her.

Emer returned the log to the wood pile, her pleasure now tempered with worry. Maybe it was a good thing that Brigid was progressing so fast. The situation in the realm was deteriorating much faster than anyone had anticipated, the sooner Brigid was prepared for her destiny the better. Emer just hoped that she and Cathbad had done enough.

'So, will everyone continue to be reborn forever?' Brigid looked into the flames again. The thought of this far-distant future unsettled her deeply. A hundred generations from now, what would the realm be like? Somehow, a glimpse of this future seemed to enter her mind as the flames jumped and danced. The strange, alien world frightened her and she shivered.

'When a soul reaches a high level of purity, it can escape from the cycle of rebirth, become One with the Goddess,' said Emer, wondering what Brigid was seeing in the flames. 'All souls will eventually complete their journeys and then return permanently to the arms of the Goddess.'

Brigid pulled her eyes from the flames and the vision they told. Hopefully she would achieve her soul-journey in this lifetime, she didn't like the look of the future world. 'Are we born only as people, or other things as well?'

'The soul can enter anything at all – an animal, a plant, a rock, a river, a parchment, a star. Everything is a part of the great creation of the Mother, and everything contains a soul, an equal part of the Mother's body and spirit.'

Brigid suddenly realised why her seashell was made of stone. The Goddess had intended her to see how her spirit was contained in everything, living and non-living. She wondered, not for the first time, if she should show it to Emer, but again something made her keep her secret to herself.

'Emer, why are some things lucky, and bring good fortune to those who own them?' she asked. She was still wondering why she'd been given her shell. 'Are lucky amulets specially blessed by the Gods, and give magic powers?'

'There is no such thing as a lucky amulet,' Emer told her. Brigid seemed particularly attached to this fanciful notion, it seemed. 'In truth it is only your mind which gives luck. When people think something is lucky, the object acts as a symbol of strength which the mind uses to focus itself. You need nothing at all outside of yourself, all objects and possessions you can live without. The Druids routinely undergo hardship and austerity in place of a life of luxury and comfort, because this is what teaches the mind to rely only on itself.'

She turned to look at Brigid. 'This was the first lesson that you yourself had to learn when you first came to the rath.'

Brigid remembered only too vividly the wrench of leaving her home and family, everything that she knew and depended on. She thought back to the first night she'd ever spent away from her home, shivering alone in the cold and longing for the warmth and comfort of her sisters. She'd come a long way since that night.

Emer also thought back to the first time she'd seen the girl. Despite her worries and doubts, the light of her soul had filled the rath. She was the one, they'd all seen that.

The fire was burning low, it was time for the lesson to end. The sun was nearing the horizon, the day was drawing to a close.

Emer and Brigid went out into the rapidly cooling air and towards the highest point of the rath. Nods and smiles passed between the two women and many others in the rapidly growing crowd. Silence fell as all eyes turned towards the dying sun, a daily ritual observed since time immemorial. As the glowing orange disc became a sliver of light and then vanished, Cathbad's voice rang out across the hilltop.

*As day turns to night,*
*As light starts to fade,*
*Let us pray for the return of the light,*
*From which our souls are made.*

After this ancient prayer had been recited, Brigid silently repeated the words in her mind, translating the message into her heart and sending it outwards towards the heart of the Goddess.

The observation of the sunset ritual would be something she would mark for ever.

# Chapter 14

*For everything has its season, and for every activity under heaven its time. A time to be born and a time to die. A time to plant and a time to uproot. A time to kill and a time to heal. A time to pull down and a time to build up.*
Ecclesiastes 3.1-3

It was early spring, although it was hard to imagine on the exposed hilltop. It had been a hard winter, bitterly cold, and deep snow still lay on the ground. Everything was suffering and men kept a close eye on their vulnerable livestock; hungry wolves were forced unnaturally close to human habitation.

Brigid was wrapped warmly but the icy wind still found its way through her clothing to chill her skin. The iron fist of winter was showing little sign of releasing its grip on the land, although today, for the first time, she could see the faint glimmer of the approaching sun in the east.

As with every morning, she was going to see to her hens, wish them good morning and gather the eggs to break the fast. Chickens, sheep, cows and goats were kept at the rath, used for meat, milk and eggs.

Brigid had been given responsibility for the care and tending of the chickens, a task she loved, and over time developed a close affinity with them. The proud cockerel, feathers standing tall and gleaming in the sun as he corralled his hens, was her favourite. One hen had laid a nest of eggs hidden inside a thick bush, and when she'd first appeared leading a troupe of little fluffy chicks, Brigid was delighted. They'd rapidly grown and learned to scratch in the dirt under the hen's watchful eye.

Although it was still early, many people were about. As she hurried across the rath, trying to stave off the cold, she glanced out of habit at Rhod's hut, but it was dark and still. Then she saw Cathbad walking towards her. Despite the cold, he was wearing the same thin robe which he wore in summer, seemingly oblivious to the biting wind howling around the darkened settlement. As he got nearer, Brigid could see ice crystals on the hairs of his beard. He would have been at his meditation, she knew. He spent an hour meditating very early each morning, in rain, snow or sunshine. She didn't believe he ever slept.

'Greetings, Brigid,' he smiled. She made the correct obeisance to the great Druid, and he touched her head in blessing as he did at their every meeting.

'There will be a break in the weather today. This cold will end and spring will finally awaken from her deep sleep,' he told her.

Brigid was amazed. 'How do you know that? Today seems the same as every day for the last two moons!' she exclaimed, her polite manner forgotten.

'I know how to read the signs in the weather and the sky, the signs most people wouldn't even notice,' he replied. 'Tomorrow will be the first day of spring.'

'Good,' she said. 'This cold spell has gone on long enough. It'll be nice to see some sunshine.' She was heartily sick of this cold weather.

'But you must accept whatever happens with light in your heart,' he admonished her. 'Do not wish for things to be different, the Gods have chosen this way for a reason.'

She looked down. She tried to always think this, but sometimes it was very hard, and she wished things could be just slightly easier. An involuntary shiver struck her with a particularly icy blast of wind.

'Are you cold?' asked Cathbad.

'A little,' she admitted reluctantly. In truth, her fingers and toes were beginning to go numb, however much she tried to will herself warm. But she knew Cathbad had conquered such trivial feelings, could warm his body through his iron will, and she didn't want to seem weak in front of him.

'You must carry on with your tasks,' he said, following exactly her train of thoughts. 'We will speak more later.' He touched her head again, and the two parted.

The first sign that something was amiss was the unusual amount of feathers scattered around, coupled with spatters of blood. Then she saw one of her hens huddled on a low branch, immobile with shock.

With a cold feeling of dread Brigid looked further, and found the once proud head of her favourite cockerel, snapped like a stick from his body. Tears already running down her face, she then saw feathers she recognised from one of the half-grown chicks. Every hen was either dead or missing.

She carefully picked up one of the feathers, a strangled cry escaping from her mouth as she saw specks of blood flecking it, diluted and dispersed by her falling tears. She dropped to her knees. The pitiful remains of her poor hens, which she had put so much work into, was too much to bear. She scrambled to her feet and ran sobbing to where she'd seen Cathbad moments before.

'It was the work of a wolf,' Cathbad told her, surveying the scene with detachment. 'A she-wolf has been seen scavenging near here. She birthed early in the year, and now cannot find food for her cubs. In desperation, she came here in search of a meal.'

'But why did it kill them all, why did it not kill something else?' she cried pitifully. In her grief she could not feel any empathy for the starving wolf.

'It is the way of nature, Brigid,' Cathbad told her. 'Your hens are dead, but they gave their lives to sustain the lives of the wolf cubs. If the hens had lived, the wolves would have died. No life is more important than another.'

Brigid looked despairingly at the ground, her arms wrapped round herself protectively, alone in her grief. Cathbad also folded his arms. He would not comfort her. She was no longer a child, she must learn to control her emotions.

'All things that live must die,' he said, ignoring her grief-

97

stricken state, 'and all things that die go on to nourish others. This is the circle of life. The sacrifice of life must be made to sustain life.'

Brigid knew that no comfort would be forthcoming, and made a big effort to control her emotions. She must accept what had happened. She wasn't a child, she was almost an initiated Druid. Druids did not cry over their losses. She saw in her mind's eye the forged sword in the blacksmith's furnace and wiped away the tears with shaking hands, then looked up at Cathbad.

'I understand,' she said with barely a tremble in her voice. 'The Goddess chose that the wolves should live. She always chooses the best way, and I will accept it.'

Cathbad was extremely pleased, although he took pains not to show it. His pupil was almost ready for her initiation, he thought with pride. And for what was to come afterwards, he added with a pang of regret.

'What happened today was an important lesson that Brigid must learn,' Cathbad said to Emer later. 'But it was unfortunate though, that she was forced to learn it in such a difficult way. Her grief was overwhelming.'

And it was a truly hard lesson for her to learn. But it is one thing to learn a lesson, and another to understand and truly believe it.

And no one, not even Cathbad, realised the paramount importance of this lesson; how imperative it was that Brigid must learn, and understand, its wisdom.

# Chapter 15

*The root of education is bitter, the fruit is sweet.*
Aristotle

'It is time for you to complete your training, Brigid,' Cathbad said to her. 'At the next full moon, you will face your initiation ritual. When you cross to the otherworld you will meet with the Goddess, who will instruct you as to your life purpose.'

Brigid nodded seriously, her face carefully blank, masking her excitement and rapidly beating heart. She was filled with pride, elation, nervousness and doubt, although deep down she'd been long expecting this. The trial of the wolf and her hens, she believed, had told Cathbad she was now ready.

'It won't be easy, but you've been taught everything you need to know. There's no point in learning unless you make use of what you've learnt, and this is the purpose of this ultimate Test,' he continued. 'From now on, you'll stay in the initiates' lodge until the time comes. You will not return to your own hut until you've completed your Test.'

*If you complete it.* The unspoken words hung clearly in the air. Brigid automatically felt for her stone shell, silently asking it to bring her luck. Cathbad noticed her movement and his eyes narrowed slightly, although he said nothing.

Over the next half moon Brigid reviewed every lesson she'd ever learnt. Emer and Cathbad came to her each day but they were careful not to say too much – it was important that Brigid use her own skills and knowledge to complete the Test.

And another thought filled her mind during this time. Rhod. After her initiation she would be free from the prohibitions of the trainees. She could marry, set up home with him. Although most Druids didn't do so, in view of their responsibilities, it would be possible. Many happy hours were whiled away dreaming of her future, of her home, her children, how she would successfully combine both her duties and her dreams. She'd already decided where their hut would be built. She saw herself crossing the threshold with Rhod's arm around her waist. He would turn, gaze at her with his eyes filled with love, bend to kiss her, entwine her with his strong arms... A familiar warm feeling spread through her body. Her future would be perfect.

The day of her Trial corresponded with the full moon following New Year's Day, the time when day and night were in perfect harmony before the rule of the night gave way to the rule of the day. Marking the end of the old and the coming of the new, it was the most fortuitous timing for an initiation ceremony. Although Brigid didn't know this, it was reserved only for those candidates with a great future written in the stars.

The day drew to a close. As the sun set, the full moon rose in the east. Dizzy from the herbs in the sacred drink she'd been given, and also from nervousness and fasting, Brigid and two other trainees entered the stone circle near Maelmin, circled the stones three times and sat in the centre. They were dressed only in simple white tunics, symbolising purity of body and mind, and carried the wooden staff of the trainee Druid and the knife that all wore at their belts.

The stones, proud and upright, were carefully aligned to channel the earth's spirit, given by Ceridwen to nourish the land. The First People had laid out the sacred monuments and stone circles, Brigid recalled, to channel the flow of this spirit, ensuring the land and all that it supported were fertile and healthy.

This circle was a node on a major energy line – she could feel the power coursing beneath her feet. It fused with her soul, filling her spirit with divine energy. Already she could feel the barriers between worlds begin to fall.

'All that you need for the Trial is in your heart and mind,' intoned Cathbad. 'Nothing else is needed, and no other object must be taken on the journey. Do you all understand?'

His eyes settled on Brigid as the candidates all nodded. She'd secretly brought her stone seashell, but that was not a problem, surely? Cathbad's eyes remained on her a while longer and she shifted uncomfortably, but at last he moved on.

Brigid heard the sound of drums. The sound filled her head, pulsating through her whole body. She saw the air begin to flicker, distorted images appearing as if the light were breaking up. The incessant drumbeat pulsed through the air causing multicoloured patterns to appear. The combination of ritual herbs, fasting, rhythmic music and the rush of energy through her soul caused her to slip into a trance. The images and lights surrounding her became more pronounced, more vivid, more real.

Then – there was silence. Not a breath of wind, not a blade of grass stirred. And the world around her altered. She found herself in another land, green and vibrant. The sound of bird song filled the air, and she could smell the delicate scent of apple blossom. Walking forward, slightly disorientated, she saw a huge wood of apple trees, larger and more vibrant than those she was familiar with.

'So I am in Avalon, the otherworld,' she said to herself with a thrill in her heart.

She found a path leading into the trees, the entrance to the abode of the Goddess. Her intuition told her to be wary although everything around her seemed quiet, with not a hint of life. She walked carefully, like a cat, every muscle tensed for sudden danger.

As she crossed the threshold of the wood, out of the bushes exploded a monstrous black dog, jaws agape and teeth bared, hurtling for her exposed throat. Brigid flung herself back into the field as razor sharp teeth slightly grazed her neck. Leaping to her feet in terror to run for her life, she was surprised to see that the dog made no further attempt to attack. It just watched her, waiting on the edge of the trees, hackles raised in warning. Brigid looked in confusion and raised her shaking hand to her throat, feeling the wetness of welling drops of blood. A split second later, her intuition less keen, she would now be bleeding to death. She offered up a prayer of thanks.

The Guardian, she recalled. He prevents all those entering the sanctuary who are unworthy. He is frightening only to those who allow themselves to be frightened. She hesitantly approached the entrance again. Immediately, snarling teeth warned her back. She wondered if she should try to find another path.

But whichever path I take, the dog will be there, waiting, she thought. He must allow me to enter. What do I have which he doesn't accept?

She thought of her knife and her staff. Weapons are not allowed within the sanctuary, it is a place of peace and light. She laid them on the grass beside her. The dog watched inscrutably. She stepped forward again, confident that the dog would allow her entry. It snarled, louder and louder. This was the test, she thought, she must conquer her fear. She stepped across the threshold and, fast as a striking serpent, the jaws clamped on her bare calf. She yelped with surprise and pain and fell back, quickly jerking her body back onto the grass. She sat up and examined the row of welling puncture marks. The dog had let go immediately; it had been merely warning her. She was uncomfortably aware that it could have crushed her leg to a pulp if it wished. What was wrong? Why would it not let her past? Surely she wasn't to fail her Test already?

She thought of her charm, the stone seashell. Was that the problem? She couldn't bear to part with it – she needed it for strength. But Cathbad had said they must take nothing else with them.

'Emer told me all luck comes from yourself, this stone is just a reminder of my strength,' she reasoned. 'A Druid has no need of these things.'

So with much regret, she laid aside her charm as well. Then, with nothing but her plain dress, she walked towards the dog again, aware of the throbbing pain in her throat and leg. It rose to its feet, poised to attack. Ignoring its growl, but uncomfortably aware of its razor-sharp fangs and glistening pink gums, she knelt on the ground in front of it.

'I come here as myself, with no talismans, objects or weapons to hide my true self. My soul seeks to speak with the Goddess. Will you let me enter the sanctuary?'

In answer, the dog licked her exposed throat, licking off the congealing drops of blood, then turned and walked into the forest.

When you are worthy to cross the threshold, the dog will be your guide, Emer had said. She followed him along a twisting, turning maze of paths through the trees. She was grateful for his help; she could never have found her way alone.

'It's better to face a problem than try to avoid it,' she said to herself. 'If I'd tried to avoid the dog, as I first thought, if I'd turned from the path in search of an easier way, I would never have found the way through the forest. Without passing the first test, I would never reach the next.'

Many things that she'd been taught and had learnt, Brigid was now beginning to truly understand.

They eventually left the trees and reached a river running through an open valley, with a very narrow bridge across it. Here, the dog lay down. He would go no further – from here she would have to make her own way.

The river was wide, fast and deep, impossible to ford or swim. The far bank was over a hundred paces away. She could see huge branches swept downstream, testimony to its great power. The bridge was the only way, she'd already learnt there was no point looking for an easier one.

She saw nothing threatening and deliberately placed one foot on the bridge. She was immediately flung backwards to the ground.

'No one may cross the bridge who does not prove worthy,' boomed a voice. Picking herself up, she saw a small, ugly man with a peaked hat and a wicked looking knife in his hand. Defenceless, she would have no chance against him. She looked at the dog for help – he lay there impassively. He would be no help, she must fight this battle alone.

'Who are you, and what is your purpose here?' asked the man.

'I wish to cross the bridge and speak with the Goddess.'

'To cross, you must answer a question. If you answer correctly, you may cross. Wrong, you will die. You can still turn back from the path. Do you accept the challenge?'

It was the only way forward, she knew she must face the test.

'I accept it,' she said at once. A gloating smile spread across the man's face and Brigid wondered if maybe she'd made a mistake.

'What is the longest thing in the world, and the shortest; the fastest, and the slowest; the most squandered, and the most rued?' He spoke carefully and deliberately, running his thumb along the blade of his knife.

She thought about it for a while and the man's smile grew gradually wider, making her uncomfortably aware of her predicament. Life was the longest thing she could think of, and could also be the shortest in the world. Was that the answer? She looked up with excitement as she made her choice.

'The answer is l...' She caught her tongue at the last second. The man's eyes had lit up greedily as she began to speak, now they clouded slightly. He hadn't won yet.

Life didn't fit with the rest of the riddle. Was she wrong? She had one chance, she couldn't afford to make a mistake.

She thought longer. Sweat began to bead on her face as the moments ticked by. She must be sure before she spoke.

Finally the answer came to her – *time*. Of course! Time lasted for ever, and for an instant too short to grasp. It was the fastest thing – nothing could outrun it, and also nothing could move slower than time. It was also what people most wasted, and what they most regretted wasting. She hoped against hope her reasoning was correct as she gave her answer to the second guardian.

'That is correct,' he said, his eyes filled with hate and his smile gone. 'You may cross the bridge.'

She placed one foot on the bridge, and then the other. The guardian smirked as she wobbled slightly, but she managed to regain her balance. As she glanced back she could see he was willing her to fall.

She ignored him and focussed as spray struck her face from the churning torrent. The bridge was very narrow, only one foot's width in span. One wrong move and she would be washed away. Every muscle in tune with all the others, she carefully felt each step across. She didn't dare look down into the rushing, foaming water – the disorientation would make her fall. She shut her eyes instead, feeling her way across. Slowly, one foot and then the other, the far bank grew closer, and then she was there. She had completed the second test.

The path reached a cliff face, tall and impregnable. There was no way of climbing it so Brigid walked along the base. The sun beat down on the bare rock and the heat was stifling.

After a long while she began to wonder if she was going the right way – the cliff face was identical to where she'd started, it seemed she'd made not an inch of progress. She looked back – the rocky ridge stretched as far as she could see, there was no way round it in either direction. She carried on walking, now slower as doubts assailed her, until at long last she came across the mouth of a cave. A symbol of the womb of the Mother. Brigid felt a rush of energy and walked into it without a moment's hesitation.

It was dark, damp and gloomy, a pleasant contrast to the heat outside. She explored it further – it stretched back deep into the cliff and then appeared to end. She could see no way forward, no tunnel or exit. She searched the rough rocky walls again, straining her eyes to pierce the gloom. The cave *felt* right – it had to be the way. And her surety paid off. Between two jutting rocks, near invisible, she found a small opening – a tunnel just big enough to crawl into.

She lay down flat and, using just her fingers and toes, wriggled into the entrance. She inched forward. The rock pressed around her on all sides. The tunnel was longer than she expected and she felt a stir of panic as it seemed to narrow. What if she got stuck? There was no way she could squeeze back out again.

As her heart beat faster the tunnel seemed to constrict, her fingers scrabbled without effect. She began to thrash about as much as she could, but to no avail – she couldn't move. There was no air, she couldn't breathe. She was going to die!

With a huge force of will, Brigid forced herself to be calm. She concentrated on her breathing, in and out, in and out, slowly and calmly, and eventually her heart rate slowed. Digging hard with her fingers and toes, with a huge effort she squeezed forward an inch. And then another inch. The skin scraped from her hands and knees, but after what seemed an age the tunnel began to widen.

Soon she could stand, and she moved carefully forwards in complete darkness until the tunnel opened into empty space. There was not a glimmer of light but she could sense she was in a vast chamber.

Deep underground, in the womb of the Mother, she faced her final test before her symbolic rebirth.

# Chapter 16

*Your treasure trove is inside you, it contains everything you ever need.*
Confucius

What should she do now? If she left her spot she would soon be lost. She decided to circle the entire cavern, using the wall as a guide, and began to scrape loose stone and earth into a pile to mark where she had started.

She soon found another tunnel opening into the rocky wall. Was this the way? She didn't know, so she carried on. She found another tunnel, and then another, twelve in all before she reached her pile of stones again. Which one was the way?

She sat down, allowing her intuition to fill the cave, tuning in with the earth energies, the life-force of Ceridwen which pulsed through the cave.

She heard a noise – a slight rustle, a movement of earth. Something was there. She strained all her senses and heard a faint hiss. It was a serpent, the symbol of the Goddess and her life force, and also the symbol of rebirth.

She listened to it drawing closer, and then there was silence. It had stopped, perfectly still, perhaps waiting for her to make a move. When there was no further movement, Brigid felt forward with her intuition. The serpent wasn't waiting – it was no longer there. Maybe it was a clue, a sign from Ceridwen sent to aid her.

An idea came to her. The snake *was* the key. Its sinuous movement mirrored the entwining, ever twisting path of life from birth until death. She stood up and concentrated on the sensation of the floor with her bare feet. And sure enough, she felt a pattern – a path – her feet barely discerning it on the uneven floor.

She focussed all her senses on the faint sensation beneath her feet. The path twisted and turned, crossing over and under other strands, just like the threads of life. She couldn't afford to lose concentration for an instant.

Brigid went forwards, backwards, and doubled back on herself until she was sure she'd lost the way. But at last the path reached a tunnel entrance, the head of the serpent.

The snake sheds its skin and is rejuvenated, reborn. And so on the path of the serpent, her third and final trial, Brigid shed the skin of her old life and became a true initiate of the Goddess. She had found The Way.

From then on it was easy. The tunnel was wider, she could walk almost upright. She walked until a faint glimmer of light appeared, which grew stronger and stronger until the tunnel opened into bright sunshine, blinding after her long period in utter darkness.

When she could see, she found herself in a glen of trees. The sun shone brightly on the leaves, the flickering light forming entrancing patterns on the ground. The sound of running water came from somewhere nearby and she could smell the sweet scent of flowers on the air.

As her eyes adjusted to her new location, she saw a woman standing among the trees, bathed in light. The glade seemed to be lit from her presence alone. Her gown was silken, flowing and silvery, from which the very stars appeared to shine. The light forming round her head was like the sun. Brigid dropped to the floor in reverent obeisance to the Goddess.

'You have completed your Trial, my daughter.' Her voice reflected the songs of the birds and the trickling of mountain streams. 'You have succeeded in everything that was placed before you. But remember, this is only the beginning. Do not think highly of yourself for succeeding – it is only through the will of the Gods that you do so. All gifts are given freely, and as such may be taken away.'

The light filled Brigid's heart and soul, she felt she would burst with ecstasy. Then Ceridwen began to speak again, her tones rich with honey and silk. 'The Road chosen for you will be long and hard, but the Gods will always be at your side. If you turn from The Road in search of ease and comfort, the Gods will turn from you. Will you accept your destiny?'

Brigid's heart was filled with love, duty, resilience and determination along with the empowering light, but she could not speak. Her words just would not come. She felt a flare of panic – what should she do?

'Do not worry,' said Ceridwen. 'The words spoken by your heart are clear. I have your answer.'

The light in the glen seemed to intensify even more, and Brigid couldn't look at the dazzling figure in front of her.

'Times are changing, the world is changing with it,' the Goddess continued. 'War is coming, a war like no other. You must ensure the world remains whole. Strife and bloodshed must be avoided. A great upheaval is approaching, all we've worked for may be lost. A guide is needed, someone who will light the world through its darkest hour and prevent our world from being destroyed.' 'And I am to do this?' Brigid ventured to say, but it was as if she hadn't spoken.

'I've watched over you since you were born, since you were chosen for your destiny. You've fulfilled everything we hoped for. Now, you must start your journey properly, your journey towards your destiny.'

The Goddess placed her hand on Brigid's forehead. 'My blessings on you, my daughter. May the light travel with you always.'

Brigid felt an intense burning sensation and then the world flared up in a dazzling light. She was blinded, and when her vision cleared she found herself again among the sacred stones of her home. The birds were singing, the sun was rising. All around the valley, people and animals were preparing to start the new day.

Emer was by her side. 'She has awoken,' she called, and

Cathbad rushed to her. Apart from her teachers, the stones were deserted.

'You were gone so long, we thought you'd succumbed.' The strain was evident in Emer's voice and eyes. If Brigid had failed...'Your test has been hard, very hard.' Cathbad's sharp eyes probed the depths of her soul. 'This is the third day that you've been gone.'

Brigid sat up, too dazed to take in Cathbad's words. A three-day initiation ritual was unheard of. She was tired, very tired, but she also felt something else – a sense that a great power had infused into her soul.

Emer handed her a cup of water and she it sipped gratefully – she was desperately thirsty. She could taste sweet honey and something else and immediately felt refreshed. She began to recount her ordeal and her meeting with the Goddess, and her teachers looked at each other and nodded. She was now to walk the great Path of the Gods, as they'd known from her birth that she would.

Cathbad hoped he'd done enough to prepare her for the journey that was to come. A huge responsibility had weighed on his shoulders for a long time; he'd played his part to the best of his ability. Now, his role in the future of the world was at an end.

'You've been chosen by the Goddess, her mark is on your brow. We've taught you everything we could during your training, you're now an ordained Druid, it's time for you to walk The Road alone.' Cathbad was silent for a moment, he knew his next words would come as a shock.

'You must leave. Your destiny does not lie here. I've read the stars, you must travel south, to the centre of Prydain, where people gather from across the world. This is where your future lies.'

Brigid felt crushed. The breath was knocked from her by the entirely unexpected shock and she stared at her teachers in dismay. After everything she thought she'd achieved, she realised it was just the beginning. There was to be no let-up on the trials of The Road. She would have no chance to enjoy the benefits of what she'd done.

The exhaustion hit her again hard, and she looked down at the ground, unwilling to let them see the surge of emotion. She felt as if her life was being ripped apart, just when she should be basking in her achievement.

'But my family, friends, home, they're all here.' *Rhod.* His name she couldn't speak out loud. She fought hard to keep the trembling from her voice. 'This is all I know, I can't leave.' 'No.' Cathbad's voice was hard and stern. He had to quell this surge of self-pity in his former student at once. 'All that you need is inside you. When you've left behind all that you have, you'll truly realise this. Only when your soul is stripped bare will you realise who, and what, you truly are. And only then will you find the way to complete The Road for which you've been chosen.'

# Chapter 17

*I shall not fall under flashing knives. I shall not burn in the cauldron.*
The Egyptian Book of the Dead

Brigid stood at the top of the hill near Maelmin as she'd done so many times before, breathless from the hard climb. She gazed at the surrounding landscape, trying to drink in every last detail of the home she knew and loved, which she would never see again. She gazed long over the landscape, at the Wyldwood, leaves flickering in the wind, the tiny figures of the men working in the fields.

Across the moors, swathes of purple heather showed among the jagged rocks, and occasional splashes of yellow where the gorse bushes were in flower. In the furthest distance a blue shimmer marked where the land ended and the sea began.

A hawk rose from the wood and soared up in the air, higher and higher until it was a speck in the sky. She envied the bird for a moment, for its happy, simple life. He will gaze down on his homeland for the rest of his life. He has no responsibilities, no reason to ever leave. I wish I could be like him, she thought. Then she immediately rebuked herself.

'A Druid lives for the greater good of the world, she does not put her personal feelings before her duty,' she told herself. 'My destiny is to keep the world safe. Without the Druids, without my walking The Path, the hawk would have no home to soar over.'

She would not turn from her destiny, and she would face whatever was necessary with strength and acceptance. She would not complain about her hardship. She would walk The Road with light and peace in her heart.

With this firm resolve in her heart, she turned and climbed back down the hill. It was time for her to leave, to say goodbye to the only home she had ever known. She would never call a place home again – she would always be yearning in her soul for the land of her birth.

One day, I will return, she promised herself, knowing in her heart that she would not. A sudden thought came to her. She took out her lucky amulet, the stone shaped like a seashell which she knew she no longer needed. She'd been almost surprised to find she still had it when she awoke from her ordeal, but of course it had been a soul journey, not a physical one. Her body had remained exactly the same.

She went to the stream, originating high up on the hill, and dropped it into the water, the life force of the world, returning the gift to the Goddess from whence it came.

'May you keep it until someone else has need of it,' she said. It lay on the stream bed, twinkling as the clear waters rushed over it. It is something for the land to remember me by, she thought. The bond I have with this place will never be broken.

Emer and Cathbad were waiting for her at the beginning of the southern road. They embraced her, and Cathbad raised his hand in blessing.

'May the Goddess walk beside you, may she never leave you. The Road may be long and hard, but you are never left alone. Travel safely on The Road.'

Brigid bowed her head in thanks and gazed for one last time across her homeland. Then, as the sun rose high in the sky, she set off on her long and lonely journey.

# PART III

# Chapter 18

*History is a cyclic poem written by time on the memories of man.*
Percy Bysshe Shelley

The path was steep, faint and narrow, used more by sheep than people. Loose rock made the climb difficult but I relished the pull on my muscles and lungs. I'd always loved pushing my body to its physical limits and I revelled in the feeling that it was working to its utmost capability. Soon I reached the top of the hill, Yeavering Bell, the highest hill of the northern Cheviots and the site of one of the largest hill forts in the country. My feet seemed to instinctively know the way as if they'd walked this way many times before.

I could see the remains of the once grand hill fort. A long line of stone encircled the hilltop – once it formed a huge wall, and indentations of lighter grass marked long-lost buildings. But now and for many centuries it had been just a grazing ground for black-faced sheep.

The surge of excited expectation I'd felt as I climbed was replaced with something strange. An odd feeling of sadness, shock and loss. What had once been a revered and sacred site – I sensed on some level that this had been one of the greatest – was now just a grass-covered mound, long forgotten and abandoned by man, restored to the earth from whence it came. A pain struck into my heart and tears blurred my eyes. How could this imposing and unshakeable place have fallen to this state?

It seemed a poignant reminder of the fragility of our existence, of what we consider important, permanent, that becomes as meaningless as a speck of dust in the grand scheme of time, so easily swept from our grasp like a wisp of smoke and leaving us to helplessly mourn its loss.

I blamed my watering eyes on the gusting wind and gazed out across the rolling expanse, struggling to regain my breath. The wind whipped my hair back wildly and specks of grit struck my face. To the south the hills continued, rising and falling well beyond the horizon. To the north lay the wide flat valley of the river Glen, where once lay the capital of Northumbria. Then further to the north lay more hills stretching into infinity.

A voice seemed to whisper in my head, *go round to the other side.*

I scrambled over rocks and rough grass and following a faint, almost indiscernible trail, I reached a small rocky outcrop which formed a three-sided enclosure. I squeezed into the natural alcove and twisted round. The sounds of the outside world had vanished – I was almost entirely closed off from the local surroundings but could see out for miles. I gasped as I took in my first detailed look at the view – it was breathtaking.

Raw and jagged mountains slashed the vivid blue sky, and a dazzling blaze of vibrant purple and yellow softened and contrasted the ferocious bleakness. Through a gap in the hillside I could see an azure shimmer – the North Sea. It was miles away, I knew – it must be a freak of perspective that allowed me to see it. In the distance I could see a group of walkers, faint black specks struggling up a steep hillside.

There was nothing man-made or man-altered in my view at all. I realised that this view had been changed by neither man nor beast for centuries. I could imagine myself anywhere in the past three thousand years.

I spent a long time drinking in the view of my homeland, the soul of the land merging with my own and filling me with an intense feeling of peace and well-being. I felt uplifted, ecstatic almost, a tremendous buzz. I could understand why the ancient people had decided to build their settlement here, on top of this inaccessible hill.

But surely, I thought, for practical reasons they would have chosen somewhere more convenient and accessible, if less awe-inspiring? What was their intention for choosing this spot? I resolved to find out as much as I could about the local history.

At last I walked back down the hill. The return journey was much easier but I slipped and almost fell more than once. The sun was already sinking in the sky and I needed to hurry. I picked my way carefully across the rocky path, and then sped up into a slow jog-trot. One problem with public transport was that I had to stick to a set timetable, and I was used to finding myself running for several miles to make the last bus.

As I passed a clump of small dense bushes, I was startled to catch a glimpse of a face. I turned my head quickly and for a split second we had eye-contact. The thing felt strangely primeval and ancient, but I had no feeling of fear or concern. It seemed strangely human, but at the same time, not – a wild, untamed air about it suggested otherwise. I had an impression of thick, shaggy hair framing its face and a pair of small horns.

I caught my foot on a rock and stumbled. My eye-contact was broken and when I turned back an instant later the thing had vanished. I went over to the bushes quietly, alert for any more sign of it, but there was nothing. I carefully looked through the bushes – they were empty. I could see no bolt-holes and I couldn't hear the tell-tale rustle of something running away. A trick of the light, there was nothing there, I told myself, and put it from my mind.

I could hear the sound of running water across to the left as I reached the base of the hill, and I listened for its source. *Find it*, said that voice in my ear.

I came across a fast-flowing stream, originating far up on the heights. The water had carved a narrow gorge for itself out of the rocky hillside. I walked along its course, watching how the light flickered through the water onto the stones below, then I came to a deep pool. Caught up in the rocks was a carrier bag. It was just a piece of litter, and even this far from civilisation litter was a common occurrence, but something about it annoyed me. I climbed down the bank and retrieved it.

Then an unusual shape caught my eye. Lying at the edge of the pool, doubtless washed there in a storm maybe hundreds of years ago, there was a fossilised seashell, the exquisite detail in form and pattern visible even through the water. As I bent down to pick it up the water lapped over the top of my left boot and I jumped quickly back to the bank, shaking my soggy foot ineffectually.

I turned the fossil over in my hands. It resembled a sea-snail and its form and lines were still perfectly clear, entirely unworn by the elements. Its beauty was exquisite. I could see the spiral circling inwards, tighter and tighter to form an infinite point in the centre. I wondered if they were common in the area and scanned the stones for more, but could see none.

I idly wondered how a single fossil had come to be in the stream, and as I held it tightly an image came into my head. I saw a young woman dropping the fossil into the water, watching it sink to the bottom, long, long, ago. She looked a bit like me.

I pushed the daydream from my head and put the fossil in my pocket, a souvenir of a happy day.

The shadows were lengthening and the air was cooling as I came down the final hill into Wooler and civilisation. The sounds of cars and voices, and the glare of street lighting provided a strange contrast to the feeling of absolute aloneness, and I could taste the acrid fumes of modern life on my tongue. Within a few minutes I passed a phone box with all its glass smashed. It almost seemed obligatory these days, with this constant raging against life.

When I passed the door of a still-open newsagent, I went inside. 'Do you have any books on local history?' I asked the man behind the counter as he coughed into a handkerchief.

'Excuse me,' he said. 'I seem to catch some disease from almost every customer these days. They're over there, by the far wall,' he indicated.

I didn't respond to his comment – everyone was ill these days anyway – and found some books on the archaeology and prehistory of the once metropolitan area. I chose two and paid for them. I was tired, I'd covered nearly twenty miles today, I reckoned from the map, and didn't want to go out again tonight, not that there seemed much to do here anyway, so I decided to spend the evening reading instead.

As I walked out of the shop I turned back and picked up a few chocolate bars. They'd do for energy for the next few days' walking.

'That's £3.40 please,' sniffed the man. I fished in my pocket for change and pulled a handful of coins along with the fossil shell.

'Now that's unusual,' he said, forgetting his illness for a moment. 'Where did you get it?'

'I picked it up in a stream on the hills,' I replied.

'Can I see?'

I handed it to him and placed the coins on the counter.

'It's perfect isn't it? Beautiful!' he exclaimed. 'The seashell is one of the best examples of the exquisite perfection of nature. Did you know that the width of each spiral is exactly proportionate to the previous? The Golden Ratio is God's number, the number that all nature resonates to.' 'I remember that from *The Da Vinci Code*,' I said, looking towards the door. I was knackered, the last thing I wanted was a lecture.

'A great example of how popular fiction can educate people,' he said, somewhat condescendingly, and I felt annoyed. Why couldn't he just do his job and sell stuff?

'This number is harmonised to our very souls, a fact that all architects, artists and designers know.'

'Oh, that's very interesting.' *Just give it back and shut up.* I had enough of this from Anna. My legs ached, a blister was developing on my right heel, and my soaked foot was getting trench foot.

'There's the money for the chocolate,' I prompted.

He handed my fossil back. 'The Cheviots are volcanic, fossils are very rare here. Look after it, it must be your lucky charm.'

I laughed. 'There's no such thing,' I said. But I kept it safely in my pocket anyway.

The area was in its hey-day during the Iron Age, just over two thousand years ago, I read later, lying on my guest room bed with my feet up. I was showered, warm and dry, and full of the exhilarating tiredness that comes only from a day's hard exercise.

The area then declined until eventually it became the outlying, sparsely populated land it was today. The ancient site on Yeavering Bell, it seemed, was once greatly revered by the Celts as the spiritual centre to the kingdom's capital, Maelmin. The heart of the kingdom of the Selgovae which stretched from northern England into Scotland, the area was one of the most populous in Britain.

I shivered despite the warmth – it seemed so familiar, as if I was reading from my memories. The words conjured vivid images in my mind, I could picture the land exactly; full of people, buildings – round, wooden and thatched, herds of cattle, oxen, pigs, women grinding grain, men tilling fields, I saw far more detail than I read.

The Yeavering Bell site had contained more than a hundred buildings and the stone wall was nearly a kilometre in length, the book continued. I looked up at the ceiling, seeing in my mind's eye the cripplingly steep hillside and treacherous paths I'd recently battled against, and my respect for the Celts grew immensely. I already knew they were highly advanced – my research on Pythagoras had told me that. Maybe he'd come here, to Yeavering Bell, to form his theories? Maybe I'd been walking in his very footsteps? No, of course I hadn't.

What on earth had inspired them to build the place, I thought again, laboriously carrying tonnes of stone and wood so far up the mountain? I could feel the answer, niggling just beyond reach. I'd felt its immense power singing through my blood, and like a name you can't quite remember, a long-lost and ancient memory was tugging just below the surface. I could almost see it, *almost*.

After struggling with my memories for a moment, I gave up and returned to my book. The outdated name of 'hill fort' was once given to any ancient, enclosed structure on high ground, I learned, and their true function is now thought to be religious rather than defensive.

*That's right.* I saw a split-second image of hundreds of white-robed people on the hill. I shook my head to dispel it, my imagination was getting far too active. But when I turned the next page, the strange niggling feeling of something, some eerily disquieting process from far beyond my ordinary life, returned with a vengeance.

Yeavering Bell was once known as Ad Gefrin, meaning The Hill of the Goat, because of its association in ancient times with the wild goat-like spirit Pan, otherwise known in Britain as Cernunnos, the God of the Green.

Pan was the nature spirit haunting the wild and lonely places, representing the untamed and uncontrollable essence of nature. He was depicted covered in thick hair, with two small goat-like horns, and dancing on his cloven hooves to the music produced from the instrument to which he gave his name – the pan pipes. The terror inspired in unwary travellers who unexpectedly encountered him also gave rise to the word 'panic'.

That strange creature I'd seen in the bushes on the hill.

It couldn't be, I thought, simultaneously as I connected it with the ancient description of Pan. How could I explain that? Once again, I had the unnerving feeling that behind the facade of my life, vast cogs were turning, directing events far beyond my control, for what purpose I couldn't begin to imagine.

'It was my imagination, I know it was,' I told myself firmly, trying to hold on to my rapidly disappearing surety that my life was my own and under my sole control. 'It's pure coincidence that the two descriptions seem to match.' But all the same, I wasn't totally convinced.

That night I dreamed again. I walked the same way as during the day, but now the landscape was different. The hills were wilder, more overgrown with heather and gorse with fewer sheep to graze it. The valleys were thickly wooded and there were small fields dividing the lower areas. A hawk soared overhead, becoming a speck in the sky. I was seeing the land was how it used to be, the last time I saw it. A last memory, held for all eternity.

On Yeavering Bell I could see the stone walls circling the fort, solid, intact and gleaming white in the sun, a monument to human endeavour designed to stand out across the landscape. The walls were much higher than I expected, it wasn't possible to see any building beyond them. Nothing but a faint pall of smoke suggested anything was there at all.

I could see a man leading a pair of oxen hitched to a plough, slowly making his way across a field, forward and back, the field turning from green to a rich black at his passing. Seagulls followed behind, landing on the freshly turned earth to catch worms. I was struck by this picture, which I'd seen so many times in the modern world. Over hundreds, thousands of years, nothing has changed. Man still makes his living on the land, and other things live from man, the eternal and timeless cycle of existence.

I went further, past Yeavering Bell and along a long valley until I reached an ancient circle of stones, a large ring on the valley bottom. I could see around sixty stones made up the ring, each carefully placed to form a perfect circle. They were tall and angular, rising proudly towards the sky. The stones glowed bright, they emitted an eerie light. They seemed to call me to them.

I understood.

# Chapter 19

*When the student is ready, the teacher appears.*
Buddhist proverb

The stones were ancient, many weathered and broken, fallen through the actions of man and nature, but I could still see the boundary of the circle marked by the remaining stones, now overgrown by grass, neglected and forgotten for many centuries.

The circle didn't even have a name now, but I'd found it mentioned in one of the archaeology books, the only stone circle in the Cheviots. This detective work and some map-reading had led me to the right spot.

I circled the stones, clockwise, wondering how it would have looked when it was a part of people's lives, a centre for worship, for speaking with the gods. I could feel a certain power associated with the stones, a sense of majesty – although the circle was broken and disjointed, its original purpose still held true.

I reached what I intuitively knew to be the entrance, where one stone stood out more prominently. As I looked at it, I saw faint marks cut into its edges, notches and grooves of different lengths and angles. I felt a sudden flash of recognition. *They meant something. Words.* The thrill of excitement then faded quickly, try as I might I couldn't recall the memory I was looking for.

The sun was sinking low towards the horizon, about to disappear behind the hill tops. Soon it would be dark. I didn't mind being here alone, at night. I'd never feared the dark and the sense of peace and tranquillity made me long to stay.

An amazing orange-pink glow filled the whole of the western sky, the air seemed to resonate with energy. It was the most beautiful sunset I'd ever seen, the atmosphere seemed to be full of magic.

Strong scents came to me – the sharp, fresh tang of the nearby pine trees, the rich smell of damp earth as the dew began to settle. The full moon began to rise, blood-red at first, then cooling to a sharp, silvery grey. I looked up at her timeless face, gazing down on me as she gazed on everyone and everything in the world, all that is and all that has been. I thought of Anna, and knew that she too would be gazing up at this same image in the sky.

I sat in the centre of the circle, listening, feeling, *being*. The wind whispered among the leaves of the trees, and in my imagination they seemed to take on words.

*As day turns to night,*
*As light starts to fade.*

The words seemed to repeat themselves over and over in my mind.

I could hear nocturnal insects stirring and awakening in the grass as I became at one with the place. I could sense the vibration of the whole valley and everything in it, I could feel the currents of energy and life coursing through its veins. I sank down into a trance-like state and became aware that things were changing. The stones became different – angular, upright, polished, as they had once been before millennia of weather degraded them. I was aware of distant, rapid drumbeats. I saw the sacred processional way approaching the circle, following a river-like torrent of energy.

Then, I was elsewhere again. I was in a wooded glen, the trees, sights and sounds more emphasised, glowing and energetic, much more than I was normally familiar with. The sun shone brightly, I could hear the sound of water running, and the scents of apple blossom and wild flowers filled the air. It seemed very familiar. From a long lost, long forgotten memory, a sense of recognition flickered in the depths of my heart.

*I know this place.*

For just a second, the memory returned clearly. I travelled back over two thousand years, to another time, another life. The feeling was intense – I was overwhelmed by emotions of elation, pride, hope and joy, of a difficult task now completed, of the culmination of years of training and work.

*The first step of a lifetime's journey.*

I walked through the trees, guided by some unknown force – I knew where I was going. After a few minutes, I began to sense another presence nearby and the path emerged from an impenetrable, dense thicket into an open glade.

I saw a figure standing there, waiting for my arrival. A woman, but I knew she was more than just a woman. She radiated energy, power and magnificence; she seemed to shine like silver. A powerful aura of peace, serenity and purity washed over me. She shimmered, her features altering and flickering as my mind took in a view of something it couldn't hope to comprehend. Eventually, my mind settled on an image with which it could identify. The Virgin Mary.

I'd attended a Roman Catholic primary school – my grandparents had been devoutly Catholic and my parents less so. My religious belief and upbringing had fizzled out in my teens but the images of my childish, simplistic devotion were still buried deeply within me.

'Welcome back, my child,' she said. Her voice reflected the sound of birdsong and mountain streams. 'I have been waiting for you to return, I felt the time was near.'

'I've never seen you before,' I started to say, but then I knew it wasn't true. A half-memory of a similar face, seen lifetimes ago, came to my mind. I knew her on a deep, spiritual level, in the very molecules of my being.

*Mother.*

'You are Mary, Mother of God,' I said.

'I am known by many names – all men know me, and all men

name me. I am known as Ceridwen, Demeter, Gaia, Isis, Ishtar. But in your land, yes, I am known as Mary. You, Bridget, are one of my children. You were initiated into my ways, long ago. Who you are, what you are, can never be taken from you.'

*I know. I remember.*

Images began to flood into my mind, broken and distorted, as the dam in my memory burst. I saw myself standing in this glade, travelling far away from home. I saw the horrific ravages of war and barbarity, I saw myself struggling, fighting, refusing to give up on what I'd been tasked.

*I cannot fail.*

I saw an overwhelming light, felt a tremendous power, infinitely greater than that I felt from the Goddess, more than had been hinted at in my dream.

*My goal.*

I saw that last desperate flare of light as a candle is extinguished, I felt the aloneness, the loss, the failure, the despair.

*I failed.*

I sank down to the ground, overwhelmed by the torrent of memory and emotion. My breath caught in my throat and I let out a choked, gasping sob.

The Goddess placed her hand under my chin and raised my face up. The dazzling light bleached my vision and the images faded. Her touch filled my soul with peace.

'You were chosen for a purpose, my daughter, a great purpose, which you have yet to fulfil,' she continued. 'The world is changing, and its future is your destiny. You began this journey long ago, and now you are nearing its end. The pieces in this game were set in motion long ago, many threads of many lives have been woven together to converge on this one final act. Now it is time for you to fulfil your destiny.'

She took her hand from my chin and stepped back. Her gaze was fixed on me; I knew she was gazing deeply into my soul. I felt everything bare to her intuition – every thought, every deed, every feeling – she saw them all.

'The auguries have been here for a long time, we knew you had returned. Your location was hidden, but a message was sent out into the cosmic mind, a request that you receive the early lessons you needed, that the first steps of your Journey were paved smoothly. Then, all we could do was wait – wait for you to remember, to find your way back to your home, to your heart.''That dream... you sent it?' Many things now began to fall into place.

'No. It came from yourself, it was your soul remembering who you are. You yourself decided that it was time to awaken. You've been sleeping for a long time, and now you must begin your task again.''What is it that I must do?' This task seemed totally natural to me, as if I knew I'd face it. It was only later I began to doubt it.

'You must complete a Journey. You lost your way, you have strayed from your Path. I can see the battle within you, you fight against yourself.'

I felt a sense of chastisement emanate from her, and remembered that Lucy Luck had said almost the exact same words. In the silence I had the feeling that she was gazing into the threads of the past and future, and at last she began to speak again.

'This battle must be resolved. You must complete a new Journey, one that will guide you back to what you had before.'

I felt a sense of shame, worry and doubt at her words. Failure and hopelessness flooded into my mind.

'Do not despair,' she consoled. 'You have already started upon The Path, otherwise you would not be here now.

The Journey ordained for you to complete, it has seven stages. These stages were assigned, by the First People in ancient times, the names of the seven heavenly spheres. The Earth is the point from whence you began your Journey, the point where all people begin. But many souls will never take the first step through the Gateway to reach the first Sphere, the Sphere of the Moon.

Although it's the first and also the easiest step, many people will never make it. They are rooted to the Earth and never raise their eyes to the heavens, they never realise the Gateway is there. This, simply, is all that must be done.'

I remembered that day in the park, seeing all those people fixated on their feet and their iPods, and I realised the precise moment when I'd passed through this Gateway and begun my Journey.

The Goddess continued, 'You've completed the tests of the Moon and Mercury, and you've now reached the Sphere of Venus. When you have completed the tests of all seven Spheres, you will reach the Eighth Sphere, that of the infinite stars. Only then will you be able to complete your Task, your destiny. Only then will you find the Goal that your soul had been set.'

I felt strength, surety and confidence filling me.

*Your will is the most powerful I have encountered.*

I knew I could complete this Task, I felt the power of my soul rising like a flood.

'What is this Task that am I to do?' For some reason, this question had only just occurred to me.

'Everything you need is inside you; your heart, your mind and your soul. The Way will be clear if you listen to your heart. You will find the answers when you need to, when you are ready.'

This vague and cryptic answer satisfied all questions in my dream-like state. The Goddess placed her hand on my forehead and my mind was filled with a vision of the universe as a system of eternal cycles. Planets eternally orbit their stars. Galaxies are in constant orbit around black holes. Electrons circle around subatomic nuclei. Everything that exists, big and small, is a holographic representation of this model. I saw life as following this same pattern, cycling from birth to death to birth to death, but here there was a difference. It spiralled inwards as it cycled, faster and faster like a whirlpool, to eventually converge on one central infinite point, the divine.

The vision faded from my eyes, although remaining indelibly imprinted in my mind, and the light surrounding her began to intensify. It grew brighter and brighter until it was dazzling and I couldn't see. All my senses were overwhelmed, I knew nothing but the light.

Then I was among the broken stones again, cold, damp and stiff. The sky was still faintly lit, but the sun had moved – it was just before sunrise. I'd spent all night among the stones, and had a strange dream.

But I knew it hadn't been a dream.

# Chapter 20

*I will go with thee and be thy guide, in thy most need to go at thy side.*

Everyman

I got up awkwardly. The dew had soaked through all my clothes and I began to shiver with cold. I jumped up and down a few times, trying to shake the stiffness from my muscles, then ate one of the chocolate bars from my rucksack in lieu of last night's dinner and today's breakfast. I'd better start walking back to town, I thought.

I walked slowly for about a quarter of a mile and then sat down again on a rock. I thought about my meeting with the Goddess, about the Task and the Journey I was to do. I listed the main facts in my mind, checking each one on my fingers. As a scientist, I was used to analysing and dissecting problems in a logical way.

I had been set a Task, I noted, a Quest, that the future of the world depended on.

To complete it, first I had to complete a Journey, the Journey of the Seven Spheres, a Journey into myself and my soul.

By way of this Journey, I would learn what this Task was and how I was to complete it.

I listened to the voice of my heart and what it was telling me. I heard acceptance, knowing, understanding and determination, as if I knew this was going to happen.

*I have waited all my life for this moment.*

I'd passed through the Gateway from the Sphere of the Earth, and I'd completed the Spheres of the Moon and Mercury, the Goddess had told me. What these trials were that I'd completed, I had no idea. Astrology was ridiculous, everyone knew that. Especially me. I knew that Mercury was the planet of scientists and knowledge, I should have mastered that test well, what with my job and everything, but I couldn't see exactly how I'd done it. And I didn't have a clue about the Moon.

I then sat up straight, the reality of the situation suddenly striking me. It was testimony to how much I'd changed, even in such a short time, that I was even considering the Task. Even a fortnight ago I would have dismissed it out of hand as a dream and got on with my life. Now I was applying my scientific skills to solve the Quest.

I laughed self-consciously, grateful that no one was here to see. Anna would have a field day, The Ladies would die laughing, Simon would sack me outright. *Oh, yes, he already had.*

I laughed again. Things were playing out just perfectly. I felt confident and sure that I could do it, and as if in answer the sun suddenly appeared from behind a distant hilltop, bathing me in an ethereal yellow glow as it slowly rose higher in the sky.

*But it was only a dream. You don't believe in dreams*, whispered the Voice of Reason.

At once I began to feel disheartened and lost, a sense of failure and foolishness replaced the confidence. The persistent voice began to pull me down into despair.

*You know it wasn't a dream*, countered its opponent, the Voice of my Heart, the Voice of Instinct. *You have been here before.*

The everlasting conflict, the battle which would pull me apart, it had to be resolved. The sun rose higher, I felt my soul absorb its light, and I began to feel happier, uplifted. My heart won.

The memories were there, on the edge of my mind. During the past few days, flashes had been coming to me, just for a split second before vanishing again, of scenes which I'd seen before, of places I *remembered*. It seemed as if the memories were reawakening, were rising to the surface. When the Goddess spoke to me – *I'd known her as Ceridwen* – I'd seen clearly. My Path, both past and future, was opened out. But like in a dream, it was lost now I was awake, the memories were again obscured and veiled. I strained to remember what I'd seen, but the memories just wouldn't come. I pulled at my hair in frustration and smacked the rock with my hand. I *knew* I could remember. *I knew.*

I stood up and started to run, slowly at first then gradually picking up the pace. I always thought more clearly when I was moving, running had helped to solve all my life problems so far. My movement was cumbersome, being laden down with heavy walking boots, coat and rucksack, but I soon got into a rhythm. The steady movement cleared my frustration and I began to relax.

*Don't think and the answers will come.*

After around half an hour the rough path reached a narrow road and I slowed to a walk, feeling much more centred, both physically and mentally refreshed and alert from the exercise. I got my map out and calculated it was about five miles back to Wooler – a two-hour walk. I started along the road which would eventually lead to a small hamlet in an isolated valley.

I rounded a corner and was surprised to see a small church set back from the road, entirely alone except for a stone farmhouse further along the valley. Why would anyone build a church here, entirely without a congregation, I wondered, and then felt a feeling of profoundness as if the answer would be greatly important.

I went up the overgrown path and opened the door. It was silent and deserted, the atmosphere pressed in on me, it almost seemed alive. I picked up a small guidebook describing the building and sat down in a pew.

Apparently the original structure dated to Saxon times and had been built on a Bronze Age burial mound, a site regarded with a superstitious respect and fear. The site was avoided by the unenlightened pagans before they were brought to the fold of the Church, and a remnant of this superstition, or history, had survived to the present day. According to local legend, the fairies can still be seen on moonless nights conducting their funeral processions up the church path, by those unlucky enough to see it.

After absorbing this snippet of useless information and eating some more chocolate, a little guiltily at profaning the place, I left the church and walked on. This section of moor was charred and ruined, no doubt the result of a discarded cigarette during last year's drought-ridden summer, and I fixed my eyes on the road so I wouldn't have to see it. As a species, we seemed to be the world's worst nightmare.

Not much further on, in a mercifully thriving area, I came across a Holy Well, a circular stone structure with a tiled roof, supposedly the site of many healing miracles. The shiny coins in the water were testament to people's continued faith in its spiritual power. This was also once an ancient pagan shrine, according to the notice, which took on a Christian format only relatively recently.

The niggling feeling returned that I'd seen something important without realising it. There were so many clues, so many thing I knew were important, but I couldn't piece them together. What was the answer?

As I headed towards the town, I wondered what it was that gave some sites their sacred identity that transcended time, culture and religion. I remembered the newspaper article which said that in both Egypt and Sumer, temples were built on the sites of earlier temples. It wasn't just in Britain then – it recurred the world over. Maybe it was simply showing dominance over old ways and religions, a new culture displaying its superiority over the supplanted one by taking over its sacred sites.

But as I was to find out, the true reason was far more profound than that.

It was mid-morning when I reached the town. I was exhausted and starving and the morning's exercise was making my stomach rumble loudly. I weighed up my options and decided food was most important, so I went to a small cafe where I'd eaten before.

'Morning!' said the teenage waitress, smiling with recognition.

'Can I have two bacon sandwiches and a coffee please?''Sure, sit down and I'll bring it to you.'

I sat in the corner, contemplating all that had happened since yesterday. If I could understand what had constituted the Trials of the Moon, Mercury and Venus, then I would be better able to understand the next ones. I heard some shouting outside as a few loitering teenagers began to scuffle on the pavement. I ignored them – I was used to London, after all.

The waitress brought my coffee, glancing out of the window, and I sipped it absently. There were only two other customers in the place, and a TV on the wall was broadcasting the news. The word 'Venus' caught my ear, and I turned round to watch and listen, surprised at the coincidence. The report was about a transit of Venus, a rare astronomical phenomenon where the planet would pass directly in front of the sun, rather like an eclipse, due to happen tonight.

As I listened, one of the other customers left the cafe. The second customer, a man of around thirty, I noticed was looking at me with obvious appraisal. He caught my eye and smiled confidently. 'Venus, the planet of beauty and love,' he said, his eyes lingering on my chest for a little longer than necessary.

'Oh.' I pointedly returned to my coffee. He was not to be deterred.

'I've always been interested in astronomy, I thought I'd set my telescope up, watch it take place. Perhaps you'd like to join me?'

'No thank you, I'd rather be in bed.' I immediately kicked myself. *Why did I have to say that?*

Thankfully he missed the innuendo, and continued unabashed. 'It's a funny thing, you know, that in all cultures around the world, the planet Venus has been assigned a female identity, the Star of the Goddess. It was Freya to the Norse, Ishtar to the Babylonians, Inanna to the Sumerians and Aphrodite to the Greeks, who of course became the Roman Goddess who lent the planet its present name.'

He drew my attention sharply. Why was it he'd given me exactly the information I was looking for? But I already knew why.

This was obviously why I'd met the Goddess as part of the Sphere of Venus, and presumably a clue as to what I was to do next. I wondered what else the lecherous creep could tell me.

He came over to my table, encouraged by my sudden interest. 'I'm Jason.' He held his hand out.

I hesitated then took it, resisting the urge to wipe my hand on my trousers afterwards. 'Bridget,' I replied.

'Are you interested in astronomy, then?' he asked.

'I know nothing about it, really,' I replied non-committally.

'Astronomy, and its ancient origins in astrology, are pet subjects of mine. In fact, I've written a book on the subject, *Lucky Stars*, which is just in publication now.' Jason looked at me as if expecting a round of applause.

'Congratulations,' I replied automatically. 'That's a good achievement.'

He settled back in his seat now he was sure of my full attention, a pose I was familiar with from countless university lectures. 'And there's another interesting thing,' he continued.

*Oh God. I'd only been in Wooler five minutes, and already I'd attracted the local nutter. How did I do it?*

'Another interesting thing, in many cultures, the moon is considered the sister of Venus. They are the only two female planetary bodies. Now why would so many people independently think the same thing?'

My heart leapt as understanding dawned on me. The Trial of the Moon – intuition – feminine intuition – following my heart to find my home – it all made sense now! I knew instantly when I'd completed the Sphere of the Moon, it was that day when I'd boarded the train north!

I looked at Jason with grateful admiration and I saw him visibly preen. No doubt he thought I was awe-struck by his wealth of knowledge, which in a way, I actually was.

'So, what are you doing in Wooler?' he asked.

'Just travelling.' Then I added, 'I lost my job the other week – cutbacks – and I came this way for a break, to work out what to do next.'

'Oh well,' he said. 'That's life. Look at the dinosaurs.''The dinosaurs? What's that got to do with anything?'

'They are the key,' he said tapping his nose.

I returned to my sandwiches, his smug attitude was rather annoying, and he was forced to elaborate.

'The dinosaurs were a perfect system of life, they ruled the world in perfect harmony. There was nowhere left to go, no room to improve. Then that asteroid destroyed this harmony. That led to the evolution of mammals and humans, we rose from the dying remnants of the previous world.

You can't make an omelette without breaking eggs, from the dinosaurs came the humans, and from your redundancy will come something much better.'

I smiled, quite cheered at this analogy. I'd already had the idea that I was on a Journey to something, and was pleased to find someone else agreed. I began to look at Jason in a more favourable light.

'So you don't mind being out on the moors alone?' he asked. 'They're so creepy, just bleak nothingness and the wind and rain.' He shuddered. 'I prefer places with some life in them.''They're beautiful!' I leapt to the defence of my beloved homeland. 'I find it inspiring, the raw intensity of the hills, I've never felt so alive as when I'm out there!'

Jason shook his head. 'I'm not convinced. I'll stay near the town, it's safer. When I was a kid, I heard stories about a Beast that lived out there, preying on unwary animals and people.' He almost whispered the last sentence, looking round as if the Beast were lurking beneath the coffee machine.

'Yeah, well I'm not afraid of fairy tales, I'm not five any more.'

I saw the gleam in his eyes. *Ooh, feisty. I like it.*

I picked up my coffee and refused to respond. We talked for a while longer until my eyes began to shut of their own accord, despite the coffee. I stood up.

'I'm knackered, I'm going back to my guest house,' I said.

'Come with me to watch Venus tonight,' Jason persisted. 'I'll be going up onto the moor behind the bridge, there's no interference from street lights, and it's not far to take the telescope.''Maybe, I'll see,' I replied. 'It might be interesting, but I don't know.'

I walked from the cafe. The yobs were gone, the coast was clear, apart from a collection of cigarette ends.

'See you later, hopefully!' Jason called after me.

# Chapter 21

*All are but parts of one stupendous whole, whose body nature is and God the soul.*
Alexander Pope

I looked up at the inky sky, punctuated with pinpoints of light. Orion, Sirius, The Plough; I could pick them out easily, with the blazing glow of Venus surpassing them all. It was just visible in the east behind the backdrop of silhouetted trees.

I watched it for a moment and then turned away from the window. Without a telescope I could hardly see anything anyway. I wondered where Jason was, whether he'd seriously expected me to meet him. It was strange – I felt a real pull to go, I half felt like dressing and rushing out onto the moor. My heart was yearning to go, as if I were about to lose a great opportunity.

But of course I wasn't going – meeting a near-stranger on a darkened moor, at five o'clock in the morning – I had a bit more common sense than that.

But still... I turned back to the window. My heart, my instinct, was telling me to go, I felt a strange attraction to him. I didn't fancy him – God no, I hated arrogant men like that, but there was something...

I imagined pulling on my jeans, my boots, running from the guest house, along the road, up to the moor. 'Jason! Wait! I'm here!' He would turn and smile, smugly, he knew I would come.

I mentally slapped myself. I was behaving like a love-struck teenager. With a last, regretted look of regret I turned from the window and got back into bed.

Three days later, I made the next step on my Journey. When I went back to the guest house the landlady was hoovering in the hallway.

'Hello Bridget, dear! How was your walk today?' she shouted

over the noise.

'Hello Betty. I didn't go far really, I'm just enjoying relaxing,' I said.

'You've been waxing?' She looked both confused and shocked and I cracked up at her comical expression.

'Relaxing!' I shouted as she turned off the hoover.

'No need to shout, dear.'

'It's beautiful here,' I said. 'I've never felt such a feeling of belonging.' I couldn't find the words to describe what I was feeling, now that after so many centuries, I had finally come home.

Betty smiled, warm and friendly. She could sense what I couldn't say. 'You should go the Wychwood,' she said. 'It's beautiful there, I recommend it to everyone.'

My heightened instincts flared brightly, I felt a tingling sensation in my fingers. 'What's that?'

'Go further along the valley, to the east. The whole valley's full of ancient woodland, the original Wyldwood, never touched nor changed by man. Just thousands of years of nature.'

My heart cried out with yearning.

'We used to go there a lot, me and my husband, on Sunday afternoons,' she said wistfully. 'It was beautiful, you felt as if you were the only people in the world.'

I had seen no sign of anyone living here with her, where was her husband?

She forced her habitual cheery expression back onto her face. 'Well, I must get back to work! Give me a shout if you need anything!'

I set out the next morning. When I reached it I was surprised to find an Iron Age roundhouse in front of the wood. A notice explained that a roundhouse had originally stood here – archaeologists had found post holes and signs of a hearth fire – and it had been reconstructed by an enterprise called Fractured Lives, rehabilitating inner-city gang kids into normal life.

I walked round the outside and saw exactly how it had been made – the main posts were interwoven with smaller sticks and coated with clay, roof timbers raised, and then the whole thing was thatched to almost ground level.

I ducked through the narrow entrance into the darkened interior. Someone had lit a fire inside it recently, the smouldering remains lay in the centre. The thick smell of wood smoke hit my nostrils and immediately awakened something inside me – a memory, hovering just out of reach. The scene seemed intensely familiar, and for less than a split second, I remembered repeating this exact same movement. I could smell other things now – stew cooking over the embers, the rich smell of curing skins, the aromatic scent of drying herbs.

But, fragile as an autumn leaf, the memory crumbled into dust, blowing away forever on the winds of time. The round-house again became what it was – a rebuilt memory of a long-ago home.

I was quite unsettled by the sudden sense of loss that came over me and I was glad to leave the rather eerie place and return to the sunshine and the twittering birds. I walked on into the wood, trying to push the strange incident from my mind.

I crossed a vast carpet of flowering violets, the magical blue haze seemed quite otherworldly. I was glad to see them, I felt as if I'd been eagerly anticipating their appearance. My last glimpse from behind the veil had left the doorway ajar and a whispered feeling came to my mind. *My favourite food of all.*

A diverse range of mature trees stretched into the distance – oak, ash, beech, holly, wild pear, interspersed with hawthorn, blackthorn, and dog rose, left untouched by man for generations. The full scale of the transcendent beauty of nature was displayed in all its infinite glory, the great natural cathedral of existence.

There was no sign of tree felling, and I wondered how it would cope with the horde of new diseases sweeping across the country. Here and there, with a jarring sense of discord, I saw the skeleton of a dead tree, leafless, white and bleached. I imagined whole swathes of woodland looking like that, then shook my head to clear the horrible image.

As I wandered, drinking in the immense power of the place, I came across a near perfect circle of trees, almost seeming arranged by man. How had that happened naturally? Inside, no trees or shrubs grew, strangely out of place with the rest of the wood. There was instead a carpet of woodland flowers, mainly violets and wood anemones.

I sat down in the circle, leaning against a tree trunk and watching the light flickering through the leaves. The natural energy flooded over me and through me until I felt quite dizzy. I don't know how long I sat before I heard the sound of footsteps brushing through the undergrowth. I listened curiously, too at peace to be worried.

A figure appeared on the edge of the grove. His features flickered in the sunlight, just like the leaves of the trees, so I couldn't see him clearly. He stepped closer and his features took on a solid form. His wise, kindly face was framed by clothing entirely of green and I had the sense that he was a part of, rather than separate from, the surrounding woodland. His eyes, ancient, timeless and infinite, held mine. Strangely, he looked like my childhood hero, Robin Hood. I'd loved that story when I was young.

I felt an urge to speak but found I couldn't. I seemed frozen, unable to move. I wasn't bothered though. Like in the grove of the Goddess, everything just felt right.

'You are coming to the end of your Journey,' he said, his voice like the wind in the trees. 'The time is near for the final act. Everything in your life has been preparing you for this moment. You know what to do, you know the answer to the final test, you must realise this before it's too late. You must find the answer from within yourself. But I will tell you this – I am the key.'

With this final cryptic message he turned and walked from the grove, seeming to merge and become one with the vegetation, and then I was once more alone.

'Is there an internet cafe anywhere in Wooler?' I asked Betty.

'No there isn't,' she said, looking up from her accounts. 'Everyone has iPhones, there's no need any more.''Oh.' There goes my only way forward, I'd have to go back to Alnwick.

'I have a computer here, the modem's a bit slow, but you can use it if you want.' Betty took in my worried expression.

'OK, that would be great.'

Betty led me to a sitting room that doubled as an office, then left me to it. I opened Google and typed in 'Robin Hood'. After a few minutes of interminable waiting, the page opened. Most of the sites were linked to folklore and fairy tales, which I'd been expecting, but the second-most common hit was related to paganism. I leant back in my seat. Why was I not surprised?

Robin Hood was a fourteenth-century folk story derived from the ancient archetype of the Green Man or Dying and Rising God, who dies before being reborn or rising from the dead. He represented the life that flourishes in spring and dies in autumn. This ancient spirit, named and recognised in all cultures, was portrayed as a folk hero to resonate with the soul of Medieval Britain.

The same lesson was repeating itself yet again, waiting for me to understand it. Like the churches, the temples, the burial mounds, there was some common link transcending culture and religion. What was I missing? It was obviously important, something which was key to my Quest, if I could but understand it.

I tried to open another page. After a minute I impatiently closed it and tried another – she wasn't wrong about the modem – and eventually I had success. The ancient spirit of vegetation, I learnt, had been given many names – Odin, Wotan, Dionysus,

Pan, Tammuz and Herne the Hunter to name but a few, but in Celtic Britain he was most commonly known as Cernunnos, the Horned One.

Pan. Cernunnos. Robin Hood. The *thing* I had seen on Yeavering Bell. They were all one and the same.

That same feeling of cogs turning, screws tightening, things converging on one point beyond my control, returned stronger than ever. What was I going to do? I was way out of my depth, I desperately needed help.

I thought about ringing Anna. She of all my acquaintances would understand what was happening, she'd be able to explain what it all meant. My oldest, and craziest, friend would hold the key to the Quest I was undertaking, ironic or what?

Of course it wasn't. That was why we'd met, over ten years ago. Obviously. We were just pawns in the game of life, chance had nothing to do with it.

I laughed out loud. Frustration, bitterness, the feeling that I was a goldfish in a bowl, the knowledge that the world was vastly more complicated than I as a scientist had ever allowed myself to believe, it suddenly seemed so ridiculously funny.

'Are you alright, dear?' Betty was standing in the doorway looking askance.

'Oh, um,' I thumped back into the real world and flailed for an explanation.

She came to my rescue. 'Someone emailed you a joke?'

'Yes, that's right.' It was a joke. Me. My life. Everything. The funniest one ever. At least she didn't ask me to tell it to her.

I picked up the phone and began to dial Anna's number.

'Hi Anna, it's me. I've just met two archetypal ancient gods, they've told me I'm on a spiritual Quest to save the world. I'm a superhero – fancy that! Actually no, I'm just a puppet, so are you. But anyway, I need help. You're the nutter, I thought you'd be able to tell me what to do next.'

I put the phone down before I finished dialling. I'd never even mentioned my dream to her, how was I supposed to tell her the latest instalment of the story? The rational scientist in me prevailed, I just couldn't admit to anyone else what I was still struggling to admit to myself. It was a phone call I couldn't make.

What was I going to do next? At one time I would have dismissed these visions as fantasy, delusion, but now I knew better. They *felt* right, the universe was speaking to me through my heart. I knew the veil of disillusion had fallen from my eyes, despite my sceptical feelings of before.

I returned to the internet and spent the next two hours trawling through Pagan, Spiritualist and Metaphysical websites, searching for the answers on my own until my mind was boggling with facts.

Eventually I turned the computer off and went outside into the fresh air. I had my trainers on and I began to run, along the road and onto the footpath that led alongside the river, and with the sound of shallow water rushing over the stones and the blood rhythmically pounding in my head, I mentally reviewed everything I'd read, organising and filing a multitude of facts.

This God is the partner or metaphysical opposite of the Goddess, the eternal life force of the world. This Mother Goddess has been known over the course of history, as she herself had told me – Danu, Isis, Gaea, Demeter, Ceridwen, Mary, etc. The God is her son, or alternatively her lover. And I'd just met them both.

With this first step clear in my mind I jumped over a stile, landed heavily in the mud and ran on. I began reviewing the nature of this Mother Goddess.

The earth was traditionally seen as a living entity. The Mother Goddess was both the earth and the totality of its life. This idea resurfaced in the 1960s – the Gaea Hypothesis, which again linked back to Pythagoras. I was back on familiar ground here with the research of the scientist James Lovelock. He found that the earth's climate and atmosphere, in particular the vital balance of water and oxygen, were regulated and maintained by life itself. Oxygen wouldn't exist unless life, in the form of photosynthesising plants, was there to create it. So it is life which sustains life. Without life, the earth would become barren.

I'd pored over various metaphysical websites, almost sensing Anna's laughing, for once seriously considering their ideas, and learnt that this delicate co-operation of life is the esoteric meaning of the Sacred Marriage between the God and Goddess, marked around the world. The Dying and Rising God represents all life that lives and dies in constant flux. He unites with the eternal virgin Goddess who represents all the subtle factors for life – the winds, the rain, the sun, the nutrients in the soil, the climate, the temperature – the essentials for life which are in turn moderated and maintained by the actions of life.

As I ran, experiencing first hand the Goddess as the river at my side and the wind in my face, and the God as the vegetation and scurrying rabbits around me, I saw how the entire world's ecosystem is a delicately balanced compromise between the two opposing factors, God and Goddess, which come together to form that beautiful manifestation of the Divine, that which we call life.

I wondered if this was the lesson of the Sphere of Venus, the Goddess, to understand the true nature of life and existence. But it still felt as if something was missing.

The footpath crossed a metal bridge and turned along a road, and I took this as my cue to turn back. The wind was behind me now, pushing me along, and I ran faster and faster, breath ragged, heart pounding. The green flashed by in a blur. I relished the smooth, incessant movement of my muscles, I loved feeling like a smoothly functioning machine. The sun filled my eyes, the air filled my lungs, the wind enveloped my body. I became at one with life, I was moving effortlessly, almost floating along the path as I ran. The Runner's High is a rare and transcendent experience.

A long forgotten memory came back to me from when I was barely able to walk. I'd wandered into the woods and got lost. The trees and bushes were huge and frightening, reaching out to scratch my skin with their thorny limbs. The rustling leaves were to me the laughter of ghostly beings looming in on me.

After an age a friendly little person had appeared, he'd taken my hand and led me home. He was wearing green and smelt of the forest and undergrowth. If it hadn't been for him I could have been lost forever. After the panic had subsided, no one had believed my story, and over time I also came to believe that I'd imagined it. Now I knew that I hadn't.

The sense of being a pawn, a puppet played by others, also subsided as I ran. I was guided, pushed, led. Many factors were at play, more than I'd ever realised, but that didn't matter. A teacher guides a child, but the lessons learnt are the child's own. The stile flashed past underneath my feet as I raced onwards. The road was rising to meet me, as it had done all my life. I just hadn't realised it.

# Chapter 22

*Out of the darkness that covers me, black as the pit from pole to pole,
I thank whatever gods there be, for my unconquerable soul.
It matters not how strait the gate, how charged with punishments
the scroll,
I am the captain of my fate, I am the master of my soul.*
William Henley

The bleak and dismal weather acutely mirrored my mood as I
trudged slowly along the path. I was tired, fed up and uncentred,
the rain soaking under my collar and through my sleeves did
little to lighten it. The Voice of Reason had reawakened in my
mind, and was becoming more vocal. *What are you doing? Stop
chasing a fairy tale, go home. Get on with your life.*

As my mood deteriorated further, the Voice grew ever more
ferocious. *You should know better. You're a scientist, you live in the
Real World, not some silly fantasy. Two dreams, some coincidences, and
now you think you're about to save the world. It's ridiculous. Utterly
ridiculous. Pathetic.*

My foot caught a stone on the path and I kicked it savagely,
watching in perverse satisfaction as it ricocheted down the steep
slope. At that moment I hated myself – for thinking I could
change things, that I could be someone special. For following a
path that no sane person would do. For leaving my perfect
existence in London, where I could have had everything. I'd
thrown my life away, on account of a dream. A *dream*, for God's
sake. That niggling voice was right. It was ridiculous.

To cap it all, hail stones began to fall, smashing painfully into
my skin. Hail, at this time of year? The universe itself was
mocking me. But freak storms had been happening for ages now,
bizarre things like this were almost expected.

As I laboured over every tortured step, wishing I was
anywhere but here, I noticed a woman on the path ahead of me.

I was quickly gaining on her – she seemed to be struggling and was stopping every few minutes to rest. I saw her lean forward on her walking poles, head down, struggling to find the energy to continue, before forcing herself onwards.

As I drew closer to her, she stumbled and almost fell before catching her balance, then sank down to sit on to a rock. I hurried up to her, my self-hatred forgotten.

'Are you all right?' I asked, my eyes raking over her.

She looked up at me, smiling tiredly. She was around fifty, her face drawn and haggard. 'Yes, I'm fine, I'm finding it a bit hard going today, that's all.'

'You don't look well though,' I said with concern. 'Do you think maybe you should get back to town?' As I spoke, I saw what I'd thought was a hat was actually a head scarf. *Chemotherapy*, I immediately realised with a guilty shock.

She followed my gaze. 'I was diagnosed with ovarian cancer last year. I'm walking long-distance footpaths to raise money for cancer research. I'm walking St Cuthbert's Way at the moment, I hope to arrive at Lindisfarne by next week.' As she spoke, she forced herself to her feet, what was clearly a tremendous effort.

I'd spent my life running and walking long distances, I knew well the iron will needed to force your body to keep moving when every step was torturous and every muscle was screaming, but I knew I'd experienced nothing like this lady was going through. Something stopped me from insulting her by offering her help.

I walked alongside her, matching my steps to her snail's pace. 'How long has it been since you were given the all-clear?' I asked, smiling.

She didn't smile back. 'It's terminal,' she said at length. 'There was nothing they could do, they gave me six months. So far I've managed fifteen.'

'I'm sorry,' I stammered. I couldn't believe I'd said something so wrong.

'Don't be,' she said with admirable strength. 'I'm not. I'm determined not to leave the world with any regrets, I'm using what time I have to do everything I possibly can. So far, I've raised £10,000, I've aimed to make it £20,000. While I'm still strong enough to walk, I shan't give up.'

We reached the top of a small rise and the landscape was displayed before us. The fickle temperament of the Cheviots displayed itself as the clouds suddenly parted and the sun shone through. The heather was in full bloom and the sun lit the purple haze beautifully. The air became alive with the sound of bees targeting the rich nectar with unrivalled enthusiasm. We both stopped to absorb this vision of heaven. My companion, I saw, was smiling, a fervent light in her eyes. *Love. True Love.* I almost began to envy her.

Further on were a few black and white animals which I assumed were sheep. As they saw us they immediately took flight.

'Cheviot goats,' said my companion, leaning again on her poles. 'They're the only true wild goats in Britain, only a handful remain.'

'I thought they were sheep,' I said. 'You know a lot about them?' They were now looking back towards us. They had huge horns, I now noticed, quite unlike sheep.

'I've learnt so much about the world in the last year,' she said wistfully, looking at the goats as if she might never see them again. 'Far more than I have in the rest of my thirty-five years.'

I was shocked. She was only thirty five? Not that much older than me.

'I was complacent,' she continued. 'I let the world pass me by. It was only the thought of death that gave me the impetus to enjoy life. Now I make the most of every minute.' We slowly walked on, easier going on a downhill stretch.

'I heard a story once,' she said between breaths. 'A great king did a favour for the wisest man in the world. The wise man said,

'Now in return, I'll give you the greatest gift a man can ever have.'

The king went to claim this gift with huge excitement, thinking of gold, jewels, the secrets of the gods, who knows what else. And the wise man said to him, 'This is your gift. You will die in three days time.''

The woman caught her breath as we overcame yet another rise in the path. 'Now I too have received this gift, I understand what the story meant.'

I had to look away so she couldn't see my face. I was filled with shock, sadness, guilt. But most of all, shame. Shame that I'd let myself despair over minor, petty things when this lady was suffering unimaginable problems and still kept going, one foot in front of the other, undefeated and indefatigable. I felt awful.

The path reached a minor road with a car parked on the verge. A couple standing beside it were looking our way.

'That's my brother and his wife,' she said. 'They meet me at every road junction on the way. We'll have lunch together now, then I'll complete another leg this afternoon.'

I looked at her awkwardly. We'd walked in silence since she'd finished her story, and I couldn't think of any suitable parting words to end our impromptu meeting. Encouragement, sorrow, sympathy, all were things she didn't want or need. Thanks, for kicking me up the arse and lifting me from my black despair, I couldn't bring myself to give.

She saved my problem. 'Enjoy the rest of your walk then, I enjoyed your company. Sometimes a chance meeting on the path can be most uplifting.'

I nodded, now feeling more ashamed than ever. 'Goodbye then.' These greatly inadequate words were the only ones I could think of. I didn't even know her name.

The car drove off, the three of them waving. I waved back and then returned to my path. I was alive. I still had the greatest possession of all, and the only one that ever mattered. If I'd taken a wrong turning, it didn't matter. I had the rest of my life to put it right. And unlike my companion, the clock was not yet inexorably ticking, louder and louder. I had all the time in the world to find the way.

# Chapter 23

*To those who see but one in all the changing manifoldness of the universe, belongs Eternal Truth.*
Indian Wisdom


A gradual sense of unease, a feeling that something was not quite right, began to creep into my mind. It was more a deep, discordant resonance that I could sense on the edges of my perception.

I could see no reason for this at all, I couldn't understand it. I was walking along my favourite path, picking off the now familiar landmarks. There was the stunted tree with one branch pointing towards Wooler, there was the rock where I'd sat to eat my sandwiches. Here was a stream where I'd washed mud from my hands after I'd tripped. The sun was shining, the birds were twittering deep in the gorse bushes, I could see no one about, no life at all except some distant grazing sheep. The world seemed as normal, but still I felt on edge.

There was a flicker of movement to the left and I jumped round, nerves jangling. For an instant I saw that same wild face in the bushes; immediately it merged with the surrounding vegetation as if it had never been there at all. This wasn't the threat I was somehow aware of, I knew that, and I continued walking, all my senses on high alert. I could feel adrenaline seeping into my blood and my heart rate began to rise. I was walking carefully, tensely, every step controlled, like a deer scenting a whiff of danger. The feeling grew stronger.

Then, I saw it. Standing motionless on an outcrop of rock, silhouetted against the sky, growing to fill my vision. A monstrous black dog. Fear swept over me, my skin prickled and the hairs on my arms stood on end. A deep chill swept down my spine.

I stood frozen to the spot, my eyes riveted on the beast. Its malevolent stare was fixed on me, its hatred was palpable across the distance. My first instinct was to turn and run, but a higher intuition told me that if I did so, I would be torn to pieces in an instant. I wouldn't outrun it, it would breach the distance in seconds.

I searched desperately in my pockets for something – anything – that could be used as a weapon. I had nothing. I risked breaking eye contact and looked on the ground for a tree branch, careful not to move anything except my eyes. I could see a heavy rock about the size of a brick, but I wouldn't even reach that before the dog's fangs ripped through my exposed flesh.

My panicked fingers eventually closed on the fossil seashell I'd found in the stream. As I touched it, the lucky amulet of a long gone person, a sense of strength flooded my soul. I felt empowered, I was no longer afraid.

Of course, the stone did nothing. It was just a symbol of luck which my mind focussed on. It merely emphasised, manifested and awakened the strength that I already had. I knew that the true power in lucky charms, amulets, the sign of the cross, all those things, was yourself.

This insight came from somewhere outside of myself and my knowledge. *Where had it come from?* It was as if something, somewhere, had sensed my panic and lent me a guiding hand from beyond the reaches of the world.

But I didn't realise any of this at the time, my mind was too preoccupied.

Still shaking slightly from the remnants of adrenaline but determined not to show any fear, I held onto my sudden feeling of confidence and surety, and I walked forward. I crossed the hillside towards the dog, slowly, surely, never breaking eye contact. Its fangs, gleaming white, I was uncomfortably aware were razor-sharp. It hadn't yet moved an inch, it was just fixed, immobile. *Waiting for me.* There was something of a supernatural air about it. I knew it was not of this world.

I walked right up to it. I knew in my heart that whatever it was guarding, *protecting me from*, I was now ready for. And because I knew that, it let me pass.

As I drew level with him, I gazed into his eyes, the windows to his soul. I saw blackness, chaos, the void. But not evil. Because there is no evil in the world. Everything is an integral and necessary part of the divine plan.

*There is no light that does not cast a shadow.*

Life and death, positive and negative, day and night, attraction and repulsion, yin and yang, male and female. The God and the Goddess. All of existence comprises two opposites in perfect and delicate harmony.

The missing link for the Sphere of Venus.

Hearing this strange and reflective insight whispering inside my mind, another message made itself heard from the far bounds of the universe. A light began to grow inside me. A light surrounded by darkness.

As everything is a reflection of everything else, our soul is also comprised of dark and light. The darkness must be reconciled, not defeated. Our life quest can only be fulfilled when these opposites are united, when yin and yang form an entwined symbol of harmony.

Having understood this dark side of my soul, I moved on, I began the next stage of my Journey. As I climbed Yeavering Bell, I felt the great power surge through me. *Something* was going to happen.

# Chapter 24

*A skylark wounded in the wing,*
*A cherubim does cease to sing.*
*A dog starved at his master's gate*
*Predicts the ruin of the state.*
William Blake

I looked towards the distant sea and the hilltops stretching far away. I was aware, with my newly heightened sense of awareness, of a current of energy beneath my feet. I could feel it flowing and tugging at me, as if I were standing in a powerful stream of water. I reached out with all my senses, my intuition, and suddenly I saw it in front of me, an electric current, the divine spirit of the land, flowing through the hilltop. A silvery, glowing, sinuous stream poured through the ground, I could see it snaking far across the land.

*The ley lines, dragon paths, Feng Shui, the universal power. The blood of the Goddess.*

As I watched I could feel the power pulling stronger, my feet began to waver. My first instinct was to resist, I pulled myself back and the vision began to fade.

*No!* said my heart. *Let go!*

I relaxed, I felt the power tugging at me even more in response. I felt my feet shift and, letting my mind go, I let myself be swept away.

My mind flew across the world at breakneck speed. I saw everything, was aware of everything, I became a part of the whole of existence. I saw myself standing on the hill top, both from close up and from an infinite distance away. I saw soaring cathedrals, pyramids, majestic temples, ancient stone circles, hill forts, carved stone heads, all laid out in an immense global network.

As I saw all places, I also saw all times. I saw ancient mounds become stone circles, which in turn became temples and then churches, cathedrals and mosques. I saw people and cultures come and go, dying and rising, all nourished by this eternal power, the blood of the Goddess.

I understood then the universal religion of which all faiths are a diverse manifestation of, forging the timeless bond with this divine spirit, the spirit of the earth. Our Mother.

I saw how the unbroken chain of wisdom had survived for millennia, since the first people had looked up to the sky. The ancient builders had been the guardians of this Truth, the sacred Spirit of the Land, and this they bequeathed to their descendants through the medium of religion.

They in turn had left their legacy to the next people, the new religions, and it is still held by people with understanding today. This was the true reason why so many sites remained sacred for millennia, why the God and the Goddess continue to exist in myriad forms.

Before I could fully assimilate what I'd seen, the vision changed yet again. My mind expanded to see the earth as a single being, a microcosm of the universe, the all-encompassing, vast, cosmic being, stretching into infinity and eternity. The All, the One, known in many belief systems as –

God.

My mind then spiralled inward, smaller and smaller until I saw that, as the earth is a microcosm of the universe, so all life is a microcosm of the earth. I saw the earth reflected in the eyes and souls of people, plants and animals. Every living thing was a minute, holographic scale model of the earth's spirit, and anything affecting one, affects all.

In another flash of insight, I saw how the energy current, the Spirit of the Earth which all life depends upon, had weakened over time, that it had reached its lowest ebb in millennia. The corresponding decrease in men's soul energy had caused the disconnection, chaos, warfare and bloodshed of our time. It had caused all the problems that were ravaging the earth.

Then I knew. Everything became clear.

This had happened before, and I had tried to change it before.

I understood the message, the challenge, the summons. I now knew what it was I had to do.

The stars had realigned – it was time to play the game again.

# PART IV

# Chapter 25

*Everything is perfect just the way it is.*
The Buddha

My life is denoted by movement. I am endlessly moving, flowing, rushing through the land. Through my body I am connected to the whole world – at once I can feel the humid heat of jungles, the frigid cold of the ice caps, the warmth of the coral reefs, the freshness of the springs from the highest mountain peaks. From the largest to the smallest, I am connected to all. Movement is my life. As my waters flow to the infinite sea, so they give birth to the clouds which nourish my birth. Without my death, I cannot live; without my life, I cannot die. I am the circle of life.

I grow weak and sluggish under the summer sun, and in winter I relish the fall of cool raindrops, swelling my body which rushes fast to the sea so I can grow ever bigger.

My body is formed from smaller bodies, identical to mine in form and shape, which combine and join to form one. And their bodies in turn are formed from smaller ones. Eventually, my body as well will join with others to form a yet larger being.

Like all things, I have two faces – that of life, and that of death, for without one the other cannot be. My nature is that of opposites – I can ripple gently, a haven for all, so many take refuge and nourishment from my body. I nourish all, and all revere me as the giver of life. And I can rage wildly, ravaging and devastating the land, smashing all before my unstoppable power. All then flee my wrath, for my touch is death.

People revere me, worship me, offer me gifts. Some entrust treasures to my guardianship. Once, a young woman stood on my banks, as she had done many times before. I knew, though, this would be the last time I would see her. She left me a parting gift, a talisman which she dropped into my body. *'Keep it until someone else has need of it,'* she whispered to me.

I kept my promise. Years became decades, decades became centuries, and still I guarded my ward. Then another woman stood on my banks, gazing at my body, and I knew – she was the one. I relinquished my ward into her care, and she continued her Journey, as I continued mine.

My constant cycle of birth and death does not last forever – over time, my body will perish. As my life causes my death in the shorter frame of time, so it does in the larger frame of existence. My constant movement erodes the land, filling my body with sand, silt and debris. This clogs my body, choking my flow so eventually my body will die. No more will I rush along the ever twisting landscape on my eternal quest for completion. My body becomes a haven for marsh plants, trees and animals, until I am no more, nothing but a fleeting recollection in the memory of the earth.

# PART V

# Chapter 26

*The wheel is come full circle.*
William Shakespeare

The town was buzzing with excitement. A ship had been sighted approaching the shore – a big ship, a trader most likely, travelling from the warm lands far to the south. Cernyw had been the centre of trade for over a thousand winters, trading its valuable tin for countless other exotic items.

The ship rapidly drew closer – the wild and desolate land which reminded Brigid so much of her home was easily visible far out to sea. On board would be exotic goods – cloth, rare foods, jewels, wines, plates – and also exotic people with news and stories. There would be excitement in the town for days.

Word had rapidly spread – it seemed like half the town were here watching. Trading ships had become rare in recent years, and with the fighting and wars that were breaking out across the realm, people now spared little thought for luxury goods anyway.

Brigid edged through the massing crowd. She shaded her eyes and watched the strange bird-like structure pass a small island. It was quite unlike the fishing coracles she was used to. A cloud of seagulls swooped around it as it sliced through the water.

A group of boys rushed past her, pushing and shouting, eager for a good vantage point, and she stepped back. She knocked into another bystander and smiled an apology. Despite spending several winters at the Cernyw rath, she had not quite settled into life in the bustling town. The biggest and most advanced kingdom in Prydain, people gathered here from all round Prydain and the world.

The babble of noise was almost overwhelming and Brigid moved to the edge of the crowd. She looked up towards the moors and saw a gushing torrent pouring through a ravine, tiny across the distance. She longed for the peace of the heights, but at the same time her desire to see the approaching ship kept her riveted.

The ship entered the harbour, furling its sails as Brigid watched, intrigued. Ropes were thrown to shore, eagerly seized, and the ship made secure. She could see men on board, dark skinned and black haired, and she did a double-take, amazed at the sight – she'd never seen people like that before. Nefer-re, a priestess from the distant land of Khem, had jet black hair like that, but her skin was almost as pale as Brigid's.

'Have you ever seen a ship like this before?' A man standing next to her took in her obvious surprise. He looked rather like Rhod, Brigid thought with amusement. His face and long hair were just the same.

She shook her head with a wry smile. She'd realised on her long journey south that her childish infatuation had been exactly that. Cathbad had been right, she'd learned the difference between the things she needed, and the things she wanted. After she'd thought she'd lost everything, she'd realised on one of her endlessly lonely days that she was still exactly the same. She still had everything she needed. It had taken this especially harsh lesson to truly understand that.

'These ships come far from the south, where the sun travels. It barely skims the earth there, it's close enough to touch, you know.' Her neighbour spoke with the lilting tones of the land of Eirinn across the western sea. 'It burns the land to an arid desert and the men's skins are burnt black. I've met many people from the Far Lands, they all look like that,' he concluded with solemn gravity.

The dark men leapt to shore, no less glad for their arrival. They'd spent weeks at sea, the journey was long and perilous. The master poured a libation of wine into the sea to give thanks for their safe passage.

Already, crates and caskets were being unloaded and carried

to specially built storehouses. People crowded round for a glimpse of the exotic goods – bundles of cloth, far finer than Brigid had ever seen, chests of mysterious substances. For the watching crowds, these glimpses would be all they would see – later would come the chieftains and rulers who had the gold to buy these highly priced goods.

'Those chests are full of fairy coins,' informed her neighbour wisely. 'There are people who travel to the otherworld, to trade with the Faerie for mead and honey, which they greatly desire.'

Brigid nodded absently, her eyes still on the ship. She well knew that the man's information was based on superstition and childish stories.

Another man appeared on the deck. His eyes flickered over the scene, taking in every detail, but he remained apart from the bustle. He was also fairly dark-skinned, but otherwise he seemed different. He was older than most of the sailors and less at home aboard the ship. The sailors were automatically adapting their movements to mirror the pitching and swaying vessel, and Brigid noticed as well their calloused hands and sinewy arms, quite different from this stranger.

A particularly heavy wave struck the moored ship, causing it to roll heavily. The man stumbled and nearly lost his footing, but the sailors didn't even notice the movement, used as they were to violent storm surges on the open sea.

Brigid watched him with interest as he carefully made his way to shore. Her intuition told her he was of the priesthood. He wore a white robe as the Druids did, but made in an entirely different style which gave him an exotic and foreign appearance.

'Who is that man?' she asked her neighbour. He stood up straight, delighted with the new opportunity to show off his worldly knowledge.

'He'll be one of the great sages of the Far Lands. The greatest of them come here to speak with our Druids, to learn of our wisdom which was bequeathed us directly from the Gods,' he said importantly, implying that he himself was well versed in such wisdom.

Over the distance, the sage's eyes met and held hers. An unspoken communication passed between them. Both knew that this was the person they had journeyed so far to meet.

Brigid left her neighbour with an absent nod of thanks and edged through the crowds to the harbour. She made the proper obeisance due to a chief Druid in respect of the rank she was sure he held.

'Welcome to our land. I hope your journey was free from difficulty, and may the Goddess bless you with strength.' She recited the greeting formally. All foreigners were accorded a welcome by the Druids and she was the highest ranking Druid present. She noticed his robe was made of a highly unusual material, quite unlike the wool she was used to.

'Thank you,' said the sage with a bow, the exotic pronunciation of his speech further enhancing his foreign air. 'The journey that has led me to these shores has been long and hard, but I sense it may be near to an end, for which I offer thanks to the Gods.'

There was a flurry of movement and shouting as one of the great chests fell from the ship, smashing the side and spilling a cascade of coarse powder onto the ground. A sweet aroma filled the air as the crowd rushed forward, hoping for treasure and gold, before disappointedly retreating. The spilled powder was rapidly salvaged by the merchants – spices were too valuable to be wasted.

'I have journeyed long from my homeland of Ellas in search of Truth,' the sage continued. 'I have debated with the great sages and wise men of my homeland and the great land of Khem across the Middle Sea, and now my destiny has led me to these shores. My name is Pythagoras.'

# Chapter 27

*My heart is with me, and it shall never come to pass that it be carried away.*
*I live in right and truth and I have my being therein.*
The Egyptian Book of the Dead

Brigid took Pythagoras to the rath outside the main town. Although it wasn't on a hill, the topology of the land gave it a natural prominence. Pythagoras strode across the planked causeway broaching the surrounding ditch, so deep that a tall man standing on the shoulders of another wouldn't see over the top. He looked down, surprised at the level of craftsmanship, although he said nothing, and then the two of them entered the sturdy wooden gates. Inside the high stone wall, the sounds of the outside world vanished. An atmosphere of intent purpose pervaded the rath, many people hurried about their business. A medley of voices could be heard – as well as the local dialect, Brigid could distinguish the rich tones of Albany, Eirinn, Cymru and the more distant land of Gaul.

Pythagoras looked around with interest. The buildings in particular were most unusual – round, squat and thatched almost to ground level, designed to retain warmth in the harsh climate. They were very different to the airy structures of his homeland.

'It's time for the midday meal, if you would like to eat,' Brigid said, still retaining her formal air.

'I would be grateful to share your hospitality,' he replied, equally formally. 'The food aboard ship is poor to say the least – rats, weevils and salt water make short work of the quality.'

After Pythagoras had eaten his fill the two sat near the fire. They attracted many sideways glances, particularly from the younger Druids – Brigid was highly respected and the exotic newcomer was obviously of renown. None, though, dared approach the pair.

'I came here to learn of the wisdom of the Druids,' he told her. 'I heard that the people of these shores are closer to the Gods, and that your knowledge of The Truth has been preserved close to its original form.''Our traditions have been preserved since the time of the First People,' said Brigid. 'They are committed to memory by every initiate and the alteration of even one word is forbidden.' She sat up straight, unconsciously smoothing her woollen dress around her knees.

'Our mystery schools and those of Khem are thought the best in the world. The priesthood of Khem, the original home of the Gods, goes back nine thousand winters and holds intact all the sacred Truths.' Pythagoras said this simply, without pride. He gazed into the leaping flames in the great hearth, seeming lost in thought and lost in the world.

'But there is something missing. It's too long since the Gods last walked amongst us, many changes have come over the land. Some important pieces I believe have been forgotten, and I've searched far and long to find them again.''And so you've come to Prydain.' Brigid understood entirely his perpetual search for wisdom.

'I feel that Prydain holds the key, that here I can find what I'm looking for. The Druids are well known and respected in our country; this is why, many moons past, I set out on this journey.'

# Chapter 28

*The only true wisdom is in knowing you know nothing.*
Socrates

The flames crackled and spat as the draught swirled round the hearth, the bitter wind easily finding its way past the heavy door drapes. Brigid and Pythagoras sat close to the warmth. Brigid found the blazing heat almost too much for comfort and longed to move into the cooler area of the building, but Pythagoras, used to the fierce heat of the Far Lands, moved even closer to its warmth.

They had talked long about the philosophy of the Gods, the Goddess, life and death over the past moon, one initiate to another, discussing all that they'd learnt, heard, intuited and discovered during their respective journeys. Brigid spoke of the wisdom of the God and the Goddess, the mortal body and eternal soul, that all things contained the divine spirit and therefore a soul. She felt that Pythagoras was a wise man who could fully understand their spiritual Truth. She also sensed, on a deep level, that Pythagoras was to be instrumental in her own journey.

'I know of your Goddess,' said Pythagoras, wrapping his robe tighter around his body. 'You know her as Ceridwen, but in my country she is known as Demeter, the people before us called her Gaea. In Khem she is known as Isis. Please tell me more about her.' 'She is the All, the spirit which infuses all things, her presence is everywhere,' answered Brigid. 'This is why anything, living or non-living, can house the soul during its many lifetimes.'

A blast of wind rushed in as someone ducked into the building, and Pythagoras winced. 'Are your winters always as harsh as this?'

Brigid smiled. 'This is not winter. Winter will not be here for two moons yet.' The draft ruffled her long hair, but she was oblivious to it.

Pythagoras shuddered. 'The things I do for Truth!' he complained. 'My robes are designed for the warm winters of Ellas, not for the bitter summers of Prydain.' 'The men can give you robes, if you wish,' said Brigid seriously. 'The winter fleeces of the mountain sheep lend the best warmth. What animal does the wool in your robes come from?' She'd been fascinated with the strange material ever since she'd first seen it.

'It's not an animal, it's a plant. It's called cotton, it comes from Khem. It's soft, cool and hard-wearing, ideal for the warm lands.' He gave an ironic smile.

Brigid felt the cotton with interest. She knew of clothing made from plant fibres, of course, but they were rough and coarse, nothing like this. How unusual these Far Lands must be!

'But you believe a soul can enter living or non-living beings?' Pythagoras asked, returning to their previous conversation. 'We, of course, believe that all living things are equal and contain the essence of the divine soul, but we've never considered that non-living objects are equal to the living.'

He looked into the depths of the fire in thought, tugging absently at his beard. 'In Khem they say the soul travels on a three-thousand-year cycle through animal and human forms, but never through non-living things. I wonder if this is the missing link I've been searching for.'

After a moment of contemplative silence, Brigid stood up. 'I must go to the town, I need jars to brew mead. There was a good crop of honey this year, we're making a lot more than normal.' 'This is the season, is it?' Pythagoras asked with interest. He'd sampled the famed drink of course, but had no idea how it was made. 'Our wines are made much earlier, when the sun still warms the land.' He shivered again to emphasise his point.

Brigid had never tasted wine, although Pythagoras extolled its value, and she wondered if she would ever make the journey to these strange lands. 'I'll show you the process, if you wish.''Yes, I'd like that.' He stood up as well, imagining the reaction to this strange drink in Ellas. 'I think I'll go for a walk as well, help drive the cold from my bones. I'll find a warm cloak first, though.'

The two made the customary parting gesture and Brigid went quickly from the building. She loved the feel of the wind as it whipped around the edge of her dress and teased free wisps of her hair.

It strengthened as she crossed the exposed and bleak moor and she slowed slightly. It reminded her strongly of her long-ago home and she felt the usual sense of profound peace wash over her. The wind lashed her face with tiny particles of grit and she smiled, remembering with fondness countless other memories.

A short distance away she noticed an old woman gathering plants. She was bent with age and even from a distance Brigid was aware that her fingers were swollen and stiff, but still she exuded an air of vitality and intelligence. As she watched, the woman spotted a small plant almost hidden beneath a rock and hastened to pick it.

Brigid left the path and crossed to where the woman was working. 'Greetings to you, Mother.'

The woman straightened as much as she was able and looked at Brigid. Her face was lined and weather-beaten, but her eyes sparkled and she seemed not to notice the bitterly cold wind.

'Greetings to you too, child,' she replied.

Although Brigid had been an adult for over ten winters, she wasn't insulted by the greeting – the woman likely had grand-children older than her.

'I see you're gathering the rock samphire,' she said, gesturing to the crude basket at her side.

'It preserves eggs and root plants like no other,' said the old woman. 'I like to eat eggs when the snows come!'

She cackled. Eggs, a spring-time treat, were almost impossible to preserve until winter, and Brigid looked at the woman with increased respect. Her herb-lore was obviously first rate.

'I should like to learn your method,' she said with genuine interest. Her love of herb-lore, inspired by Emer, had never waned.

The old woman looked sly. 'My secret was taught to me by my grandmother, and she learnt from her mother. I don't divulge it to just anyone.''I've used samphire to cure the winter-sickness, but I know no other use for it. I'd be grateful if you would teach me.' Emer had told Brigid of this bleeding sickness, and the curative of green plants. The last winter had been unusually long and she'd been grateful to Emer for this knowledge.

'My cottage is a half day's walk from here,' said the old woman. 'If you care to make the journey sometime, maybe I'll teach you the secret.''Thank you, Mother. I will.' Brigid looked at the sky, which was boiling with angry clouds. 'There's a storm coming, it's not a time to be out here.'

The woman picked up her basket. 'I was going now, anyway. My cottage is past the Big River, next to the Derw-Wood.'

Brigid nodded and raised her hand in farewell. 'Good bye then, for now.' As drops of rain began to fall, she hastened on her way.

But even before she reached the town, she could feel there was something wrong.

# Chapter 29

*And when the dogs gather together let me not suffer harm.*
The Egyptian Book of the Dead

A hostile crowd had gathered, unsmiling looks and muttering were directed towards three young men from the village and two sailors from the Far Lands.

'What has happened?' she asked someone at the back of the crowd.

'The dark men wanted to make offerings at the shrine of the Goddess, some people didn't like it.' The man spat on the ground. 'They shouldn't offer to our Goddess – she doesn't recognise them. They think their dark Goddess is equal to ours – ridiculous!' He turned away in disgust.

Brigid was shocked. When had this intolerance begun to develop? If there was one thing the Druid lands were known for, it was tolerance and peace. Brigid made to push through the crowd but someone caught her arm.

'There's nothing to gain by intervening, the argument is already over,' said Pythagoras quietly. 'You will not change men's hearts, the problem runs much deeper than that. The solution lies with the stars.'

Distracted by what was happening, Brigid wondered what he meant. He was obviously referring to the time of calamity that was approaching, she would have to ask him later. She needed answers – the realm was beginning to slowly fall apart.

The two sailors backed away and hurriedly left for the safety of the docks. They had no wish to start a fight – they just wanted to get home safely. The young three men strutted round with triumph.

'They know not to mess with us, we're better than them any day. Pity we didn't get some dark blood on the ground to offer the Goddess,' gloated one. An older man clapped him on the back with pride.

'I must speak with them,' said Brigid to Pythagoras as she began to hurry after the sailors. What was going on? There was a festering undercurrent of hatred developing in the community. It had been there for a while, but this was the first time she'd seen it so blatantly.

The two sailors were already a good way away and she had to run to catch up with them. They suddenly heard her footsteps and jumped round nervously, expectant of more trouble, but then relaxed and smiled as they appraised the elegant woman. The first opened his mouth to speak, a wicked gleam in his eye, but then his companion hastily nudged him silent. More knowledgeable, he'd realised she was of the Druids.

'Greetings to you,' she said, looking at them with interest. Their skin was more a dark brown than black, she could now see, rather like the rich colour of earth. Their eyes were nearly black and their wiry hair was also unlike anything she'd ever seen.

The sailors returned the greeting politely, now looking at the ground like a pair of nervous boys. They were very young, she could see. As an icy blast of wind struck them, their skin raised in bumps – they obviously felt the cold as much as Pythagoras. Well, it was a bit chilly today, she conceded.

'What happened in the town?' she asked, smiling to put them at ease.

'Well, we usually offer gifts to the native Gods where we visit,' the first said, looking up at her. 'We need a safe journey home.' He hesitated, unsure how much to say to the foreign Druid woman.

'I don't know what happened. Some people think we shouldn't do it. Normally we're welcomed everywhere, people look forward to the ships arriving. This is the first time something like this has happened.'

The second sailor fiddled with his tunic as he began to speak his worries. 'There are changes happening. People are frightened, worried, so they get angry. Everywhere on this voyage, there was hostility in the air. They look to place the blame somewhere. The seas were terrible too, stormy and wild, it was a nightmare crossing. The Gods are growing angry with us.'

He looked up at the sky furtively as if expecting an imminent show of this anger. 'That's why it's so important that we appease them.'

Brigid felt a shiver down her spine, for the first time the icy gusts of wind felt quite unpleasant. She had also felt the discord, the disharmonious hum which was affecting people's hearts and minds. So it wasn't just Cernyw, it was the same across the world?

'The shrines aren't that important. All the world was made by the Goddess and so is sacred to her. Wherever you are, she will always hear your prayers.' It was imperative she reassured the sailors, negative thoughts breed and spread like a forest fire.

They both turned to look at her, searching her face for signs of untruth. 'In our country, the Gods are worshipped only in the temples, at the will of the priests. It's only the priests who are worthy to intercede with them.'

It was Brigid's turn to be shocked. As if any man were better than another in the eyes of the Gods! She shook her head. 'That is not right,' she said forcefully. 'Everyone is equal, everything is equal, only in the matters of men is rank and position important.'

They'd reached the harbour and Brigid raised her hand in blessing. 'May the Goddess watch over you on your way, and the wind of good fortune carry you home.'

The sailors bowed their heads in thanks, grateful that their homeward trip would be less arduous. But as Brigid watched the waves already tugging greedily at the ship, she was aware that in the soul of the world, something was going very wrong.

As Brigid went back to the town, she could hear shouting. She began to run, holding her skirt up so it didn't impede her speed. She was panting hard when she reached the edge of the crowd and she pushed her way through. People reluctantly moved out of her way – despite her dishevelled appearance, most still recognised and respected the Druid woman. She could see the figure on the ground, mud and blood staining his white clothing.

Oh Goddess no, it couldn't be! Brigid dropped to her knees, pulling that strange material called cotton away from the body. She looked up and saw three figures furtively moving away, the crowd moving to block her view. *Them* again. But they weren't important now. Pythagoras was breathing, although not awake. The blood pouring from his head told her why not and she quickly folded a pad of cloth and pressed it to the wound.

'What happened?' she demanded. There was a murmur but no answer. The crowd pressed in slightly closer. 'What happened?' she said again, standing up. A sea of hostility faced her and Brigid raised her chin. She was a Druid, none would dare harm her.

After a moment's face off, one man spoke. 'He fell,' he muttered.

She ignored the lie, Pythagoras' life was more important. 'Bring a cart,' she ordered. Nobody moved, and not one person would meet her eyes.

'Now!' she shouted. She glared round at the crowd, daring them to defy her. Someone reluctantly heeded her natural authority, and a cart was brought through the crowd.

She struggled to heave her friend aboard. Only one man came to aid her, and he was none too gentle with the unconscious man. 'Dark bastard,' he muttered as he dropped the body down.

Brigid ignored him – she would gain nothing from confronting him – and climbed up with Pythagoras, resting his head on her lap. The cart driver began to force a way through the crowd for the slow and bumpy journey to the rath.

He was breathing peacefully, the bleeding had stopped, and as far as she could tell there was no damage to the skull. But despite that, it had been three days and Pythagoras showed no sign of waking.

Brigid had barely moved from his side, hoping against hope her friend would awaken. She'd done all she could, it was in the hands of the Goddess now. If he didn't awake... Brigid thought back to his last words to her. *The problem runs deeper, it lies in the stars.* He may be her only hope. And now, because she hadn't spoken of it earlier, that hope was lost.

She forced her dark worries aside. The Goddess would choose the best way, of course, she must have faith. She offered up a silent prayer.

And her faith was rewarded. As she looked up, she saw two dark eyes looking into hers.

'Pythagoras! How are you feeling?' Brigid almost jumped up with gladness.

He smiled, gentle, happy and serene. 'I have seen it,' he said dreamily, light and excitement filling his eyes. 'I saw everything. I saw the answers.'

Brigid didn't speak. She knew what answers he meant, and was truly glad for her friend. She saw the light radiate through his body as his soul returned, and he began to speak. Her first thought was that he should lie quiet and rest, but she could see he was desperate to tell her his story.

'I became aware of my soul as separate to my body. I could feel the ground beneath me – I *was* the ground. A part of me could feel the heat of the sun on me, the rain washing over me. Another part of me could feel that I was a part of the earth, rooted deep into the ground.

I was aware of all time, from the beginning of the world to the end, all laid out as one. The rain ran over me for aeons, cutting grooves in my body. The sun dried and warmed me. Plants used me for support and protected me from the sun and rain. When they died, their seeds grew in their place. I became aware that all things live, some for a short time, some for longer, but the spirit of life lives forever.'

He paused and reached for a cup of water, and Brigid helped him to drink.

'This vision has opened a new doorway in my mind, I've now seen things I was never aware of before. I have meditated on all my knowledge, and have concluded that this is the missing part of our wisdom. The soul can indeed reside in non-living objects, as all things contain the divine spirit.' He looked around the building in wonder, as if seeing the world in new eyes. He sat up, then rose to his feet, reaching for his staff, his vision empowering him with strength.

'I have done it! I have the answer! I will teach the priests of Ellas, and Khem! I will make sure this great gift of wisdom is never again forgotten. I will set up a school in my homeland, a school of philosophy where students from across the land will travel to learn. What I now know can never again be forgotten.'

He thumped his staff on the floor to emphasise his words. All eyes in the room turned to him, and the attention of others, albeit unseen, was also invoked. 'I will make sure that my name and my teachings will be renowned forever.'

The passionate force of this vow sent a tingle down Brigid's spine. She did not doubt that the Gods would honour his pledge.

They sat together beside the leaping flames, a bond between them forged for all time. Brigid was quiet. It was time for her to act, to do something, but what?

'I am worried,' she said to Pythagoras. 'What happened in the town has emphasised the problem, but it's been around for a long time.'

He nodded in agreement.

'And you know of it too,' she stated. 'You said it was linked to the stars.' She looked up from the flames, a silent plea in her eyes. 'When I met with the Goddess, she told me the world would one day fall apart, and my destiny was to stop it. I think this is that time, but I don't know what to do.''Yes,' Pythagoras replied, rubbing the rapidly healing wound on his head. 'It is written in the stars, we also knew it would happen. We have a vast knowledge of star lore, we learnt it from the priests of Khem – their astronomers have tracked every star for thousands of winters. I can tell you exactly what is happening.''I would be grateful for your help.' Brigid's formal reply did not betray the blaze of hope that filled her heart. Despite the best efforts of the Druids, the tinder box situation realm-wide was rapidly deteriorating, and no one seemed to know what was causing the chaos, or why. Only last week, it had been reported that the two kingdoms to the north, the Catamandae and the Somerae, had descended into full-scale war, although for now it seemed to be localised.

Pythagoras looked at the fire for a moment. It had taken many winters' learning to fully comprehend the complexities of star lore, it wasn't something that could easily be explained in one evening. 'The stars that surround the sun on new year's day are shifting,' he began, 'and soon a new set of stars will occupy this position. This is called the cycle of the Great Year, which traverses twelve long Ages in each cycle.'

Brigid looked confused, and Pythagoras picked up a wooden tablet and carved a circle with his knife, adding twelve boxes around the edge. 'The sun is presently here,' he said, adding a circle into one box, 'in the stars of the Ram. But it is about to move into the next box,' he added a second circle, 'that of the Fish.'

Brigid nodded, understanding.

'The Age of the Ram is drawing to a close, and the Age of the Fish is dawning. But each change triggers great changes on earth. At the end of the Age of the Bull, the last Age, there was a devastating war in Khem, their temples destroyed and much sacred wisdom lost. This is when, I believe, our wisdom was corrupted, the pieces were lost that I've travelled so far to find.''And the end of the Age is causing our troubles now?' Brigid was riveted to his words.

'The earth is a mirror image of the heavens; as the heavens change, so must the earth. She must retune with the sacred song of the stars, but not without difficulty. Times of change are always difficult. Countries will fall, others rise from their ashes. Gods, religions, people, they must all change in accordance with the new Age.''How can it be stopped, then? It is fate, no one can prevent the wheeling of the stars.' Brigid looked down in resignation. What could she do? Not even the Gods could prevent the coming war. 'I feel as if, I don't know, all my life I've been searching for something. I thought when I started on the Druid Path I would learn the answers. But as far as I've come, I feel no further forward. What my soul searches for is still far away on the horizon, like a rainbow you can never reach.' Brigid shook her head slowly. She would never succeed in her Quest.

'The war may be foretold, but its outcome is not. You will find your Path.' Pythagoras looked firmly at her, his eyes full of determination and resolution, but Brigid could not meet his eyes. Despite her unwavering faith in the Gods, her task now seemed impossible.

'Although the change is hard, devastating, it will be survived. The heavens will continue to turn and the earth to spin, despite the choices we will make.' He put his hand on her shoulder, comforting, assured. 'Life will endure. It always has and it always will.'

That night Brigid tossed and turned, sleep refused to come. Her mind went over all that had happened lately, the changing times, what she could do about it. She went over and over the problem until she fell into a fitful sleep and began to dream.

She saw the whole land bathed in sunshine, glowing and green. And then she saw a huge black cloud was drawing over the land. She looked up and saw it wasn't a cloud but a monstrous black bird, wings outstretched, soaring above the land. It gazed down malevolently, a hostile, evil presence infecting all that lay below it. It covered the entire land in the darkness of its shadow, dropping ever lower and closer.

Brigid jerked awake, a deep sense of dread taking hold in her. She rose and went to the door. The full moon bathed the deserted rath in a cold glow. Somewhere, an owl hooted. The cool air was refreshing and she longed for the peace of the woods, so she walked barefoot from the rath and into the trees. Leaves crunched under her feet and she felt a twig snap. It was dark, but like a wild cat she could find her way safely. A rustle in the leaves betrayed a small vole. Further away, a larger animal crashed through the undergrowth. Sounds were clearer at night to compensate for the darkness, she remembered Cathbad telling her.

She found the trail of the larger animal followed it. She could hear running water ahead and soon reached a fast flowing stream, glowing silver under the moonlight. She heard no more of the animal and was unaware of a pair of eyes, ancient, timeless and infinitely wise, watching her from the undergrowth.

A flash of movement darted upstream. A salmon. They spend their entire lives travelling from the sea to the place of their birth, searching for the home that in their souls they know is there, she thought. Just like us.

She looked after the fish, silently wishing it well. Everything in the world is searching for something, she realised, a relentless, never-ending search for fulfilment. Some find what they are looking for, some never will.

Regardless of the troubles in the world of men, the fish would continue on its journey. As Pythagoras had said, life was strong. It would always survive. Although the time would be hard, it was really nothing but a flicker, a passing moment soon lost in the sands of time.

She would trust the Goddess, everything would be the way it was meant to be.

# Chapter 30

*I asked God for happiness. God said no. I give blessings, happiness is up to you.*
Anonymous

Brigid walked through a secluded valley on her way to the home of Allie, the old woman she'd met on the moor. Everywhere was unnaturally quiet – no people, no roosters and no cattle could be heard or seen, all were removed to a place of greater safety. The wilds of the countryside were no longer safe.

The nightmare had come to pass, war was ravaging the south. Some people in the neighbouring kingdom had been raiding across the border, provoking outrage by killing men and carrying off women, children and livestock, burning entire villages to the ground. The chieftain had ridden out and surveyed the smoking, blackened wreckage with seething anger.

'Raise the banners!' he cried, turning to face his men. 'This deed shall not go unavenged!'

The young men of the realm, bored of everyday life, flocked to his banner in search of fighting, excitement and loot. The army marched north to the cheers and admiration of those left behind. Children watched with sparkling eyes, wishing they were old enough to join them, and young women stood on the sidelines, eyes searching in adoration for that particular special face.

Not all those watching were so exuberant, though. Mothers worried for their sons, wives for their husbands. A dark undercurrent ran under the celebratory atmosphere.

'War promises glory and gain, but gives only despair, devastation and loss,' muttered an old man darkly, turning from the festivities.

A chance to settle old scores, gain land and riches, or to give excitement, the fever was rapidly spreading. Raiders and bandits were also roaming the countryside, taking advantage of vulnerable settlements, their menfolk far away.

Brigid had become close to Allie over the recent moons and was concerned for her safety – she'd be very vulnerable to the preying thieves. Druids had a responsibility towards their communities, but it was more than that – Brigid genuinely cared for the old woman. Allie had an unrivalled repertoire of healing knowledge, she'd discovered, learnt through a long lifetime of treating illnesses in her extended family and the animals they tended.

At noon Brigid stopped to quickly eat the bread and cheese she'd brought with her. She had a good appetite after the long walk and she was not yet half way there. She heard shouts and galloping horses in the distance and listened warily, but mercifully they came no nearer and she relaxed. Her intuition would tell her of any danger so she didn't feel unduly worried, despite her isolation – she'd seen no one since she'd left the rath.

As she walked along the rough stone road, fog began to descend. Soon she could barely see twenty paces, it was as thick and impenetrable as she'd known on the hills in the north. She recalled one of the Druids telling her that thick fogs would come in from the sea, but this was the first time she'd seen it for herself.

Soon, everything was dripping wet. Beads of water formed on her hair, eyelashes and eyebrows, dripping to the ground, and her clothing was coated with a film of moisture. The world became eerily silent, the fog dulled all sounds so nothing but the constant drip of moisture could be heard.

Brigid wasn't worried, she knew the path well and wouldn't get lost. If anything, the fog was a benefit – it would help hide her and prevent sounds she made reaching unfriendly ears. She continued walking confidently until she reached the small, strangely shaped rock which she knew marked the turning point. On the right, just visible in the fog, she saw a faint track leading through some bushes. She thanked the Goddess for blessing her with fortune and began to pick her way along it.

After she had enjoyed the tranquillity of the foggy world for a good distance, it came to an abrupt end. It began to thin slightly, and then she walked through a defined edge and into bright sunshine. She looked back at the sharp edge to the blanket of fog, amazed at how abruptly the world was swallowed up. She smiled in delight – it was incredible how it could have such clarity.

She walked on through a vastly different world. The sun shone brightly and, in abrupt contrast to a moment before, she could clearly hear the sounds of birdsong and running water from the nearby river. She saw with pleasure that the gorse was flowering brightly, then hesitated. Something was wrong. It was quiet – despite it being perfect foraging conditions, there was not a bee in sight.

Slightly unsettled by this strange turn of events, she walked on towards the river. The sound of rushing water seemed clearer than ever after the fog, and as she rounded the wood she realised why. Instead of the shallow and easily fordable river that the path usually led to, a ferocious, tumultuous cascade of brown muddy water churned past, branches and debris dragged along with it. The result of heavy rain high on the moors, the river was now impassable.

Brigid looked, aghast. There was no way she could ford it. A tree trunk swept just three paces from her confirmed her supposition. She would have to walk upstream to where it shallowed. She wondered about turning back, but immediately dismissed the idea. She didn't give up that easily on what she had tasked herself.

It was nearly four thousand paces before she reached a likely place. The river widened out and she looked across it critically. It was just about passable, she decided, and she removed her boots and tucked her skirt up high then began to slowly step through the water. It came high up her shins in the centre and she struggled to keep her balance, all the time checking for branches and other hazards. It was chilly and she was quite cold when she reached the far side, and she quickly replaced her boots and began to run until she was warm again. Despite that, the delay meant the sun was nearing the horizon when she finally reached Allie's home.

It was empty. It looked like no one had been here for days – there was no perishable food around and the hearth was cold. Fires were kept burning perpetually all year round, extinguished only on Beltaine Eve, when the symbolic relighting corresponded with the Sacred Marriage and the reawakening of the Land.

Brigid remembered the first time she'd seen the Beltaine fires, a sight she would never forget. At midnight, when everywhere was in total darkness, a spark had appeared high up on the Hill of Cernunnos, rapidly fanned into a roaring fire. Sparks flying up into the air were visible even from the valley. In response, other fires began to flare up on other sacred peaks – Rosscastell, Bywyck and many others – she could see over a dozen from her spot alone.

The sense of awe and majesty she had felt was overwhelming. She had hung onto her mother's hand, almost frightened to even breathe. It was her first understanding of the living breathing earth, its life-force, its blood, connecting all the sacred points in a vast network. And it was also the first inkling she'd had, at three winters of age, of the great future which the Gods had chosen for her.

Brigid pulled herself back to the silent and cold building. Allie must have gone to stay with her family for safety. She had three sons with farmsteads nearby and five married daughters – any one of them could have taken her in.

Brigid looked up at the sun – it was almost set. It was too late to return to the rath, she would have to stay here for the night, so she turned her mind to basic necessities. She went into the wood to gather firewood. She believed she was alone in the glade, didn't hear the slight movement of loose stone over the sound of her breaking sticks, or the faint sound of feet, or see the form of a shadowy being, barely distinguishable from the surrounding vegetation.

She lit a fire in the cold hearth and cooked some grains she found in an earthen pot. She knew Allie wouldn't have denied her this hospitality, she'd bring her a like gift when next she saw her.

She sat by her fire late into the night, staring into the flames, thinking deeply. Pythagoras had left Prydain half a moon before, carrying the piece of his soul that he'd travelled so far to find. He'd fulfilled his role in Brigid's future, and she'd fulfilled her part in his. The time had come for them to part. Brigid had watched the ship sail away, carrying the friend and mentor that she'd come to love and respect. She was glad for their meeting, and the guidance she'd received and given. Its effects would ripple through the future in ways neither of them could ever begin to imagine.

As the ship disappeared from view, she sent a silent blessing after her friend, and a prayer of thanks to the Goddess who'd provided for her in her need. She wasn't sad to see him leave – their paths had crossed and now parted, this was just the way of things.

Entirely lost in thought, she was unaware of the approaching danger. She was vaguely aware, on an unconscious level, of slight sounds outside but didn't register the warning. She snatched her awareness back and leapt up, but it was too late. The men were already inside the room.

'Well, here's a pretty young thing,' one grinned lewdly through broken teeth. 'A good price for a night's work!'

She clamped down on her fear as the men's eyes flickered round the room, appraising what they would take – to panic would be fatal. The lesson of her long ago night in the Wyldwood came to her aid, she took a conscious breath to calm herself and focussed her attention on them. The three men were unkempt and sloppy, not trained soldiers. She could also smell stale ale. Opportunistic bandits, they must be, relying only on her assumed fear to retain the upper hand. Maybe, if she was quick, she could gain the advantage.

Two men were searching the poor dwelling, the third was smiling cruelly at her. He was in no hurry – he was sure of his prize. There was a direct line between her and the entrance.

As fast as a wild cat she leapt forward, grabbing and throwing the earthen jar of grains in his direction with all her might. It struck the man in the head, shattering into pieces. She saw a snapshot of blood beginning to pour, and then she was outside, running. Her advantage was minimal – with surprised and angry shouts, the men were soon behind her.

She reached the edge of the trees and paused for the merest instant, reaching out with her intuition. The path split in two. Along one fork, she glimpsed a fleeting black shadow – was it the shape of a large dog? She took that path without further hesitation. Although running at speed, she was careful to avoid stepping on twigs or anything else that would betray her. Soon darkness surrounded her. She paused in her flight and listened carefully.

Two men had taken the other path, and one followed hers. They were moving carefully and adeptly, a short distance back. They were well used to travelling through woods at night, she could tell. But no match for a trained Druid.

She listened further, perfectly still, and then the man was right behind her. He'd silently crept through the trees as she'd been listening to the other two blundering around, and she realised to her cost the price of underestimating her enemy.

His hand closed on empty air as she turned and sprinted through the trees, panic speeding her feet. She had no thought for carefulness this time, she crashed through the trees as if the Hounds of Annwn were after her. The man was close behind her, and gaining. She could hear his breathing over her own gasping, barely laboured at all – he was enjoying the chase. He would surely catch her.

Her foot caught in a root. She fought to retain her balance, took two, three, lunging steps with her arms thrown out, and then began to slowly topple towards the ground.

Then, as all was lost, a cool, damp hand caught her and pulled her into a dense clump of vegetation. She sensed at once that it was a friend and instinctively lay still, trying to breathe as quietly as possible. The presence surrounded her, she seemed to sink into the vegetation, merge to become one with it.

The man stopped, breathing hard, unwilling to believe that he'd just seen his prize vanish from under his eyes. He turned, parted the entangled vegetation, and looked directly at her – but did not see her. He was also unaware of another pair of eyes looking back at him from among the leaves. He searched a while more, then walked away.

'Lost the bitch,' she heard him mutter.

Slowly, she returned to herself, separated from The Green. The Green took on a form, man-like. A wreath of leaves framed two wise, timeless eyes, a set of antlers crowned his head.

'Cernunnos,' she breathed. She stared at him, shock overcoming her respect.

'No one may violate my sanctuary with evil intent,' she heard, a voice like the rustling of leaves. 'You are safe now. You have a purpose, it was not my intention for you to pay for this mistake.'

Cernunnos. She couldn't believe it. It was a life-changing moment that Brigid would remember always. The Green waited, he had all the time in the world.

'All the time I was in the north, in your sacred place, I never saw you. Why have you appeared to me now?' Brigid hardly dared to speak, she was so overawed by the immense sense of *presence* which she felt, but she had to know.

'You did not see me, that's true,' he answered. 'But I was always there.' The leaves in the forest rustled in agreement.

'I have watched over you, all your life. I have always been at your side. You didn't see me, because you didn't want to. You saw the world the way you wanted, the way you expected. Now the veil has fallen from your eyes, you are seeing the true nature of existence.'

Many things now fell into place. The countless times she'd sensed the presence of something, the unusual creatures she had seen. She realised that she had indeed met Cernunnos, many times before.

'You hadn't opened your heart to me, although you believed you had,' the rustling voice continued. 'You were focussed on your lessons, using your mind rather than your soul. This wasn't wrong,' the voice answered her unspoken question. 'You had to do this to learn discipline and knowledge. But this was only the first step on a timeless journey. Now you've learnt to live with your heart and soul, to feel the spirit of the Goddess within you. Now you're able to see what is hidden from the blinded eyes of men.

'Your Journey is coming to an end. What was set in place long ago is about to converge, the End Time is approaching. Everything that we have is at stake.'

The Green began to fade, merge with the surrounding vegetation. The rustling voice grew fainter as it spoke. 'The key to life is life. As long as there is life, there is hope. You must remember this. You must act, and soon.' 'Wait!' cried Brigid. 'I don't know how to change things. Help me!'

But the voice was gone. She was alone in the darkened wood. She would have to find the answer on her own.

# Part VI

# Chapter 31

*What the caterpillar calls the end of the world, the Master calls a butterfly.*
Richard Bach

The warm and balmy sea washes over my body as I float, carried by the tides of the ocean, governed by the tides of time. As I swim I gain nourishment from the water, a never-ending quest. My life has one purpose – to live.

As I move through the waving fronds of green, I see a swift movement. Instinctively I cower, I withdraw my body back into its shell, my home, my haven. I catch a glimpse of a multi-coloured pattern dash past and I relax. The fish are everywhere and we live happily side by side.

As the sun and stars wheel overhead on their eternal cycle, so my life continues to its end. After my life is gone, my body provides nourishment for others, but for my shell, my refuge and sanctuary, the universe has a very different plan in mind. It sinks through the shallow waters to the sandy ocean bed, and here it lies.

My shell is slowly covered by sediment. The sun and stars continue to wheel, the eternal cycle continues, day after day, week after week, aeon after aeon. The sea retreats, the sediment hardens. What was once a warm ocean becomes dry ground, a base for soil, roots and plants. A new era begins.

But in the scheme of eternity, nothing is eternal. The rock begins to decay, aeons of wind and rain take their toll. One day, my shell, now hardened to rock, emerges from its dark resting place where it has lain for so long. By the actions of water, ice and wind, I begin to journey again. My shell reaches a rough mountainside where it lies for another infinite period.

One day, a girl finds me and claims me for her own. She bestows a great meaning on me, for which I am amused. But she is young, so young, and I do not begrudge her innocence.

One day, when she learns the Truth, she returns my body to the waters and here I wait. After another infinite period my rest is again disturbed. She returns to reclaim me and I begin a new journey, my role is not yet over. In eternity, nothing is eternal.

# Part VII

# Chapter 32

*Let the great wheel turn. A man's fortunes rise and decline. When the moon is full, it shall grow thin.*
The Egyptian Book of the Dead

I gazed down at the rushing water, entranced by the shimmering, swirling patterns made by the dancing sunlight. It was impossible to describe how I was feeling, now and ever since I'd returned to my mortal body on Yeavering Bell. Since that visionary experience, where I'd briefly become One with the Earth's Soul, seen into the past and the future, the near and the far, the big and the small, it was like I held the power of the world at my fingertips, like a dazzling light blazed within me. I knew without being told that I'd reached the Sphere of the Sun.

I turned suddenly, aware of a presence behind me, a flickering concentration of energy. I'd now become more perceptive and sensory, for one I was aware of an energetic aura enshrouding everything, more an awareness on the edge of my conscious vision, sudden flashes of colour in the corners of my eyes.

My eyesight showed me what my other senses had alerted me to. An elderly man with a dog had stopped on the bridge and was looking at me with quizzical interest.

'Looking for salmon?' he asked, indicating the water below. 'They're migrating now, lots of them about.' I noticed the near indiscernible tremble in his voice, a faint shudder in his hands. He was not well. Not ill either, but his health was definitely fading. His aura was flickering, I knew, although I couldn't see it. His body was failing, as was his soul. He was lonely, isolated, and wanted someone to talk to.

'I can hear the fish splashing, but they're not easy to spot. Do you know where they come from?' I focussed my energy towards him and he smiled broadly, cheered by the prospect of conversation.

'From hundreds of miles out in the Atlantic. They make their way to the river of their birth to breed, a true miracle of navigation and memory.'

The salmon was of course just another thread in the great web of existence, linking everything with everything else. There were examples of this wonder everywhere, why had I never seen it before?

'I used to spend hours out there with my fishing rod, when I was younger,' he continued. His smile faded. 'But standing waist-deep in that icy water, I've got terrible arthritis now. And diabetes, to cap it all. I haven't been out for years.' 'You can still enjoy the beauty of the river, though, nothing has taken that from you,' I said.

'Yes, there's precious little else I can do now. Who would get old?' he asked bitterly. 'Sit down!' He jerked the dog's lead and poked it with his walking stick. It stopped its harmless snuffling and crept behind him.

I imagined him bathed in the golden rays of the sun, the quicksilver of the earth current rising up around him. The severed connection with the Soul of the Earth began to heal.

The old man straightened up a little. 'But one mustn't complain, I suppose. Things could always be worse. I must be off, anyway, I'm going to my book club later. We're reading *Life of Pi*, at least I'm not stuck in a boat with a tiger! Come on, old boy.' He chuckled and walked away with a new burst of strength, the dog trotting happily at his side.

I leant again on the stone wall of the bridge, looking down into the water. The rushing stream was loud in my ears. This encounter was fairly typical of the past few days. I seemed to be drawing people to me; people who, in their own unique ways, were lost in the world.

This must be the great power that the ancient saints and visionaries held, I mused, that attracted the masses to their feet. They sensed the light that they themselves were lacking and were drawn to it like moths to a flame.

Betty noticed the change too. 'You seem different,' she said that evening. 'As if you've won the lottery, found the love of your life and landed your dream job all at once.'

I laughed happily. 'Everything just feels perfect.' 'My husband said everything's always perfect. It's just that you don't realise it.' She looked rather sad again. Sad and alone. 'Would you like a cup of tea, dear?' she said, a plea in her voice.

I was tired, hungry, and desperate for a hot shower. 'That would be lovely,' I said. I genuinely meant it.

Betty looked immediately happier. She just wanted someone to talk to, I thought. Hers must be a lonely job really.

She ushered me into her kitchen and fussed about arranging a tray, cups, saucers, teapot, tea cosy. All very elaborate and very unnecessary. I glanced up at the clock.

Eventually she was ready and placed the tray on the table with a flourish. As she put a cup in front of me a huge ginger cat leapt up out of nowhere and knocked it flying. Tea went everywhere and I just managed to dive and catch the cup as it flew off the table. Betty looked mortified.

'*Tiger*! Get away! I'm so sorry, Bridget dear!' She looked at me with her hands to her mouth. 'It didn't burn you?' 'No, no. I'm fine.' At least my reflexes were on the ball. 'I didn't know you had a cat?' 'Tiger, my only companion now.' She fussed around with a tea towel and issued me with a fresh cup. I kept a wary eye on the floor, where the cat was now pointedly facing the Aga.

Betty picked him up and settled him on her knee, and I ruffled his head. The look of absolute disgust he gave me was something only a cat could be capable of.

We talked for a while about our lives, families and friends. 'My daughter, she never wanted children of her own,' she said. 'Said there's enough children in the world, unloved and malnourished. She adopted a couple of darkies from Central Africa.' She shook her head. 'Each to their own, I suppose, but it'd make the heads turn, wouldn't it? Better they at least look the part. What do you think?'

Luckily I'd just taken a mouthful of cake and was spared proffering my opinion on the 'darkies'. I deliberately over-chewed it and then swallowed.

'These cakes are wonderful!' I enthused, finding the icing particularly fascinating. 'Did you make them yourself?' 'Oh, no, I don't have time to bake. They're from an enterprise I'm involved with in the town, called Fractured Lives. It teaches disadvantaged kids useful skills, it's having a real positive impact. I support them all I can – kids are the future, after all. It gets them off the streets, they seem to have nothing to do but hang around these days, don't they?'

I remembered the roundhouse and nodded, it was a subject very close to home. If only my brother had had something like that to help him. He'd gone from hanging round to shoplifting, drug experimentation and gang life. He'd gone to my father's at sixteen, I didn't even know where he lived now. I wondered how he was.

Betty was thinking on the same lines. 'At least my daughter's children will have a good future, better than in Africa anyway.' She looked into the distance, absently stroking Tiger. 'We fell out quite badly. We haven't spoken for a long time. Perhaps I'll give her a ring, try and patch things up.'

We each sat with our painful memories for a moment. 'It's sad really, isn't it,' said Betty. 'The world has shrunk to a fraction of its former size, we can travel anywhere and contact anyone, anywhere. We have the internet, email, mobile phones, Blackberries, Facebook, but we're more alone than ever. We don't even speak to our families any more.' 'That's the curse of modern life.' I shook my head. 'Money, electronics, bright lights, they've replaced the old values.' 'But are we any happier for it?' she asked. 'We have everything we could ever want, at our fingertips, but are our lives fulfilled?' 'No,' I answered, thinking of the ongoing wars, all the troubles in the world, all caused by an incessant, desperate need to fill the gaping hole within us. 'We're not happy at all. No one is happy. No one has been happy for a long time.'

When I turned on the TV, the news was on. The problems in the Middle East were fast spiralling out of control, an apt illustration of the conversation we'd just had. Every country was closing its borders, battening the hatches. National armies and local militias were readying themselves. The screen was filled with soldiers in heavily fortified positions and men in isolated hideaways, all bristling with whatever weapons they could lay their hands on. Western ambassadors were involved in desperate peace talks – if war broke out, how long before they turned on the West? It was imperative that the situation be calmed.

I half listened as I filled the kettle and opened a packet of sandwiches, and the report switched to the Atlantic hurricane. Already storms were lashing the US coast, people were evacuating from low-lying areas and flood barriers were raised. Footage of wrecked boats and overwhelmed defences was already coming through. *The world is falling apart.*

It certainly seemed as if the world were bent on destruction. Where man was not trying hard enough, nature was finishing the job.

I now understood what the problem was. The earth-energies were weakened and fragmenting, our souls were unnourished. A dog bites because of fear, and this sense that something was amiss, deep in our minds, translated as a desperate urge to protect ourselves. And as our weakened souls are a microcosmic part of the earth, so the earth grows sicker.

And it was not just men who were affected. Extinctions, sterility, diseases, freak weather conditions, they were all symptoms of this cosmic sickness. My project at PharmLab involved the influenza virus which had appeared out of nowhere and was proving as deadly as the Ebola Virus. And this was just one of many disturbing diseases appearing in recent years, affecting not just man but animals, plants and trees as well.

'It's as if nature's trying to wipe the slate clean,' Simon had joked at a seminar. 'Life is no longer wanted on earth.'

I turned off the TV and went to the window. In the inky darkness, I could see the stars shining brightly. Anna had told me about the Precession of the Equinoxes, the cycle of the Ages which was linked to chaos on earth. The stars were slowly moving, they were no longer in harmony with the earth. As I watched, a bright star dimmed and then vanished behind a roof top as the earth spun on her perpetual axis. The new Age was dawning, but like the dinosaurs, the old harmony had to be destroyed before the new one could form.

When the Age of Pisces had begun, a war had begun, a war to end all wars, I *remembered*. Now, two thousand years later, the dawning of the Age of Aquarius, events were repeating themselves. And if events continued on their present course, it could mean the end of the world. Not figuratively, but literally.

# Chapter 33

*No man is an island, entire of itself,*
*Each is a part of the continent, a piece of the main.*
*Any man's death diminishes me, for I am involved in mankind.*
*So therefore never send to know for whom the bell tolls; it tolls for*
*thee.*

John Donne

Eventually I fell asleep, lying on my bed fully clothed, my mind still full of images of war, death, disease and bleakness. I dreamed I was standing on a tall hill, watching over the entire world. I saw time passing like a film reel, as it whizzed past I saw how the chaos and bloodshed infected everything and everyone in these times of disharmony. Then things gradually recovered, harmony and peace returned. I saw people begin to forget the troubles they'd faced, they became nothing but memories, legends told to their children.

Then everything changed. I was transported to a parallel world. Gone was the peace, the happy families and settled lives, the harmony and light.

It was replaced by nothing.

What had been green and pleasant was now scorched, barren and dead. What little lived, did so in torment and despair, suffering to sustain its meagre, tortured existence. The light of the world had died. Permanently. The twisted blackened ruin of the world was all that survived. Damaged, broken people wandered in a hopeless daze amongst damaged, broken buildings. Nowhere survived love, peace, happiness or laughter, it was like gazing into the mouth of Hell.

I woke with a jump, drenched in sweat. The room stiflingly hot, I had a stale taste in my mouth and my belt buckle was digging into my stomach. My heart was pounding and I felt sick. I was more disturbed and frightened than I'd ever been in my life. I had seen the future. Two options. One for if I succeeded in my Quest, and one for if I failed.

It was imperative that I did not fail.

I got up before six after lying awake for the rest of the night. I turned on the TV for something to do and my eyes riveted to the picture. I felt physically sick, unable to believe what I was seeing. I wondered for a minute if I was still dreaming, but no, I was awake. It was real.

I was seeing exactly the same scene of devastation as I'd just dreamed.

I watched the news report with a mounting horror. During the night several missiles had been sent into two Israeli cities, obliterating huge residential areas. The camera panned round, showing broken, shattered buildings, masses of rubble, and amongst it all wandered dazed people, all dirty and grimy, all with tattered clothing, many covered in blood. In the background I could hear a child crying, untended and ignored.

I was too shocked to listen to the report but the image said more than words ever could. The cameraman was now in a vehicle, driving deeper into the devastated area. The camera paused for a moment on a scorched car that had obviously smashed into a wall before bursting into flames. Out of one shattered window hung an arm, a human arm, blackened and charred. I could still see the shining gleam of a wedding ring.

After a few seconds the camera moved on to the next horror. Three dogs were fighting in a street, pulling and tearing at a small bundle. I knew it could only be another body, a child most likely by its size. The camera didn't even bother to pause.

After what seemed an age, the report ended. The news studio appeared, the presenter flanked with politicians and foreign affairs experts. The most pressing concern, it seemed, was how this development would affect our security.

'A horrific scene, utter carnage.' The presenter paused for a second, suitably moved, before moving onto more important matters.

'So, Robert Smith, the Advisor for Security in the Middle East, what measures are being taken to prevent a similar incident on UK soil?'

The grim looking man to her left began to speak. 'I must offer condolences to all those affected. But the likelihood of risk to UK citizens is minimal. We have exemplary security measures already in place.' He turned to fully face the camera for emphasis. 'There is no threat to British security whatsoever.'

I hit the off button and stared out of the window. Then I went downstairs and outside into the street. The sun was just rising above the horizon and early morning mist enshrouded the fields and moors, lending an ethereal beauty as the sun gradually began to penetrate it. There was no one about, no cars, no activity, just the sounds of nature. The birds were singing loudly and as I walked down to the river a beautiful russet-coloured fox ran in front of me. It stopped and looked at me for a second as if silently greeting its fellow traveller, then continued on its way.

Despite the turmoil in my mind, I began to relax. The world was comforting me, telling me in the only way it could that The Way would become clear.

I reached a still pool of water near the river and sat down, ignoring the dampness soaking through my clothes. A film of oil lay on the surface, reflecting rainbow colours as the sun caught it. Man was always so careless, his tainted presence left nothing untouched.

I gazed into the timeless waters, letting my mind wander, searching for the answers. I was supposed to change things, to change the world.

But how? It was only superheroes who saved the world. I wasn't Superman, I wasn't a world leader, I had no influence whatsoever. But somehow, I had to do something. How was I to do it?

Anna had wanted to change the world, and I'd ridiculed her.

I picked up a stone lying by my foot and threw it into the water. The mirror-like stillness of the surface was instantly shattered. Droplets scattered widely onto the water, the overhanging leaves and the plants. Some splashed onto my face. The oily rainbow shimmered as ripples spread outwards, rushing towards the far bank, picking up momentum, power and speed. I watched as a fallen leaf was carried far across to the other side and caught on a willow branch, washed up like a boat in a storm surge. Other leaves on the bank were swept into the water and began to float towards me. One leaf was swept right out into the main river, caught by the current and whisked off downstream. It would eventually reach places the stone had never dreamed of. Where the stone had hit the bottom I could see sediment rising. The cloudy haze gradually spread outwards throughout the whole pool. No part of it was left untouched by the stone.

As I continued to watch and think, silent and motionless, my mind as still as the pool had formerly been, the ripples gradually faded, weakened and vanished. The sediment began to clear, settling out in new places. The pool returned to normal. It was as if the stone were never there.

Then a light burst into my mind. The answer had come to me, in a flash of such amazing, dazzling insight, that I could hardly stop myself from leaping up in ecstasy.

The stone *had* been there, and it had changed the pool for ever. The pool could never return to how it was.

All people, all things, every thought, action, idea and movement, they all alter the world in a small, subtle, but definitely real way. The butterfly flapping its wings in Europe causes a tornado in America.

Everyone changes the world. Everything is connected to everything else, all is a part of the whole. And what changes one, alters all.

# Chapter 34

*For a man to conquer himself is the first and noblest of all victories.*
Plato

I knew I had to find something. That immense power source I'd encountered, was this it?

Things were coming together in my mind, I was finally beginning to understand, but what exactly I needed to find, the key to the Quest, I still had no idea. I may as well be searching for the Holy Grail, I thought crossly.

Then I began to smile. Maybe that wasn't such a bad idea.

The Grail was the chalice which collected the blood of Jesus, I remembered well from my Catholic upbringing. It was later the focus of many medieval hero-quests, in particular those of King Arthur, and the only knight pure enough to reach it was Sir Galahad.

This idea of the sacred Quest seemed very familiar, and the blood of God could easily be a metaphor for the life-energy of the earth. I began to believe that I'd actually found the answer.

I was on Betty's computer within minutes. I waited impatiently for the modem to connect, the cat laughing smugly from his sunny windowsill, then it took only five minutes with Google to fill my mind with myriad esoteric and metaphysical ideas, linking the Grail to eternal life, the Philosopher's Stone, alchemy, hidden treasures, conspiracy theories, the Knights Templar and UFOs to name just a few.

I logged off the computer in frustration. This was hopeless, a needle in a haystack. There was only one thing I could think to do.

'Anna!' I could hear thumping music and a babble of voices in the background.

'Hang on a minute,' she said. 'I can't hear.'

The noise faded somewhat. 'Anna, where are you?' 'Brig! I was wondering where you were! I'm in Glastonbury.'

Of course! I remembered. She was at what a few weeks ago I would have called a 'weird-fest', a mass gathering of all the country's assorted nutters and tree-huggers.

'Anna, a lot of stuff's happened lately.' That would win a prize for understatement of the year. But I persevered, and half an hour later Anna knew everything.

'The Holy Grail?' she mused. 'The most sought-after talisman of all time. Its present chalice format is thought to have originated from a Celtic cauldron, the Cauldron of Ceridwen.'

*Ceridwen?* Another thread drew tight in my mind. I was definitely on the right track.

'These are just two names for the spiritual Heart of the Earth, the destination of the Soul-Quest,' Anna continued, 'also known as the Philosopher's Stone, Nirvana, Tir-na-Nog, Paradise, Enlightenment. During the Renaissance it formed the basis of alchemy. Alchemy wasn't concerned with the literal synthesis of gold, contrary to the desires of many greedy rulers. Its true nature was concerned with the transformation of the soul, from its leadened state to the golden state of divinity.'

I was hanging onto her every word. Normally I would have switched off long ago, accustomed as I was to Anna's notoriously rambling lectures.

'So this Heart of the Earth, known by whatever name, is what feeds all the souls on earth, and is where the ley lines come from?' I questioned.

'Yes, the ley lines are like the veins of the body, transporting the blood of the earth from the Heart. Of course, it's not an accident that the body of the earth is described the same way as the body of a man.' She chuckled.

'So where can this Heart be found?' I asked, too eager to know the answers to think about the humble pie I was eating by the plateful.

'That, I can't tell you. There are many possible places, where the earth-energy is particularly strong – Canterbury, Stonehenge, Westminster Abbey. Here in Glastonbury – that's why we're here. They're all possibilities. But really, it's inside yourself that you must find it, the physical location is merely an aside. They say anyone can find it, anywhere, if their heart is pure enough.''So, what do you think I should do, then?''Come to Glastonbury. Here, if anywhere, you'll find the people who can help, some of us were discussing it only yesterday. Everyone's feeling the energies fail, even experienced dowsers are having trouble picking them up. The world's never known anything like this before. I wonder if it really is the end of the world.' Her voice took on an unfamiliar edge, she really was getting stressed about her beloved planet.

'We'll find a way, it won't be the end,' I said. 'Think of the dinosaurs.'

# Chapter 35

*Pride goes before destruction, and a haughty spirit before a fall.*
Proverbs 16.18

So I set off to Glastonbury. I left the home I'd so recently found, but this time I wasn't sad. I knew I would see it again, that when I'd completed my Quest, finished the Journey that would provide me with the key, I would once again come home.

Anna met me at the train station and rushed to hug me as I stepped onto the platform. She was wearing a purple dress and a scarf which flew behind her as she ran. She looked the typical New Age hippie but they complemented her features perfectly. She looked beautiful.

She took a step back and looked at me critically. 'You seem different.'

'I've travelled a long way.'

'Yes, I can see that.'

We walked away from the station. 'I know some people you ought to meet,' she said seriously. 'They'll be able to help you find what you need. But first you need somewhere to stay. My tent's full, but I've been looking round all morning and I've found a guest house with vacancies.'

I heaved a sigh of relief – I didn't really want to be squashed in a tent full of hippies. And it seemed every window stated 'No Vacancies'. I was glad I hadn't had to search for a room myself – the town seemed exceptionally busy.

Then when we reached the festival site, I saw why. The huge open space outside the town was filled with a sea of tents, marquees, stages and thousands of people. I stopped and stared in amazement – I couldn't believe the size of it. No wonder the town was full.

I could hear rock music, drums, pan pipes and what sounded like Morris dancing, almost overwhelming the hum of voices.

Ironically, or appropriately maybe, I could hear that iconic REM song, *it's the end of the word as we know it.*

'There's a lot of people here,' I said, unnecessarily.

'There's a lot of people who care,' she replied tartly.

I looked again over the panorama, and this time I could see something different. I could see a pulsating, vibrating aura of energy encompassing the entire festival ground. A mass of colours swirled together, every shade imaginable but somehow all coming together to form a perfect display of harmonic radiance. Something of my awe must have shown on my face as I looked at the incredible scene.

'You can see it too?' asked Anna softly. 'That's the effect we want to have, to unite all the energies into one and feed it into the entire world.''It looks amazing,' I agreed.

Two men were walking towards us and Anna waved. One was in his twenties with dreadlocks, a ripped denim jacket, combat trousers, and more piercings in his face than I'd ever seen before – I could hear him jingling as he slouched towards us. The second was older, with white floor length robes and carrying a wooden staff.

'These are my friends, Brig,' said Anna. 'Earthman and Arthur Merlin Invictus Redragon.'

I didn't need to ask which one was which.

'Nice to meet you,' I said, as if meeting a prospective employer. I felt proud of myself for not noticing their, um, *unusual* appearances. We shook hands politely. Earthman seemed unable to make eye contact and he thrust his hands back in his pockets immediately. I wondered if he was slightly dysfunctional.

'Let's go walk round,' said Anna, taking my arm.

'So, what do you do?' I asked Earthman, a little patronisingly. Even though he'd be no help to me, I thought I'd best make an effort for Anna's sake.

He shuffled his feet awkwardly. 'I, um, I'm between jobs right now.' He found a spot in the distance intensely fascinating and turned his head away. Conversation over. I wondered about asking the Druid the same question, but decided that could be even more awkward. Instead I busied myself thinking up possible occupations, an extra in *Lord of the Rings* came out top.

Despite my new-found sympathy for Anna and her ideas, I was beginning to doubt whether I'd done the right thing. Were these the best people she could come up with?

Our tour around the camp revealed a host of people from all walks of life. There were the hippies and Druids I'd been expecting, but also smartly dressed people, people in saris, turbans, hijabs, and a moment later I saw what looked like three Masai warriors.

'All people from under the sun,' said Arthur Merlin Invictus Redragon to me, smiling slightly. 'All people are One in the eyes of God, and all have a birthright to live on, and love, our planet. This festival was designed to unite all people from all cultures under the common banner of humanity. A perfect lesson for the Sphere of the Sun.'

I looked at him in surprise. Did everyone know about this Path of the Seven Spheres?

'I can see the power of the sun radiating in your soul. It's obvious to everyone that you're walking this Path,' he said in response.

It was true, I realised. People had been looking at us with more than a passing interest. I'd thought, presumptively, that they were looking at my rather strange companions, but I realised now that the attention had been directed at me.

'I don't really know much about the Spheres,' I admitted. 'I don't understand the astrological reasoning behind them at all.'

Arthur Merlin Invictus Redragon looked surprised before struggling to contain his unwanted display of emotion. 'Then you've done very well, reaching the Fourth Sphere with no training whatsoever.'

He looked at me with added respect as Anna and Earthman made a beeline for a nearby crystal stall. 'The Sphere of the Sun is concerned with unity, oneness, the knowledge that all things are an equal and individual part of a vast being, and so all resonate to the same cosmic frequency.'

He planted his staff between us and glared at me, and I took an automatic step back. 'The Sun is dazzling, brilliant, and full of pride. This is where many people fail, because of their arrogance and pride in their achievements.' He had a habit of carefully enunciating each word like he was talking to a child.

'Everyone walks the same Path, regardless of where they've got to,' I answered carefully. I could sense a fierce passion within him, I didn't want to provoke his disapproval when I probably needed his help.

He looked mollified. 'At least you've learnt that,' he said gruffly.

I went over to the crystal stand to end the awkward conversation and looked over the display.

'I find that lepidolite is best for stabilising the earth-energies in meditation,' said Anna seriously. 'I find it much better than obsidian.' 'But used in combination with bloodstone, it's the most powerful crystal I've ever known,' countered the proprietor.

I idly picked up a few crystal-trees while they finished their debate. I could almost sense an energy circulating around them – one felt quite warm and pulsated in my hand, and I felt a slight sense of loss as I put it back down. After a moment's hesitation I picked it up again.

'I'll take this, please,' I said. 'It's very pretty,' I added for the benefit of anyone watching.

'Well, I think it's about dinner time,' announced Anna. 'Let's go to the Green Dragon. That's a cafe just round the corner,' she explained to me.

The cafe had a huge ornamental dragon in the window. I ordered coffee and a ham sandwich, Anna ordered herbal tea and chocolate cake, and Earthman settled for organic flapjack and Earl Grey (chemicals are poisoning the world). I was surprised to see Arthur Merlin Invictus Redragon choose a massive plate of all-day breakfast. Did Druids eat meat?

Now I'd warmed to them a bit, I could see that the two niche members of society, or weirdos as I normally called them, were not actually psychos and were genuinely concerned for the future of the world. I supposed that really, we were all walking the same Path. A lesson from the Sphere of the Sun.

'So, are we ready for tomorrow?' asked Earthman, a crystal ring in his eyebrow tinkling slightly as he spoke. He seemed to be coming out of his shell a bit more now.

'Yes, everything's prepared, we need to go an hour before sunrise so we're ready at dawn,' replied Arthur in between mouthfuls of bacon and egg. Could I call him just Arthur, or was that too familiar?

'There's a ceremony on the Tor tomorrow,' Anna explained to me. 'The sun aligns with the ley line at dawn, its power will flood down it and we'll channel it through the whole of the earth. It's not much, but it'll help.' 'We have to awaken the land,' continued Earthman, twirling a studded panther-head which was hanging from one of his many earrings. It caught in a dreadlock and Anna untangled it for him. 'The new Age has weakened its energy – it's sluggish, almost dead. We've got to awaken the King somehow.' 'The King?' I asked dismissively. Although loath to admit it, I was definitely out of my comfort zone.

'The Sleeping King,' he clarified. 'It's how all this was named in myth – the prophesied end of the world in the new millennium. The earth-energy, the Spirit of the Land, it's always been personified by the land's leaders – the king or the emperor, and also as Charlemagne, Quetzalcoatl, Viracocha, Jesus, King Arthur Pendragon.'

I looked at the second King Arthur who was liberally

covering a pile of mushrooms with brown sauce. He showed no reaction at the mention of his namesake. I thought Charlemagne may have been a French king, the other names meant nothing. 'So why 'sleeping?''Everyone knows the story about Arthur sleeping in a cave, to be awakened in a time of great need. But what most people don't realise, the same story is told for all the other saviours. They were all prophesied to return one day.' The last sentence was delivered with such gravity that I struggled not to laugh.

'Some nutter in London told me Jesus was coming any day now,' I said.

'Yes, and the return of all the others is imminent too. They were driven away, killed, sacrificed, whatever – but all will return. Any day now. The same story told the world over. Whaddaya think of that?' Earthman sat back in his seat triumphantly.

'So, that this supposed end-of-the-world would happen was known centuries ago, and ancient people everywhere left clues telling us about it, in myths, religions and stories? And waking the Sleeping King is the same as finding the Grail? It's all about reactivating the earth-energies?' I was drawn into the conversation despite myself and realisation dawned. 'So this is why the Grail is so closely linked with King Arthur, then! And Jesus too!''Exactly! In the country's darkest hour, a hero will ride forth,' Earthman intoned. 'This is that time. The Sleeping King will be awakened. We don't know how, but we *will* find a way.' A few heads turned to look our way as he thumped his fist onto the table, making his tea slosh out over the veneer. His passionate speech was interrupted while we mopped it up with napkins.

'Well, anyway,' he said, screwing up his napkin into a ball. 'We do what we can, every little helps. Much as I hate quoting from a multinational chain-store.'

I stood up. 'Does anyone want another drink?''I'll have some tea,' said Arthur. He pulled an elaborate leather pouch from a fold in his robe but I waved him aside. What would he have given me – a gold doubloon?

Everyone else shook their heads and I went to the counter. When I returned the conversation had moved on to psychometry.

'The stone's memories are also your memories, because we are all part of the same One Being,' Arthur was saying. 'The whole universe knows that stone was a meteor flying through space, just as your whole body knows your toe was burnt in hot water.'

I stirred my coffee and I watched the inky blackness swirling around, thinking about a meteor hurtling through space before crashing into earth. A sudden image came to my mind of the universe as a vast, living, conscious being. Each part had a dual nature – a complete structure in itself, and also a single part of something much greater.

I thought about how a single nerve cell or muscle cell contains all the DNA needed to form a human being, and the universe following suit. Like a vast hologram, each part contains the whole.

'Are you all right Brig?' asked Anna. 'You've been stirring that coffee for about five minutes.'

I jumped, my reverie broken. 'I was just thinking,' I said.

'The lower order of existence is a mirror image of the higher. 'As above, so below,' as Hermes Trismegistus said,' Arthur responded, looking at me gravely. I had the disturbing feeling he'd seen exactly what I was thinking.

I felt the same tingling in my skin as I'd often had since Yeavering Bell. I could feel light flooding through my veins as a result of that new vision, despite that nagging voice telling me I'd now taken up reading tea leaves. A golden rush of energy made me feel more alive than ever. Arthur and Anna were looking at me with interest – they were obviously aware of it too.

'So, the way forward,' mused Earthman to himself. 'Bridget, perhaps you're the key,' he said, only half joking. 'How's it to be done?'

The energy grew stronger, I suddenly felt amazing, charged, empowered. I could do anything. I was aware from the edges of my vision that I was glowing, a shimmering coruscation drifted from my hands as I moved.

I looked at the other three around the table – they seemed flat and dull in comparison. What could they know? I held the power, I was the one given the Quest, I had the answers in me. At that moment I knew, as clearly as I could feel the pulsing light, that I was on the wrong path, there was nothing they would be able to teach me. And time was running out, the clock was ticking.

I pushed back my chair and stood up. 'We won't get anywhere just sitting talking, will we?' I said impatiently. 'I think this is a waste of time. I'm going round the town, see what I can find.''Brig?' said Anna in surprise. 'Brig!' she called as I walked from the cafe.

I glanced back and saw that she'd risen from her seat but Arthur had his hand on her arm, holding her back. I momentarily wondered why he'd done so, but then pushed it from my mind and focussed on what mattered.

The golden shimmer began to dissipate and I felt normal, human again. I walked around the town for a while, wondering what I was to do next. I wished I knew more about the astrological references which seemed to be so crucial. I almost wished Jason were here, he'd know the answers to everything. Then as if in answer, I remembered. He'd written a book. What was it called? I racked my brains – it was something catchy – but I couldn't remember. I didn't think, somehow, I could go into a bookshop and find it with just his first name, and I struggled for a while before giving up.

As I was walking towards the Tor, thinking about climbing it, the name burst into my mind. *Lucky Stars*! I doubled back on myself and went in search of a bookshop. Being Glastonbury there was no shortage of shops selling the weird sort of stuff, as I still called it, and I soon found one stocking books.

'I'm looking for a book on astrology, called *Lucky Stars*,' I said to the hippie-looking woman, after checking no one was watching. 'The author's called Jason, I don't know his surname,' I continued apologetically, but the woman was already pulling a book from a shelf.

'It was only out last month, but it's flying out. It's set to be a best-seller.'

I took it from her. It was a thick book full of diagrams and illustrations, it looked very comprehensive. Jason Smith was his name, I saw. A familiar face smiled suggestively from the fly-leaf, and I tried not to smile back. 'OK, I'll have it.' '£12.99 please. We don't issue bags any more, it's our environmental policy,' she said in response to my expectant look.

A good idea, of course, but I was still a bit surprised. My bedtime reading was sorted for a good few days, anyway.

I went out, found a bench in a small park, and opened the book. It was surprisingly intelligent, not just full of horoscopes like I'd expected. He gave some examples of how astrological conjunctions have a scientific basis – traditionally detrimental conjunctions, such as an angle of 120 degrees between two planets and the earth, greatly weaken radio signals, I was interested to read. Astrology was not just for quacks after all.

I soon learnt how each Sphere represented the stages of the Journey I'd already completed. After looking up from the ground, the earth, and seeing the Gateway, the Sphere of the Moon was about following my intuition, my heart, as I'd already guessed.

The Sphere of Mercury related to knowledge, philosophy and understanding, the opposite to the Moon. I saw how the facts I'd learnt – from the books, the internet, people, coupled with my new intuition, had enabled me to move on to the Sphere of Venus, the Goddess.

Venus was about seeing the light in all things regardless of my personal feelings, and the black dog was the final test of this Sphere.

The Sphere of the Sun was the spirit flight from Yeavering Bell, and learning to see all things and all people as part of the One Being.

In the geocentric model of the solar system, Jason wrote, the fixed stars, the Eighth Sphere, were equated with heaven and God. I realised then why the Journey had been named for this model – because the journey of the soul, from earth to heaven, is a mirror image of the Solar System. I looked up at the endless blue sky, to where the stars would begin to appear in a few hours time. My destination.

Then I read something which made me pause for thought. The feeling grew until it felt like I'd been kicked in the stomach, and it dawned on me that I'd made a terrible mistake.

The most common fallacy of those born under the Sun Sign was pride. Did that also apply to the Sphere of the Sun? I thought back to when I'd walked out of the cafe. Was it the right thing to do? Or was it pride that had driven me to do it? Did Anna's friends actually hold the answers I needed?

I remembered something Anna had said to me a while before – 'I'm glad you're finally beginning to see the light.'

Other accusatory voices also began to speak in my mind.

'...you think you're so perfect...'

'...you always have the answers...'

And then Arthur's words rang out. 'People always fail here, because of their pride and arrogance.'

My greatest personal strength, I'd always thought, was my strength of mind. I only believed in what could be measured and proven scientifically, I didn't believe in what I considered fallacies, and my opinions weren't swayed easily. Now I began to wonder, was that actually my greatest weakness? Even though since Yeavering Bell I was thinking differently, seeing things differently, I was still slipping back into my old habits, my rather superior attitude to the others and their way of thinking. I was still struggling to accept that I'd been so wrong for so long.

I thought about the times when I'd accepted those 'fallacies' as real. That was when I'd moved forward on the Quest. Now, I was stuck. Had I just thrown away my only chance?

I got up and almost ran back to the cafe. I pushed and rattled the door before I noticed the closed sign. It was dark and empty. I looked up and down the street but of course they weren't in sight. I pulled my phone from my pocket and dialled Anna's number, but it clicked to answer machine after two rings. She wouldn't speak to me. It was over. My arrogant pride had ruined everything.

# Chapter 36

*With one foot always forward, a man reaches heaven.*
Chinese proverb

It was an hour before dawn and the procession wound its way up the ancient sacred way of the Tor. Around one hundred people were present, many in Druidic robes but an equal number in other dress. The eerie, silent, candle-lit procession seemed almost sinister. The shadows leaped from the flickering lights and the shadowy, orange illuminations of many silent faces looked positively creepy, and I felt an involuntary shudder as I looked back down the hill. The procession moved slowly and I began to shiver, despite my coat. The pre-dawn air was heavy with dew and I wondered, despite its importance, if the ceremony would last long.

Anna had been out of signal, on my fifth desperate call she'd finally answered. I was almost crying with relief and babbled an incoherent explanation, but it seemed almost like she was expecting the call; she dismissed my waffle immediately. I wondered if Arthur had had something to do with it.

When we at last reached the top, the sky was starting to lighten in the east, fingers of grey pushed up from the horizon and somewhere, far below us in the countryside, a lone blackbird began to sing.

We all gathered in an uncoordinated huddle. Anna and someone I didn't know were arranging crystals and other objects around the perimeter, to channel the sun's energies when it struck the horizon, apparently. Arthur and some other Druids were making other preparations, what exactly I could only guess at.

Then, all present were arranged into a horseshoe shape, pointing to the east. All this was done in total silence, barely the rustle of a footstep or a coat could be heard, just the melodic song of the blackbird.

We waited, in perfect silence and total stillness. The horizon grew brighter, the grey turned to deep blue, then a shimmer of orange appeared. The blackbird was joined with other voices, soon the dawn chorus was in full swing. Not a sound could be heard across the vast swathe of countryside except the welcoming song for the new day. It seemed strangely appropriate that only the sounds of nature and harmony would precede the ceremony.

Then the long-awaited moment arrived. The orange glow had grown steadily stronger, and then a tiny speck of light appeared in the east. As one, the horseshoe of people raised their arms to the air, silently willing the power of the sun to channel into the hill. I stared at the sun as it rapidly grew bigger and the light dazzled my night-accustomed eyes. The stark contrast made it seem as if the whole site were filled with a bright light, absorbed and funnelled by the mass of people. The arrangement of crystals flared and shone in the sun, unnaturally so.

At that crucial moment, when the disk of the sun sat exactly on the horizon, it seemed as if the site was bursting with energy. A buzzing filled my ears and the course of energy which flooded down my arms, through my body and feet and into the ground was almost unbearable, I felt like a battery charged to the limit.

I looked away from the sun disk and gasped. I could see a river of multicoloured light flowing through the land, from the direction of the sun towards us. I knew without looking that it would continue behind us far into the west. The swirling, shimmering, rainbow-coloured torrent of energy tore through everything in its path, a spectacle that was simply awe-inspiring to watch.

The transcendent moment seemed to last for an eternity, and then the sun separated from the horizon and the day was born. The river vanished, although I could still feel its tremendous presence. The ritual was complete.

A few moments later the group began to break up. I looked round. Everyone was wearing the same expression of awe and wonder on their faces; they'd all seen what I'd seen.

With the breaking of the spell, normality seemed to return. As people began to speak, the sound of a car engine could be heard far below us. The world of man had awoken.

Anna came up to me, filled with triumph at the overwhelming success. 'Did you see it? The St Michael Line, the most powerful ley line in the country, the main artery of Britain.'

I was stunned into silence. I couldn't think of anything to say, but she could sense what no words could express.

'It worked, perfectly. We've boosted the earth's power immensely and maybe things will be a bit different now.' She laughed and bounced on her heels.

People were starting to head back and I stood looking across the perfectly flat landscape, broken only by this single hill, an island in the spiritual flood plain.

'We're going now,' said Anna. 'Only three hours and it'll be breakfast time.' I looked at my watch and was surprised to see it was only just past five o'clock.

I started back down the hill with the group, but then turned back. All the crystal arrangements were left in place, and I still had the crystal tree that I'd bought in my pocket. I could feel its warmth in my hand, could almost see it pulsating with light. I went to where I felt the centre of the tor was and knelt down, scraping a shallow hollow. Then I placed it in the ground, pulling soil around it. 'Grow,' I said to it. 'Grow into a big tree and bear fruit.'

I saw Anna a short distance ahead with Earthman and Arthur, and I caught up with them. They looked at me without speaking. Although Anna seemed to have forgiven me, the other two perhaps hadn't.

'That was incredible,' I said, inadequate words to break the ice. I hoped my intention would be communicated with my feeble words.

'The most amazing ritual I've ever seen,' enthused Anna, almost dancing down the hill. 'Don't you think?' she said to Earthman.

His natural jubilant personality came through and he agreed enthusiastically. 'I feel so alive now!' he said happily, his metal adornments jangling in agreement.

'So now it's down to waking the Sleeping King,' I stated. 'That's what we have to do now.'

The three of them looked at me and I looked back beseechingly. My bubble of pride had burst. It was confirmed, these people knew a lot more than I ever would.

I swallowed. There was no other way.

'I was wrong. I'm not so weak that I can't admit it,' I said, licking my dry lips. 'Will you help me? Please?'

# Chapter 37

*For evil to prevail, all it needs is for good men to do nothing.*
Edmund Burke

Two fried breakfasts, a bowl of muesli and a plate of wholemeal toast were on the table and everyone was tucking in with enthusiasm, still buzzing from the ceremony. Even Arthur seemed almost cheerful.

'Once, that happened all along the line, on every sacred site,' said Earthman through a mouthful of muesli. 'Think what that would have felt like! What we felt today was just a trickle of the line's true power.' He smiled at me happily and I smiled back, a bond between us that comes only from sharing something amazing.

I couldn't begin to even imagine what that would feel like. 'It would be like a direct line to heaven,' I said, looking out of the window towards the tor.

'It would. That's the idea, that this power, traditionally channelled by the King, would fertilise and rejuvenate the entire land. Everyone, everywhere, would feel its benefit.' 'What about other ley lines, elsewhere?' I asked.

'The same ritual would happen, but on the appropriate day of the year. The dragon-slaying ritual is universal.' Earthman scraped his bowl noisily, attracting an irritated look from Arthur.

'Why don't you just lick it out, it'd be quieter.'

Earthman smiled angelically and Arthur returned to his own plate with a snort.

'Dragon? I don't follow,' I said, confused.

'The dragon is the ancient symbol of the ley energy. The mastery or channelling of the energy is known in myth as the slaying of the dragon. This is the St Michael Line, and St Michael killed a dragon. But he's actually an adaptation of the Celtic God Beli, also a dragon-killer. And today is St Michael's feast day.' 'You seem to know an awful lot about myths and their meanings,' I said.

'Oh, I did my doctorate at Oxford, 'Myth, Folklore, and its Universal Message to Mankind'.' He reached for a piece of Anna's toast, giving me a chance to mask my surprise at this casual revelation. He had a doctorate? From Oxford? I'd just assumed he was a drop-out.

'I did a two-year fellowship then funding ran out. Cutbacks and all that.' He glanced at me and I nodded in empathy as Anna slapped his hand away.

'Get your own!''So, tell me more about the myths of ley lines,' I said with more interest and respect.

'The first thing is that ley lines are not a myth. They are a fact. But every line and node can be identified through folk-stories,' he said seriously. 'Any mention of miraculous beasts, strange events, dragons, fairies, Gods, ghosts, UFOs, they all have one meaning.''So they're not all just stories then?''All stories have a meaning,' snapped Arthur. His earlier cheeriness had died a death. 'They were formulated in remote ages to safeguard sacred information, when it was foreseen that war and devastation would obliterate all texts and teachers. It is just a case of whether you are wise enough to see their true meaning.' His tone offered no doubt as to whether he thought I was.

I looked down at my bacon, determined not to let my indignation rise. His caustic instruction was rather riling but it just seemed to be his natural manner. At least I wasn't one of his Druidic pupils.

I remembered my vision of sacred buildings which rose and fell on these eternal nodes of energy, and understood how the ley lines and the life force they channelled were indelibly engraved on our hearts and souls. *A building is not sacred unless built on the site of a previous sacred building.*

'The ley lines came to modern awareness in the 1930s,' said Anna. 'A man called Alfred Watkins realised that the ancient

British roads were arrow-straight across vast distances, and he gave them their current name. They were linked to the energy currents later, but this was just rediscovery of ancient knowledge.''So it was the Romans who first tracked the lines, when they built their roads?' I remembered this much from school.

'No! That's not right at all!' Arthur's words were like bullets and I derided myself for flinching. 'The roads were there long before the Romans. The Old Straight Tracks, as Watkins called them, were already centuries, maybe millennia old when they arrived. They've been given credit where no credit was due.' He turned back to my rapidly vanishing food and stabbed a mushroom with unnecessary force, blaming it for all misunderstanding in the world. I didn't dare say I was still hungry.

'The St Michael Line was once a road,' said Anna, 'running from St Michael's Mount to Norfolk, although only bits still survive.''And St Michael's Mount has more myths than anywhere,' Earthman burst in. He leant forward, jingling enthusiastically. In the same movement he swept Anna's toast onto his plate. What was it with men and food?

'Legend has it that St Michael's Mount is the surviving remnant of the lost land of Lyonesse. Its Celtic name, Carreg Luz en Kuz, actually means 'Hoar Rock in the Wood'. And the giant Comoran lived there who was slain by Jack the Giant Killer. Another synonym for dragon-killer.'

A whirl of information swept round in my mind. So many pieces of the puzzle, all floating randomly, just waiting to coalesce into a meaningful picture.

As Earthman devoured the toast, Arthur chipped in. 'The Mount is also where Jesus and Joseph of Arimathea landed on their journey to Glastonbury. You are familiar with William Blake's *Jerusalem*, I assume? And at the Second Coming, he will follow the same route,' he continued without waiting for my answer.

'And Jesus represents the Sleeping King, and walking this ley line means it'll be reawakened by his presence,' I finished. I thought I was following the reasoning correctly.

Arthur looked at me with grudging respect. 'Yes, exactly. Yet another encoded myth.' Earthman stood up to get more toast. His appetite seemed insatiable. 'Will you get me some coffee?' I asked, pulling some money out of my pocket. My hand came back with the fossil seashell from the stream. I'd forgotten all about it.

'That's interesting,' said Earthman, taking it from me. 'Where'd you get it? No, don't tell me, I'll practice my psychometry.'

He made an elaborate show of feeling and reading it, then frowned. 'It feels quite strange. First I thought you'd just found it recently, and now it feels like it's been part of you forever.'

I remembered my mental image of someone dropping it into the stream. Someone like me.

'You lost it in the water,' he decided. 'Then found it again? I don't know. It's very conflicting.' 'I did find it in a pool,' I said slowly. I knew the true situation was far more complicated than I would ever understand, and for some reason I then recalled Pythagoras' previous life as a rock.

Arthur was looking at me strangely again and I felt quite uncomfortable. Earthman frowned and handed the fossil back to me with a strange look of both awe and fear.

'Everything in the universe is connected to everything else,' said Arthur, as if trying to make sense of a difficult problem. 'The past and future are irrevocably entwined.' He smiled thinly. 'A fact that sees me well all the time at work.' 'What do you do, then?' I said, too eagerly, just wanting to break the uncomfortable atmosphere. He was a fortune teller then!

'I'm an allocations manager at an investment bank.'

My jaw hit the table.

'One's preconceptions can be just a *little* misleading, on

occasion.' His voice dripped with acid.

As all eyes turned to me, my face began to burn. 'Um...' My mind went blank under the scrutiny and I dropped my toast. A buttery smear streaked down my leg and I bent to the floor. Thankfully I was saved further embarrassment by the sound of sirens. Three police vans hurtled past, blue lights flashing, and we all turned to look.

'That's not good.' Anna frowned. 'They're heading to that protest march.' 'What's that?' I asked.

'There's an anti-war rally in the town, some of our people were going, but it looked like others were too, outsiders. We'd better go and see what's happening.'

We went outside into the street. From the direction the vans had gone, already people were streaming towards us, looking worriedly over their shoulders.

'There is trouble,' said Arthur. He looked at me and smiled grimly. 'Your initiation to the Sphere of Mars.'

Mars was the God of War, I remembered.

We hurried along the road, a robed and staffed Druid, a hippie, a metallic pin cushion and a relatively normal hiker. We must have looked a very odd set even for Glastonbury, but people were more concerned with what was happening behind them.

I could hear the noise now – shouting, screaming, breaking glass, topped by more sirens. As we turned the corner, the chaos hit us full on. People were scattered everywhere, some running, some cowering, the once peaceful march had descended into anarchy. Placards lay abandoned on the ground amongst lost sandals and smashed bottles. A wall of riot shields blocked the end of the road and twenty or so people in balaclavas were hurling bottles, bricks, signs, plant pots and anything else they could at them. A dustbin had been set on fire and thick black smoke was drifting across towards us. Then I noticed a little teddy bear abandoned in the middle of the road. More shouting and yelling rose from another street, along with the clash of weapons on shields and bodies.

'What happened?' whispered Anna. 'It wasn't meant to be like this.'

A brick flew past us and smashed a shop window, scattering glass everywhere and setting the alarms ringing. I flinched back and looked over my shoulder towards safety, and then a young woman ran past, blood running from a cut on her face. She stopped and turned back to us.

'Cheryl!' cried Earthman. 'What's happened?' With a practised movement he steered her into the shelter of a doorway.

She rubbed at her face with her sleeve, leaving a smear of blood. 'I don't know,' she sniffed, tears running down her face and mingling with the blood. 'There were others here, it must've been them, but then the police came and all hell broke loose.' Anna put her arm round her shoulders and hugged her.

Earthman looked round. 'We ought to go, the cops'll nick anyone who looks suitable. It's out of control, the tear gas'll be out in a minute, you can see the cops are on the back foot.'

I wondered uncomfortably how he knew so much about riots. More sirens screamed up and we were ushered back from the street by black-uniformed officers. 'Back! Now!' they shouted. They flashed a look of pure hatred at Earthman. He was right, what he'd said. They didn't like the look of him at all. We hastily backed further out of sight as a fire engine and an ambulance appeared in the street.

'It's ruining things, it was supposed to help!' Anna was almost crying. 'This negative energy will ruin everything.' 'It'll be OK,' I said, not knowing what else to say. Could this actually have any effect on anything? I didn't know any more.

A police van screamed up to a few people further down the road, people like us who were watching in disbelief. Black-clothed officers jumped out and immediately wrestled two of them to the ground. Within seconds they were thrown into the van, and a young woman who remonstrated with them, obviously protesting their innocence, was also handcuffed and dragged away. I watched with horror – that could have been us.

'They're just attacking everyone, just because we're different,' whispered Anna. I was glad we weren't near the front line.

'That's always the way,' said Arthur grimly. He was gripping his staff in both hands like a weapon. 'To make a uniform society, everything and everyone different must be ostracised. If there's only one mould, everyone is forced to fit it.'

I was shaking, I realised. I'd seen footage of riots on the TV, but the reality was a complete shock. I remembered the sheer hatred on both sides, directed at anything and everything in their path, and automatically checked over my shoulder as the shouting grew closer again. But still I didn't see the bottle coming.

Anna screamed as a deep cut split her face, blood pouring down her dress. She put her hand to her face, dazed, as a mob barrelled towards us. We had to get away, now.

'Anna!' I shouted. 'Come on!'

When she didn't respond, I grabbed her arm, shielding her from the approaching mob and we ran down the road and along a side alley, Arthur on her other side. Earthman appeared a moment later as Anna sank down to the ground, shaking like a leaf. She looked a right mess, but considering she'd had a bottle smashed in her face, she was probably quite lucky.

I looked back the way we'd come, expecting the mob to appear any second. 'We need to get further away,' I said, shifting from one foot to the other.

'They've gone further on,' said Earthman, shaking his head. 'They'll head for MacDonalds, Burger King, we always do. The symbols of the Establishment. Torching a dustbin in a back alley isn't the same.'

His confidence reassured me, and it was only later I realised he'd said 'we,' not 'they'. Just what did he do in his spare time?

Arthur was kneeling down with a folded cloth pressed to

Anna's face, and she tried to smile up at us. 'It's not too bad,' she whispered. 'I'll be OK.' 'She needs stitches,' stated Arthur. 'The hospital's only round the corner, we can walk there.'

He helped her up and she swayed to one side, Arthur steadying her. I took her other arm and soon we were waiting in A&E.

'She'll need to stay in overnight,' the doctor informed us. 'She's had a head injury, maybe some concussion, it's standard procedure.' 'Can I see her?' I asked.

'Yes, but briefly, she needs to rest.' 'Oh, God, Anna,' I said. She was sitting in a bed, looking pale and drawn in her hospital gown, a huge dressing taped to her face. 'This is turning into a nightmare.' 'It's OK,' she said gently. 'Just a cut, that's all. I haven't even got a headache.' She smiled tiredly and I felt relieved.

'Do you want anything?'

'No, I'll be out in the morning. Go and enjoy the rest of the day, don't dwell on this. Negativity breeds.' 'It doesn't feel right, just leaving you here.' 'Focus on the positive, no matter how small it is. That's the only way we'll ever get there.' She smiled again, stronger this time. 'You've still got a long way to go, you can't let anything pull you from The Path. Go back to the camp, keep looking forward. There's a lot depending on it.'

I kissed her good cheek and we left the hospital, walking in silence back towards the camp.

'Don't dwell on the negative,' said Arthur, hearing my unspoken thoughts. 'The light is always surrounded by darkness.'

*There is no light that does not cast a shadow.* I felt a bit more positive, and less guilty about leaving my friend languishing in hospital. She'd told me to look forward, not back.

A group of young people passed us, looking at us and giggling to each other. 'Beardy-weirdy,' I heard. I glanced at Arthur, he showed no reaction but his tightened lips told me he'd heard as well. I felt so angry that I was about to turn back and confront them, but Earthman's silent hand on my arm stopped me. Instead I seethed in silence for a while. What was wrong with being nice?

We passed a shop that looked like an army surplus store. Dried food, camouflage nets, knives, hunting equipment, I looked in the window in amazement. Inside it was packed.

'A prepper's shop,' explained Earthman.

I was none the wiser.

'Preppers, they're preparing for the end of civilisation – stock-piling supplies and stuff.' He nodded to a couple of people just leaving.

'Do you really think this is the end?' I asked.

He was quiet for a moment. 'It doesn't have to be, but yes, I think it's very likely.'

I nodded, rather grateful for his positive answer.

'I'm thinking of going out to Thailand. Doing conservation work in the rainforests. You know, educating the locals about ecology, ensuring it's preserved for the future.' He looked at me seriously. 'It's always been a dream of mine. Now there's nothing holding me in England, I think, why not?''Go for it,' I said. 'Follow your dreams, listen to your heart, it's the only voice you can trust.' If I'd learnt anything, it was that.

When we got back to the camp we found an improvised dance taking place, a cross between country dancing and Eastern belly dancing. A strangely good mix of fiddles and drums set a fast tempo and people were whirling around ecstatically. Earthman looked on, eyes shining, then grabbed my arm. 'Let's go, Brig!'

He dragged me into the midst of the crowd which seemed to be entirely improvising the dance. I felt incredibly out of place and thought guiltily of Anna while attempting to shuffle around awkwardly, but after a moment I began to relax and then enjoy myself. Look forward, she'd said. The rhythm filled my head and my whole body began to resonate with it. I saw the auras around people again, the room began to pulsate with light. Earthman was also enjoying himself, throwing himself around like a madman. He was jangling wildly as he moved and I began to mirror his movements. As the music took over my body more and more, I began to feel as if I were floating, I seemed to be almost weightless, and my dancing got more and more ecstatic.

After what seemed an age the music came to an end, and with it my feeling of weightlessness. I came back to earth, finding myself among a tent full of similarly bemused people. Earthman pulled me into a damp hug, and I laughed tiredly, rubbing sweat from my eyes as we went back outside.

Arthur was watching us, his arms folded. 'Well, you really know how to let yourselves go!' he said drily, one eyebrow raised.

Earthman and I looked at each other and laughed. I pushed back the strands of hair which clung to my face. 'Well, I'm knackered now. That music's quite something, it seems to fill your entire body. It's amazing.'

It was beginning to get dark and my stomach was rumbling. 'Shall we get some burgers?' A familiar and mouth-watering smell came from a nearby van.

'I don't eat burgers,' said Earthman, a look of disgust on his face. 'Trans-fats, E-numbers, cholesterol, a heart attack in a bun,' he clarified.

'Well, I'm starving,' I countered, and returned five minutes later with a dripping greasy bun. 'I think I'll have an early night tonight, it's been a long day.' Anna was the glue which held us together, I realised. It seemed a bit awkward, just the three of us.

I walked back to my guest-house and switched on the TV, by a strange coincidence the screen was showing an image of St Michael's Mount. *Nothing happens by coincidence.* I turned the volume up.

'This huge rock was supposedly dropped by the wife of the giant Comoran,' the presenter said, indicating a monolith beside her. I felt a sudden tingling at the now-familiar name.

The documentary revised for me all the facts I'd learnt earlier, and then gave some of its history as well.

It seemed that St Michael's Mount had a long history with ancient mariners. The Phoenician seafarers from modern-day Lebanon traded for tin here as far back as four thousand years ago. The Mount had been the commercial heart of Britain. I made a careful note of all this, knowing in my heart it was to be important.

When the news came on, I saw the global situation was becoming increasingly fraught. The US had raised its terror state to High Alert and finally launched missile attacks against key military sites in Pakistan, after months of threatening. I didn't see how our ritual that morning would be enough to make any real difference to anything.

# Chapter 38

*Light one candle, don't curse the darkness.*
Chinese proverb

There was an atmosphere of worry and fear about the town as we headed towards the Green Dragon to celebrate after collecting Anna. Everyone seemed suspicious, nervous, for some reason my companions particularly seemed to be attracting hostile looks. I noticed more than one person crossing the streets to avoid walking past us. It was strange – Glastonbury was known for its tolerance of the weirdos, and it was obvious from the bandages that Anna wasn't well.

The waitress at least smiled in happy recognition – we were fast becoming her best customers. 'All-day breakfast?' she stated before Arthur could speak.

'You've got it!' he said. 'Extra mushrooms as well.''And extra everything else as well?' she quipped. 'I'll see what I can do.''I'll have the same,' I said. 'I'm sure someone will manage what I can't eat,' I added, raising my eyebrows pointedly at Arthur. He looked affronted and we all laughed, Arthur begrudgingly smiling as well after a while. I felt an intense bond with my friends, a real sense of companionship that I'd never felt before. Now Anna was back we were whole again.

My barriers, the walls I hid behind, they'd been crumbling, and we'd become close by way of our shared view of the world. I was really enjoying my time in Glastonbury, I thought as I carried my plate to our table. I could stay here forever. I'd never felt so happy in my life.

Earthman pulled out a copy of *The Times* and sat engrossed with the crossword for a while.

'Here's a clue for you, Brig,' he said. ''Dragon-killer to climb in this place'.''I'm not much good at cryptic ones,' I said evasively. Too cryptic, too weird.

'Two, eight, five letters.''St Michael's Mount.' The coincidence was not a surprise.

'Correct! Now time for dinner.' He threw the paper on the table, the completed crossword uppermost.

I picked it up and read some of the clues, and then the answers. They meant nothing to me and I shook my head in incredulity.

'Earthman does the crossword at home while his eggs are boiling, and he hates hard-boiled eggs,' Anna explained.

I smiled wickedly. 'He's hard-wired to the internet with all the metal in his face.'

Anna spluttered coffee into her lap and Earthman looked theatrically hurt. I could see Arthur was trying to hide a smile as well.

I put my arm round his shoulders briefly as an apology then looked down at the headlines in the paper, immensely proud of my wit. In Syria and Afghanistan, it seemed some progress had been made, there was a hope of peace talks. But it was tentative, very tentative. Because of our ritual? I wasn't sure.

'Things are looking a bit better,' I said hopefully. 'Maybe things can be sorted out.'

'It'll take a lot more than that,' said Arthur, ever the grumpy old man. 'You saw what happened at the rally. Violence punctuates everything at the moment.''Why? Why are people getting so violent? Why is nothing ever settled amicably any more?''People are frightened.' Arthur's unexpected, soft answer made me look up. I'd never seen such an expression on his face before – sad, sorry, with a hint of hopelessness and failure. He seemed to have lost his appetite, was just moving his food disconsolately. 'They're frightened, lost, and isolated. Afraid that our way of life, our culture, our religion, all that we use to define who we are, as individuals and as a society, is wrong. Afraid that our entire existence has been based on a lie.''So what's the answer then?' I asked quietly. 'How do we stop being afraid?'

'The soul lives forever. When you realise that, you have nothing to fear. This is what Jesus tried to teach – that we should seek the reward of heaven, rather than a reward on earth.'

I was surprised and looked at his face to see if he was serious.

'What?' he said, his prickly demeanour firmly back in place. 'Why shouldn't I read the Bible?'

I sandwiched my bacon between two pieces of toast to cover my embarrassment. 'So you all believe the soul is immortal, then?'

The answer was unanimous.

'Birth is not the beginning of life, only of an awareness,' Anna stated, as if it were the most obvious thing in the world. 'Death is just the ending of this awareness. Most people have forgotten this, so are afraid of death, but really death is just a new beginning.'

Arthur pushed his half empty plate away. 'At one time, everyone knew that, all men knew God and the Truth for themselves. Now the earth is sleeping, God is a distant memory for so many, and the Truth has become distorted and false ideas added. This has caused the world to become what it is today.' He stabbed a stray mushroom on the table.

'People are frightened of going to Hell. They don't realise that we are all already there.'

'Everything we do will help,' soothed Anna. 'We're making a difference. We *are*.' Her heartfelt, determined words seemed to ring quite empty.

We all sat in silence for a while, absorbed in our own thoughts, until Anna and Earthman stood up.

'We're going to a seminar, on the charging of crystals and their uses in acupunctural healing,' said Anna. 'There's some brilliant speakers there, I really can't miss it, especially now I've escaped the sick-house. You probably wouldn't find it that interesting,' she added apologetically to me.

She wasn't wrong. 'I'll just hang around for a bit, go for a walk or something,' I said, grateful I didn't need an excuse. 'What are you doing, Arthur?'

'I don't have any plans. I'll stay here with you for a while,' he said, rather begrudgingly I thought. Perhaps I should be more grateful for his attention.

We sat in silence for a while. 'So, you're initiated into the Fifth Sphere, the Sphere of Mars,' he said. 'Do you feel as if you're making progress on your Journey?''I'm learning things every day,' I answered slowly. I didn't quite see him as a confidant yet. 'I think I'm going forward.''Learning is not enough. You may reach the Doorway of Truth, but you won't pass through it. I presume you've never read *The Hermetica*?' He raised one eyebrow, daring me to prove him wrong. Unfortunately I couldn't.

'One of the greatest texts of ancient wisdom ever written. You should read it,' he admonished. I nodded meekly. Yes, sir.

'You will find what you're looking for, as long as you never give up hope. The light in your heart is the only thing you need.'

I looked up at his suddenly gentle tone. He was looking at me intensely, as if there was something vitally important he needed to say. 'You'll be moving on soon, I can see that. I have to make sure that you've gained everything you can from your sojourn in Glastonbury.''I have gained a lot. I think I know where I can find the Grail.''The Grail is inside you. It is the light of Truth in your heart. Anyone can find it if they can unlock the door in their soul. This is the true purpose of the Journey.'

I nodded. 'Anna said much the same thing.''Anna and Earthman are walking very different Paths. I hoped I could speak to you before you left, I knew when I saw you that you were the one.' He looked wistful for a moment. 'I had hoped I could find the Grail in this lifetime, but now I know I will not. Instead, all I can do is hope that you will find it, for the sake of mankind.' He leant forward urgently.

'Time is running short. We gained but a little time with our ceremony, enough for you to complete the final stages of your Quest. But you cannot afford to dally. If you know the Way, take it. *Now*. There is no time to lose.'

I remembered the news reports lately – growing bleaker and more desperate by the day. He was right. There was no time to lose. I'd lost my focus somewhat, I'd been simply enjoying my time with Anna and Earthman, and I felt a sense of regret.

'I must go now, I have matters to attend.' He stood up and offered me his hand stiffly. As I took it, he wrapped me in a fierce hug. His surprising gesture crushed the breath from my chest, saying more than his words ever could. Then, embarrassed at his weakness, he stalked away without saying goodbye, his staff tapping on the tiled floor as I stared after him.

I finished my coffee then stood up and got some chocolate cake, anything to avoid making the irrevocable decision. I had to leave. I unhappily crumbled my cake, wishing I didn't have to burst my happy bubble. I was closer to Anna than I'd ever been, now I could see the world from her point of view. The barriers between us, the ones I'd so carefully built up, were gone. Earthman had also become a firm friend, and even Arthur I'd miss.

I got up and went outside, aimlessly wandering the streets. Couldn't I just stay here, forget the Quest, just live my own happy life? What if I did that? The thought seemed deliciously appealing and my mind played with the decision. My life would be perfect, even more perfect than before with what I'd learnt. My naive optimism cheered me up, for a moment.

I could hear voices on a radio inside a shop, several people were huddled round it in stony-faced silence. I felt cold – something had happened. My dream-vision of the end of the world, the option should I fail, crept insistently back into my mind.

I went inside and began to listen. From what I could gather, a bomb had been detonated in New York, a huge bomb in a subway. The damage had been devastating – hundreds killed, and the collapsing tunnels and buildings above meant no rescue operation was possible. No one knew who was responsible, but speculation had inevitably turned to Syria or Pakistan, or alternatively religious fanatics and end-of-the-world-ers. I remembered those earlier hostile looks.

Even more sinister, the few survivors had fallen ill – people walking alive from the tunnels had collapsed and died, leading to theories of a biological, chemical, or even nuclear weapon.

'We will keep you posted with all developments,' said the disembodied voice.

I walked from the shop in a daze. Time was running out, Arthur had said. I tried not to question the selfish decision I'd made just a moment before.

The next shop sold TVs and my regret and doubt amplified. Parallel images of lines of soldiers blocking every street, head to foot protective gear and respirators, automatic weapons at the ready. No one, at any cost, was to leave the contamination zone. Survivors were handcuffed and forced into trucks – 'for their own safety,' apparently.

I turned away and carried on walking, eventually reaching a viewpoint looking out across the countryside. I leaned on the railings and gazed far away, towards minute cars on a motorway, a tractor working in a field, white dots of sheep in a grassy pasture.

Then I saw a horse galloping hard. It was too far away to see clearly but even so I could sense the urgency in its pace. Its rider was bent low over its neck urging it on, and strangely he appeared to be wearing a long, old-fashioned cloak which streamed out behind him. The horse effortlessly leapt a hedge as if it were nothing.

I watched them for a few minutes. The scene niggled at my mind as if it was something important. Somehow, it seemed familiar. I'd seen it before somewhere, but the fleeting sense refused to be pinned down.

Horse and rider disappeared behind a low clump of trees, and then the rider reappeared on foot. He was running hard, a tremendous effort put into his fierce pace. It was strange, eerie almost. As if I'd witnessed something from another world, another time. I didn't know why I thought that, but something about the scene was not quite right.

A moment later, the rider, his cloak folded round his body out of the way, disappeared into the distance and although I looked for a long time I didn't see him again.

I walked back to town and idly looked into a few shop windows, my mind deliberately blank to avoid thinking about the decision that was coming. In the third I saw a huge picture of St Michael's Mount and as my eyes riveted to it, it seemed to glow as if coming alive.

I heard a voice whisper in my ear, as faint as a breath of wind. *If you desert the Path, the Gods will desert you.*

My feelings had reversed, I realised, when at last I let myself think. I was no longer contemplating abandoning the Quest. I had a duty. My life had a purpose. I couldn't turn my back on it. My earlier wistful vision of a perfect life I now saw as a reality; ravaged, war-torn and desolate. The Path was my future. It was also the future of the world.

St Michael's Mount. The start of the mighty ley line, the myths and legends had hidden the answer. Here was the Heart of the Earth, where I would find the Grail, the Cauldron, the Stone. I thanked Earthman in my heart for telling me the answer, and whatever Gods there be for letting me understand it.

'You're leaving already?!' cried Anna. 'You can't go yet!' 'It's time to go, Anna, I have to.'

She was almost crying at the bombshell, but I had by now accepted the decision and was feeling serenely calm and peaceful. All things have an end. In eternity, nothing is eternal.

'It's been nice to stay here, I'll miss you all.''Earthman will miss you too.' She looked at me significantly. I was mortified to feel myself begin to blush and Anna burst out into giggles. I smiled sheepishly at my oldest and truest friend. Her wicked look confirmed the bond between us. She'd done more for me than anyone else ever had, I just regretted I'd never realised it sooner.

'I'm going in the morning. I'll catch a bus south, see where it ends up,' I stated, bringing the conversation back to safer ground. 'It was good to see you again, and thank you for everything you've done.'

Anna hugged me fiercely as if I were going away for ever, and then stepped back. 'I hate saying goodbyes,' she said with tears in her eyes.

'It's not goodbye forever,' I said firmly. 'You can't get rid of me that easily.''I'll tell Earthman that, he'll be pleased.' She smiled wickedly again and then turned and walked away. As she disappeared from sight, I turned back to my Path and the next stage of my Journey.

# PART VIII

# Chapter 39

*Who sees the Lord? It is himself he sees.*
*For what ant's sight can discern the Pleiades?*
*Could an anvil be lifted by an ant?*
*Or could a fly subdue an elephant?*
Farid ud-Din Attar

I am heat, an infinite, unimaginable heat. In my heart is the womb of the universe, where all things are created, all the building blocks of life. They flow out over huge distances, bathing the entire universe with my essence. My immense power attracts others, who encircle me and live off my strength. My heat, light, power and energy flow freely from my body to nourish everything around me, all that is entirely dependent on my gifts. My heat and power is greater than anything.

I exist for aeons. Nothing in existence lives for as long as me, and so worlds grow up around me, worship me, offer me gifts, prayers and sacrifices. I see people build monuments to me, buildings, temples, anything to absorb my might and bring themselves closer to my power. I hear and see everything, but still I do not answer those prayers.

I am the form that they have assigned the term of *God*. But in truth, I'm just a speck of dust in the face of the True One, despite my awe-inspiring might, so I watch with indifference the antics of these myriad tiny creatures who swarm to my light.

Any which venture too close to me are seared, burnt and destroyed, absorbed entirely into my body. Nothing can touch my body and survive in itself. I am worshipped only from a distance.

But eventually, like all things, my time must come to an end. The immense energy which gives my power is exhausted, my heat begins to wane. My body begins to shrink, contract, faster and faster until it implodes, and then my body is blasted outwards, an explosion which sends shock waves across the entire universe. I am atomised, my unstoppable death throes destroying everything in my path. All those prayers had been to no avail.

But my death has a purpose, a great purpose. For on the infinite scale of the universe, my body will seed, form the basis of many new bodies, which will in turn attract supplicants, worshippers, prayers.

And so the wheel of existence turns.

# PART IX

# Chapter 40

*Whether you think you can or you think you can't, you're probably right.*
Henry Ford

I reached Dartmoor, the wild, bleak, untamed wilderness of Devon, one of the few unspoilt havens in Britain where as far as the eye could see there was no sign of man's presence.

I got off the bus in the middle of nowhere, on a rough, pot-holed section of road, unrepaired for years. The driver looked at me as if I was mad.

'You sure you want to get off here, love?' he asked. 'You'll be walking for miles before you even see another person. You don't want to be lost out here.''Yes, I'll be fine,' I said. 'I know where I'm going.'

Actually I didn't, but a sudden impulse had told me to stop here. The bus had passed a gushing waterfall descending from a sheer cliff, a sudden flash of exquisite beauty in the midst of the bleakness, and then we reached a junction, a second road shining white in the sun ran arrow straight across the moor into the distance. I thought I saw a multi-coloured glow running alongside it. I immediately jumped from my seat, grabbing my rucksack and ringing the bell to stop.

'Well, there won't be another bus along until tomorrow if you change your mind.' The driver looked at me doubtfully for a second then opened the door.

I stepped onto the road. The doors shut behind me with a hiss and then the bus pulled away. I watched it recede into the distance and then vanish, my last contact with civilisation for who knew how long. A flicker of doubt came into my mind – was that a good thing to do? I pushed it firmly aside – it was too late now anyway.

I walked back to the crossroads. The glare of the sun made any subtle colour patterns impossible to see, but I could feel the energy coursing under my feet like a rushing torrent. It was subtly pulling me towards the west. I settled my rucksack firmly onto my shoulders and set off.

I was loving the feeling of peace and harmony and revelled in the rare experience of aloneness, with not a soul visible for miles around. The only sounds I could hear were the faint hum of the wind and the occasional eerie cry of the curlew. Its haunting sound was said to be the lament of those souls lost on the moor, never to find their way home. A sudden chill hit me as a cloud covered the sun, and I shivered. The moor was baring its teeth slightly.

I walked for around an hour then stopped to eat one of the sandwiches I'd brought. I sat on the grass at the side of the road, looking out at the expanse of landscape. What sign there was of men was mostly ancient – prehistoric farmsteads, the remains of bygone field systems, ancient roadways and tracks. It seemed to me that no one else had lived here in two thousand years. There wasn't even a vapour trail in the sky – an ash cloud from a volcanic eruption near Iceland had grounded all planes.

I lay back and looked up at the sky, thinking about the road on which I was walking. It was the same ley line that ran through Glastonbury, I was sure. As I relaxed and slipped into myself I could feel it singing in my veins.

I was on one of the Old Straight Tracks, an ancient sacred road. According to legend, Earthman had said, they were laid out by the Goddess of the Ways and were an inviolable sanctuary for travellers. This stretch of road, then, must have a heritage of thousands of years, I mused. I was walking in the footsteps of an inestimable number of feet.

I was surprised then to see someone coming – I was quite sure no one had been there a moment before. It was a woman, with long, flowing, blonde hair and an elaborate dress, unusual for a hiker. There was something strange about her, a subconscious prickling which I couldn't put my finger on.

She stopped beside me. 'How are your travels on The Road going?'

I had a feeling she wasn't talking about the road we were both walking along. 'I'm enjoying the walk. It's a beautiful day.'

'When joy fills your heart and the sun lights your path, you cannot lose your Way,' she replied, her voice melodious and beautiful. I immediately felt a sense of peace, like I was being lulled to sleep.

'I am Elen, I watch over all those who walk this Road.'

I wondered rationally if she lived locally and provided information for walkers and hikers, but I knew she was more than that. On some level she seemed intensely familiar. 'I feel I'm nearing the end of The Path, that the final hurdle lies just ahead,' I felt drawn to say.

'You're right, the final goal of a lifetime's journey is close at hand. The final step lies ahead, where you must prove you've learnt and understood everything life has taught you.'

I stood up. The woman seemed to flicker slightly as the sun caught her, I couldn't quite focus on her.

'You have all that you need, inside you. It's now up to you to use it.'

An intense feeling of relaxation and purpose filled me as she spoke. I could do it, I could succeed, I knew I could.

A delicate smile played across Elen's lips as she heard every word I thought. 'When you chose your Path, you knew you could succeed. It's only later that the doubts come. That's where faith comes in.'

When I *chose* my Path? 'But I thought I'd been chosen?' I looked at her in confusion. There was no longer any doubt to whom I was speaking.

'The choice was always yours to make, but it was the Gods who laid the choices in front of you.' Her body seemed to be absorbing the sun, she grew brighter as she spoke. 'It was your destiny to face The Path, it was your choice to walk it.'

A breeze seemed to shift her dress slightly, although no wind touched me. I felt as if something, somewhere, in the inner vestiges of the universe, had just clicked into place.

Elen smiled and raised her hand, a gesture of farewell, or of blessing. 'It's time for you to continue your Journey, the end-game is approaching.' She walked past me, and when I turned a few seconds later the road was empty.

I spent the rest of the day walking across Dartmoor with a renewed vigour. The miles seemed to sail past under my feet, the road was rising to meet me all the way. The world was buzzing with energy, and I was buzzing too.

In mid-afternoon I saw a hill standing out of the moorland topped by a small church, proud against the skyline. A timeless monument to the universal religion. My heart began to sing, this was the place it had been aiming for.

There was a small group of houses, too small to be called a village, clustered near the base, all stone-built with a farm house at the centre. Probably the vestiges of an ancient farming community, scratching a living from the bare bones of the moor.

A sign told me I'd reached Brentor. A notice in a cottage window said 'Rooms to let'. I'd never doubted my guardian angel would provide for me.

My first step was to climb the steep hill towards the church. I wasn't surprised to see it was dedicated to St Michael. I opened the heavy wooden door and went inside, feeling the great surge of power coursing through the building. The atmosphere seemed to vibrate with energy, accumulated from millennia of devotions from so many people.

The church was deserted and I sat in a pew, drinking in the heady power of the building, channelled and amplified by the careful location and layout of the building. In the east window was a depiction of St Michael slaying the dragon and I looked at it with interest. The spear transfixing its heart was the transfixed node of energy in this very place. I sent a silent message of thanks to Earthman for informing me about this. The design was surrounded by an intricate woven pattern of Celtic knotwork, the endless knot representing the twisting, turning, threads of life.

Above my head on a stone pillar was an image of the Green Man, a pagan yet very common symbol in churches, another representation of Cernunnos, God of the Green. An ancient face gazed outwards from a wreath of carved stone leaves. As I looked at it, it became animated, alive. The leaves appeared to move as if blown by the wind, and a pair of timeless eyes met mine.

I heard the door open behind me and the spell was broken. The pillar returned to how it had always been. I turned and saw a man in his late fifties standing in the doorway. I felt an immediate sense of surety, peace and confidence about him. Then I noticed the dog collar around his neck. The rector, I assumed.

He glanced round as if looking for something and then noticed me in the shadows. He smiled with a genuine warmth and came and sat down next to me. 'I'm James, the rector of this church. Are you enjoying the peace of our beautiful sanctuary?'

I felt slightly annoyed by the intrusion but his genuine friendliness appeased me somewhat. 'Yes, it is beautiful. The atmosphere here is electric. I've walked a long way today and I can feel it nourishing and feeding my spirit. Just sitting here I feel so much better.'

'There's great power in this place, the Grace of God is given freely to all,' James answered, with the confidence of a man of faith. 'Where have you come from?'

I wasn't sure how to answer. Should I say that I'd caught the bus to Exeter, then at a whim jumped off in the middle of an uninhabited moor, walked fifteen miles at random, then just happened to arrive here? He'd be on the phone to the nearest mental institution. But in the end I decided on the truth.

He accepted my explanation without comment, thankfully. I

supposed he was used to people's irrational actions in the name of God. 'Many people are guided to this place, it's a place of great sanctity. I saw someone climbing the hill, I have a principle of welcoming all seekers so I came in search of you.'

Seekers? I wondered with a thrill if he was referring to Grail seekers. 'Seekers of what?' I asked, my heart in my mouth.

'The Holy Spirit,' he answered.

I looked down at my hands. Something of my disappointment must have shown in my face for when I looked up he was looking at me slightly quizzically, his eyes narrowed. 'Some of them will find what they are looking for,' he said slowly.

'And the others?' 'Many seekers go away empty handed. Not because they don't find what they seek, but because they do not recognise it when they have,' he added enigmatically. This time I was sure he was referring to something different. He leant back in his seat and folded his arms. *Your move.*

'I hope I will find what I'm looking for,' I replied carefully. We seemed to be playing some cryptic mind game, I hoped this implied that I understood what I thought he was saying. Maybe I should have paid more attention to Earthman's crosswords. We looked at each other for a moment, many unspoken words passed between us.

'I've seen many seekers over the years,' James said. 'I've come to know which will succeed, and which will fail. I can see that the light is on your side.'

He stood up. 'Will you be needing somewhere to stay tonight? Mrs Jackson in the village lets out rooms for pilgrims and seekers, you would do well to try there.'

I thanked him for the advice and got to my feet. My leg muscles screamed in protest, their long rest had sent them to sleep, and I hobbled painfully from the pew.

James put his hand on my elbow to steady me. 'Come back in the morning when you're rested, we'll talk more. At around eleven?'

I nodded. Now I just wanted food and sleep and I was thinking longingly of a hot shower. I struggled down the steep hillside, holding firmly to the handrail for support. I gritted my teeth for the final push – fifty torturous metres to the alluring cottage.

Soon I was falling asleep in a steaming bath in Mrs Jackson's guest room. 'You're in luck,' she'd said to me. 'Last week I was full. All birdwatchers come to see some rare bird – I've no idea what – blown here by that hurricane. But one of them said it's all those satellites. The, um, radio communications –' she looked at me for confirmation – 'that interfere with their navigation. That's why so many birds end up way off course now.' She nodded enthusiastically but I was more interested in the hot meal she'd promised me.

When the temptation of that food overcame the desire for sleep, I got out of the bath and got dressed. On the TV I saw a smiling, exhausted woman waving happily at the camera, the island of Lindisfarne in the background. Her top was emblazoned with a cancer research logo and her headscarf rippled in the wind. She'd made it then. I sent her a silent message of congratulation, and knew she would hear. Then I went downstairs to where a bowl of hot soup was waiting.

'It's my husband's favourite, chicken and tarragon,' said Mrs Jackson cheerfully. 'I hope you like it.'

I took a spoonful, my mouth already watering from the rich smell. The flavours exploded into a cacophony of delight. 'The best I've ever had!' I enthused, feeling its warmth spreading through my exhausted body.

Her face split from ear to ear in a huge smile and she hurried out to bring in the main course. A huge plate of lamb casserole, mint dumplings and new potatoes was just as delightful, and she watched delightedly as I cleared up every scrap. Then, despite being only eight-thirty, I climbed into a soft feather bed and was soon sound asleep.

# Chapter 41

*To see a world in a grain of sand,*
*A heaven in a wild-flower,*
*To hold infinity in the palm of your hand,*
*And eternity in an hour.*
William Blake

I arrived at the church at ten o'clock and sat down to do my daily mental revision of everything I'd done, seen and learnt – my old scientific habits died hard. Then, exactly on time, James arrived.

'You slept well, I trust?' he asked.

'Yes, thank you, I feel much better today.' 'Here the energy of the land can nourish and heal your soul, even at this dire time,' he said.

*At this time?* I wondered if he was aware of the changes in the land, the Sleeping King, the cause of all the trouble. After the last few weeks, I wondered if there was anyone who wasn't. I'd had enough of the cryptic guessing game and decided to take the plunge.

'Do you know about the Sleeping King, his link to ley lines and the world's soul-energy, that all this trouble is caused by the broken link between man and earth, and will only be put right when the King is awakened?'

James looked at me steadily without answering. I began to feel uncomfortable – perhaps he didn't.

But at last he nodded. 'This is a time of great suffering. Global wars, the threat of nuclear strikes, natural disasters, it's all everyday news. The world is governed by hatred, intolerance and greed. Even the great religions which are tasked with guarding our spiritual essence have been debased and corrupted, fighting in factions between themselves. These are dark times indeed.' He sighed and shook his head.

'I believe there is a way to change things,' I told him, feeling slightly foolish – what if he thought I was mad, just another nutter? But he accepted all I said.

'The Grail, whatever you like to call it, is certainly the key. If it can be found – *if* – then the Spirit of the Land will awaken, harmony will be restored. If not, then the future will be beyond our worst nightmares.' James sighed and polished his glasses on his sleeve. 'Man has gained, and learnt to abuse, much power. For the first time in history, he has the means, and more importantly the inclination, to wipe out the entirety of life on earth.''Many people are trying to make things better.' I told him about Glastonbury.

'Yes, I couldn't go to the festival myself, but it will have helped, certainly. Everything will. But will it be enough? The world has seen nothing like this before, and I pray to God, never will again.' He crumpled up a hymn sheet in his hands with frustration. 'The world may not even exist tomorrow – think about that. Some power-crazy nation may have destroyed every last vestige of life.'

'Everything will be the way it's meant to be. Forged in the fiery furnace of life, we become stronger than ever,' I said fervently. My sense of purpose and rightness, invoked by my meeting with Elen, hadn't diminished.

James looked at me in surprise, taken aback by my words. But not as much as I was. *Where had they come from?* As I wondered, I saw a sudden flash of memory in my mind – a smith frantically hammering a sword before plunging it back into the furnace. I shook my head in consternation and it was gone.

I looked up at the slain dragon in the window. What were these profound flashes of insight that were coming to me? They seemed to come from a place outside myself, ideas which appeared fully formed in my mind. It was like I was tapping into a kind of universal database, containing past, present and future, everything, everywhere. The dragon gazed into my eyes with an immense wisdom as I recalled that experience on Yeavering Bell.

'You are right, of course,' said James.

I looked back at him. I had to think for a moment what I was right about.

'But it's not nice to witness the furnace at close hand. Of course we must suffer, to prove we're worthy to reach God. It's adversity that brings out our true soul, transcends our selfish desires and unites us under the common banner of humankind.'

I agreed. 'The Blitz Spirit, the Dunkirk Spirit. I've noticed when a plant has a stem broken, several more shoot from the wound.' 'Exactly. When life is tested, it becomes even stronger than before.' James looked at the dragon for a while. 'I shouldn't doubt the Will of God, this is all happening for a reason. But my faith is being tested like never before. People take for granted what they have, without any thought that they may one day lose it. All that matters is money, no one cares about Truth any more. My congregation's dwindled to a handful, people have turned from the God of Love to the God of Money.' He looked angry and frustrated.

'People never look up from their feet, never see the heavens above their heads. All they see is a life with cars, grand houses and money.' I again remembered that day in the park, the day when I'd first looked towards the sky. 'We've used and abused the world and all that's in it for our own selfish gain, and now we're faced with the biggest wake-up call of all. Our very survival, and that of all life, is at stake.' I was beginning to sound like Anna, I thought fondly.

'Would you like tea?' James asked. 'I have a kettle and supplies here for parishioners' meetings, and some biscuits as well, I believe.'

I agreed readily, and soon he returned with two china cups and a plate of biscuits. 'What do you know about my Quest, the Quest of the Seven Spheres?' I asked as I sipped the tea. I winced – no sugar. I thought about asking then decided against it.

'It is not just your Quest,' he admonished gently. 'All men are equal in the eyes of God. Everyone is on a Quest, the Quest to reach God, their divine source. And this source, or the means to the source, is known to some as the Holy Grail.''The Sphere of the Sun,' I recalled. 'Don't fall into the trap of fallacious pride.' I'd nearly fallen at this hurdle before, but it was still easy to feel just a bit proud of myself for being chosen.

'The way to God lies with yourself, and only with yourself – what you have in your heart and your soul. No man holds the key to heaven for anyone but himself. The idea that it can be otherwise – through baptism, confession, last rites – is a lie created by men.'

I was surprised at his decidedly unchristian words. 'Isn't that a bit heretical?''Heretical in the eyes of the Church, or heretical in the eyes of God?' He looked at me with a challenge in his eyes. 'That was the message preached by Jesus when he railed against the Pharisees and the Scribes. But now the Church has fallen into the same fallacy that its prophet tried to prevent.'

I wasn't really interested in a theological debate. It seemed to be a topic that would lead to the loaded question, 'So, do *you* go to church?' I looked around nervously, wondering about my next step. I wasn't sure if I'd passed through the Sphere of Mars or not yet. I really needed to finish Jason's book. Maybe I'd now reached the Sphere of Jupiter, king of both the Gods and the Planets. I put my empty cup down on the pew.

'I'm sorry about the lack of sugar,' said James. 'An oversight on my part, I never take it myself.'

I looked at him in surprise – how did he know?

He smiled slightly. 'Human nature and its weaknesses are my vocation.'

I laughed uncomfortably. What other weaknesses and secrets had he intuited in me? I studied the hymn-sheet in front of me with careful attention.

'How do you feel, in yourself?' he asked suddenly. 'Do you feel as if you can succeed?' His face was warm and open, I felt I could lay bare my soul to him. Well, he was the master of the confessional. Except he didn't believe in that, of course.

I thought carefully, wondering if he already knew from the weaknesses he saw in me. 'It's not an easy road. I wonder sometimes why I've been chosen for this Quest.' I looked up at the dragon again. 'I just feel as though, I don't know, all my life I've been searching for something, what I don't really know. That's why I loved science and history at school, I was trying to understand something. But as far as I travel, what I'm searching for is at the same distant point on the horizon, like a rainbow you can never reach.' I noticed the Green Man gazing down at me again.

'But the road is rising to meet me, I must be on the right path.' My deep-seated doubts gave an air of hesitation to my words.

'You know the story of Robert the Bruce and the spider? The world abounds with stories of ordinary people who, against all odds, survive and flourish in the face of crippling adversity. They suffer devastating illness, loss of limbs, find themselves stranded or shipwrecked. They face trials that most people would shatter under, and come through them with the light of life still in their hearts. These are the hardest tests of all, but they awaken something inside you, force you to a new level of existence, to transform yourself and the world. You become what you never felt was possible.'

I could see a deep-seated resilience in James' face, a surety and confidence that I'd felt only once in my life. After I remembered the strength of *Brigid*, I recalled what Jason had said about the dinosaurs. Then that lady on the moor who'd turned her illness into a force for good. And I understood exactly what he meant.

'The true definition of a superhero,' I said, a lump in my throat. 'An ordinary person, who deals with whatever life throws at them and comes out on top.' 'That's right.' James reached across and squeezed my shoulder for a brief second. 'You never know when you may be called to the battlefield, or what the battle may be that you face. But there is no escaping your life, no matter how hard you try.'

He held out the plate of biscuits and I took one automatically. I'd thought it would sweeten the bitter tea, but that seemed trivial now.

'Some people don't fight the good fight, they turn, run and hide. And then their lives are nothing, meaningless, grey and dull, a mere existence until death.' James paused, his gaze far away, then he turned to face me fully. There was a strange look in his eyes and I felt quite uneasy.

'They turned from The Road,' he said. 'And The Road, God, life, turned from them.'

I shivered. I'd heard these words before, whispered in my mind, when I watched that horseman galloping across the fields. *Where had they come from?* It was almost frightening that James had repeated them almost exactly. Was it a warning? A memory? Something buried deep within my soul, fighting to be heard? Another whisper from the cosmic mind? My head began to spin and I felt quite sick. I stood up and lurched sideways.

'Are you all right Bridget?' asked James urgently, standing up quickly.

'Just a bit dizzy, suddenly. I need some fresh air.' I got to the door, moving from pew to pew for balance and pulled it open. A blast of air struck my face, a relief from the suddenly stifling atmosphere inside. I leant on the wall in the sunshine, breathing in deep gulps of fresh air, and began to feel better.

'What happened?' James was standing beside me.

'I don't know. What you said, it was as if – I don't know. It was like it meant something, something important. I don't know,' I finished lamely.

He looked worried. 'Sometimes words can resonate with the soul, a forgotten memory, a motto, a credo from lifetimes ago. Maybe that was what happened.'

I felt a faint whisper of sound and saw his lips frame something, as if he'd thought something to himself. I heard his unspoken words. *She remembers. She is the one.*

# Chapter 42

*The boundaries between the animate and inanimate worlds are becoming increasingly blurred.*
Jagadis Chandra Bose

As I looked down the hill, still struggling to regain my composure, I noticed two men resolutely forging a way up the hill. I breathed deeply and my senses cleared and sharpened. I could sense an aura of strength, power, arrogance and determination about them.

James followed my gaze. 'If I am not mistaken, these two are also seekers. Many people come here in the naive hope of finding buried treasure, rumoured to be buried nearby. Of course, it's not physical treasure, but the treasure of the soul, but many don't understand. They're blinded by greed and cannot even see into their own hearts.' He shook his head, the weary gesture of one who has seen it all, many times. 'I wonder which these will be.'

The two men, in their fifties and dressed like Victorian adventurers, reached the gateway. They looked around with a practised air and then nodded curtly to me.

'Good morning,' I said. 'What brings you to this spot?' I already knew the answer but both men smiled importantly.

The first pulled himself up taller, his belly straining against his trousers, an assertive posture to impress this silly woman. I looked around for support but James had disappeared. Never mind, I could handle arrogant men.

'We are on an important mission,' he announced, emphasising every word. 'The world is about to end. China, if not Syria or Pakistan, will unleash their nuclear weapons any day, then the world will no longer exist.' His voice was wheezy and nasal, I immediately thought of overindulgence in single malt and cigars at old-boys' clubs.

'But this war –' he checked round for eavesdroppers and leant towards me. I could smell tuna on his breath and wondered where he'd got it – tuna was near enough extinct now according to the environmental experts. 'This war was foretold, millennia ago. It's beyond the power of man to stop it, as it was beyond man's control that it started. It is the result of a great astronomical cycle, far beyond man's understanding.'

He checked I was hanging on to his every word. 'All men that is, except us. We've discovered what is happening, and we've discovered how to end it. We've dedicated ten years to this Quest, and this is why we're here now.'

I nodded, trying to look impressed. I wondered exactly what they expected me to say. Probably nothing, just simper with wide-eyed admiration.

'We're searching for the Holy Grail, which it may surprise you, is also known as the Philosopher's Stone and Nirvana. This place is linked to the Grail, this is why we've come here. There are many hidden clues, if you know how to read them.' 'The dragon,' I volunteered helpfully.

He looked affronted. *How dare you know something.* I felt pleasantly smug.

The second man, who hadn't spoken yet, looked at me sharply. 'Then you also walk the Path,' he observed. 'Perhaps we should share our experiences.' 'No one has searched more thoroughly than us,' said the fat man, glaring at his companion, who looked back evenly. 'We've travelled the length and breadth of Britain, we've read every myth, every legend, every ancient text from across the world,' he explained to me. 'There's just one final piece in the puzzle remaining.' 'What do you intend to do with the Grail, should you find it?' James had reappeared at my shoulder and we exchanged looks.

'We will restore the true rulers of the world,' said the fat man proudly.

'And who is that?' 'The philosophers. We will instigate a perfect world following Plato's theory of the perfect city.

No greed and jealousy – no one will have personal property. No neglect – children will be brought up collectively. Everyone will be allocated a spouse and occupation according to their personality, so no divorce or discontentment. The philosopher-rulers will lead a world in perfect harmony. Everyone will selflessly work together for the good of all.' He smiled confidently.

I felt quite unsettled by this proposed totalitarian regime. 'Are you sure this is the right way?' 'Yes, of course.' He began to bluster. 'A strict, governing hand is what the world needs. A world governed for the good of all is a world free from war and hate. Isn't that right, Clive?' He turned to his companion for support.

'Do people really need to be ruled?' asked James. 'What if everyone follows the universal laws of truth, beauty and harmony?'

Clive, who hadn't really contributed to this conversation, looked at James with interest. I wondered if he really subscribed to his companion's ideas.

'We've studied everything ever written about The Path.' The fat man was losing ground fast and he didn't like it. 'This is the way forward. This is the purpose of the Grail.'

James held his hands up in submission. 'Of course. I'm sure you're right.'

I was feeling increasingly unsettled. These two men were walking The Path, that was certain, but they'd obviously not passed the Sphere of the Moon – they were treating the Grail like an intellectual challenge. They'd looked upwards, realised the Path was there, but they hadn't understood the first lesson, to follow their hearts and their intuition. Until they realised this, they would never come any nearer to their goal, for all their learning and knowledge. They would just circle around it forever, as the moon and other spheres perpetually circle, never getting an inch closer. I saw yet another layer of symbolism in the

Path of the Seven Spheres.

I had to tell them. They needed to be set on the right track, but the fat man at least was unlikely to see reason. Just as I had been, I thought uncomfortably.

The meeting seemed to be over. 'I'd like to hear more about your theories,' I called after them as the two men began to walk away. 'Maybe we can help each other.'

'The first point is that the universe is a vast intelligence, a conscious being, of which the Grail is a manifestation of. Plato described it fully in *The Timaeus*.' The fat man, who had introduced himself as Colin, was sitting in the central and dominant position of a picnic bench. Clive, James and I were arranged around him like pawns. I felt like I should be taking notes and preparing for spot questions.

'Pythagoras, obviously, was the first to teach this idea in the West, but it's also found in other global philosophies, the Old Testament and Vedic texts, Buddhism, and of course *The Hermetica*, which went on to influence Christian and Muslim philosophy and thinkers such as Blake, Newton, Jung and John Dee.'

I'd heard of this text before, I thought maybe Arthur had mentioned it. Perhaps I should find it some time.

James gazed into the distance, looking bored. Colin took a mouthful of water from a plastic bottle, giving the inferior minds a chance to catch up before continuing his lecture. 'So therefore, every object, thought, action and being exists as a product of the Great One's mind, infused with this cosmic energy, every one no less than perfect.'

I remembered this profound insight from when I'd faced the black dog, what I now knew was the test of the Sphere of Venus.

'I worked as a metallurgist,' said Clive. 'This was what first set me on The Path, when I learnt that modern science has actually proved this concept. I heard of an Indian scientist named Bose, who showed that metals have learning abilities and reactions to different stresses.''That's not possible!' I couldn't contain myself.

'That's what I first thought, too. His data was checked by dozens of other scientists, there's no doubt about it. Trying to understand how, and why, set me on the long road that led me here, today.'

I could empathise with him – my own story was even more fanciful. I nodded in understanding and he smiled, relieved I hadn't ridiculed him further.

'Plants as well, they have feelings, emotions, likes, dislikes, awareness of pain, threat and stress.' He was warming to his theme.

'Well, anyway,' interrupted Colin, annoyed by his loss of limelight. 'Let's keep on track.' Clive looked down at his hands.

'The physical body of any object obviously has a finite lifespan, some longer than others, but as all scientists know, energy cannot be made or destroyed, it is merely changed from one form to another. A being of pure energy – the soul, both individual and collective – must be immortal.''So you believe the Grail will convey immortality?' asked James, the first time he had spoken.

'Of course. The purpose of the Philosopher's Stone was to grant immortality, obviously. The Hindu king Yudhishthira ascended bodily to heaven after a spiritual pilgrimage. As did Galahad when he found the Grail, the prophet Enoch, the Buddha, Mohammed, Elijah...''And Jesus, the Sleeping King,' I interrupted. 'Who is a symbol of the Grail.'

Colin wasn't sure whether to be annoyed at the interruption or pleased that I was following so closely. 'And the Persian-Roman God Mithras the same, they both represented the key to heaven for mankind. In finding, or becoming, the Grail, they escape the cycle of life and death, they become eternal. Also the main esoteric message of the Mahabharata, obviously.'

CHAPTER 42

I looked round. Everyone else seemed to be following the argument. 'Um...' I raised my hand, and immediately hated myself for it. *Please, sir?* 'What's the Maherater?'

'The Ma-hab-har-ata.' Colin spelt it out slowly, as if talking to a backward child. 'It is the most ancient sacred epic of the Hindus.' He looked at me with one eyebrow raised.

'So, every myth, religion, medieval romance, esoteric and occult text, across time, culture and place, actually encodes the message of the Grail?' I confirmed, determined not to let Colin rile me. 'Everyone knew about it, and everyone recorded their knowledge for the future generation – us – who would need to find it?''Correct!' said Colin with a flourish. 'And we –' he looked at Clive – 'are the ones who will find it.' He hesitated for a moment. 'Fifteen years ago, I was working on a linguistics project, recording the dying languages of the New World. I transcribed a story which was near identical to the Biblical story of the Tower of Babel. That made me think – how had that come about? I read deeper and deeper, and found repeating motifs the world over, all with a common message.'

I was listening with more interest, but then his arrogant attitude returned. 'Now, using that message, we will restore it to its true order.'

James stood up, looking decidedly unimpressed. 'Well, I have matters I must attend, I'll have to leave you now.'

Colin also stood, gesturing to Clive. 'We also must continue, we've delayed far too long.'

As they strode down the hill, James and I looked after them. 'They will not find the Grail, they will fail,' James said.

'I know.''Many people have come here on their search, but all go away empty handed.'

I looked back to a time when I was as lost as they were, when I was drifting, rudderless on the tides of life, and felt empty.

'There's one myth that they've overlooked, or failed to understand. The myth of Icarus,' James said.

267

'He was given wings by his father, melted them when he flew too close to the sun, and then fell to his death.' I recalled a long ago bedtime story.

'Yes, but there's a message encoded there. The sun represents the divine light, the Grail. The wings are the knowledge he had, which he didn't understand or use wisely.'

'So when the gift of wisdom is abused, then failure, death, will follow?''Exactly. It's what's in your heart that counts, not what's in your mind. You can only achieve the Grail when you complete The Path. If you reach it when you are not ready...' He let the answer hang. 'There are untold dangers of progressing too far, without truly understanding what you've learnt. Those two men are heading into dangerous waters.' James turned away.

The feeling of emptiness grew stronger. I looked down the hill as they disappeared, full of conflicting thoughts. I was at a cross-roads, the choice I made here was vital, I knew.

I could set them right, share my wisdom. Why did James not try to do this? He knew more about The Path than I did, perhaps they were meant to fail, I shouldn't interfere. The path to success was through failure. But that just didn't seem right, was James so disillusioned by the many seekers he met that he just didn't care any more?

The two men were at the bottom of the hill, Clive was unlocking a car. James said they would probably die in their attempt. I couldn't let that happen. They cared, after all. Cared enough about the world to try to put it right. Just like the rest of us. Their motives were pure. Pure enough they would succeed regardless? James was not worried, so why was I? Was I wrong? Was he?

I looked around, James was preoccupied with the church noticeboard. The men were both in the car, the engine was running. I sprinted from the churchyard and down the hill, almost flying down the steep slope, arms out wide for balance. The car was moving, I still had over a hundred metres to go. It gathered speed. I was too late. Leaping like a mountain goat, I reached the road. The car was gone. Breathing hard, I ran to the corner, but I knew it was too late.

I walked slowly back to the car park, empty and desolate. A test, and I'd failed it. An opportunity, and I'd lost it. I felt terrible. I sat down on the grass to regain my breath and then noticed a bag partially hidden under a bench. Clive had been carrying one very similar. I leapt to my feet with a bursting light of hope. It was his bag, I recognised the logo, a strange cluster of linked hands. When I heard an engine behind me, I didn't even need to turn round.

Clive wound down the window and we both looked at each other with relieved gratitude. 'I only put it down for a second,' he explained with a heartfelt smile.

I handed it through the window, my expression mirroring his exactly. As he tried to take it I hung onto it, and he looked at me quizzically. I had a second chance, I couldn't let it go. 'I have some information that may help you,' I said quickly. Both men looked at me and I finally relinquished the bag. 'You're doing it wrong, completely wrong, you're going to fail.' *And die.*

Clive was waiting and Colin was pointedly studying his notebook. That told me he was also listening.

'In alchemy, the most important step to produce the Philosopher's Stone was purifying one's own mind and soul,' I said. 'Without this, no amount of work or dedication would gain anything. The Grail doesn't show itself to those who don't prove worthy. Maybe this is why you can't find it, after years of search. You must look first to yourself, find it in your own heart.'

It was to protect them, not itself, that the Grail didn't appear, I realised. Like Icarus, they would be destroyed. The Grail had their best interests at heart.

I was met with a stone wall of silence, but I gauged a flicker of encouragement in Clive's eyes.

'Listen to your heart, your instincts,' I persisted. 'Don't try to impose your own will on the world, accept that you're just a part of it.'

They'd heard my words, it was up to them to understand them. After we looked at each other in silence for a minute I turned and walked away from the car. There was nothing more I could say.

As I went, I heard a voice call after me. 'Thank you.'

# Chapter 43

*There is no religion higher than Truth.*
Helena Blavatsky

After a moment's hesitation, I decided to call Earthman.

'Brig!' He sounded delighted to hear from me and I felt a pang of loss. Anna had been right – we'd forged a close bond. 'Where are you now?'

'Brentor, in Devon.'

'I know it well. You're getting closer then,' he stated.

'How are things in Glastonbury?' 'I'm back home now, in Manchester. The festival's over.' I counted the days, it was already nearly a week since I'd seen him. 'So, how's it going, really?' 'Two men came here today, Grail seekers. I was talking to them for ages.' 'And?' He could hear the worry in my voice.

'They knew everything, everything about the Quest. They'd spent years researching it. But they'll get nowhere, because they're treating it like an intellectual puzzle rather than a Soul-Quest.' 'And you're worried you're doing the same? That you're not pure enough in spirit to find it?' He intuited exactly my problem.

'Why me, Earthman?' I asked desperately. 'Why was I given this task? There are much better people in the world, I know nothing about the Quest. I'm just making it up as I go along. I wonder sometimes if I've just imagined the whole thing.' 'You were *chosen*, and the universe chose the best possible person. It doesn't make mistakes. And by knowing nothing, you were forced to follow your heart and your instincts. There's nothing that isn't real, whether we've imagined it or not.'

Spoken like a true nutter, I thought affectionately. I could hear the unshakeable confidence in his voice, why did everyone seem to have that except me?

'If I was meant to follow The Path, then why did the universe make me a scientist? Why not something more relevant – a mythologist, a historian, a Buddhist monk?' Or just another hippie nutter, I mentally added.

'That's something only you know the answer to,' he said. 'But doubting is only human. 'My God, my God, why hast thou forsaken me?' Even Jesus doubted he was on the right path.'

In the distance, I could see three horses on a bridleway. They startled a flurry of pigeons which rose up in a cloud.

'Think about what qualities you've gained. I don't mean the practical or scientific skills, what did you gain inside you, how has it developed you as a person?'

I swapped the phone to my other ear and thought for a moment. 'Well, I learnt to be analytical, to make my own judgements, not just blindly accept as the truth what others said. I suppose I learnt to form my own questions, and then discover the answers for myself, to be mentally independent. I learnt to see everything as a continual development – science is about going forward.'

'Well, don't you see? This is exactly what you needed on this Journey. You've had to forge your own path, there was no one there for you to follow. This is why the universe made you a scientist.

I told you, the universe doesn't make mistakes. This is all the proof you need that you're on the right path.'

His triumphant explanation made me feel so much better, I hadn't thought of it like that. 'Thanks, Earthman. You've cheered me up no end.' I smiled at a couple who were walking past my seat.

'You yourself played a role in deciding your life, you know. It was partly your decision as well. Why might that have been?'

*That sense of failure*. I failed last time. Because I was forced to follow the Path of others, it was the only Path available. So I would not make the same mistake again, I had to develop the skills to find my own Path.

'Brig? Are you still there?''I don't know why that might have been,' I said slowly.

'Well, nothing happens without a reason. Have faith.' I heard a voice in the background, a woman, and he was distracted. 'Look, I can't talk any more, I have to go. I'll speak to you another time.'

I put my phone back in my pocket, wondering who the woman had been, and went back towards the church.

'Ah, Bridget! I was wondering where you'd got to.' James was arranging a pile of parish magazines on a table. 'Did you learn anything from your meeting with the seekers?'

He looked at me intently over his glasses, and I felt slightly uncomfortable. 'I spoke to them again, I tried to set them on the right Path. I thought they shouldn't be left to wander in the dark.'

James looked a little startled, then somewhat doubtful. Was he doubting my actions, or his own indifference? I shuffled my feet then met his eyes steadily. I knew I'd done the right thing.

'I was just about to stop for lunch,' he said finally. 'Would you like to join me?'

James installed me in his living room, tastefully decorated but with no personal touch except for several hundred books, some shelved but most just heaped on the floor.

I browsed some of the titles, surprised by the diversity. Apart from the Christian based texts that I was expecting, he had copies of *The Origin of Species, The Rig Veda, The Koran,* Richard Dawkins' *The God Delusion, Bible Myths and their Parallels in Other Religions, The Prose Edda, A Brief History of Time,* the list went on and on. It seemed that he'd read, or at least owned, every book relating to the Truth that he could find. And I thought Christians had a reputation for being narrow-minded.

I jumped as James opened the door and dropped the thick tome on Pythagoras I'd picked up, remembering the part he'd played in all this. It landed on one precarious stack and I watched in horror as an avalanche slowly begun. Other piles were dislodged as momentum built up and then books were strewn across the entire floor.

James slammed down the tea tray he was carrying and rushed to the rescue of his beloved books. He picked up one casualty and stroked it comfortingly before laying it gently on the table. I could only look on in mortification.

'I'm sorry,' I stammered. 'It was an accident.' *Like I'd kicked them over deliberately.* I knelt down and tried to rebuild the stacks, hoping he hadn't noticed my particularly childish excuse. 'It's quite a collection you have.'

He waved his hand dismissively. 'I've been meaning to put up more shelves for a long time. Leave it, the tea will be cold.'

'You really have an amazing collection,' I tried again when we were seated.

James now smiled with pride, looking at his collection lovingly. 'The result of many years' study. All religions teach the same Truth, I learnt that a long time ago, when travelling in the Middle East. The most eye-opening experience of my life.'

He looked wistful and I wondered if we all remembered the moment when we'd looked up and seen the Gateway to the Spheres.

'There's a twelfth-century Sufi poem, *The Conference of the Birds*, which is an especially great illustration of this Truth. You should make a point of reading it.' He rummaged among a pile of books and pulled out a slim volume. 'You may have this, I have several copies somewhere.'

I took the proffered book with dutiful thanks. I still had Jason's book to finish. 'It seems a recurring theme, that the same archetypes and messages are repeated constantly. Do all religions tell the same message as the myths?' 'Absolutely,' he replied, sipping his tea. 'All religions have one purpose, to guide souls to the Truth, and God. As times, places and cultures change, so the religions must adapt so this message is still understood. Do you know the story of the Pedlar of Swaffham? Or Paulo Coelho's *The Alchemist*?'

I shook my head.

'Well, they actually tell, in a veiled way, this same Truth, the message that evolved to give as much diversity of religion as there is diversity of people. The outer impressions may change, but the underlying body and spirit is ever the same. The same flesh under the clothes of time, place and culture.'

The Sphere of the Sun, I realised. 'All people are equally part of the human race, regardless of race, colour, background or creed, and all the Gods are equally a part of God. Just as a stream, a sea, an icicle, a dew drop and a cloud of steam are all diverse manifestations of water.'

James offered me the plate of scones. 'There's jam, butter and cream in the dishes, if you wish. All fresh from the farm.'

I took a scone and buttered it, and James continued, 'The teachings are there as a guide, they're a means to an end. They're not the end itself, as many people believe. Without the true connection with God in your heart, all you gain is admiration, praise and respect among men, but nothing from God. Do you know Goethe's play *Faust*?'

I did, coincidently. I'd been to see an obscure production of it with Tom, one of his friends had produced it. 'Faust had the same problem as Colin,' I stated.

He smiled thinly. 'The wisdom of the Sphere of the Sun is also its curse.'

I realised with a sudden sick feeling what a fine line I and all of us were walking on The Path.

James put down his cup as if he'd come to a decision. 'There are many of us who remember the old ways, who are at one with the Truth. We're meeting to discuss awakening the Sleeping King. You have an important role in this, that's certain. I believe you should join us, perhaps together we can find a way to restore the world to harmony.'

275

'Where is this meeting?''We're going to Boscawen, a stone circle near St Michael's Mount in Cornwall, where once the *gorsedd*, the great meeting of the Druids, took place.'

I started and the same dizziness came over me. I put the china cup down before I dropped it. I hadn't mentioned my idea that St Michael's Mount was the Heart of the Land, the home of the Grail. I was being drawn along by a force outside my control, sucked in by a whirlpool, but I knew better than to fight it.

The decision made, I looked out of the window at the rolling green pastures of my homeland. Sheep were scattered about, grazing peacefully in the sunshine. 'Animals are always so happy,' I mused. 'I wonder if it's only humans that are cursed with negativity.''We alone know fear and regret. Our greatest blessing, and our greatest curse.' James joined me at the window. 'Regret for the past, fear for the future.'

The strange dizziness made my vision flicker slightly and my thoughts were in strange confusion.

'Paradise – eternal life – an eternal now – no past and no future. That's why it's such bliss. Animals live only in the present, so they're already in paradise. Whereas we've made our world a living hell.'

James agreed. 'There's a lot that we can learn from a simple animal,' he said.

# Chapter 44

*In that old potters shop I stood alone*
*With the clay population round in rows.*
*And suddenly one more impatient cried–*
*Who is the potter pray, and who is the pot?*
Omar Khayyam

I spent the rest of the day finishing Jason's book on astrology. It was really uncanny how the aspects of each planet seemed to mirror exactly what had been happening in my life. In the chapter on Mars, I learnt about magnanimity and treachery. On one side it related to guiding your fellow man, and on the other to selfishness and abandonment. My warning to the two seekers – obviously the final test of this Sphere.

And now I'd reached the Sphere of Jupiter, the King of the Gods. The Sphere where nothing is lacking, where all pieces come together, the stage set for the final act.

I looked up and felt the sun shining on my face. It would have been much easier if I'd known all this from the start, I mused. If I'd trusted my instincts and watched the transit of Venus with Jason, I could have had a clear path to follow instead of struggling through this uncharted, murky water.

But then, of course, I was used to that. That was why the universe made me a scientist, after all.

I remembered something my tutor had said to me when my dissertation project was racked with problems. He once had two students; one's project proceeded flawlessly and he got a top grade. The second had trouble from the word go with problem after problem. Everything that could go wrong, did, and he got a low grade. 'But,' he'd said, 'in their future careers, it was the second student who went the furthest. His problems had given him so much experience and insight, and it paid off. His mistakes had given him the knowledge to never make those mistakes again.'

All roads lead to Rome, as they say. There are no wrong turnings, no wrong paths. This was the way it was meant to be. My Journey had progressed perfectly, no matter the problems – they'd been there for a reason. There was no other way I could have done it.

I turned on the TV as I was packing my rucksack. The almost inevitable news report showed soldiers massing into their bases ready for mobilisation against the enemy, whenever the enemy could be identified. Soldiers waved happily to the cameras, others looked grim faced and important. Reservists were being called up on both sides of the Atlantic and air strikes had been launched against strategic sites in Pakistan and Libya to vehement protest. The only victims were women and children, were the righteous claims. The emerging photos of crude villages destroyed by this supposed justice along with the broken bodies of young children only fanned the flames further.

*And so the world slowly falls apart.*

I hit the off switch, I couldn't bring myself to watch any longer. I needed to find The Grail, and I needed to hurry. The world couldn't wait much longer.

I struggled up to the church with my rucksack, eager to be off. At last I understood everything. Thanks to Jason, I knew all about the Seven Spheres, and I knew what to do and where I had to go. The road was rising to meet me, everything was suddenly so easy. I thought back to that day when I'd first learnt about Pythagoras and his theories, it seemed a lifetime ago. I'd come such a long way since then.

'Morning, James!' I dumped my rucksack down.

'I didn't mention it yesterday,' he said, 'but I'm travelling to Boscawen with another friend of mine, an adept of neuroscience who's studied a lot about the spiritual workings of the mind.' I wondered about the strange terminology – *adept*.

As he spoke, the door opened. 'Speak of the devil, excusing the pun.' He smiled at the woman, who had massive blonde hair. She'd probably been a beehive fan a few years back.

'This is Joanna,' he said. 'I was just talking about you. This is Bridget, who'll be travelling with us. I must speak quickly to the churchwarden, we'll leave in around half an hour?' He looked at us with raised eyebrows and we both nodded agreement.

'Why don't we go for a walk?' suggested Joanna. 'It's a lovely day, and I love walking across the moors.'

'Yes, that's a brilliant idea,' I agreed readily. I'd been dreading a conversation about hairsprays – I'd never been a girly girl. We walked down the hill and followed a footpath across a field and into open moorland.

'So you're an adept of neuroscience, then?' I began, hoping she'd explain.

'Yes, I've done a lot of research into the nature of the human brain and its perception of what we call reality, and how that relates to the spiritual or mystical experience. Because of the subject I prefer 'adept' to 'lecturer'. Do you know much about how the brain works?' 'Not really,' I admitted. But as she said it I realised – of course! This was the missing link, the unifying key for the Sphere of Jupiter! The brain was the home of the mind, the soul, the spirit, what everything I'd discovered hinged upon. I wondered with excitement what she could tell me about the Quest.

'It's a fascinating subject, the brain is the pivot the world revolves around, the reason I chose to read the subject.' Her eyes lit up as she spoke and I silently urged her on. 'Did you know that what we perceive is actually a very limited snapshot of the world? We filter out the vast majority of what we see, hear and sense, allowing just ten per cent of it to reach our conscious mind. The rest we are unaware of, except when the small quiet voice of the subconscious is heard over all the chatter. This is where our gut feelings arise from.'

Joanna turned to look at me and smiled knowingly as I looked across the landscape, drinking in every detail. I could see everything, I thought, I was aware of a lot more than ten per cent of it.

'Have you ever recognised someone's face when you've no idea who they are? Have you ever walked into a room, noticed something has changed, but can't put your finger on what? How do you know that, when it's quite obvious you don't know it?!'

Of course I'd been there, but I'd never thought of it like that before. I laughed and waited for her to continue.

'And this explains the god factor. For example, a man walks through a wood each day when the birds are singing. He never listens to the birdsong, isn't aware that the birds are even there, but his subconscious hears, and remembers. Then one day they're not singing. He doesn't notice – he'd never heard them anyway. But the subconscious does, it warns him with an uneasy feeling that something is wrong. He doesn't know what – the voice of the subconscious is too quiet. But nevertheless, as he is prudent, he proceeds with caution.' Joanna paused while we climbed over a stile, jumping down onto the soft muddy ground.

'Go on,' I urged, when we were walking on. She stooped to admire a little white flower, lifting its face towards her, and I began to feel annoyed.

'A large predatory animal, a lion maybe, was laired in the bushes,' she eventually continued, 'and it frightened the birds into silence. The man's extra caution pays off – he sees the lion before he blunders into its jaws, makes good his escape.'

Joanna stopped in the path to deliver her punchline. 'He then thanks whatever gods he believes in for warning him and saving his life. But in fact, the only god he need thank is himself. This leads us to the key question; do you believe in the gods because they are real, or are they real only because you believe in them?''I don't know.' I couldn't think of anything else to say. My previous happy bubble had just been shattered, I felt lost. In a few words she'd called in to doubt everything I'd learnt so far. The gods weren't real, after all. Perhaps nothing was. This wasn't at all the conversation I'd been expecting at all. I looked away towards the horizon, trying to distance myself from the unwanted challenge to my theories.

'Because you now believe in the gods, you notice their perceived influence in your life,' she continued, and I tried not to hear what she was saying. 'They become more real, you create a mental image of them. Then you begin to see them in dreams, visions, trances, real life, and this proves to you their reality. But, the million dollar question, do they really exist outside your mind? Are they anything but the voice of the subconscious striving to be heard?''I don't know,' I said again. I felt quite unhappy. Joanna had reawakened my doubts, the thought that my whole Quest had been imagination. I *was* mad, I'd thrown my whole life away for nothing.

'The gods, angels, whoever people believe to guide them, they appear in times of need, that's a fact,' Joanna said. 'This projection of the subconscious gives you confidence, faith and strength. The same goes for death-bed visions of a parent, Jesus, whoever.'

Just as I'd seen Mary, Robin Hood, Elen. And I thought they'd been real. I shook my head as I descended into a deep black hole. 'I can't believe that. Doesn't this take away the mystery and meaning of life, reducing the gods and our spiritual existence to nothing but imagination and fantasy?' I asked desperately. I suddenly realised how much I'd changed, now my newly gained beliefs and world-view were once again being challenged.

'Not at all,' she reassured me. 'You're seeing it the wrong way. The Mind is the greatest God of all, it's a reflection of the divine consciousness. We're not denying God – on the contrary, science supports and complements the divine. The great sage Hermes Trismegistus told us to use science to understand the universe and to understand God. Scientists are more likely than anyone to appreciate the true perfection of the universe in the form of crystal structures, cellular arrangements, far distant star nurseries, the perfect harmony of co-existing life.'

Joanna stopped and indicated a dandelion on the path, its bright yellow face shining upwards towards us. A bee landed clumsily on it – at least one still survived, then – and I smiled. A tiny, beautiful, miracle of nature.

'Everyone wonders at nature, for example how plants manage to turn and face the sun. Then this non-specific thought is forgotten as one of life's mysteries. But science has found that plants contain a growth hormone called auxin. Auxin is inactivated by sunlight, so the side of the plant facing the sun grows slower than the dark side. Therefore this uneven balance causes the plant to form a bend.''Towards the sun!' I finished. A light began to shine in the blackness of my mind as I forced the problem of reality into the background.

'Exactly. Nature designed a perfect solution to the problem, but we only appreciate the intricacy of this through science. Scientists believe in exactly the same marvel as the mystics, but simply know it by another name.'

All religions teach the same Truth, James had said. Science was just another modern religion. 'The purpose of life is to learn, and understand,' I said. 'Through understanding what we see, we understand who we are, and what we are.'

The lesson of the Sphere of Jupiter, I thought.

# Chapter 45

*All those who come before my splendour see*
*Themselves, their own unique reality.*
*How much you thought you knew*
*And saw; but you now know that all you trusted was untrue.*
Farid ud-Din Attar

Joanna stopped suddenly. 'Shut your eyes', she ordered. After a second's hesitation I did so. *Now what?* I was expecting some bizarre mind trick and waited for her to do something.

'Describe the path we've been walking on for the last half hour. The details – the plants, trees, birds.'

I could hear the amusement in her voice and felt quite rattled, but thought carefully. I hadn't really been paying attention, just looking at the scenery in general, so I had no idea really. 'Dandelions,' I said lamely. 'Daisy, willowherb, daffodil.' Gradually my mind gathered momentum. 'Oak.' I remembered crunching over acorns. 'I remember a blackbird, and some goldfinches.' I ran out of ideas.

'Now open your eyes.' She was even more amused now.

I looked round and then laughed in disbelief – it was nothing like my mental image. Immediately I recalled ash, blackthorn, bramble, dog rose, a flock of geese, a pigeon in a tree, I couldn't believe I'd forgotten them.

'What you think you see is often just what your brain thinks should be there. This picture is based on belief, past experience, but not necessarily reality. I said you see ten per cent of what's there, I should think, in your case, it's actually a lot less than that.' Joanna looked at me scathingly. 'When did you ever see daffodils in autumn?'

I laughed with embarrassment and Joanna offered me a packet of mints.

'So, we see what's not there, do we also have a habit of not seeing what *is* there?' I asked, half joking.

'Of course,' she replied, as if I was stating the most obvious thing in the world. 'You airbrush things out all the time, when your brain just assumes they're not there – 'you can't see for looking'. How often do you feel a right idiot for missing the blatantly obvious?'

At that moment a pheasant exploded into the air from just under my foot. I yelped in shock and lost my balance, landing heavily on the ground.

Joanna offered her hand to pull me upright. 'Of course, the camouflage of nature is an entirely different matter,' she observed as I dusted myself off.

We turned back towards the church. The hill burst out of the landscape, the church gleaming in the sun. I could see the shadow-pattern of light and dark racing across the wilderness as the clouds scudded across the sky, and stopped to take in the incredible panorama.

'Make the most of it, it won't be here long.' Joanna sounded bitter. 'They're building a nuclear dump, somewhere to store radioactive waste. It'll be concrete and razor wire instead, then.' 'But why here?' I was gob-smacked. 'They can't!' 'It's out of the way, you can't have ugly things near people. Better to spoil the wilderness instead.' She thrust her hands into her pockets.

It was easy to hate mankind, I thought. Very easy.

We walked in silence for a moment and my mind was dragged back to the depressing problem Joanna had thrust on me. The gods I'd seen weren't real, my mind had imagined them. It had imagined the whole Quest. I'd seen them because I wanted to see them, and everything I didn't want to see, I simply didn't. I'd been like that my whole life, I saw bitterly, I was making the world up as I went along. And now I was on a wild goose chase to the loony bin.

'So everyone sees the world the way they want to see it, not how it really is,' I concluded miserably. This was turning into a nightmare. 'What actually is real?' The question was directed more to myself than Joanna.

'But how do you define real?' challenged Joanna. 'Reality is just what the majority believe.'

'But some things are definitely real, aren't they?' I looked towards the church on the hill. That was real, even if everything it represented wasn't, which was what Joanna seemed to be saying.

'Everything you perceive, now, at this moment, you believe is real, yes?' she said.

Of course it was.

'But when you're dreaming, you again think that's real, unless of course you're lucid dreaming. But the moment you wake up you realise it was *not* real. How do you know you're not dreaming at this very moment? That all your life until this moment was a dream, and reality is something very entirely different?'

I'd been led into a trap, and the feeling of doubt returned with a vengeance. The comforting light of the sun had vanished behind some clouds. Was anything really real? I just didn't know any more.

# Chapter 46

*Can something as impermanent and transitory as earthly existence be anything other than an illusion? How can something be real which never stays the same?*
The Hermetica

'Did you have an interesting and enlightening walk?' James was standing with his arms folded next to his car, the door already open. 'You were gone a very long time, I've been trying to ring you, Joanna. We really needed to get off to a good start.' He looked at us with annoyance.

'Joanna was telling me about her work,' I replied. 'How the mind invents the world it sees, interprets it the way it wants, and how probably nothing is based in reality.' I looked at him, waiting for him to refute this idea and tell me my beliefs were right.

'And you find this hard to grasp? But it's been known all along, by those who could understand.' James sounded dismissive as he yanked open the boot and threw in a small holdall. 'Look, put your rucksack in here, it'll just about fit,' he said. 'If we're all ready, we really need to go, now.'

I quickly squashed my rucksack into the boot as Joanna got into the passenger seat. It felt like hours had passed since I'd dropped it down, full of confidence and faith. I opened the rear door, feeling much worse for James' casual agreement with Joanna's bleak theory, and James jumped behind the wheel and slammed the door. He crunched the gears and we were off, down the steep hill and on our way to our destiny.

'It'll take several hours to get there, we really can't be late,' James said to justify our abrupt departure. He checked the clock for the umpteenth time but his natural relaxed demeanour was quickly returning.

'What's actually happening at Boscawen?' My questions had been left maddeningly unanswered every time I'd asked before.

James smiled slightly and Joanna also stirred in her seat. Neither spoke and I felt quite annoyed. Was their disciple not fit to understand? But after the last half hour, I agreed I probably wasn't.

At last James began to answer. 'There's a ritual taking place, the timing's crucial. But I can't really say any more than that.''Can't say, or won't say?' I couldn't help myself.

James just smiled at me in the mirror like he was pacifying a child as he took a sharp bend at speed. 'Everyone sees the world in their own way, what happens to you may be entirely different to anyone else, it's impossible to say. But whatever happens, you can take it in your stride.' *Reality again.* He glanced at the clock and pushed his foot to the floor a bit harder. The engine whined in protest. 'But we've a long way to go yet.'

We travelled a few miles before James broke the silence. 'Well, back to reality. As we were saying, everything in the world you collate into a grand picture, centred on your perceptions.' He seemed happier and more expansive now we were well on our way, although he was still looking at the clock every few minutes. 'If you're not aware of anything – through sleep or coma – then for you the world no longer exists. But, your mind is limited by time and place, you're aware of only a small fraction of the universe.' He waved his hand at the landscape in illustration.

'Imagine your mind is free to travel to the far reaches of the universe, into the smallest atoms, to the past, the future, without limit. It can experience all things and all times as one interconnected image.'

I looked out of the window at the expanse of moor, imagining my view stretching across the world, across the universe, into the past, the future. Lives, cultures and worlds rose and fell.

'This is what it's like to be the Mind of God,' he said when he judged my vision to be complete. 'The One which unites the All, the fundamental unity between all that exists. The reality.''Like in the Hermetic texts!' said Joanna. 'Everything we've learnt about reality was actually known millennia ago, we just didn't realise it!' She produced a nail file and began to carefully rasp away.

I looked out of the window. The gorse bushes and stunted trees which lined the road flashed past in a blur, we were going too fast to truly grasp a clear picture. This was exactly how I was feeling right now. I chewed my thumbnail distractedly. I'd never got round to reading *The Hermetica*, and now there were so many things filling my mind, how could an ancient sage possibly understand the universe better than we did today?

'It's not such a leap to accept this.' James appeared to be reading my mind. 'The truly enlightened mind, free from the trappings of its physical body, can become One with the cosmic mind, and then the answers to everything are laid out in front of you.''Carl Jung's collective unconscious', stated Joanna, who having finished her nail, opened a bottle of purple nail varnish and balanced it on the dash board. As James rocketed round a bend, it tipped dangerously and I flinched, but luckily it remained upright. I wondered if he drove like a maniac all the time.

'Science may have taken a vastly different path to the mystics, but it has arrived at exactly the same place,' he said quietly.

As if in answer to this profound conclusion, the sun burst out from the dark clouds, illuminating a forest of wind turbines away to our front. They flashed rhythmically in the sun as they turned, the work of God combining with the work of Man.

I heard a low rumble in the distance, rapidly growing louder, then with an ear-splitting roar a dozen or so fighter jets blasted directly over us. We watched them rapidly disappear, their intrusion into that perfect vision reminding us exactly what we were playing for.

'There's an Air Force base not far away, they've just come back from a tour of Afghanistan,' said Joanna. 'Now they're getting ready for the next.' There was a slight tremble in her voice and James squeezed her arm. My unspoken question echoed round the car.

'Barry, my son, he flies one of those planes.' Joanna looked after them wistfully. 'He's only twenty-two.'

The end-times were close to everyone's hearts, everywhere. We travelled in silence for a while and I wondered about the end-times and the negativity seeping into the collective unconscious.

'Often, when I pray, I hear the answers I need, deep profound insights which I know haven't come from my own mind.' James looked at me in the mirror and noticed my unguarded expression of recognition. *A cosmic message from the universal mind.*

'You experience the same,' he stated.

'Sometimes, yes,' I said slowly. 'I see visions, hear whispered words which have an important meaning, or no meaning at all. I have strange feelings, I say things which seem to come from outside myself. It's hard to explain really.'

I saw James' eyebrows lift slightly, and Joanna also shifted in her seat. They were both surprised, and I felt a bit uncomfortable. What were they expecting me to say?

There was silence for a moment, and then James began to speak. 'I've put a lot of time into thinking about these insights. They're also known as the Akashic records. And, I believe, instinct.'

I brightened, now back on familiar ground. 'A new born animal immediately knows to find its mother's teat and suck. Fledgling birds fly to their wintering grounds thousands of miles away, navigating precisely to the right area at the right time. Eels swim to the Sargasso Sea to breed. And animals and birds seem to sense earthquakes and tsunamis long before people are aware of them.'

James and Joanna seemed quite impressed at my knowledge. 'There was a programme on the Discovery Channel the other week,' I explained sheepishly.

James laughed heartily, slapping the steering wheel, and Joanna smiled as well, looking round from her nails.

'Well, it shows you were paying attention! And as you have very aptly summarised, the voice of instinct is very obvious in all forms of life. How can this be possible, unless a quiet voice is whispering in their ear? This alone shows that all life, not just man, is intimately connected with the universal mind.' James glanced in the mirror at me, looking very serious, and I braced myself for a particularly profound revelation.

'Pass the biscuits out of that basket, Bridget, I'm getting peckish. We really haven't time to stop.'

A little disappointed, I rummaged under the tea towel next to me, amongst Tupperware boxes of sandwiches, fresh fruit and sliced tea cake, and pulled out a packet of digestive biscuits. I took one and passed the packet to Joanna.

'Oh, only plain ones? I was hoping for something more inter-esting,' complained James, but he took two anyway, steering one-handed. 'It's easy to explain how all information is stored, just how this cosmic database can exist,' he continued. 'It's in the form of light.'

He paused for a moment, to let this sink in. 'All sight comes from photons of light, travelling at infinite speed through space. What you see has a time delay on it, the time taken for the light to travel from the object to your eyes. On earth it's so small it's all but non-existent, but on the scale of the universe, it's greatly important.'

James slowed to let a dozen sheep wander across the road in front of us, tutting in impatience. They showed no reaction to the revving engine. 'It takes eight minutes to get from the sun to the earth, so you see the sun how it was eight minutes ago. For a star fifty light-years away, you see it as it was fifty years ago. For intelligent beings on that star's planets, this sight is a distant memory, the star may not even exist now.' 'Now we have telescopes picking up stuff from billions of light-years away,' I added. 'Time-wise, from near the Big Bang.' I remembered seeing a report on it some months back.

'That's right, Bridget, the universe holds records from the beginning of time, if only we could see them. And going back to those intelligent aliens, if we had a powerful enough telescope we could watch their every move. And we would be aware of the bigger picture, all the things they missed – where they lost their keys, who killed their president, everything.'

'And the opposite is true,' I said. 'Aliens could answer our undying questions – JFK, Elvis, Atlantis, whether I left my purse on the bus.' I looked up at the clear blue sky. Was something watching us at this very moment?

'The universe is aware of everything – every thought, every action, every deed, it can see into our very souls.' James smiled, about to deliver his master-stroke. 'Just like the universal concept of God.'

God. The final concept to be explained. The overriding principle of the Sphere of Jupiter.

But it didn't seem to quite add up. 'All these photons are light-years away, it's only those distant aliens who'll know the answers to our profound mysteries! How could we ever access them to learn anything?'

James chuckled and smiled at me indulgently. I felt like he was waiting for his star pupil to pose the obvious question. 'Have another biscuit, dear.' He offered the packet over his shoulder and I took one, reluctantly and impatiently. He glanced at the clock again – we'd been travelling for nearly two hours. And it felt like it too.

'Again, modern science has found the answer. Are you aware of the concept of entanglement?'

I was not.

'Einstein called it spooky action at a distance. It's the concept that photons, or any other particle for that matter, have an unbreakable bond between them, or entanglement. Anything affecting one will affect the other, instantaneously. It's been suggested by some eminent physicists that every particle in existence is entangled with all others – everything links with everything else, and anything affecting one, affects all.'

I remembered the ripples spreading out through that pool of water and the insight that came from it. Another message from the cosmic mind. Had that flash of insight into *entanglement* come to me through entanglement itself? That was just too weird.

'So we could instantly connect with the far-distant photons,' I said slowly. 'See the history of all things and all places, what's happening elsewhere on earth, what others are doing, thinking, feeling.' More and more pieces began to click into place. 'We could sense the history of objects, their past owners and past functions. We could know of approaching danger beyond our visual perception. We could predict future events. See the ghosts of times past.''A perfect description of everything associated with parapsychology and the so-called pseudo-sciences!' responded Joanna.

'But it's just weird, hard to grasp,' I said, distractedly crumbling a biscuit in my fingers. 'In the physical world of atoms and molecules, how can they have bonds bridging most of the universe? It doesn't seem to fit with our understanding of reality.''But like I was saying,' said Joanna, 'how do we define what's real? Is real actually real?''The physical world is just an illusion,' said James. 'All matter on a fundamental level is just small pockets of energy, attracting and repelling other pockets to form the myriad illusions which we call solid objects. Solid matter doesn't actually exist.'

I just couldn't take in any more at the moment. Everything I knew when I left Brentor had been turned upside down. I now knew absolutely nothing about anything. I leant my head on my hand and stared out of the window at the world rushing past.

'But this illusion does arise from an underlying permanent

reality.' James smiled reassuringly. *Oh good, that's nice to know.*

'We see only the shadows, but they're produced from a permanent reality behind the scenes, the eternal and unchangeable laws of science which govern everything from the largest galaxy to the smallest atom.'

The final biscuit was gone and James tapped a rhythm on the steering wheel, driving at a more controlled speed. 'Have you noticed how, in nature, all things repeat themselves in fixed patterns, varying only in scale? If you look closely at a twig, you see its bark, nodules, smaller branching twigs. It's identical to a main bough from a distance. The same fractal structure on different scales. Or look at a river, made up of smaller tributaries, a rocky outcrop formed of smaller rocks. The same rules govern the formation of atoms that govern the formation of galaxies.'

James looked at me in the rear-view mirror, and smiled enigmatically. I had the feeling he was saying something hugely important, but I just could not follow what.

# Chapter 47

*The building blocks that the universe is put together from are more delicate, more startling, and more fugitive than we can catch with the butterfly net of our senses.*

Jacob Bronowski

'Four wise men were blindfolded by the king, who wanted to see how wise they really were. He told them to identify what was in the room with them. The first stepped forward confidently, felt the object, and said, 'It's a pillar, it's hard, solid and round.'

'The second stepped forward and said, 'No, it's a winnowing fan, I can feel how it flaps though the air.'

'The third stepped forward and said, 'No, you're both wrong. It's a plough share, it's long, curved, pointed, just right for rooting through the soil.'

'The fourth came to his turn and said, 'You're all wrong. It's a rope, feel how it whisks through the air, it's pliable, hairy, and flexible.'

'After much argument without reaching a consensus, the king ordered the men to remove their blindfolds. They found, to their shock, an elephant.'

Joanna laughed and I racked my brains trying to remember where I'd heard it before.

'This story was told by the Buddha,' James continued.

Of course! I remembered it from a seminar on the virtues of co-operation between different scientific disciplines.

'It demonstrates how, although what you see, feel or sense may be correct in itself, it's not necessarily the totality of the truth.'

My mind was whirling, I couldn't take any more. I couldn't understand why James had recited this story, although he obviously thought it important. I rubbed at my face in frustration, I could feel a headache building up. I felt suddenly desperate for some exercise, I hadn't been running for ages.

We reached the top of a hill and the whole vastness of the moor was displayed in front of us, stretching far into the distance. A network of light and shadow raced across the landscape and in the distance another forest of wind turbines lent an eerie sound to the scene. I looked with longing at the expanse, wishing I could be out there.

Yet another sheep ran across the road in front of us and James swerved to the side of the road to avoid hitting it, cursing under his breath. The car travelled over the rough stones and debris for a few metres before regaining the tarmac while the sheep looked at us with disinterest.

'They always seem to get in the way, don't they,' commented Joanna. 'Stupid things.'

James shook his head, glancing at the clock again. We'd travelled only a few hundred metres before the car began to pull to one side, the movement noticeably rougher. James pulled over, already knowing the problem. I was shocked to hear him swear under his breath – I didn't think a vicar would know such words.

'Must have been a nail in that stony stuff.' He leapt out of the car and round to the boot. Joanna and I got out and surveyed the sagging tyre, the hiss of air very audible, as the bags were dumped on the road. James rummaged for the spare wheel and the jack then looked up and noticed us watching him awkwardly.

'We've got a few minutes before I'll be done, we've made quite good time so far, there's less than an hour to go. Why don't you stretch your legs for a minute? Our stop may be fortuitous.' 'Tell that to the stupid dammed sheep,' sneered Joanna. 'It'll do it all over again.'

The breeze lapped round my face and clothes, enticing me out across the moor. 'Yes, I'll do that,' I said gratefully. I turned and quickly walked along a narrow trail before Joanna had a chance to join me. I just wanted to be alone with my whirling thoughts for a while.

With my arms wrapped tightly against the wind and the world, I thought about everything I'd learnt, read and heard lately. The journey to Cornwall was proving very arduous. The trial of the Sphere of Jupiter, the King of Planets, to reconcile all opposites and form the ultimate unified answer – of science and Gods, real and imagined, material and spiritual, it was the hardest trial of all.

I thought about the concepts of the spiritual universe, oneness, entanglement, the equally divine nature of all things, how science, religion and mysticism all seemed to be pointing to one answer, but I could not see what that answer was.

Every time I thought I understood, I formulated an idea of the order of existence, another level of complexity opened up showing that I'd barely yet scratched the surface. I had a huge way still to go.

I remembered a poster which had been on the wall of the Faculty, with a quote from Isaac Newton. I'd walked past it every day for a year, and it seemed to sum up exactly what I was going through. I recited the familiar words to myself once again.

*I seem to have been like a boy playing on the seashore,*
*diverting myself with a smoother pebble or prettier shell than*
*ordinary,*
*whilst the Great Ocean of Truth lay undiscovered before me.*

I knew just how he felt, and his was a much greater mind than mine would ever be.

The sun, fresh air and movement helped to clear my mind and I began to think clearly and logically. I thought about the story of the four wise men, and saw what James had wanted me to realise. The mistake of both science and religion is that they each hold a part of the puzzle, but believe they hold the totality, like each of the wise men. Both sides have taken opposite approaches to reach the same goal – the understanding of the nature of the universe.

I thought about the eternal conflict between science and religion, traditionally mortal enemies when in fact they complemented each other, offering a different means to the same end. I hadn't realised how much science seemed to prove the ancient mystical views, rather than destroying them as many people – including me – assumed. As Joanna had said, the traditional way to God is through science.

I reached an ancient dry stone wall, an age-old boundary built by a long ago farmer. I leant on it and looked out at the beautiful view. The wind whipped hungrily at my hair, I could taste the salty tang of the ocean, distant as it was. Air, the most insubstantial form of all, it held a tremendous power.

I realised that science and religion have progressed as far as they can, and only when the two unite, accepting and encompassing all areas of the traditionally unexplained – parapsychology, psychometry and the rest – will we ever understand the true nature of existence.

The first two Spheres, the Moon and Mercury, represented intuition and knowledge respectively. That must be why.

As I looked across the full glory of the miracle of creation, I wondered if we would ever understand everything, or even anything. It's said that physics aimed to form an exact picture of the material world, but it actually proved that this aim is unattainable. The scientists themselves say that the universe is too complex for anyone, even them, to ever understand. Were we just blind men groping around in the dark, with no hope of ever finding our way from the maze? I was thinking this more and more, that the main aim of humanity – understanding – was just a will-o-the-wisp, a fleeting shade, unreachable and unattainable.

I reviewed all I'd learnt as I rested my face on my arms and gazed, unseeing, across the landscape. Quantum mechanics has shown that, far from following the rules of physics as we know them, particles act according to their own rules. They can exist in two places at once, or two opposite states at once. Apart from the four dimensions that we know – width, height, depth, and time – the universe may have as many as eleven more dimensions. As we can have no concept of what we can't perceive, explaining their nature is rather like describing colour to a blind man or sound to a deaf man.

Every idea has been by necessity simplified to a level which we can understand, but paradoxically, it becomes too simple to be correct.

But one definite conclusion has been reached, I thought, as the wind caressed my skin. Science has emphatically proven that from the largest stellar object to the smallest subatomic particle, existence is the most wondrous, most magical, and most beautiful thing that can be imagined.

And, I mused, looking across the most beautiful snapshot of this existence, this is exactly the conclusion that religion has developed over millennia, naming this wondrous phenomenon as...

God.

# Chapter 48

*Every form, no matter how crude, contains an image of its creator concealed within it.*
Helena Blavatsky


As I continued to contemplate, leaving at last my stone wall and walking on further, I remembered what James had said about fractals. I'd reached a small stream and, probably for the first time in my life, I looked at it closely. I could see that the main stream was fed by three other smaller ones, and each was indeed a scale image of the other. I looked further down the hill and saw where the stream had enlarged, merging with yet others to form an even bigger version of itself.

I crouched down close to it and could almost imagine that I was looking at a huge Amazonian river, stretching right across my field of vision, pouring over the huge boulders in its bed. A tree trunk was swept downstream, torn from its roots by the ferocious cascade. The pounding tumult in my ears was deafening.

As I sat back on my heels the boulders reverted to small pebbles, the tree trunk to a twig, and the tiny stream was once again babbling down the hillside.

I was reminded of the Mandelbrot Set, the most famous example of a fractal image, my high school maths teacher had been forever talking about it. I began to see that this strangely humanoid image seemed to resemble the secrets of the universe in ways that not even its creator, Benoit Mandelbrot, had imagined.

Or maybe it was just another example of a human mind accessing information in the vast cosmic mind, and creating an image representing it... my mind was boggling.

I walked onwards across the moor, deep in thought, and as I rounded a slight rise I heard a sudden rush of movement. I'd surprised a small flock of sheep which ran off across the moor, twenty or so leaping down a steep slope to lower ground. Then I saw one had been left behind. It was standing looking at me from a few metres away, seemingly unafraid. I looked back at it, and then walked up to it, wondering if it was ill or something – I couldn't see any reason why it would have stayed behind. It walked away from me as I got closer, but then stopped and turned back to me again. I was quite puzzled, it seemed as if it wanted something.

Then I realised what the problem was. I saw another sheep, caught in a patch of brambles and stuck fast. It was well hidden, wouldn't have been seen by anyone unless they were exactly where I was. If the other hadn't stayed there with it and alerted me to its presence, it could probably have died from lack of food or water.

I went up to it quietly. It struggled ineffectually for a moment then stood still, looking up at me helplessly. I could see its flanks heaving as it panted desperately. I tried to pull the brambles from it but they were stuck well into its wool, there was no way they were coming out. I winced as a strand of thorns raked across my hand and drops of blood welled up. I wondered what to do – I couldn't just leave the poor thing there. I looked back in the direction of the car then remembered I had a penknife in my pocket. I managed to slowly cut through the main stems, wrapping my sleeve round my hand to stop more thorns sinking in and eventually I'd cut through most of them. Sensing freedom, the sheep began to struggle again. A moment later it pulled itself free and struggled away, pieces of bramble trailing behind it.

I watched as it went away, pulling a thorn from my thumb with my teeth. It went up to its friend and they rubbed their noses together. *Thank you.* Then it went to a small pool of water and drank deeply. I wondered with a pang how long the poor thing had been trapped there. Then with one last look at me they were both running towards the rest of the flock.

For a long time afterwards, I didn't move. This seeming act of compassion by the first sheep, it was amazing, incredible. It so clearly demonstrated all I'd been thinking about. Do animals really have such attributes, traditionally considered as human only? This simple act clearly brought home that they did.

The Truth suddenly dawned on me. I realised the true nature of oneness, that all things are equally a part of the whole. In a sudden intense vision, where my mind freed entirely from my body, I saw how every individual thing is a complete image of God, the Universe, combining with others to form an identical image, which combined with others in turn, expanding onwards into infinity.

I saw how each thing contains a spark, a part of the divine spirit and the entirety of the divine spirit. I watched as a vast sun exploded into an infinite number of fragments, from which an infinite number of new suns were born. These souls, these new suns, contained the entirety of the essence of the original. I saw how everything, *everything*, is entirely One with the divine, with God.

From a simple act of compassion from one animal, I had found the final piece of the puzzle. I had learnt the lesson of the Sphere of Jupiter.

# PART X

# Chapter 49

*The dust returns to the ground it came from, and the spirit returns to God who gave it.*
Ecclesiastes 12.7

I am one among countless others, invisible, inseparable, but still individual. I was once a part of a whole, a solid rock of eternal existence, until gradually I was split off from my whole to become a small speck in the infinity of the universe.

I am on a constant ever-moving journey, being washed, buffeted and pushed as the sun and stars wheel overhead. I am moved by the immense oceanic force which takes me to new locations, forward and back, forward and back, until I am left to rest for a time, and then the cycle begins again.

I am not alone, I am a part of an infinite number of others, all of whom dance to the same rhythm. Together we form a complex diverse structure of being, although individually we are nothing.

Many come to us to wonder and to marvel. They stand, watch, contemplate, try to understand, but always they leave empty-handed.

I remember one man, he visited every day, standing searching on the shore of the great ocean. He found stones, shells, pretty pebbles, but he too eventually left empty-handed. I could have told him the answers, if only he had understood my words.

I continue this cycle for an endless time until gradually I begin to coalesce, unite with the immense whole from which I once came. I become fixed, immobile, solid and eternal, as I once was. I was one, and I am still one, but now I am One formed from countless others, a transcendent One which encompasses and includes all other ones.

# PART XI

# Chapter 50

*It's the end of the world as we know it.*
REM

Brigid shook her head in shock, her hand over her mouth as the messenger's news was relayed to the rath. A ripple of hushed voices swept through many of the Druids, but the older ones remained stony faced and impassive. It was unprecedented, unbelievable, even in the face of recent events.

The rath in the next realm had been destroyed, the messenger had said. The women carried off by soldiers, the men slaughtered, every building razed. This unthinkable act of sacrilege no one had ever considered, even in the darkest days of the war.

Brigid looked up at the sky in dazed shock, absently noting the flight of a far up hawk. Everyone, no matter how base or criminal, respected the sanctity of the Druids. *Everyone.* Without their sacred Law, the country would be nothing, a barbaric wasteland with no respect for man nor God. For the first time she realised the true importance of the task she had been given. Entire villages had been obliterated, their inhabitants massacred, outlaws and exiles were ranging with impunity, but she'd never, ever, considered this, even her darkest moments. Suddenly, she felt quite sick.

She looked round at the silent huddle of refugees who'd flocked to the rath in desperation, hollow eyed, hungry and ragged. What would become of them if their only hope of sanctuary was violated? The answer did not bear thinking about.

This must be kept from them, she thought desperately, hope was the only thing they had left. But already she could see it was too late. It was passing through the huddle, the change in their faces said it all.

Brigid felt exhausted. The constant stream of refugees from the countryside, all with their own bitter stories to tell, kept her and all the Druids stretched to their mental and physical limits. Many were sick, wounded and malnourished, a lot of them children – the rampaging warriors made no distinction between man, woman or child. Food was running short, the few crops planted were untended, and even with the Druids' vast repertoire of edible plants and fungi many people went to bed hungry.

She forced herself to look calm and unruffled. She knew people would be looking at her to gauge her reaction – if she panicked, so would they. With a huge effort, she walked calmly back to the building of the sick, smiling at those she passed. Despairing would get her nowhere, and the sick ever needed tending.

A young woman looked up frantically as she entered, her face filled with utter relief. She rushed over to Brigid. 'A young girl has arrived, alone. She's very sick, in her soul as well as her body, I don't know what to do. Please help!' Gwen, a healing woman who looked much younger than her eighteen winters, gestured frantically towards a wooden bench.

'I will look at her,' Brigid said, rubbing her sore eyes. Gwen slumped and her eyes filled with tears, she felt such relief that someone had taken over. She'd really been thrown in at the deep end these past few weeks.

Brigid pressed her hand to Gwen's back in comfort. 'You're doing well. You'll come to be an excellent healer some day.'

Gwen smiled through her tears, then laughed a little. Brigid remembered how proud she herself had been when Emer said almost those exact words to her during her training.

She went over to look at the child. She was sitting blankly, rocking back and forth, locked inside the nightmare in her mind. She could be no more than six winters, covered in mud and scratches, and with a deep festering cut to her arm. Her long blonde hair was hopelessly tangled and full of leaves and dirt. Brigid felt with a pang of sadness that she looked just like her younger sister Bethan, who'd been about her age when she'd last seen her.

She thought with a sudden dread about her own family – whether they were safe, whether they even lived. No word had reached the Cernyw rath from the far north for many moons – what messengers set out never reached their destination now.

She would do her best for this child, she resolved. She was someone's sister, someone's daughter, and maybe someone would do the same for her own family.

She washed her festering wound, applying a poultice of woundwort, rosemary and betony, just as Emer had taught her long ago. Then she crouched by the child's side and forced her to look at her.

'My name's Brigid, what's your name?' The child just stared blankly into space, unseeing and unhearing.

Brigid got a small piece of honeycomb, a great treat, and held it out to her. When she got no reaction, she forced it inside her lips. The sweet, sugary taste provoked a reflex in the child and she began to suck and chew her treat. When she'd swallowed it she looked around, more alert to her surroundings than before.

'What's your name?' Brigid repeated.

The girl looked at her despairingly. 'Deirdre,' she whispered.

'Are you hungry? When did you last have food?' There was silence. When Brigid was about to speak again, the reply came.

'When the soldiers came.'

'Where are your family?' she asked gently.

'The soldiers killed them all. They are all dead.'

The simple, weary and resigned reply from so small a child, stripped forever of all innocence, was simply heartbreaking and Brigid struggled to control her surging emotions.

Brigid put a comforting arm around the girl and was immediately filled with an intense vision. She saw men running, swords drawn, slicing and hacking indiscriminately at the people around them. Men, women and children ran in terror, cut down as they fled. A terrible, agonising screaming tore the air. One man, braver

than most, ran at two soldiers brandishing a pitchfork. He was
cut down before he could even raise it, a sword blow through his
neck nearly severing his head. Blood spurted through the air.

Smoke stung her nostrils – the wooden buildings were alight,
and flames tore through the tinder-dry thatch like wildfire. Yet
more screams came from inside the blazing inferno.

Brigid saw Deirdre standing in the entrance of a hut, too
frightened and bewildered to move. A woman with the same
long blonde hair snatched her arm violently.

'Run!' she screamed. 'Get away! To the woods and hide!' She
began to run, dragging the child behind her, but within twenty
paces a sword came from nowhere and hacked through her body,
then cutting deeply into the child's arm. Blood spattered across
Deirdre's face from her mother's dying heartbeats as she looked
down in bemused shock. With her last vestiges of strength, the
woman raised herself up. 'Run!' the almost inaudible plea came.

Deirdre turned and ran, faster than she'd ever run before,
leaving the shouting, the screaming, the roaring flames far
behind her. Soon she was in the depths of the woods, lost, alone
and frightened, only the desperate need to escape from that
infernal scene driving her on, until days later she stumbled into
the rath and safety.

Brigid was shaking as the vision ended, but she still held
tightly to the girl. Deirdre had relaxed and was starting to drift
into sleep, her nightmare exorcised from her mind. Brigid sat
there until the girl was breathing deeply and calmly, and then
covered her with a warm blanket so she could sleep in peace. She
gazed down at her for a long time, hoping against hope that her
own family was safe.

'The realm is fracturing, chaos reigns. Father fights against son,
brother against brother. That this would happen was written in
the stars, but it is playing out much worse than I feared.' Bran,
the oldest Druid in the rath, sat stiffly in the dimly lit building,

seemingly unaware of the cold air seeping through the walls.

Brigid listened attentively, tucking her skirts underneath her against the damp floor. She was meeting with the greatly venerated Druid for the first time – he spent much of his time in isolation and meditation, preparing for the last great test of his long life. He, if anyone, would be able to offer her guidance. Time was running out and the latest atrocity had spurred her to at last seek him out.

Although she didn't know it, he'd been waiting for her approach ever since she'd arrived in Cernyw – he knew much more about her destiny than she did. He knew she would come to him when the time was right, and so he waited patiently. The future would work out the way it was meant to, and no amount of worrying or impatience would change it.

'People are losing their connection with the Spirit of the Land, this is what's spawned this bloodshed. All life lives from this Spirit and the gifts it freely gives us.' Bran paused as if to regain his breath, but in truth he wanted Brigid to speak.

'But this Spirit is weakened,' she stated, remembering what Pythagoras had told her. 'People have lost their connection with the Gods, so their sacred Law is forgotten and ignored.'

Bran nodded, pleased. She had learnt well, she was wise. He'd met few who truly were in his long life, and he'd been white haired since the present chieftain was a babe in arms.

Brigid shook her head, remembering with awful clarity her vision of Deirdre's ordeal. 'To end the war, the Spirit must be strengthened. But this will only happen when the change is done and the new Age begins. How can I do anything to help?' Although she knew in her heart that she would succeed – the Gods would never task her with something of which she wasn't capable – the voice of doubt still niggled in her mind. She looked up at Bran and his faded blue eyes met her gaze calmly.

'The Spirit can be strengthened by another means. Its power will then infuse through the world, purifying men's souls, and then the war will end. This is what you must do – the purpose for which you were born.' Bran's intense look belied his near blindness, his dimmed eyes saw far more than she could ever realise. He saw the burning light in her soul, the light of the Goddess. This light had filled the rath with divine strength, although Brigid was unaware of it. This was why, he mused, it had remained safe for so long.

'How can I do this?' asked Brigid.

Bran was silent. She could feel his gaze upon her soul and she hoped she appeared worthy. What if her doubts let her down? What if her weakness meant Bran would not help her? She looked at the floor nervously. The silence drew on interminably, then she raised her eyes to meet with Bran's. In that moment, their gazes locked unwavering, their respective powers combined. The room was filled with light, a pulsating maelstrom of orange and purple, flecked with foci of gold and silver. Both felt as though they were being sucked into it, but despite the tumult neither would break their gaze.

Bran saw what he needed to know. 'You must travel to the Heart of the Land, the source of the Spirit,' he said at last. 'There is wood outside, make up the fire. The air grows cold.' He closed his eyes and breathed deeply. He'd spent his lifetime preparing for this moment, he thought with a profound sense of destiny.

Brigid stood and did as she was asked, giving the old Druid the time he needed. A moment later the fire was blazing well and she seated herself again.

'The manifest form of the Spirit is known by different names in different lands,' he continued, speaking slowly so his words would be absorbed fully. 'But we know it as the Cauldron of Ceridwen, the source of the *awen* of the bards, the origin of all life, formed from the Great Spirit of the Mother.''The cauldron of the Ancients that brought their dead warriors back to life!' exclaimed Brigid, remembering the Sacred Histories. 'When a body was placed in it, the soul would return.''From the Cauldron flows the life force of the land,' said Bran. 'This is the true meaning of that story. It nourishes and nurtures everything that is, was, and will be. When this flow is weakened, the whole world is affected.'

Brigid nodded. This was what she'd learnt from Pythagoras, and its truth was now self-evident. 'How can I reach the Cauldron?' she asked. 'It's possible to reach it in the otherworld,' she mused. 'There are stories of people – great heroes – who've done so.' 'That is it,' stated Bran. 'If you can find the Cauldron, if you are of pure enough spirit – for none find it who aren't worthy – you can harness its power to harmonise the land.'

Brigid nodded, resolute and determined. She had been chosen by the Gods for this task, she would not fail.

'I knew this time would come in my lifetime,' he continued. 'For this reason I learned, from all the wise men I knew, everything regarding the Quest for the Cauldron. Over many years, slowly piecing together everything held in the collective wisdom of the land, I have gained a vision of The Way.

But it's not me who is destined to make the Quest. I must pass on all the wisdom I've gained in my long life, for it is you who must make this Journey.'

# Chapter 51

*What man can teach another of this truth? We must seek it in You, ask it of You, knock at Your door. Only then shall we receive what we ask, and find what we seek, only then shall the door be opened to us.*

Saint Augustine

The sun set, the stars slowly wheeled around the infinite sky, and as dawn was lightening the skies in the east, Brigid finally left the old Druid, having gained as much of his great wisdom as he could impart in the little time available.

Bran rested, exhausted. Now he'd fulfilled his life purpose, played his part in the future of the world, he felt his time was near. He hoped he'd done enough, given her the guidance she needed. For now it was up to her to find The Way for herself. This she could only do with her own intuition – The Path cannot be taught, it has to be learnt for oneself. He knew what she must do to succeed, but could not tell her, for unless the wisdom came from the heart, it had no meaning.

There was nothing more he could do. He had shown her The Path, now she must walk it, alone. All he could do was hope, and pray, that she would succeed.

All eyes were on Brigid as she crossed the rath, although no one would speak to her directly. All contact was prohibited until after – *if* – she completed the Quest. The younger ones whispered behind their hands, feasting their eyes on the legend in the making and composing the stories that would one day impress their peers. Others, older and more mature, silently offered her blessings – they knew too well what was at stake.

The Journey to the Cauldron of Ceridwen was known to many only as a story from the Heroic Age. It hadn't been attempted for many hundreds of winters, and that a Druid was to attempt it, here and now, had sent a feverish buzz through the rath. For the first time in over six moons an air of optimism and hope hung in the air, children ran and played, heart-torn refugees smiled and chatted.

Brigid was uncomfortably aware of the attention on her and she kept her gaze blankly ahead until she reached the sanctuary of her hut. She mustn't even look directly at another person during her preparation. She tried to avoid going out if possible – she disliked the sudden awe and almost worship she was receiving. Her spirit was only a gift from the Goddess after all, she should be the subject of their worship. But her enforced isolation was, however, giving her ample time to prepare, physically, mentally and spiritually, for the greatest trial anyone would ever face.

As the sun began its downward descent in the sky, Brigid slipped from the rath. In the distance she could hear the babble of merry voices and the smell of wood smoke wafted towards her. It was the festival of Samhain, marking the start of winter, when animals were slaughtered for the coming lean months and a great feast was held to warm the body and soul. The entire rath was involved with the feast, for most people Brigid was forgotten. Only the elders knew fully what was to happen tonight, and their occasional glances back towards the deserted rath betrayed the subject of their thoughts.

For this was also the day when the veils between the worlds became thin. For those making Spirit Journeys, this sinister and dangerous day would aid their crossing to the otherworld.

The sounds of merriment faded behind her and were replaced by the wind in the heather, the cry of gulls and the surge of the sea. As Brigid reached the top of the cliff she could see the sacred rock of Carreg Luz, surrounded by the grey swell of the sea. Reached only at low tide, the Sacred Histories said the island was once the Sacred Mountain of a great land now drowned by the sea. Only this one part survived on account of its great sanctity.

Here lay the Heart of the Land, Bran had told her. The cave symbolising the Womb of the Goddess, found on the tideline marking the unity of earth and sea, would lead her to her goal.

She scrambled down the steep path to the shore and there she waited. The cold wind lashed sea spray against her skin but she was unaware of discomfort. The sun sunk lower, soon it would be sunset. Brigid looked to the east but she knew the full moon wouldn't yet be visible. To attempt her ordeal the world must be in perfect balance, mirroring the perfect harmonic state of her soul. The polar opposites, the sun and moon, day and night, light and dark, earth and sea, must all unite in harmony.

As the day slowly drew to a close, the atmosphere grew brooding and unfriendly and she could sense many eyes watching her. It was not considered wise to be out on Samhain Eve. All people would now be safely in their homes, surrendering the land to the beings of their nightmares.

Far off on the distant hillside Brigid could see dark shadows, beings which appeared to have little substance as they flitted along. A sudden ray of the dying sun struck the spot, and where she'd been looking an instant before, there was now nothing. Somewhere, a wolf howled, long and eerie. They too could sense the night wanderers. Brigid looked back towards the sea, now rapidly receding. She knew the Sceadugengan were not hostile towards men.

The path to the Sacred Rock was emerging from the waters of the Goddess. The Way was opening.

A chilling scream produced by no earthly voice split the air, coming from far across the lonely, deserted moors. Those who heard it in the town would huddle closer to their fires, instinctively check the door was secured, that the baby was sleeping peacefully, and feel grateful they were not outside on this night. The Beann Sidhe, the soul of the earth, cried for all harm and torment done to her body. She was often heard, but never seen.

Brigid rose. There was nothing more she could do; a lifetime's preparation had already been done. It was time.

Many sets of eyes watched her cross, many of them wishing her well. The future of all depended on the outcome of this night.

Deep inside the cave, the Womb of the Mother, she sat cross-legged in total darkness and began to relax, freeing her mind from its earthly trappings. Soon, lights began to appear in front of her eyes, coalescing to form flowing streams, and then rivers of blue fire. She followed the rivers with her mind, tracing their paths to reach their source.

She knew she would face trials on the Journey, and they would be hard, but she knew she was well equipped to succeed – she had all the knowledge she needed.

But she was wrong in one respect – there was only one trial she would face, but it was the greatest trial of all. And there was no guarantee that she would succeed.

# PART XII

# Chapter 52

*Do not let the left hand know what the right hand is doing.*
Matthew 6.3

The storm clouds built up – menacing, uncontrollable, raw energy, waiting to explode. The sky grew dark, despite it being only mid-afternoon. The power and charge in the air was almost terrifying. A warning rumble crossed the sky – to remind us of our weak, feeble insignificance in the face of the storm's might. Rain began to fall, heavy spots, cold after the heat of the day, rapidly gathering intensity until we were soaked to the skin. The storm intensified with deafening crashes of thunder. I'd always loved thunderstorms, I revelled in the electric buzz in the air, but this was the most powerful storm I'd ever experienced.

It grew steadily darker. It was almost impossible to see across the ring of stones now, except when they intermittently appeared in brilliant flashes of lightning. For a split second, I could see the faces of the others, all only too aware of the immense power swirling round us.

If our ritual worked, this power, the divine spirit of the universe, the macrocosm, would descend to unite with that of the earth, the microcosm, and this transcendent energy would revitalise the earth. This ritual, James had said when we reached Boscawen, was known as the Ritual of the Star of David.

The storm was directly overhead now, everyone present was tense with anticipation, fear and excitement. The raw energy in the air was coursing through us all. A great crash split the air, reverberating across the valley and echoing back. A bolt of lightning had struck a tall oak tree some distance to the left, splitting it into two. A second brilliant flash revealed one half slowly falling to the ground, smoking and blackened, before the vision again vanished.

The intensity of the storm became near unbearable but no one left their spots. The climax was approaching. The power was circling, swirling, attracted to the stones which would absorb it, fusing it with the earth current to cause a surge of energy through the land. It was hoped by all present that this was enough to awaken the Sleeping King.

I looked round at the other faces. Apart from James, Joanna and myself, there were nine other people arranged round the circle. They all seemed to know each other – I was the odd one out. The tall, thin, hook-nosed man who'd led the ritual now occupied the northern-most point. He was wearing a strange black cloak which made him look quite vampirish and he exuded an overwhelming air of power. He was sitting entirely motionless, an expression of serene concentration on his face, he alone seemed not to baulk at the ferocity of the storm.

A *magus*. The word came unbidden to my mind.

He hadn't deigned to tell me his name, and the force of the energy crackling from him made me sense that he was the most powerful person I'd ever encountered. His presence seemed to heighten my own powers – for the first time I could clearly see the auras surrounding everyone, mirroring the shapes of their bodies perfectly. The *magus* I could see emitted a blinding aura of orange and purple, edged with a black tinge which lent him a slightly unsettling air.

The combination of auras filled the circle with a pulsating, radiating, mass of colour, constantly shifting and swirling. For an instant, it seemed to become almost alive. I could sense an awful intelligence to it, I could feel eyes watching me, sense its fiery breath on my cheek, feel the pulse of wings. Then the terrible beast receded back into the swirling pool of energy, although its continuing presence was all too palpable.

As I looked up I could see tongues of energy reaching up, drawn towards the storm. And although I couldn't see it, I knew the energy of the storm was reaching downwards towards us.

Then, there was a deafening explosion, a burst of light so

intense I was blinded. A powerful shock wave swept over me, so powerful that I was thrown to the ground and lost awareness, I didn't know how long for.

When I came to myself and sat up, blinking, the storm had passed. The birds were tentatively beginning to sing, the sun was creeping out from behind the darkened clouds. Everyone in the circle seemed dazed, shocked, even the *magus* looked off-balance. We had all experienced the same thing.

James was looking at one of the stones – it was shattered, scorched, splintered into many fragments. 'The lightning struck it,' he said quietly, a look of dazed fear on his face. 'That's what broke the power of the storm.'

As I looked at the stone in shock, I realised for the first time how dangerous the ritual had been. We could have all been killed.

'Did the ritual work? Did we re-energise the land?' asked Joanna.

'No, it didn't. That's why the stone shattered, because the two opposing forces were incompatible on some level. The discordance broke the spell, so we've gained nothing, the earth has gained nothing.' The aura of the *magus* crackled ferociously, everyone instinctively stepped back from him.

I could see faint black tongues of fire flickering across the grass from his feet. They suddenly surged in power and the *magus* abruptly turned and stalked from the circle, leaving the rest of us to stare helplessly after him.

'What do we do now?' asked Joanna at last.

'I don't know,' answered James when no one else spoke. 'This ritual was the culmination of all our collective wisdom, knowledge and expertise. There is nothing more that we can add, to my knowledge.'

Then his resolve returned, his unshakeable optimism and faith were restored. 'But we mustn't be disheartened. We've done what we can, the future is out of our hands now. We must trust in God that this was meant to happen, that we've succeeded in playing our part.' He squared his shoulders resolutely. 'Everything always works out for the best – because of, or despite, our best efforts.'

Some of the group were heartened, others were not. I said nothing. The failure confirmed everything to me. It was my Path, and mine alone, to awaken the Sleeping King, to find the Grail, and I knew where I must go for the next and final step of my Journey.

But there was no need for them to know. It was a Quest for my own soul, which all people must complete over many lifetimes. It wasn't a heroic attempt to save the world – only superheroes did that. For the Quest to succeed, purity of soul was paramount, everything I'd learnt had told me that. If the motive was admiration, pride or respect, it would gain nothing.

So I had no reason to speak. If my Quest succeeded, the effects would become apparent in the world. If not, nothing would change. Either way it was down to me, and me alone, to continue. There was nothing more anyone else could do.

It was time for me to leave the group, and continue my Journey alone.

# Chapter 53

*But angels come to lead frail minds to rest.*
Edmund Spenser

As the group gradually drifted off I walked away. Only one set of eyes watched me go. James had realised, on some deep fundamental level, the way things were meant to be.

It was a short distance from Boscawen to St Michael's Mount, and now I just had to make the final step on my journey of a lifetime. The infinite guiding hand that watches over us had brought me almost to my destination.

I walked the remainder of the way. It seemed appropriate to use the gifts of life, health and fitness, the greatest gifts anyone can have, to finish my Journey. I felt the earth-energy feeding and nourishing my soul and I felt uplifted, alive. The breeze brought the salty smell of sea air across the open landscape and the cry of seagulls reeling overhead betrayed the closeness of the sea.

All the houses I passed were displaying carved and lighted pumpkins, images of ghosts, witches and ghouls. It was Halloween, All Souls Eve, the surviving remnant of the ancient festival of Samhain, when malignant and evil spirits would walk the earth.

A group of assorted fairies and monsters rushed towards me, shouting excitedly. 'Trick or treat! Trick or treat!'

They surrounded me as I hastily pulled some biscuits from my coat pocket and put one in each eager hand. 'Thank you!' They rushed off in search of their next victim.

I wondered if the date was auspicious – maybe the ancient festival, where the doorways to other worlds opened, would aid me in some way. But most likely not, I thought, that was just wishful thinking.

As I climbed to the top of a slight rise, I saw it. The culmination of my life journey, the point I'd been travelling towards for so long. The island rose up proud from the sea, the immortal remnant of the land of Lyonesse. Overhead, seagulls swooped and screeched and dived into the sea. The waves, whipped up by the wind, sent spray lashing against the precarious buildings on top, built as testimony to man's survival against the odds in the face of the might of nature. I saw two little fishing boats near the island, the men on board hauling in lobster pots. I'd heard they were favoured by the new fishing quotas that banished the bigger trawlers.

I saw in my imagination a wooden ship sailing in, the billowing white sails furled as she approached land, and heard a cheer of excitement as she safely moored. The Mount had been the landmark for traders since time immemorial, coming to acquire the famed Cornish tin which had been mined here for millennia. The ancient shafts and workings were mostly long buried and forgotten by all, a fact I was about to find out to my cost.

I wandered slightly off the path to gain a better view of the ancient and sacred island, picking my way around a slight mound entirely overgrown with shrubbery. I felt a slight crack under my feet, the sensation of something starting to move, but before I could react it was too late. The ground was collapsing underneath my weight, a yawning chasm opened up, tentatively covered over by centuries of plant roots, but not nearly enough to support my weight.

My mouth opened in a scream before I started falling, a last snapshot of the Mount imprinted on my mind before I was enclosed in darkness. Instinct made me wrap my arms protectively around my head but one arm was wrenched backwards on impacting the wall of the shaft. I felt my face scrape along the rough stone and earth, although adrenaline dulled the pain, and then I struck solid ground. A layer of dirt and leaves, gathered over who knew how many centuries, cushioned my fall slightly, and although badly winded I didn't think anything was broken.

I lay without moving for a moment in almost total darkness, letting the shock subside. And when the adrenaline began to recede, I looked up at the mouth of the shaft, impossibly far above my head. Then panic set in.

There was no ladder, no way to climb out.

No one would hear my shouts, even if by rare chance they happened to walk this way.

And no one knew I had come here.

I could feel warmth running down my face and I put my hand up, feeling the blood pouring from the wound down the side. My arm was killing me as well, although I could only feel minor grazing as I tentatively patted it. The air was stale and musty and full of dust but it seemed good to breathe. Enough fresh air must filter down to make it breathable, I thought gratefully.

I pulled my phone out of my pocket. As I'd already guessed, there was no signal, but I used its faint light to look around the chamber. The shaft was around two metres wide at the bottom, although the top looked narrower, and a tunnel yawned to one side.

I used the light to check my injuries. I couldn't see my face but could see no serious damage anywhere else. There was bruising already forming on my arm, and my hand was smeared with blood from my face, but I could feel it was beginning to clot.

I looked up again. A faint ring of light penetrated through the mass of vegetation and shrubbery, but despite my rude arrival it was still almost completely covered. No sign whatsoever that someone had fallen.

I thought, now a bit calmer, that it was around eight metres to the top. I was very lucky not to sustain serious injury. I looked again at the tunnel, my only realistic hope. Although my mind screamed at the thought of crawling down this ancient, blackened tunnel with its unimaginable dangers, I crawled to the entrance. I felt a sharp pain in my leg as I did so – maybe I'd sprained something after all.

I looked down the tunnel, a yawning mouth of blackness just big enough to crawl into, and I forced myself into the entrance, desperately grateful for the faint glow of light from my phone. Grit dug into my hands and knees, and my back dislodged small showers of dirt. I had to concentrate forcefully on my breathing to try to quell the rising surge of panic.

But after only around ten metres or so, the tunnel was blocked by rubble and earth. It must have caved in, long ago. My mind full of the terrifying prospect of being buried alive in here, and acutely conscious of tonnes of unstable rock above my head, I gratefully started back out. There was no room to turn round and I had to crawl backwards, the stabbing pain in my leg increasing. I put my phone in my pocket and the blackness pressed in on me intolerably. How these ancient miners coped with this, day in day out, I had no idea.

The faint, grey glimmer of light in the shaft entrance was immensely comforting when I at last reached it, and I sat down and summed up my options. There was one. No one would ever rescue me; it was up to me, alone, to get me out of this mess.

I cursed myself bitterly for being so stupid. If only I had stuck to the path! Why did I have to walk right on the wrong spot?

I forced myself to stand up. My leg screamed as I did so but I pushed the pain from my mind and felt around the shaft. There were slight hand holds but the surface was loose and crumbling, I couldn't see it accepting my weight. I reached up as high as I could and eventually felt something, protruding and solid. I couldn't tell what it was – it could be a tree root or an ancient iron bar, but it seemed solid enough. I pulled it experimentally – it didn't shift.

I hung my weight on it and began to pull myself up, using my feet as leverage on the crumbling wall. With the strength of my arm muscles, honed by hours in the gym, my eyes reached level with my hold, and I felt desperately with my other hand for a second grip.

I found a piece of jutting rock, grasped it and pulled myself higher. Already I was breathing hard with exertion and my arms and fingers ached with strain. I hung onto the first grip like a lifeline, but I had no choice. I had to let go and find a new hold. I took a deep breath, pulled my leg up and got my foot where my hand had been, using my leg muscles to push myself higher into the shaft. My damaged leg began to spasm in protest but I willed it to hold on, and amazingly, it did.

I found a new grip, but as I hung my weight on it, it gave way. I grabbed desperately for my last hold, but too late. I fell from my tenuous position and was then lying on the ground again, coughing and with a new pain shooting up my arm.

After a moment I got up and reached for the first hold again. I had to keep trying, else die here. I grasped hold of it, but my muscles were too weak this time, I couldn't do it. My arms were shaking with stress and the new pain was unbearable, it was all I could do to hang there without thinking about climbing. I let go again in despair.

I thought about fetching rubble from the tunnel, dragging it back bit by bit to make something to stand on, but the thought of disturbing that fragile structure and the image of all that weight crashing down on me made me quickly abandon the idea.

I sat down, forcing myself to breathe deeply, to relax, to rid my mind of the stress and panic it was riddled with. After ten minutes, focussing on a bright beam of silvery light in an inky blue background, that beautiful face which watches down on us all, I felt calmer and happier. I stood up serenely and went back to the first hold.

I pushed myself easily up to where I had reached before, then felt for a new grip. I found a handhold, it shifted slightly but I had no choice. I carefully and steadily put my weight on it – it held. I carefully focussed on the movements of my muscles, feeling each one operating as part of a smooth, well-oiled machine, no sudden movements, no stress, nothing that would make me fall again. This was my last chance.

I felt upwards again, but I could feel nothing this time. I forced myself to stretch as high as possible, my calf muscles beginning to shake with strain as my toes took my entire weight. I shifted, ever so slightly, to take some weight off my damaged leg, which thankfully had subsided to a dull throbbing.

My fingers scrabbled desperately then caught hold of a jutting stone. I pulled it and it came loose. I froze as my weight slipped and just retained my precarious balance on the shaft face. Dirt showered down on me, getting in my eyes and my mouth, sticking to the congealing blood across my face. I blinked painfully. The urge to rub the irritation from my eyes was overwhelming and I felt tears begin to stream, but I dared not let go my grip for an instant. I blinked again and razor-sharp fragments grated across my eyes, all I could do was force my eyes to remain still.

Sharp fragments had also lodged in my windpipe and throat and I coughed slightly, loath to make even this movement. I had to force myself to breathe evenly, to override the urge to cough. The desperate urge to succumb to my reflexes was overwhelming. I brought one hand down, slowly, slowly, and rubbed a finger across my eyes. The relief was indescribable.

My muscles were shaking uncontrollably. I was using every vestige of my mental strength to force my body to hold on. And my body, honed and fit and trained to perfection, used to obeying my mind's every whim, hung on, giving me its all. I thought of all those years of cross-country, of hiking up mountains, of pumping weights at the gym. What if I'd chosen the pub over the gym? Chocolate over pounding the streets? The answer did not bear thinking about. I thanked my lucky stars that I'd chosen the option that would save my life.

Every muscle, tendon and sinew screaming, I reached up again. I found a second rock, at the very extent of my fingertips. I stretched as high as I could, but couldn't grasp it except with the very tip of one finger.

My body was at its physical limit, and my mind the same. Every muscle in my body was shaking uncontrollably, what I was requesting of my body was way beyond its capabilities, despite a lifetime's training for this moment. I couldn't go any further. I was stuck, on a long abandoned mine shaft, with no way up and no way down.

In times of extreme physical stress, bacteria can alter their genetic make-up, switching genes on and others off, trying desperately to find a way to survive this life-or-death situation. This, as all biochemists know well, is a process known as transformation.

And it is not just found in bacteria.

At the final moment, when I had no choice but to let go, to fall, to die, I felt myself begin to change. Something was happening. My mind seemed to fill with light, I felt almost ecstatic. A sense of immense euphoria swept over me, transcending even what I'd felt when I'd danced with Earthman, or when I had flown along the ley lines from Yeavering Bell. A sound filled the air, the sound of birdsong, joyous, triumphant and vibrant.

*Even in your darkest moments, the light in your soul will show you the way.*

I looked up and I could see, perfectly. The pain in my body vanished. I felt as if I was filled with light and air. I could see clearly the hold I'd aimed for, a jutting piece of quartz, just above my fingertips. I stretched up again, and I felt as if I was lifted on a current of air. I grasped the pale stone with my fingertips, and pulled myself easily level with it.

I was powered by a strength from outside myself, the strength of the entire universe. Now, instead of fighting against the shaft, I became One with it – we were both equal pieces of creation, after all. And we worked together, a co-operation of two equals, the shaft helped me to climb itself. It showed me the holds it had gifted me, and held my hands and feet securely as I moved. I was just one fragment of creation, one shard of light, working with another.

Up until now, I had only learnt the answers. Now, I was becoming what I had learnt. The final test of the Sphere of Jupiter.

With little effort, I reached the top of the shaft. I felt a rush of fresh air coming down from above, the most beautiful sensation I'd ever felt. And then my hand grasped the mouth of the shaft.

As I did so, the ethereal light began to fade, I didn't need it any more. The shaft was once more plunged into darkness as my second hand, and then my feet, pulled themselves into the daylight.

And now I was ready. I was ready, heart, mind, body and soul for my final Test, which lay just one step ahead. I stopped and looked towards my final goal. I realised that everything in my life had been leading towards this point – absolutely everything, both big and small, had been an integral piece of my Journey. Everyone I'd ever met, everything I'd ever done or seen, the large things and the small, had been converging on one ultimate purpose, steering me towards this final test. This was the reason I'd been born, many times, to fulfil this one task.

I gave thanks, to the gods, and all things guided by them, and all that guide them, to the universal intelligence, the cosmic mind, God, for preparing me so well.

I knew what I had to do. I knew I'd done all the preparation I could, I had all the wisdom I needed in my heart to succeed.

I walked towards the causeway which led to the island. The tide was in and the island was separated from the mainland by the timeless ocean, the metaphysical barrier between this world and the otherworld.

As I reached the causeway, I heard, far off across the moor, a heart-wrenching, blood-curdling wail that caused my blood to chill. Like no sound I'd ever heard on earth before, it seemed to echo and reverberate across the valley.

'It's nothing,' I told myself firmly, 'probably a noise from a machine or a quarry,' although I felt strangely unsettled long after it had died away.

I sat on the shingle beach, tuning in to the sacred site, venerated by man for many millennia. Waves washed into the shore, crashing over jagged rocks, the snarling teeth of a wild, untameable place. Spray lashed against me, the salt stinging the cuts and scratches on my arms and face. I looked over to the island, drinking in every detail of it, and began to relax, sinking into a trance-like state. The world changed subtly, seemed to become more vibrant, ethereal, more energetic, less physical and solid.

I saw a path leading around the base of the rocky structure. I hadn't noticed it before but now it was clear, picked out in relief against the background. It led around the cliffs and ended at a small cave in the rock, near invisible against the background. A glow of blue light seemed to come from it, lighting up the surrounding area in an eerie glow. I understood what the earth was telling me.

I sat without moving until, when the day started to draw to a close, the tide had retreated far enough for me to cross to the island. Sunset was approaching – the time between times, the time when the veils between worlds become thin. The time to enter the otherworld, the land of the soul.

I'd always loved the time of sunset – the cooling air, the dampness of the forming dew, the settling scent of the green vegetation, the birds singing their final songs. I would watch the sun sink below the horizon, the colour of the sky intensifying into deep blue then black as the first stars appeared against the growing darkness. It was always my favourite time of day.

The ancient people instinctively felt the power of this time, and all the natural world feels it too. And now science can explain why. The ley lines are influenced by the sun and the moon; when the sun is on the horizon, its energy force is directly parallel with that of the earth and magnifies its power exponentially. When the moon is full, on the opposite horizon, the three-fold alignment charges the earth's energies to their absolute maximum. My soul was now ready to flow down this surge of energy, I was ready to cross the barrier between worlds.

I got up and crossed the bare rocky causeway with waves occasionally washing over my feet, traversing the barrier between the world of men and the world of the spirit.

And then I was there. I followed the path which had been shown to me and entered the sacred cave, the Womb of the Earth, the entrance to the Heart of the World.

And at the same time, I reached the Seventh Sphere, the Sphere of Saturn.

# PART XIII

# Chapter 54

*The worldly hopes men set their hearts upon turn ashes.*
Omar Khayyam

Brigid reached a great cavern which emitted a powerful glowing light from the entrance. The sense of an immense, indescribable power located within overwhelmed her, nearly forcing her back.

'Only the pure of spirit are allowed access to the Cauldron,' Bran had said. If she wasn't pure enough, she wouldn't go a step closer.

She forced her mind to still, relax, as she'd been taught to do, allowing her soul to free from its earthly prison, its material wants, needs and desires, to become nothing but the pure state of the Goddess within her. She moved forwards, towards the great soul of the Mother, her mind reaching its enlightened spiritual state and becoming a form of pure soul. And so, slowly, excruciatingly slowly, she entered the cavern, the Heart of the Goddess.

And there it was, the Cauldron of the Goddess, Ceridwen, the source of all life. It was lit up, glowing and pulsating, reminding her of the red-hot coals in the blacksmith's forge so long ago. It was larger than any cauldron she'd seen, but even so she knew her vision was deceptive, she saw only a minute fraction of its power. She held her breath as she beheld the most powerful talisman of all, something barely known of even in the Sacred Histories. How long since mortal vision had lain eyes on it? She couldn't begin to imagine. She could feel its immense power feeding into her soul, the most amazing experience of her life. In her awe she almost forgot her original purpose – to reach it and harness its power, but then she forced her mind to focus.

From the cauldron bubbled and streamed the life-force of the world, the *awen*, which flowed outwards to infuse through the entire world, the source of the energy which she'd felt flowing through the stone circles and sacred sites.

The flames which fuelled it, allowing the life force to seethe and bubble within, were themselves fed by its power – the life-force dripping into them, like fat from a cooking-pan, caused the flames to leap and spark. It was the ultimate embodiment of the endlessly cycling chain of life.

She could hear buzzing, like a huge swarm of bees. She looked around automatically but the sound seemed to come from the Cauldron itself. Brigid now understood why the bee and its gift of honey were so greatly revered among the Druids.

The Cauldron was enclosed on three sides by towering cliffs, and the fourth side opened outwards towards where she was standing. It was entirely surrounded by flame and the rivers of fire, the life-force, flowing towards her blocked any approach to it.

A short distance in front of her the river had formed a shallow and still pool, smoke and steam rising from it. Brigid walked carefully to its edge, her skin prickling from the searing heat. She looked at the unbroken surface, her vision distorted only by the rising haze of smoke. The instant her eyes touched the pool, she felt something lock inside her mind. As she gazed into the burning pool, it gazed back into her soul. A connection, permanent and unbreakable, was formed, and visions began to appear on the surface. She saw Cathbad striding across the hillside, Emer preparing herbs, her mother grinding grain. She saw the Hill of Cernunnos, Carreg Luz, the Cernyw rath. Was she seeing the past, or the present? Were these events playing out at this very moment? She didn't know.

She tried to pull her gaze from the pool, but the pool held her fast. Then she saw herself, crossing to Carreg Luz. This she knew was only a short while before. Then, another image. Herself again, walking along a line of fire, speaking to strangely dressed people, gazing again at the Cauldron. Intuitively, she felt it was the future, this was yet to come.

What were the images trying to tell her? She knew it must be important. Then she saw herself hold out her hand, she was holding her stone shell – the one she'd returned to the Goddess years before. One of the strangely dressed people took it from her. So it couldn't be the future, after all, but it was definitely not the past. The images flickered and distorted as she tried to interpret their meaning.

Brigid tried again to break her connection with the strange pool, and this time, with a huge effort of will, she managed to tear her eyes away. The surface disappeared into a shroud of smoke and Brigid pulled her mind back to the great task she was here to complete.

She knew she must reach the Cauldron, but how? The phenomenal heat that was searing her skin held her back; she could go no closer to either the Cauldron or the rivers of fire. She tried to step forward but the heat was too much, she could see her dress begin to singe. With all the phenomenal strength of her immortal soul, the purified and strengthened spirit which had been chosen to complete the Quest, she could make not an inch of progress.

She relaxed, stepped back, allowing herself to think. There was no way to cross the blazing flow, she must find another way. She knew that the answer was inside her, that there must be a way. She encircled the cavern, climbing the rise towards the cliff heights, and saw how the river of fire flowing from the Cauldron had gouged a deep ravine in the rocky floor, forming the cliff face she was now standing on. The great heat rising upwards burned her skin and stung her eyes.

It seemed impossible. Even if she found a way to climb down the sheer cliff face, she would still have to cross the river, and she would never survive the phenomenal heat.

What was she to do? There must be a way, she knew there must, but she didn't know the answer. All her training, her learning, had been to no avail – there was no way she could reach it. She could not fulfil her destiny.

It was the key, the only way to save the realm. Her destiny – the purpose of her entire life – was to reach it. But she couldn't do it.

She stood there for an age, her mind running through all she'd learnt, from Cathbad, Bran, Emer, Cernunnos, Ceridwen, but the answer was not there.

Then the image began to fade and break up. It was too late. The sun was rising, the gateway was closing. There had been one chance for her, and now it was lost.

Brigid was once again within the cave on Carreg Luz as the sun rose above the horizon. She was exhausted – the encounter with the life-force of Ceridwen had stripped her of her soul-energy, it would take a long time to recover.

She left the cave, too exhausted to do more than blindly stumble into the growing daylight. She somehow staggered across the path to the mainland and collapsed on the shore, where an early morning fisherman later found her and took her to the rath.

# Chapter 55

*No one ever really dies. You believe that? If not, for you, it's almost over now.*
NERD

And so the world slowly fell apart.

Brigid's sickness, afflicting her soul as well as her body, showed little sign of improvement over the coming moons, despite the combined skill of the Cernyw Druids. She had failed her life's Quest, the purpose for which she was born, the loss of hope was the one malady that no treatment can cure.

War continued to ravage the kingdom until it seemed that no one had been left untouched. All had lost friends, family and colleagues in the bloodshed, and the shortages of food and other necessities meant life had become intolerably hard. No one was safe from the rampaging war-bands, even the Druids were not safe to walk alone. Happiness and peace seemed things long lost.

A messenger arrived at the rath, his horse white-eyed and foaming from the hard and perilous ride, and everyone quickly gathered to hear his message. It was a rare event, for even they were no longer safe to travel. Bad news, everyone knew, before he even began to speak.

Cunedda, the chieftain, had been killed in battle. Slain ostensibly by an enemy arrow, but also by the intense grief he suffered following the slaughter of his family a moon before. The news spread slowly through the rath – people no longer even had the will to gossip.

Grim faced and silent, the Druids, especially the more worldly among them, prepared themselves for the end. It would not be long before the last vestiges of their world fell under the blades and axes of the barbarian warriors.

Brigid silently turned her face to the wall when Gwen told her the news. Her mind was too far gone to even feel despair. After waiting in vain for a response, the young Druid turned and quietly left her alone. The trauma and anarchy in the realm was mirrored by the torment and heart-break in Brigid's soul. All that she'd ever done, learnt and thought had been for one purpose. And now it was over, all was lost. She spent her time in a black shroud of despair, having not the will to speak, eat, or move from her room.

Her only companion was Deirdre, the girl who so resembled her young sister. She sat with her and brought her what little food and water was available, sharing Brigid's despair as Brigid had shared hers. The girl still rarely spoke, their relationship was one of mutual silence. Brigid gazed sadly at the little blonde head next to her, the embodiment of all she'd failed to do.

But under the blanket of darkness and despair, the light of life and hope still flickered faintly in her heart. *Surely there was another way?*

She hadn't been brought so far if she were meant to fail, surely she could yet complete the Quest. The Gods themselves had said she would.

Then one night she dreamed of Emer. Her old teacher was walking towards the distant sea. A horseman, bent low over the saddle and galloping hard across the moor, passed her and travelled rapidly into the distance before being thrown to the ground.

Then Emer changed, took on the form of the Goddess, Ceridwen, as she'd seen her in the grove of her initiation. 'Do not turn from the Road,' she said, 'else the Gods will turn from you.'

Brigid awoke, feeling more positive than she'd done for a long time. The Goddess was still by her side, guiding her. She had not failed, there was still a way.

The key must be what Emer had taught her. She ran her mind through all her memories of her training, everything she'd ever learnt. Eventually she recalled the island of Ynys Druineach, far to the north. Emer had told her, so long ago, when she was young and untried, that here lay the greatest Wellspring of the Goddess in the world, even greater than Carreg Luz. This was where she should go! Maybe she should have gone here in the first place.

She knew nothing about the place except vague stories, she wished she'd spoken to Emer about it when she'd had the chance. But it was too late now. She knew what to do, she would complete her Quest with what little she had.

The light of her soul began to strengthen. She now knew The Way.

She left her room for the first time in a moon and went to the great hall where the entire rath was gathered. All the Druids were in despondent debate, and Brigid went up to the main hearth to speak. The room fell silent as she approached, all still held her in esteem despite her failure. When she told them of her plan, a wave of shock spread through the hall, many tried to deter her from her resolve.

'This is an impossible journey, you can't hope to get there!'

'It is many moons travel to reach Ynys Druineach. You're too weak; you've not recovered from your ordeal.'

'The roads have been impassable for half a year; no messenger has reached that far north since before the war began. The countryside is no longer safe for anyone.' 'The Cauldron is lost to us now, there's no way you can reach it. The future now lies only in the hands of the Gods.'

'We've set plans in motion to alleviate the war, to elect a new chieftain who will enforce peace on the land. This is all we can do now. The world will not improve for a long time, but we may prevent things from getting any worse.'

Brigid was unswayed by their arguments. The confidence with which she'd walked the Path of the Goddess had returned with renewed vigour, although her body was still weaker than she wished to admit, even to herself.

'It's not over yet,' she said. 'It's never over while we still live – there is always hope.' Cernunnos had told her that – that life is hope. It had since come to her that this was the message he'd tried to tell her – that this would prove to be the answer to the test.

Before five nights had passed, she was ready to leave. She'd been undeterred by any reasoning and she said her farewells to the people she'd developed a close bond to. Deirdre tugged at her hand, silently trying to prevent her leaving. Brigid placed her hand on her head in blessing, silently infusing her with the Light she held within her. She would be well cared for, she knew. As well as was possible now, anyway.

Brigid had tried to give the impression that she was recovering, but although her dream had infused her with a strengthened hope and spirit, she was still in truth very weak. She pushed this from her mind – she *must* complete this journey.

'There is always hope,' she repeated emphatically, drawing out every word. 'There is always a way. We are still breathing, still walking. The battle is never over while we can still fight. We are not yet done.'

She turned from the rath, left its welcoming, inviting fires, the appetising aromas of roasting meat and fresh bread, now scant but life-saving. Comfort held no grounds with her now.

Then, slowly, painfully, she walked into the growing twilight, began the hardest, longest, loneliest journey of all.

Finally she was lost to the sight of all those watching, and was gone.

\* \* \*

Brigid would not complete her journey, she would never find what she was looking for. The price, both physical and spiritual, that she had paid had been too great.

But she was right, there had been a way open to her. And at some point, long into the future, the stars would realign, and so the game would be played again.

# PART XIV

# Chapter 56

*The first morning of creation wrote what the last dawn of reckoning shall read.*
Omar Khayyam

The sun set beyond the distant hills and the silvery moon rose in the inky sky opposite. All opposing forces were in perfect balance and harmony. In the cave on the shore, where the land and the sea were also in perfect balance, I became One with the most transcendent place and time in existence.

The air grew charged with energy – it seemed more so than normal – a sense of anticipation and excitement was charging the air. The whole of the universe it seemed was quivering with expectation. I heard a sound travelling from a huge distance, to my mind it was like the eerie howl of a wolf.

I had a sudden flashback for an instant, to a time over two millennia ago, to when I'd done this before. I'd failed in my Quest then.

But was it really a failure?

All that happens is a part of the great divine plan. I, my teachers, the gods, had all tried to bring about an outcome which in the end was not meant to be. My soul hadn't been ready to find its goal, and neither had the world. Despite the tragedy and bloodshed, the world had survived.

Unlike this time. This time, it really was the world which was at stake.

I, and all the other players in the game, were part of a much bigger game, one which was played out over the whole of eternity.

I hadn't been given another chance. In reality this was the only chance I'd ever been given.

The air grew still, the birds were quiet, the world was frozen in time for an instant, and then all changed and I was in the land of the soul. My mind reached a cavern from which an eerie pulsating light emitted. As I neared the cavern, the sound of buzzing, humming, filled my senses. It sounded as if the cavern were full of bees. I knew I must be getting close – the bee was yet another ancient symbol of the Divine Spirit.

The power from what was in the cavern emitted an immense force, pushing me back. It was as if an immeasurably strong magnet was repelling me, refusing to allow me near. This was the barrier between the transcendently pure, divine, soul state, and the base, tainted, material state. I had to overcome it, and I wouldn't do it unless my soul and heart were pure.

But I knew I could pass it, and my conviction was such that I began to make progress. The desires, memories and negative thoughts, the cloak of shadows, all things of my world, were sloughed from my soul as a snake sheds its skin, and I moved forward, slowly, slowly, my soul gradually becoming purified, *transformed*. And so, eventually, I entered the cavern.

There, I saw the talisman which I had quested for.

The purpose of a lifetime, of many lifetimes. I had done it. The most amazing feeling in the world. It glowed in infinite colours and shimmered and swirled, eventually taking the shape most commonly associated with it – that of the Holy Grail, the Chalice, the object of so many Quests over so many centuries. This wasn't its true shape, I knew – it had no form or shape that our eyes can discern, I was seeing my mind's interpretation of what it cannot hope to ever understand.

From it flowed an immense river of fire, encircling and flowing around the cavern before splitting and dissipating through many tunnels. In my mind's eye I could see them flowing across the land, around the world, the life-force of the earth, the ley lines or dragon paths as they are known to mystics around the world. The source of the life blood of the universe, the True God, The Philosopher's Stone, the key to paradise, enlightenment, which all people of all ages have searched for.

In the rivers I could see a reflection of all the cosmos. The rivers became streams of intergalactic stardust which birthed new galaxies, stars and solar systems. I could see blood flowing in the veins of a man, rivers of water flowing through a fertile land, sunlight flowing towards a verdant planet. This river of energy, of life, was a part of and at the same time the whole of all that exists. Everything was a reflection of everything else. The life-force of the earth was the life-force of the universe, and vice versa. In that image, I saw the true nature of existence.

# Chapter 57

*The Gods sing a hymn of silence, and I am silently singing.*
The Hermetica

The rivers flowed shallow where I stood, but further across the cavern, near where they originated from the Grail, they had gouged deep gorges in the rock, sheer sided and impossible to climb. The nearer to the Grail, the higher and steeper they became, the result of the immense power flowing from it. The Grail was entirely enclosed and protected by the strength of its own soul. The eerie glow of light and crackling of ethereal flames entranced me, I watched fascinated before drawing myself back to the problem I faced.

I was now facing the hardest test of all. And I didn't know the answer.

Somehow, I had to gain this immense power. I tentatively tried to touch one of the rivers, but in an immense explosion the flames leapt back and I was thrown to the side of the cavern. There was no way to cross the rivers here.

I circled the cavern around which the river flowed, looking for a way. I climbed upwards until I reached the top of a cliff from which a sheer drop led directly into the depths of the river of fire. The heat rising upwards was more intense than ever, my skin was burning unbearably. There was no way I could climb down the sheer rock, and if I did there was no way I could overcome the heat without being roasted.

Doubts assailed me – maybe I wasn't good enough? Only the pure of heart and spirit could succeed – maybe I was lacking too much. Although the whole world was at stake, I could see no way to complete the Quest.

I had failed here before, and would fail here again.

I forced my mind to still – it was not over yet, there was still hope. I could still find the answer. I let my intuition speak. And then a sense of great peace came over me. I heard the answer.

For the meaning of life is life. For life to continue, life must be sacrificed to nourish it. This is what Cernunnos had told me.

The words of that Sufi poem, *The Conference of the Birds*, which James had guessed would be so important to me, came to my mind. It tells of moths flying round a flame, a metaphor for the divine goal. The moths each fly up to the flame, then return to tell what they think they have learnt, but each is told they've learnt nothing. Then one flies right into the flame and is burnt up. I managed to remember the words perfectly for some reason, even though I didn't recall even reading them when I'd hastily skimmed through the book one night.

*You can never find the longed for goal*
*Until you first out-soar both flesh and soul.*
*But should one part remain, a single hair*
*Will drag you back and plunge you in despair.*
*No creature's self can be admitted here,*
*Where all identity must disappear.*

This was the Seventh Sphere, the Sphere of Saturn. And Saturn was the governing planet of death.

Beyond Saturn lay the Eighth Sphere, the Fixed Stars, immobile, perfect and eternal. The Sphere of God.

The key to the final test is sacrifice. It is the impurity of the physical body that holds you back – it is the only soul that can complete the Quest. Only by leaving behind my body would I complete this trial.

After all, you can only enter paradise after your death. It is only through giving up everything, *everything*, that you are and you have, that you reach the final perfect state of harmony with the divine. All that is impure, material and individual is stripped away, leaving only that divine spark which is in all things. So the man becomes identical to, One with, God.

The perfect order of the dinosaurs had to meet its destruction so man could evolve.

I knew I had the answer.

I thought briefly of what I was leaving behind – the family, friends, places, that I would never see again. I could still turn back.

But I wasn't really leaving anything – I now truly knew how the life-force was a part of everything. My body belonged to nature, so its fate was of no consequence. The irrational torments of matter were replaced by understanding.

I would be reborn, become part of something much greater. I would be a part of the universal spirit, but knowingly, consciously, as the universe as a whole is a living consciousness. All things are a part of this vast being, but are aware only of their own small section of space and time, they cannot see the bigger picture. When I out-soared flesh and soul, I would become one with everything, everytime, everywhere.

I had prepared for many lifetimes for this goal – I could not turn back now.

I turned, ran to the edge of the cliffs, and flung myself into the all consuming flames. The sensation of great, infinite, indefinable power came over me, like an exploding supernova vaporising into heat and light. But I relished the feeling and gave myself into its midst.

\* \* \*

*This Nothingness, this Life, are states no tongue*
*At any time has adequately sung–*
*Those who can speak still wander far away*
*From the dark truth they struggle to convey,*
*And by analogies they try to show*
*The forms men's partial knowledge cannot know.*

# Epilogue

The sun rose. The world continued to turn. Life went on. The sacrifice that one person had made would make the world a better place, for whatever affects one, affects all. No man is an island, everything is part of the whole. One soul finally achieved its transcendent life purpose, and so would uplift the souls of all living and the collective soul of the world.

Many people would not notice, and those who did would soon forget. But like the ripples spreading out in a pool of water, the effects would last forever. It was a drop in the ocean, but the ocean is made up entirely of individual drops.

The universe exists for ever. Events might seem important, devastating even, in our short lifespan, but who knows what part they play in the bigger picture of eternity. Everything that happens, happens for the best possible outcome. If the music of life seems discordant, it is the fault of ourselves, not the master musician. To walk The Path is to become perfectly tuned with the harmony of existence, to see all things in perfect symphony.

We may never fully understand the reasons why, the game may not play out for many generations, but existence moves inexorably onwards towards its perfect state.

We are all on a journey. The key to this is that there is no journey. We are already there. This is what we have to realise. We are all part of the divine universe, as all around us is divine and part of the divine spirit. So there can be no failure, there is nowhere to go wrong. Men, animals, gods, we are all instruments of an infinite power, working towards one ultimate goal.

This is what takes an eternity to realise – when past, present, and future all exist simultaneously as one.

\* \* \*

For all those who walk The Road, may the light of life shine always in your soul.

# Select Bibliography

*Afterlife*, Colin Wilson, Caxton Editions

*An Invitation to The Secret Doctrine*, H.P. Blavatsky, Theosophical University Press

*A Replication Study: Three Cases of Children in Northern India Who Are Said to Remember a Past Life*, Antonia Mills, Journal of Scientific Exploration

*Awakening Osiris: A New Translation of the Egyptian Book of the Dead*, Normandi Ellis, Phanes Press

*Celtic Mythology*, Geddes and Grosset

*Entangled Minds*, Dean Radin, Pocket Books

*Fingerprints of the Gods*, Graham Hancock, Century

*Introduction to Mythology*, Lewis Spence, Senate

*Myths and Marvels of Astronomy*, Richard A. Proctor, Forgotten Books

*Oriental Mythology: The Masks of God*, Joseph Campbell, Penguin

*Prehistoric Northumberland*, Stan Beckensall, Tempus

*Sir Thomas Malory's Tales of King Arthur*, Michael Senior, Book Club Associates

*Supernature*, Lyall Watson, Hodder and Stoughton

*The Book of the Dead*, E.A. Wallis Budge, Arkana

*The Conference of the Birds*, Farid ud-Din Attar, translated by Afkham Darbandi and Dick Davis, Penguin

*The Divine Matrix*, Gregg Braden, Hay House

*The Elixir and the Stone*, Michael Baigent and Richard Leigh, Arrow

*The Encyclopedia of World Mythology*, Arthur Cotterell and Rachel Storm, Lorenz Books

*The Giant Book of the Supernatural*, Edited by Colin Wilson, Paragon

*The Hermetica: The Lost Wisdom of the Pharaohs*, Timothy Freke and Peter Gandy, Piatkus

*The Hero with a Thousand Faces*, Joseph Campbell, Sphere Books

*The History of the Kings of Britain*, Geoffrey of Monmouth, Translated by Lewis Thorpe, Penguin

*The Mysteries of Britain*, Lewis Spence, Senate

*The Myth of the Goddess: Evolution of an Image*, Anne Baring and Jules Cashford, BCA

*The Occult*, Colin Wilson, Mayflower Books

*The Quest for Merlin*, Nikolai Tolstoy, Hamish Hamilton

*The Secret Life of Plants*, Peter Tompkins and Christopher Bird, Penguin

*The Serpent Grail*, Philip Gardiner and Gary Osborn, Watkins Publishing

*The Sun and the Serpent*, Hamish Miller and Paul Broadhurst, Pendragon Press

*The View Over Atlantis*, John Michell, Sphere Books

*The White Goddess*, Robert Graves, Faber and Faber

MOON

BOOKS

Moon Books invites you to begin or deepen your encounter with
Paganism, in all its rich, creative, flourishing forms.